Ariette

Written by Miranda Moeller
Cover by McKenzie Moeller

ISBN 979-8-9905157-0-3

First paperback edition May 2024
Bird and Cat Press, May 2024

Printed in the United States of America

Published by Bird and Cat Press
Bird and Cat LLC
P.O. Box 157
Columbus, Texas 78934

www.birdandcatpress.com

To those seeking true freedom.

"A GENTLE TALE THAT SOOTHES LIKE A LULLABY.

The citizens of Pernia ought to be enjoying celebrations across the kingdom for Prince Faaris on his eighteenth birthday. Instead, the royal family is attacked and the city of Asteris is thrown into chaos. The King's trailblazing new law is upended and Faaris is left vulnerable. Unsure whom to trust, the young prince takes solace in his truest friend, a small star named Ariette. Though his heartfelt wishes and her tranquil songs can only be communicated across the expanse through conversations held in verse, it is a challenge they both handle with grace and elegance. While their relationship may be unorthodox, Faaris has never been one to embrace convention. His heart wants to believe in all the tall tales and bedtime stories he's been raised with, so he continues to wish upon his remote beloved star. A dependable presence in his life, Ariette loves her human stargazer and cannot bear to see Faaris suffer. Though granting human wishes is forbidden and visiting Earth is a death sentence, Ariette can't stand idly by while her companion is in trouble. She reasons that without love there is no meaning, and she risks everything to save her precious stargazer. But Earth is no place for a creature made of stardust, especially when a hidden enemy is calling the shots.

If you've ever contemplated the expansive night sky and pleaded with the stars to grant your heart's desire, Ariette will be your wish come true. A gentle tale that soothes like a lullaby, this novel is a delight to read. While the protagonists are from two different realms, they share a common need for purpose, connection, and love. Ariette is a soulful being without a real soul. Faaris is a good person through and through, a kindhearted prince forced into a desperate situation. Their storybook romance is wholesome and beautiful, though not without some daunting obstacles. Moeller's writing style is mesmerizing in its simplicity, standing out for its whimsy, tenderness, and composure. What opens like a bedtime story blossoms into an allegorical fantasy that readers of all ages will swoon over. The plot features a kingdom in turmoil, star-crossed lovers, mythical creatures, deception, danger, and sacrifice, every element needed for a well-rounded novel. Ariette is truly poetry in motion, a shimmering fairy tale come to life with a beautiful message at its core.

Ariette

MIRANDA MOELLER

Bird and Cat

Press

1

"MY LOVE, MY LIGHT, ON THIS BEAUTIFUL night, I hope you know you are my life. Never was there a creature so fine, as my one and only love divine. Like the star that you are, you shine in my heart. Wherever I go, I will be where you are. And when the sun breaks, my farewell I'll condone, now that I know I am never alone." Faaris sighed and let his words drift into the cool night air as the twilight began to fade. He folded his hands over the edge of the balcony and glanced up at the stars, letting a soft wind brush several loose curls across his forehead. His chamber was close to the highest level of the palace, giving him a view of the entire city of Asteris, the capital of Pernia. His chamber was dim with the light of several lanterns and was by far one of the most beautiful rooms in the palace. A big, ornate rug covered a large area of the marble floor, resting between a messy desk and his big, silk-laden bed. The balcony awaited beyond opened, glass doors, veiled by sheer purple curtains. The streets below were empty and twinkling here and there from the light spilling from several windows. The grand bazaar was always full of life, even at this hour. It was when the restless came together to dance, sing, and tell stories around the central fountain. If Faaris was lucky, sometimes he could hear music. Beyond the city was nothing but pure, white sand dunes stretching far into the horizon. Only his imagination could fill in what was beyond them. He gulped and fidgeted with his hands, smiling to himself as he cast his eyes back to the stars. "Dare I ask again?"

He paused, hoping to give his hesitations a chance to pass, resting his focus on his hands. The seven gold rings he wore reflected the moon's luminescence in a mesmerizing way. "My Setareh," he said, still focused on the star, "what I wouldn't give to have you here, to know what your life is like. The mystery of your world will torment me forever."

Light suddenly crept across the balcony's floor as the doors to his chamber opened. "Faaris," a soft voice spilled through the open doorway.

Faaris turned and slipped away from the balcony's ledge. A smile came over him as he looked to the doorway. There stood a little girl, no older than four, gazing at him with two big brown eyes. She held onto the door as if afraid to enter.

"It's alright, Mushroom," he said. "You can come in."

Parisa smiled and hurried into his arms. For a moment he held her in a tight embrace as she buried her head into his chest.

"What brings you here?"

Parisa gazed up at him, her big brown eyes nearly penetrating his heart. "Happy birthday, Faaris," she whispered in her soft four-year-old way.

"Well, thank you," Faaris said, unraveling her from the hug. He smiled and tucked a loose strand of hair behind her ear, looking at her from eye to eye. "Don't tell me you've come all the way up here alone."

Parisa nodded, trying her best to hide her guilt with a smile. "I did."

Faaris grinned and lifted her into his arms. "Now, Mushroom, what did we say about roaming around the palace all by yourself."

Parisa giggled and blushed. "But I couldn't find you."

Faaris smiled. "Well, you found me now. What is it?"

Parisa yawned and gave him a helpless look. "I'm tired."

"Ah, of course," said Faaris, stealing a glance at the stars once again.

As his eyes met the moon, the wind picked up, and a cool breeze swept through the balcony. An enormous pair of wings glided across the face of the moon. Faaris gulped and hurried toward the edge of the balcony to get a closer look, leaving Parisa behind. "Did you see that?"

His eyes were fixed on the creature, trying to make out what it was as it made its way across the night sky. Just as he raised his head toward it, its shadow swept across his face, sending a chill down his spine. For a moment he froze, reconciling with the strange, cold feeling that was running through his body.

"It couldn't be," he breathed, still watching the creature before it disappeared into the stars.

"What?" asked Parisa.

"The Sima Bird," said Faaris.

"What's that?" Parisa asked.

Faaris crouched at the base of the ledge and invited her to his side. "Come here, I'll tell you a story."

Parisa hurried to his side and sat beside him at the foot of the ledge, nestling close enough to rest her elbow on his thigh.

"Alright," said Faaris, looking to the moon as if to extract the story from his memory. "Once upon a time, there was a tree. It was an ordinary tree of average stature, scrawny even. Season after season, its branches held little golden fruits that had great healing properties powerful enough to heal any wound, cure any illness, and even restore life."

Parisa just listened, eyes wide and focused as the story unfolded in her imagination.

"Not even the wisest of kings had ever been fortunate enough to find it, though many had tried," said Faaris. "As time passed and kingdoms grew, it got lost in an oasis in the Pernian desert. Still, it stood."

"Is it still out there?" Parisa asked, turning her head toward the city as if to see far into the distance toward the desert.

"No one knows," said Faaris. "I believe it is. Do you?"

Parisa nodded. "Yes. Can we go find it?"

Faaris laughed. "I've tried many times before, believe me. I never found it."

Parisa's eyes were still fixed into the distance. "Oh."

"Well, in its branches lived the wise and compassionate Sima

Bird," Faaris went on. "Like the tree, she was the only of her kind. She had lived long enough to have seen every age that the earth would ever know, gathering a wealth of knowledge from each. Her form was like that of an egret or a swan, though her neck was much longer and her beak far sharper. She carried herself with grace, traveling the skies on wings more enormous than even the great Pegasus."

Parisa gasped. "It was her. I know it was."

Faaris smiled. "Perhaps. I suppose it could have been. Shall I go on?"

Parisa nodded.

"Her feathers shimmered like opal with silvery tips, making her blend with the morning stars," said Faaris. "The strength of her wings was more powerful than any creature on Earth and rightfully so, as she spent her entire life in flight, only taking refuge when the time came to lay an egg. She had a great love for all creation, having enmity toward none except for the dark cobra, who tried to eat her extraordinary eggs."

"Is he a snake?" Parisa asked.

"Yes," said Faaris, "he was the most venomous serpent of all. One bite was the kiss of death."

Parisa gasped and moved closer to Faaris.

"In the blink of an eye, he left his victims paralyzed," said Faaris, gazing to the stars as the story played out in his head. "Within an hour, they were dead. Watching them suffer was one of his greatest pleasures, only second to delighting in his own victory. He was long and thin and as black as the night. His eyes were like two fireflies and his tongue as thin as a blade. His

5

fangs looked every bit as lethal as his bite. His hiss echoed like the sound of a siren, though it never gave warning of his arrival. He was the swiftest creature alive. Where he was feared, the Sima Bird had the respect that he desired most but would never have."

"I'm afraid of him," Parisa whispered.

"Don't be," said Faaris. "I'll tell you a secret. He's only a coward hiding behind his deadly bite. Perhaps he was jealous that the Sima Bird could fly, and he could only crawl."

Parisa giggled.

"The Sima Bird was known as a bird of fortune," said Faaris. "She had the ability to bestow kingship upon those whom her shadow passed over or whose head or shoulder she chose to rest on. Yet, such an honor was rare, for she flew at such great heights that she wouldn't possibly be spotted by the naked eye. Nevertheless, if one were to spot her, they were sure to enjoy a lifetime of joy and happiness, but if they were to kill her, they were fated to die in the days to come. You and I would therefore be very lucky, wouldn't we? If it was her, that is."

Parisa nodded.

"Once she was intrigued by the most beautiful of wishes, a wish for true love. It was this wish that inspired her to journey to the stars. It was during the journey that she died her first death. Her wings were so large that they caught fire from the heat of the sun, dissolving her to dust in an instant."

Parisa watched him intently, without saying a word.

"Nevertheless, she rose again with grace, more beautiful than before," Faaris went on. "From that moment on, she died many more times. As often as a star fell from the heavens, she burst

6

into flames, retiring to her death only to rise from the ashes each time stronger and wiser than before. Her love for the stars was like that of no other. Born from the heavens to which she would return, she served as a mediator and messenger between the earth and sky, carrying the wishes of humans to the stars and back. True love was sometimes discovered this way, but only by the ones who dared to petition the stars. Uniting lovers was her favorite of all tasks, second only to defending them against evil. It was the only cause for which she would sacrifice her own life. It was her true destiny."

For a moment, they were silent. Parisa glanced at him. "The end?"

"For now," said Faaris. "Now let me ask you this: do you believe in wishes?"

Parisa thought for a moment. "Yes."

Faaris glanced to the stars and then back at her. "Shall we make one? Shall we dare to petition the stars on such a night?"

Parisa jumped to her feet. "Yes."

"Alright," said Faaris. "I'll let you in on a secret. The stars will only hear you if you rhyme."

"Why?" Parisa asked.

Faaris shrugged. "I don't know. That's just the way it is. I figured it out several years ago. Then, all of my wishes started coming true. Why don't we give it a try?"

Parisa stood and wrapped each of her hands around two of the balcony's beams. "I'm ready."

"Alright," said Faaris. "First pick a star. Now, repeat after me. Little star up in the sky."

Parisa smiled and locked her eyes on one of the stars. "Little star up in the sky."

"I give this wish to you up high," said Faaris.

"I give this wish to you up high."

"To grant you happiness while I sleep," said Faaris.

"To grant you happiness while I sleep."

"And my every wish to safely..." Faaris paused and looked down at her.

"Keep," Parisa finished.

"Perfect," said Faaris. "Now, if ever you want to make a wish and you don't know what to say, you'll have this one to get you started."

Parisa smiled, still looking at the sky in awe. "Now you make a wish."

Faaris sighed and looked back to his star. "Setareh, my love, my beautiful star, what I wouldn't give to be where you are."

The small star that his eyes were set on flickered at the sound of his words. Faaris grinned and lowered his head, sending his eyes back to his hands.

"I'm sleepy," said Parisa, tugging at Faaris' sleeve. "Will you come sing me to sleep. Please."

"Alright," said Faaris. "Why don't you go on, I'll meet you there later. I have to go to the party first. I'll be there. I promise."

Parisa stood and headed for the doors to Faaris' chamber. Faaris sighed, watching her small shadow all the way to the door until it disappeared. He turned back toward Setareh.

"Forgive me for asking thousands of times," he said with a laugh, "but why must we always speak in these rhymes? I have more to say than I can in refrain, much more than a rhyme could ever contain."

Setareh glittered above as if she were thinking of speaking back to him.

Faaris looked up at her with hopeful eyes. "Go on, my star, say what you wish. There's no need to be shy, nor a need to resist."

He sighed and looked back at his hands, letting his eyes fall shut as the chill of the breeze sweep across his skin. The moon was high and bright as always, but tonight it was especially full and golden as it was only once this time of year.

Faaris glanced down at his hands and twisted some of the gold rings until they were all facing upward. He began to wonder what Setareh's life was like in the mysterious world that he only caught a glimpse of when the sun sank.

The soft sound of stardust trickled down from the sky. Faaris smiled. The stardust floated down into his hands in the form of a small, glittering orb. It floated with the grace of snow yet burned with the flames of a fervent fire. It was both hot and cold in a way that seemed lethal though it promised not even the slightest bit of harm by the look of it. Its beauty belonged to the stars. A shiver ran down Faaris' spine as it floated into his hands. The strange burning feeling never ceased to surprise him. When it reached his hands, it burst and let out Setareh's words. "Fear not, dear stargazer, I've heard you this time. I cannot explain why we must always rhyme. I've seen not your face and I know not your name. I hear you only when we speak in refrains. I do not know of the reason why, perhaps it is the law of the sky. Please don't stop wishing, you're doing quite well. At least as far as I can tell."

Her voice was as soft as breath, like he always imagined an angel's might be. Hearing her speak was like listening to a lullaby. There was no way for him to know if she was smiling back at him, but he was almost sure he could hear it in her voice. Just as he was about to reply, the sound of footsteps crept up from behind and two, tall shadows closed over him. Faaris dusted the icy stardust off of his hands.

"Faaris, my son," came a voice from the doorway of the balcony.

Faaris turned to see the two tall silhouettes of his parents in the doorframe. Both were poised and elegant as they always were, looking at him with gentle expressions as if they were statues that had come to life. His father wore a long, green robe made of the finest satin, with intricate gold embellishments to match the glittering crown on his head. His mother was dressed the same, but in a rich shade of violet with chains of shining beads and pearls hanging from her skirt that made noise when she moved. The moonlight cast its glow across them as they stepped onto the big, empty balcony, illuminating the beads and jewels that hung from their garments as if they'd been sprinkled from head to toe in fresh snow.

Faaris smiled and spread his arms as if asking for mercy.

"Forgive me, Father," he said. "I was just on my way to join you."

Faaris' father stepped closer and took him by the shoulders. "Never mind that, Faaris," he said. "We haven't come to scold you. It is your birthday after all. We've come with a gift."

The queen came up behind him with a mysterious object in

her hands, covered by a deep violet cloth. The king moved aside and held his hands out as if to display the gift. Faaris looked from his mother to his father. They both wore the same, knowing expression in a way that made Faaris uneasy.

"We've come to present you with this," said the queen, unmasking the mysterious object to reveal an elaborate glass bottle, stained in the same shade as the cloth, "for giving us eighteen wonderful years."

Faaris' eyes widened. The bottle's beauty was hypnotizing. He took a small step toward it and lifted it out of his mother's hands. The glass was almost as cool as the night air and smoother than ice, studded evenly with gold beads and crystals.

"It's...lovely," said Faaris, "but...a perfume bottle? I'm afraid I don't understand."

His mother smiled. "It is not merely a perfume bottle, my love."

Faaris' heart jumped inside of him. He took a deep breath and looked at his mother. "It isn't a genie, is it?"

Faaris' father laughed. "Ah, Faaris. Heavens no. But it is worth more than you can imagine."

Faaris blushed. "Ah, I see. Forgive me, but you know how I feel about things like that...genies. They're wicked. Wicked spirits come to bewitch our souls and steal our sanity. If the stories are true, that is."

The king smiled. "I couldn't agree more," he said. "But you mustn't believe all of those stories you read. They're nothing more than fantasies."

Faaris smiled. "I'm wary of fantasies, believe me. Most of

them, at least. The Legend of the Sima Bird is real, I'm sure."

The queen smiled. "Ah, we used to read that one every night," she said. "You would ask me to read it over and over again. It was your favorite one. It reminds me of your seventh birthday."

The king smiled to himself, almost laughing.

"I asked you what you wanted most, and you said the Sima Bird," said the queen. "So we got you a…"

Faaris grinned and cast his eyes at his feet. "A white peacock," he said. "And so, the collection began."

"Yes," said the king. "How many are you up to this year?"

"Eleven," said Faaris, rubbing the back of his neck, "but I think it will end there for now. I'm not asking for another one this year."

"No?" said the king. "Oh, Faaris, is something troubling you?"

"No," Faaris lied. "Well…not really…um. I still believe she's real you know…the Sima Bird. Call me childish. This year, I'll have her in my menagerie, I'm sure of it."

The queen shook her head. "Oh, Faaris, who truly knows? It says that she cannot be seen."

"Just because we can't see her doesn't mean she doesn't exist," Faaris said. "Seeing isn't always believing, you know. I for one happen to believe in many things that can't be seen."

The queen smiled and placed her hand on Faaris' cheek. "Well, stories aside, fear not about the gift, there isn't a drop of oil inside, much less a genie."

"I don't understand," Faaris said looking at the bottle. "Why such novelty? I assure you I can be perfectly satisfied with another peacock for the menagerie like all the years before. I've grown quite fond of them actually. They remind me of the Sima Bird. She and I are alike, you know. We share a great love for the stars."

The queen smiled. "Ah, you and your stars."

Faaris smiled to himself, lowering his focus toward the ground.

"This year is special," the queen said with a soft coaxing tone.

Faaris smiled. "Ah, because I'm eighteen now? It's just another year."

The king cleared his throat. "Indeed, it is, but we've been discussing this for quite some time and we both feel that it's time we…"

Another shadow appeared from the doorway. They all turned to see Faaris' older brother Sanjar leaning against the doorframe. Like the king and queen, he was tall and thin, only several inches above Faaris, who stood a little over six feet. He sparkled from head to toe in jewels. Over his shoulders hung a long green robe made of satin which gleamed in the light of the moon much like his jet-black hair which was doused in oil. It was long enough to be pulled into a ponytail at the nape of his neck, which it always was. His skin was smooth and pale like his father's and always shimmered with mica powder on special occasions. His beard fell just short of his chin and was finely trimmed around his sharp jawline. He was so polished that he almost looked unreal in the moonlight, as if he belonged to the stars themselves.

"Last I remember, the party is downstairs," said Sanjar, grinning as he popped a small, red grape into his mouth from a vine he held in his hand. His sleek, milky skin wrinkled from his dimples to his chin into two fractures as he smiled.

The queen brought her hand to her heart. "Sanjar, my child, you nearly frightened me. Is everything alright?"

He grinned. "Fear not Mother, everything is just…peachy," he said, tossing another grape into his mouth. "But I was wondering why you left. And of course, why the main man himself never showed up in the first place. What was it this time, Faaris? Nerves?"

Faaris lowered his head. "Priorities. I was on my way. I just… had to settle some things first, that's all."

"Ah, of course. Say no more," Sanjar said while twisting the black, groomed hairs on his chin. He shuffled suavely over to Faaris and gripped him by the shoulder.

"I forgot you were a…bit of a head case when it comes to parties," Sanjar grinned, shaking Faaris' shoulder.

Faaris wrestled himself free of Sanjar's grip. He sighed, looking offended, hoping that Sanjar would sense the resentment in his eyes. "I said I was coming, I only wanted to pray first. You wouldn't understand."

Sanjar laughed. "Pray? Oh. What makes you think I wouldn't understand? I could have prayed twice today. You wouldn't know."

"But you didn't," Faaris said with a straight face.

"No, I was too busy making all of this happen," Sanjar said, referring to his elaborate ensemble. "Another time perhaps."

"Well, a man only turns eighteen once in his lifetime," said Faaris. "I wanted to make this night count in my own way. I do this every year, it's nothing new. And you're right, I'll be the first to admit that I hate parties."

The king frowned. "Like kings, my sons, like kings. That's

quite enough."

Sanjar rolled his eyes.

The queen sighed. "This reminds me. Your father and I have been discussing something important for quite some time and while you are both here, I feel that now is the right time to tell you. What do you think, Azad? Shall we tell them now?"

The king, Azad, looked from Sanjar to Faaris. "Yes, I believe the time is right."

Faaris swallowed hard. "Mother, is… is something wrong?"

The queen smiled. "Not at all, my love."

Azad cleared his throat. "As you know it is customary for the eldest son to take the throne after the death of his father. It's been the law for centuries. Now that Faaris is old enough, we feel it's best that you are both aware of our wishes for the future of the kingdom."

"Father," said Faaris with a look of uncertainty.

"Now, God willing, this won't take effect until many more years, but we want you both to know that we've decided to change this law," said Azad.

Sanjar's sharp, golden eyes lit up. "What?"

Azad closed his eyes and took a deep breath. "We've decided that it would be best for the kingdom that Faaris take the throne first, even though he is not the first born."

Sanjar gulped, and a light sweat began to gleam on his brow. "Father," he said, frowning with confusion, "why?"

"Yes," said Faaris, "why me?"

The queen sighed and closed her eyes. "We simply feel that Faaris is better suited for the responsibility."

"Soraya," Azad said, as if trying to stop her from saying anything further.

Soraya sighed. "They deserve to know our reasoning."

Azad raised his chin, looking from Faaris to Sanjar with confidence. "So they do. Very well, then."

Soraya turned to Sanjar, whose spirits were looking low. "Sanjar, my love, please don't take this to heart, but how can we entrust our beloved kingdom to a man who spends all his hours throwing celebrations every time the sun sets and spending far too many funds on jewels and robes. That is not the way a true king behaves. Therefore, we have made our choice."

Faaris beamed and looked down at his feet.

"But it's unlawful," said Sanjar. "The eldest son is the rightful heir. It's been that way for centuries."

"Well, not anymore," said Azad. "I've made a change of law."

Sanjar winced. "What? When?"

"Last month," said Azad straightening his robe at his chest. "I'm making the announcement tonight."

Sanjar's heart was racing behind his cool composure. "But Father, you can't…"

"Sanjar, I am king, and it is done," said Azad. "Enough."

Sanjar was grinding his teeth behind closed lips, though he couldn't hide the fear in his eyes.

Azad took Sanjar by the shoulders and gave him a loving look. "Please try not to take it to heart, my son. It's for the best. For all of us."

"Now, my sons," Azad smiled. "We must not leave our guests downstairs without us. Come." He put his hands behind each of their backs and moved them toward the doorway.

Sanjar cut his eyes over at Faaris. Faaris managed a meek smile. He stopped walking.

"Father," said Faaris. "I need just one moment alone, please. I'll join you shortly after that. I promise."

Azad sighed. "Very well. It is your night after all. We will see you shortly, then."

Faaris pressed his palms together at his nose and bowed. "Thank you, Father. Believe me, I won't be long."

Azad nodded and motioned for Soraya and Sanjar to exit the chamber ahead of himself. When Faaris was sure he was alone, he hurried to the edge of the balcony and set the glass bottle on the ground and cast his eyes up at Setareh. "Night shall come, and I'll see you again. Oh, how I long for the days just to end. Nothing is sweeter than seeing your light. Until the next sunset, I bid you goodnight."

He kissed his fingertips and reached for the sky as if to touch her. As he turned to leave, he stumbled over the bottle at his feet, knocking it over and sending the lid all the way to the doorway. He grunted to himself while scurrying to save the small, gold lid. As he knelt to pick it up, he saw a bright flash of light from the corner of his eye. He turned to see what it was and caught a glimpse of one of nature's rarest, most enchanting sights—a shooting star.

A smile of intrigue peaked in the corner of his mouth and he stood slowly, lid in hand. He took a quick glance back up at Setareh to make sure she was still in her usual place. The shooting star streaked across the black sky as any falling star would, but there was something peculiar about this one. Rather than darting straight for the ground, it seemed to be traveling, winding, and turning on its way to Earth. The wind grew stronger and caught Faaris off balance. He squinted to get a closer look at the star. For a moment, it was almost as if it were moving closer to him, as if a wild storm were stirring. He waited for a second, deciding whether or not his eyes were playing tricks on him. But soon enough, the sizzling bright light shot in the direction of the balcony and swirled in front of him like a sparkling white flame. Faaris stumbled for the doorframe, leaving the bottle on the ground. He shielded his eyes as the star came to a blinding closeness. Stardust rained all around the balcony, and in a flash, the star collided onto the little glass bottle. Like a magnet, the lid was drawn from Faaris' quivering hand and sealed over the bottle. Faaris held his breath as the stardust cleared. The bottle shook a little but returned to normal within a few seconds.

He examined the sky overhead, which was no different than each night before, aside from the golden harvest moon. He crept toward the bottle and knelt to take it into his hands. It was warmer to the touch.

His mind was racing, stirring with all kinds of explanations as to what he'd just witnessed. He scanned the little glass bottle and tucked it away inside his robe. While bracing the doorframe, he glanced back once more at the sky. It was as still and quiet as ever.

2

"DEAR STARGAZER, WHY DO YOU NOT reply? Have I said something wrong? Won't you please tell me why?" Setareh, as Faaris called her, was anxious waiting to hear back from him. Hearing from him was like hearing stories from a faraway land, a land she longed to see.

Aelius, the strongest and brightest of all the stars, laughed and threw a fresh orb of sizzling, white stardust, a blorba, as the stars called them, at her head to get her attention.

"Hey, Ariette," he called at her from across the dark, open space, "how long are you going to let him call you that?"

Ariette sighed. "I don't mind. I think it's kind of him to give me a name. If he wants to call me Setareh, then I will be his Setareh. As long as he still calls me his friend, he can call me by whatever name he wishes."

"It doesn't bother you that he doesn't know your real name?" said Aelius.

Ariette shook her head. "I like it this way. Besides, he's never told me his name."

"Aw, are you shy?" said Aelius.

"Leave me alone, Aelius."

"So, when are you going to give up on him?" Aelius asked.

"Never," Ariette smiled. "He is my stargazer, and I am his star. We belong to one another."

Ariette whirled around the dark star-studded cosmos and rested into a more comfortable position, where she could see Earth and all its kingdoms in perfect view. Wishes were floating up all around the stars, but not one was answered. Ariette reached out to touch one. When her long slender finger nearly met it, Aelius threw another sizzling blorba at her hand, forcing her away from it.

"What do you think you're doing?" Aelius shouted.

Ariette jumped and hugged herself. "N-nothing, I...I was just curious. I've never granted a wish before."

"And you never will. So, don't even think about it," Aelius scolded. "Remember the law? No more wishes."

"I still don't understand why," Ariette mumbled to herself.

"It's simple," said Aelius. "Wishes come from humans. Humans make stars curious. Stars get curious and then we want to visit Earth. Stars visit Earth...we die. The end."

Ariette sighed and tucked several strands of her translucent hair behind her ear. Every move a star made was followed by a twinkling shower of stardust. It made up their entire bodies, flowed through every part of their being, and gave them celestial abilities of all kinds. Granting wishes was only one of these.

"I miss the days when things weren't so...cold here," she said. "The days when granting wishes was allowed. I never even got the chance to try it. If I had one wish, it would be to change that rule."

Aelius frowned and flew across the dark, open space.

In a storm of stardust, he landed beside her. "Careful what you wish for, Ariette. Those rules are there for a reason."

"A reason I don't understand," she said and turned away from him, crossing her legs as if there were a chair floating beneath her.

"Someday you will," Aelius smirked.

Ariette turned back toward him. "I doubt it."

She blinked twice making her beady, periwinkle eyes look especially innocent. "Surely you will tell me the truth soon. Earth can't be a death sentence for a star. I know you've been before. When I was small, you would return with stories of how brave you were and how all the humans thought you were a god," she said.

Aelius closed his eyes. "*You* didn't die," said Ariette.

"I'll tell you when you're ready to know," Aelius said, "and I don't think that's any time soon. Not according to the moon."

"And the sun?" Ariette asked. "What would he think?"

Aelius laughed. "I think he would agree with the moon."

Ariette glanced at the sun. "What if I asked him?" she said playing with a loose strand of hair. The strand floated out of her hand, much like everything else in space.

Aelius snickered. "I don't think you're that brave, little star."

Ariette crossed her arms. "How would you know?"

"Well, for one, you hardly move. That's why you're so weak. If you want to be bright, you've got to move around. Stir up some stardust, like me," he bragged, performing a quick, glittering exhibition of his skills right in front of her.

"I sing," Ariette said. "Do you not hear me sing to my stargazer? Sending my voice all the way to Earth takes a lot of stardust, which you wouldn't understand."

Aelius laughed and rolled his eyes. "It's not about stardust. Sound is much weaker than motion. Look, you have to keep moving. It's the only way to stay alive. Black holes always come for the weak ones. I don't want to see you sucked into one. Besides, the more you move, the brighter you'll be. Just look at me. How do you think I got so bright?"

A cold rush of stardust rang throughout Ariette's body. "I will try my best."

"You've got your whole life ahead of you, Ariette. I know you're not going to let a little shyness keep you from staying alive," said Aelius. "It's my job to look after you. If we lose a star, the Lux won't be the brightest constellation anymore, we'll just be like any other. No offense to Orion, but if you start moving, they'll have their work cut out for them. Maybe your stargazer will even see you better, although I'd hate to see you throw your life away for some human."

Ariette rolled her eyes. "Are we not meant for more than just floating around and shining? What about…you know…love? True love like the humans wish for."

Aelius put his hands on his hips. "My point exactly. One

wish, and now you're curious."

"What?" said Ariette.

"Look," Aelius laughed, placing his hand on her shoulder, "don't do it for me. Do it for yourself. You heard what I said about listening to wishes."

"Sorry, I just…" Ariette gazed down at Earth, "I want to know them. I want to know what their world is like. I want to know why they wish for such things."

Aelius frowned. "I know everything I need to know about humans," he said. "They don't wish because they love you, Ariette. Don't let their lyrics deceive you. They wish because they need you. We are more powerful than they could ever be and they know that."

"We are still nothing without love," said Ariette. "At least they have souls. Our hearts are empty. We are nothing but fire and dust, which will end with time. You know, maybe if you'd actually listen to them, you'd see what I see."

"I know everything I need to know about humans, alright? And stars don't need love, so forget it," he said, frowning. "I don't need a soul either. I have more stardust than any star that's ever existed. I've heard enough ridiculous wishes and even granted a few before it was forbidden. I, for one, like the new rule. I think it's better this way."

"So, now I'm supposed to just twirl around in this same spot for the rest of my life?" said Ariette. "Soulless and empty until the end of time?"

Aelius scratched the back of his neck. "Well, pretty much. That's what were supposed to do."

"Well, then maybe I don't belong here," said Ariette. "Who would want to live in a world without love? A world without anything. Nothing but cold empty darkness as far as the eye can see that only ends in more darkness."

"Look, if it makes you happy, I'll love you," Aelius teased, putting his hand over his heart. "What do you say?"

"I say, my heart is on Earth," said Ariette. "Besides, how will you love me if you don't even know what love is? I doubt you are even capable of such a thing. This world is dark and lonely. If I could, I would fly away to Earth and never return. That would make me truly happy."

"I'm going to tell the moon you said that," Aelius frowned. "Father wouldn't like it either."

Ariette flinched. "Aelius, please, no. Haven't you ever wondered what it's like? Am I so wrong to dream?"

"Look, at least you can still talk to the humans," said Aelius, "just no wishes. And you're a star in the Lux, remember? We're the brightest constellation in the galaxy. You mean to tell me you're not satisfied with that? It sounds like a good deal to me."

"I like wishes," said Ariette. "They are magical. Without them we are just...stars. Creatures of fire. Listeners of dreams but receivers of none."

"And what is so bad about that?" Aelius said. "We have our stardust. I think you need a little perspective, star. Then maybe you'll be grateful to be where you are. Trust me, Earth is rough."

Ariette put her hands on her hips. "Yet, somehow the humans are living there happily."

"What makes you think they're happy?" Aelius said with a

laugh. "Losing a star like the Nyx constellation just did is proof enough that it's dangerous there. I'll stay right where I am until the end of time, with a smile. And you should too."

"The Nyx lost a star?" Ariette asked, looking paler.

"Didn't you see the star that just fell?" said Aelius.

"I must have missed it," Ariette said. "I was listening to… never mind."

"Yeah, well, you can thank that star for the new rule," Aelius said, dusting several specks of stardust off of his arm.

Ariette took a deep breath and squeezed her arms around herself even tighter. "What does that have to do with wishes?"

Aelius laughed. "It has everything to do with wishes. Don't you understand? She's trapped there now because of a human's wish. If she stays there for too long, she'll start losing her stardust and fade away. Then she'll never be able to return to us. Trust me, that kind of fate is no better than death. You're better off staying where you are. Nothing, and I mean nothing is worth the risk."

Ariette hugged herself and looked at him. "Not even a soul?"

Aelius shook his head. "Nope."

"Oh," Ariette said, lowering her head. "I guess I can learn to be happy here."

3

As FAARIS NEARED THE GREAT HALL, the vibrations of drums began to pulse through the corridor, and the sounds of string instruments and chimes grew louder with every step. He pulled back the tall, red curtains at the entrance to the Great Hall and slipped into the crowd. The room was dim, drawing every last bit of light from the bronzy lanterns that were on the surrounding walls. The ceilings were as tall as the floor was wide, which, when mixed with a loud crowd of strangers would have easily overwhelmed Faaris if he weren't used to it. He weaved through the crowd, making his way to the head of the room, where he was sure his father would be. Azad was taller than most, which would make him easy to spot. Faaris decided that it wasn't likely that his father would be found seated at the throne. He was a generous king and always liked to be part of the festivities. Faaris nodded and smiled as he passed several nobilities.

"Best wishes to you, Majesty," they would say.

"What a fine young man you're becoming."

"Your father must be pleased with you."

Faaris smiled and nodded. "Thank you."

He was careful to keep his pace just fast enough to avoid getting caught in any long conversations. Like an eagle, his eyes surveyed the area, trying to spot even a single jewel on his father's crown. A short, strong arm swung around Faaris' neck and dragged him down several inches.

"There he is," came the voice from behind. The sound nearly deafened Faaris, coming just a little too close to his ear.

"Razi." Faaris laughed, turning to see the round, smiling face of his long-time friend, the look that almost always had the power to ease whatever thoughts were troubling him. Like almost everyone in the room, Razi also wore satin stained in a rich green with gold trim and a hat in a similar, intricate design over his tight brown curls. Faaris was used to this type of greeting and shook his head, knowing that he should have expected it, especially on his birthday.

"You finally came out of hiding," Razi teased.

Faaris smiled and rolled his eyes. "Having fun?"

"'Course I am. This place is always fun," said Razi.

Faaris rubbed his chin, eyes scanning the room. "Have you seen my father by any chance?"

"Not since I got here," Razi said. "I found Sanjar though."

Razi pointed Faaris to the banquet tables where Sanjar was centered among a flock of princesses, flirting and laughing as he always did.

Faaris shook his head. "I could have figured that one out."

Sanjar caught Faaris looking at him. Faaris turned and looked down at Razi. "Is he coming this way?"

"Looks like it," Razi said under his breath.

Before Faaris had the chance to escape, he found Sanjar's hand gripping the back of his neck. Faaris turned to see him grinning down at him as usual.

Razi bowed to Sanjar. "Highness. Nice to see you again." He struggled to his toes, trying to reach Sanjar's height. "Any pretty ladies over there?" he said, nudging Sanjar's arm.

Sanjar slapped Razi on the back. "Pretty, ha. Be my guest. These are princesses we're talking about."

Sanjar winked at the princesses from over his shoulder. "Don't ask me any of their names, though," he said, turning back to Razi.

"I'll take my chances," Razi said, heading toward the banquet tables. "See you, Faaris."

Faaris held a hand up as if to say goodbye. He looked up at Sanjar who was still hovering over him.

"Where is Father?" Faaris asked.

The musicians stopped playing. The crowd settled to a silence and turned their attention to where the top of two stairwells met above the thrones. Azad and Soraya stood, heads held high and regal like statues. The jewels they wore glittered even more in the light of the lanterns and chandeliers than they did in the moonlight, making them almost look unreal. The glow of the flames cast steady shadows of gold and bronze across their faces, catching their chiseled cheekbones as if their skin was made of marble. Aside from blinking, they barely moved, but it was this air about them that demanded instant respect from the people.

"The announcement," Faaris whispered to Sanjar, who had already run off. Faaris shook his head at the ground. He knew Sanjar couldn't bear to hear it. It was too humiliating.

"My good people," Azad announced, spreading his arms out toward the crowd.

Every eye in the room turned toward him. Faaris smiled. He was proud of his father. To see him standing there the way he was, and to hear his voice reach out to thousands was vitalizing.

"It brings me great joy to see you all here tonight, gathered to celebrate another year of my beloved son's life," Azad said. "It has been my privilege to watch him grow and become the young man he is today. Over the years he's shown to all of us that value lies in matters of the heart more than gold itself, and I believe that this is what truly makes a good man. We have built first our family and then our kingdom on love, and I believe whole-heartedly that someday my Faaris will carry on our legacy. So, tonight I stand before you to make it known that there has been a change of law."

Faaris' palms began to sweat, and his heart started racing. He drew in a deep breath to try to calm his nerves. He knew the minute the words were uttered that he would have the attention of thousands of guests in the Great Hall, but also the loathing of his brother. As Azad continued his speech, Faaris' eyes began to wander. He heard a soft clinking sound coming from the ceiling and glanced above. One of the lanterns had flickered out. In the shadows, it was almost as if a dark figure was perched on the lantern. Faaris shook his head and tried to convince himself that his eyes were only playing tricks on him. He tried to focus on his father's words, but his intuition was unsettled. His eyes kept going back to the lantern.

Azad continued to speak.

Another lantern flickered out. Faaris was the only one who seemed to notice. He heard more rustling sounds coming from the ceiling and glanced up once more.

"And so, we have made the decision to…" Azad went on. He turned to Faaris and opened his mouth to speak when suddenly every lantern died out at once. The crowd gasped and began whispering amongst one another.

Two silver blades spiraled across the room. Faaris was sure his heart stopped as he watched the blades fly across the air. His eyes traced their path directly from the chandelier where the dark figure had been.

"Ah," Azad's loud bellow echoed from the head of the room.

Faaris glanced to the top of the stairs as the blades plunged into the chests of his father and mother, not a second apart.

"*No*," Faaris felt himself say, though he barely remembered it as he made his way through the teeming crowd. It didn't feel real. Surely it was a dream. The dark figure was only an illusion, he thought. Surely it was his nerves. He was simply hallucinating.

Azad and Soraya melted to their knees, fading below the ledge of the balcony and out of sight. It happened as steady as leaves falling from the trees upon the dead of winter, yet all at once they slipped away—an image that Faaris knew would haunt him forever. Time itself seemed to have stopped along with Faaris' own heartbeat.

"Father," Faaris cried, struggling to make his way toward the head of the room.

"We're under attack," the leader of the guards shouted from the stairwell, drawing his sword and racing toward the king and queen. A masked man, clad in black slithered down the walls and onto the floor, scurrying toward the exits. Guests began to panic and scatter, each hustling toward the nearest exit.

"Stop him," the guard shouted.

Like a lizard, the black clad man slithered across the floor, throwing knives at anything, or anyone, in his path of escape.

Faaris glanced across the room, just as a knife flew toward him. He dodged it and found himself suddenly swept off of his feet by a pair of strong arms. He panicked and tried to fight the grip, but his strength was no match. The man threw Faaris over his shoulder and began running for the tall, red curtains at the side of the room. Faaris recognized him. It was the leader of the guards and Azad's most trusted advisor.

"Mehrzad," Faaris cried.

"All is well, all is well," Mehrzad panted, struggling to deliver Faaris to safety.

"But, Mehrzad, please," said Faaris, tugging at the back of Mehrzad's robe. "My father, my mother. Let me go. Please."

Mehrzad burst through the curtains and slipped into a dim corridor. He set Faaris on the ground, bracing him by the shoulders.

"Now," said Mehrzad, looking Faaris directly in the eyes, "stay here until I return for you. I'm going to go find your brother."

"And my mother and father?" Faaris said.

Mehrzad paused and closed his eyes. "I...I tried to save them." He sighed. "I'm sorry dear boy. I wasn't able to save them, but at least I can save the two of you."

Faaris gulped and nodded, eyes beginning to swell with tears. "Oh, God please be with me," he whispered to himself.

Mehrzad turned back toward the curtains, motioning once more for Faaris to stay where he was. Faaris sank to the ground, heart thundering in his chest. As he closed his eyes, bitter tears fell onto his cheeks. Every nerve in his body began shaking. Panic was taking over, worsening now that he was alone. Faaris tilted his head to the ceiling and folded his hands over his chest.

"How can this be?" he whispered. "I don't understand. I don't understand."

Mehrzad slid back through the curtains, dragging Sanjar behind him, both sweating and panting. Faaris stood and embraced each of them. "You're alive. I thought you'd never return. I was nearly holding my breath. I've...I've been suffocating over the thought of losing you too. I couldn't bear it."

Mehrzad shushed him. "Come with me," he said, nudging Faaris and Sanjar ahead. "Quickly."

"Where are we going?" Faaris asked, starting into a run.

"The menagerie," said Mehrzad. "You'll be safe there."

"Why don't we ask questions later, Faaris," said Sanjar with a grin, trying to stay cool. "Unless you want that killer to hear us.

Then we'll all be dead."

"He's right," said Mehrzad. "Go on, both of you. The quicker the better. I'll meet you there as fast as I can."

Sanjar grinned and raised an eyebrow at Faaris. "I'll race you."

"Now's not the time," said Faaris, focused on reaching the menagerie.

"Who says we can't have a little fun?" said Sanjar.

Faaris drew in a deep breath. "Perhaps a time when our lives aren't on the line. Besides, you and I both know the odds are in your favor."

Sanjar shrugged. "The quicker the better. Aye, Mehrzad? You wouldn't want to die now, would you, Faaris?"

Faaris heaved a heated breath, as if a burning fire were building in his chest. "I'll see you there." With that, he took off as fast as he could, eyes dead set on the path toward the menagerie.

Sanjar charged after him with all of the power he could manage, catching up to him within only seconds. They ran neck-and-neck down the hall, Mehrzad hurrying behind them with a smile on his face.

"I haven't seen you this angry in years," said Sanjar.

"I'd consider that a good thing," said Faaris. "But I have every right to be."

As soon as they reached the doors to the menagerie, each put his hand on one of the handles and pulled, their sweaty palms slipping a little. The doors were locked. Faaris grunted and slammed his fist against the door as if he sought great revenge on it. "I knew it."

Sanjar threw his head back laughing. "I thought you had the

key, bird boy?"

Faaris sighed and rested his hands on his hips. "I took it off for the ceremony."

Mehrzad hurried toward them just as they turned back toward the hallway. Without hesitation, he kicked through the doors of the menagerie and rushed them into the garden.

"With all due respect, was that really necessary?" said Faaris, striking a firm hand toward the damaged doorway.

"Someday you'll thank me," said Mehrzad.

"Granted," said Faaris, "but you didn't have to go on and destroy my only chance of privacy like that."

"Rest assured, I haven't broken it," said Mehrzad. "I intend to lock you in here for the night, after all."

The moon shone through the top of the dome, serving as the only light. The shadows of trees and bushes lurked in the darkness, masking the beauty of what Faaris usually called a safe haven, transforming it into a place of fear and uncertainty as if it were some sort of underworld that he had never known before. The familiar sound of trickling water from the fountains comforted him somewhat as the cool mist fell across his skin, but not even that was enough to console him this time.

"Stay here until I return," Mehrzad ordered.

"Do you expect us to stay here all night?" Sanjar whined.

"Only until I come for you," Mehrzad said.

"How soon is that?" Sanjar said, putting his hands on his hips.

"As soon as we know you are safe, Majesty," Mehrzad said with a bow, slipping back through the doors. "I assume you'd prefer not to die."

Sanjar rolled his eyes.

At the sound of the lock, Sanjar grabbed Faaris by the arm and slammed him against the side of the wall. He pulled a small knife from his belt and held it to Faaris' throat.

"Listen well, rat," he hissed. Faaris' breathing grew faster, and a cold sweat broke across his forehead. Faaris couldn't manage anything more than a weak grunt. He was almost sure he saw tears in Sanjar's eyes, though such a thing rarely happened. "I'm as…" Sanjar choked, the blade quivering a bit in his hand, "I'm as…aargh. I'm as torn as you are. I…look, neither one of us needed our parents to die. But they did. It happened. It's over."

Faaris gulped. Seeing his brother this way brought tears to his eyes too, some of which fell. He couldn't help it. "Sanjar. I know. It's done, but it's not our burden to carry. Please don't release your anger on me. Please. We can figure this out together."

Faaris closed his eyes. "Please."

"Alright," said Sanjar, "I have an idea. Consider your life before you say anything smart. You and I are the only ones who know about that law, so I say away with it. As far as anyone knows, I'm the next heir. Say one word about the announcement and you can kiss your life goodbye. Understand?"

"But…" Faaris choked, "it's the law. Father would never allow it. Besides, you wouldn't kill me."

Sanjar tightened his grip on Faaris and brought the knife closer to his skin, just close enough for Faaris to feel the chill of the metal. Faaris closed his eyes, prepared for the worst.

"Don't underestimate me," Sanjar said with a glare. "Now, swear you'll say nothing, or I'll kill you right here, right now.

Don't think I won't."

The cold blade was only one move away from slicing across his skin.

"You wouldn't," said Faaris.

Sanjar grinned. "Try me."

Faaris glared at him. "You are aware that killing me would derail your chances of being king, aren't you? You and I both know that no one will agree to crown a murderer as their king. You'd be banished forever or worse. I'm not afraid of you."

Sanjar moved the blade closer to Faaris. "You should be."

Faaris closed his eyes and held his breath.

"No one would ever know," said Sanjar. "For all they know, it was the assassin. I'm a lot smarter than you think, you know."

Sanjar laughed to himself and carved a small scratch across the side of Faaris neck. Faaris tried to let out a scream but couldn't manage to make a sound. His entire body was shaking. He closed his eyes. *God, please, no. Please, no*, he prayed.

Sanjar lifted the knife away for a moment and pushed Faaris into the wall, holding his hand firmly over Faaris' chest. "You know what?" he said.

Faaris released a breath and swallowed hard, looking at Sanjar with resentment. "What?"

"I think you're right," said Sanjar. "I've changed my mind. It's Mehrzad I want dead."

"No," said Faaris, his voice growing louder now that he was free of the knife. "I...I forbid it. Not Mehrzad. He practically raised us. How could you even think of such a thing? If you even so much as think of it again, believe me, I'll alert the guards and the counsel, and you'll be the one to die."

Sanjar laughed. "You think I'm afraid of you?"

"When I give my word on something," said Faaris with a glare, "you should be. The truth can't stay hidden for very long."

Sanjar thought for a moment, staring at Faaris as thoughts billowed in his mind. Faaris didn't break his glare for even a second.

"It's Mehrzad or your word," said Sanjar. "Surrender. I dare you."

Faaris was silent. Sanjar smiled at the fear that was intensifying in Faaris' eyes.

"But you're lying," said Faaris. "I know how you are. It doesn't matter what I say."

"You don't believe me?" Sanjar teased, bringing the knife to the side of Faaris' neck again. "Oh, Mehrzad," Sanjar said in a playful tone, "Faaris tried to escape last night to find you, and the assassin slit his throat. I saw the whole thing." He tightened his grip and leaned closer to look Faaris directly in the eyes. "It was bloody."

Faaris closed his eyes and held his breath. "Fine," he said, the glare in his eyes almost as fierce as Sanjar's. "I'll say nothing."

Sanjar grinned. "Wise choice." With a quick wave of the knife, he cut a small slit across the side of Faaris' neck before tucking the knife away. A small drop of blood spilled from the cut. Faaris took a breath and brought his fingers to the cut.

Sanjar stood and began walking toward the exits. "Let that be a reminder."

"Sanjar," said Faaris. "Mehrzad said we have to stay here.

Where are you going? The assassin is still here."

Sanjar grinned and whipped the blade back out. "I'm going to kill that loathesome…"

"Sanjar wait," said Faaris reaching for him. "He'll kill you."

Sanjar turned and knelt beside Faaris. "You're right, I almost forgot something."

He reached into Faaris' vest and ripped out the glass bottle. When it was secure in his hand, he threw Faaris aside and rose to his feet. Faaris heaved a deep breath and placed his hand over his racing heart.

"What kind of idiot do you think I am?" Sanjar laughed. "I know what this is."

Faaris got to his feet, looking puzzled. "What?"

"It's a genie, isn't it," Sanjar said, toying with the bottle.

Faaris braced the wall behind him. "No. I can assure you it's empty."

"Liar," Sanjar sneered.

"I'm telling the truth," said Faaris. "There's not a genie, not even a drop of oil. See for yourself if you don't believe me."

Sanjar examined the bottle. "You can't fool me, Faaris."

Faaris shrugged. "Last I saw it was empty. Honest. Genies don't exist anyway. It's only a myth. You'd know that if you spent any time reading."

"We'll see about that," Sanjar laughed, plucking the lid from the bottle.

The minute the lid came off, the vague sound of a woman's voice began to echo through the menagerie in song. Both Faaris and Sanjar fell silent, hypnotized by the sound. Clouds of deep, purple smoke began to rise from the bottle, carrying the woman's voice to a louder volume. A ghastly figure floated from the mouth of the bottle, letting the smoke carry her out in one fluid motion. Crystal stardust fell around her, giving her entire body a glow.

Sanjar turned his head and cocked an eyebrow at Faaris, mouthing the words, "Liar." Faaris shook his head and opened his arms, trying to defend himself.

When the genie had completely emerged, she opened her eyes so suddenly that both Faaris and Sanjar took a step back. In the light of the stardust, her eyes were unusually light in color, like two icy gemstones staring straight into their souls. Her skin was as pale as the moon and her hair as black as the night sky. Like a mermaid in water, she floated over the bottle, hovering by a tail of smoke. A sly smile crept across her face as she glanced from Sanjar to Faaris. Her eyes froze on Sanjar and a haunting song spilled from her mouth.

"Hear this song and you will see,
The magic that's inside of me.
My voice, my magic melody,
Listen well, it is the key.

Close your eyes and dreams ascend,
Wish and you can capture them.
Anything your heart can find
Sing to me in perfect rhyme.

Soft as dust, pure as the day,

This song will take your pain away.
Sing to me, your heart's desire,
Take this chance, lest it expire.

But when this song comes to an end,
This magic chance you will have spent.
Only thrice I'll sing for thee,
So, choose your wishes carefully.

You must speak now, this is the time,
Until my silence, I am thine.

Any wish you shall receive,
If your heart truly believes.
Limitations, there are some,
I cannot change the setting sun.

I cannot force the moon to rise,
Or take the stars out of the sky.
I cannot change what has been done,
But I can reverse what has just begun.

The natural laws I cannot change,
But only slightly rearrange.
So, if you wish to change your fate,
You must be wise and unafraid.

Your choice of words will be the key,

To any possibility."

Faaris couldn't stop staring at the strange sight before him, practically hanging on her every word. Sanjar turned his head to Faaris and shoved him out of the way.

"I wish…to be the richest man alive," Sanjar said, staring at the genie.

The woman grinned and shook her head. In an instant, she was sucked back into the bottle, and the garden returned to darkness. Faaris remained silent, trying to hide his urge to smile. He knew why Sanjar's wish hadn't been granted.

4

ARIETTE COULDN'T WAIT FOR NIGHT to come. Tonight, she would sing for him, straight from her heart. How brave of her it would be. Songs from the heart were the best ones, and he deserved the best. She took a deep breath and hummed to herself. The melody was smooth and silky. She was the spider, and the song was her web. In that moment, she closed her eyes and let the song take form. Nothing could pull her away—not even Aelius' scolding.

"If a star could have a wish, I would wish to hear from you soon, dear stargazer," she said, looking down upon her beloved Earth. She watched night's shadow fall over her stargazer's kingdom. Aelius wasn't paying attention to her. When night came, he was especially focused on being the most impressive stud in the night sky.

Several wishes began floating up, but none for her. Most of the humans gave their wishes to the brightest stars. The unanswered wishes just dissolved into the atmosphere. Aelius flicked them away as they appeared around him. He always received the most wishes. Ariette's heart nearly broke watching their precious wishes be ignored. She hated the rule more and more. She sighed and hugged herself. Still, she hadn't given up. Her stargazer had been wishing on a regular basis these days. She knew she could count on hearing from him tonight.

Sure enough his wish came, twinkling effervescently like a special little gift just for her. Stardust flurried inside of her. She almost hesitated to open it, but at the same time, she couldn't wait. She reached for it. As her finger touched it, it burst, letting out her stargazer's words.

"My love, my life, what a beautiful night," he said, "but something terrible has happened tonight. I can't explain, for fear I'll be heard, but please believe I've seen the worst. A man in black disturbed our night and killed my parents with his knife. My brother stole the gift they gave me and not only that, he tried to kill me. That is not what scares me most, for I have also seen a ghost. We call them genies where I'm from, creatures as wicked as they come. They give us wishes, but with a price. Can you give me some advice?"

Ariette's heart sank a little as the stillness of the cool dark air came over her. She took a deep breath and closed her eyes.

"Advice you ask, but I cannot give," she said. "Things are different where I live. The creatures you speak of, I do not know, but I'm sorry that they scare you so. Please let me share my remedy, my secret song, my melody. It heals my heart when I feel sad, and it will help you forget the loss you've had."

She gathered each word into a blorba in her hands, and with a big breath, she sent it down to him. Her heart was racing as she watched it fly off.

"Full of surprises you are indeed," Faaris replied, "you always know just what I need. Such an angel you are to me, of course I would love to hear you sing."

Ariette's heart filled with joy. She felt brighter than the sun. With a happy heart, she took a deep breath and let the softest melody pour out of her. As she sang, stardust spilled from her hands to carry each note down to her stargazer. She had never done this with a song before, but it felt more magical than any word she had ever sent down to Earth. When she had finished the last note, she opened her eyes and took a deep breath, watching the last of the stardust trickle down.

"Please like it, Stargazer," she whispered, holding her hands tightly to her heart.

"Ariette," Aelius called from across the way. "Do my ears deceive me, or do I hear what I think I hear?"

Ariette's heart jumped inside of her, and she turned toward him with eyes as big and bright as the moon. "What?"

Aelius flew toward her in a storm of stardust. "I don't think I've made myself clear," he said, folding his arms.

Ariette sank and hugged her knees while floating.

"No wishes," Aelius scolded. "Don't even look at them, do you understand?"

"I'm sorry," Ariette said. "I was only singing. I'm not granting any wishes. I promise."

"You'd better not be granting any wishes." Aelius frowned. "I'll be watching, so don't try anything."

Ariette sighed and crossed her arms as she watched him dart back toward his usual spot. She looked at Earth with an empty feeling in her heart. Her stargazer's response floated up to her.

"What a lovely gift you have indeed," he said. "A lullaby you are to me. In this moment you've numbed my pain, but my heart will never be the same. Your voice is unlike any I've heard, far sweeter than any bird. My world is shaken, I struggle to recover. Dare I ask you for another?"

Ariette bit her lip. She glanced at Aelius to find him staring back at her with the fullest intent in his silvery eyes. Her heart sank. Into her hands she whispered, "I cannot for now, please forgive me. But I promise not to leave you empty. Another time will come, I'm sure. Another day you must endure. I long to sing for you again, please be patient my dear friend." She sent it off with every speck of remorse that was inside of her. For what seemed like the longest time, she didn't hear back from him. She hated the rule now more than ever.

Aelius was aflame, so absorbed into his movements that there was no way he could have possibly seen or heard her. Ariette's own luminescence was glowing it's brightest too, which was still nothing in comparison to the other stars.

"I am invisible to all but you, it seems. Still, I have wishes, fears, and dreams," Ariette said to her stargazer, knowing that he wouldn't hear her.

Another glittering wish drifted up to her. The night was

nearing its end. She knew this would be the last she would hear from him until the next sunset. She welcomed his wish into her hands and let it unravel. "What a mystery you are to me, I never thought a star could sing. A song of hope you've given me, truly you have rescued me. Your voice is sweetness, your words are poetry, nothing on earth compares to such artistry. You're the melody that's found my heart and carried it out of the dark. Each time I see you in the sky, you shall be my lullaby."

5

THE MENAGERIE WAS ALMOST A different place when the sun was up. Rays of light cast through the glass dome, making it seem as if the garden were outdoors. A soft mist arose from the big rippling fountain at the center of the garden, filling the air with its soft, pleasant aroma and giving life to the plants. Fruit trees of all kinds lined the walls of the dome, stretching all the way to the top of the tall glass ceiling and lending their sweet citrus aroma to the already enchanting scent of the mist. Marble statues of the Sima Bird stood throughout the menagerie, almost blending with the live white peacocks that roamed around beneath them. The menagerie had returned to its usual beauty thanks to the rise of the sun. It was the oasis of the palace, offering Faaris sanctuary from the troubles of the outside world.

Faaris hadn't slept that night. He was careful to do as Mehrzad had ordered and waited in the garden. Fortunately, Setareh was there to keep him company until sunrise. Sanjar, on the other hand, had left with the bottle several hours before sunrise. Faaris watched his last wish fly off and eagerly leapt for the doors as soon as he heard knocking.

"Faaris. Sanjar," Mehrzad called, banging on the door.

Faaris hurried to unlock the doors and swung them open to see Mehrzad looking down at him. He let out a sigh of relief and threw his arms around Mehrzad's sturdy chest.

"Thank goodness," Faaris said, the sound muffled by Mehrzad's robe. "I prayed all night."

Mehrzad smiled and patted Faaris on the back. "Well, I want you to know that you are safe for now," he said. "We lost the assassin, but we managed to keep an eye on his escape route. Razi will look after you as your personal guard, and I will look after Sanjar. We are going to do everything we can to protect you and your brother until the masked man is captured. We've secured all the exits and stationed a guard at every door. And I'm afraid that means you cannot leave the palace."

Faaris smiled. "Frankly, I wouldn't want to."

Mehrzad paused. "What's that on your neck?"

Faaris immediately brought his hand to the scar. "What? Oh, that. I um…it's just a scratch."

"I see," said Mehrzad. "One of the birds scratched you while you were asleep, I take it."

"It's nothing," said Faaris. "I'm fine really."

"Very well. Now, where is your brother?" Mehrzad asked,

looking over Faaris' shoulder into the menagerie. "He has a big day ahead of him."

"He left during the night," Faaris said.

Mehrzad sighed. "What am I going to do with that boy? Let's just hope I can make a king out of him."

Faaris took a deep breath and closed his eyes. "Mehrzad."

Mehrzad turned toward him with a warm look. "What is it Faaris?"

"There's something I…" Faaris ran his fingers through his hair. "I need to tell you something."

"Of course," said Mehrzad. "Anything."

"Well…" Faaris gulped. "It's um…it's about the law. Last night, Sanjar…"

Sanjar crept up behind Mehrzad. "Talking about me?"

Faaris was almost sure his heart stopped for a second. Mehrzad turned to see Sanjar looking up at him. "Ah, yes. There you are, my boy," he said. "Now, we have some very important items of business to discuss, if you would join me in the Great Hall."

Sanjar rubbed his hands together. "Ah, say no more, Mehrzad, my good man. I'm all too prepared."

Faaris released an angry breath.

"Oh, Faaris, forgive me," said Mehrzad. "I almost forgot. What was it that you needed to tell me?"

Sanjar raised an eyebrow at Faaris. "Yes, I'm becoming quite interested as well."

Faaris gulped and cast his eyes at his shoes. "Um, it's…it was nothing. It doesn't matter now."

"No?" Sanjar teased. "Well, I heard my name. It must have

been important."

Faaris shook his head. "No. It was um…" He paused and glared at Sanjar. "It was about the coronation law. There's something I felt Mehrzad should know. That's all."

"Oh," said Mehrzad. "Well, do tell me if there is something regarding the law. I must know."

Sanjar slid his blade from his belt and admired it. "You know, Mehrzad," he said. "I've been carrying this thing with me since I was a boy. I've been thinking that perhaps as king, I'll require an upgrade. What do you think?"

Faaris gulped and clenched his jaw, watching the blade with the sharpest focus. "We shouldn't have our weapons out inside the palace, Sanjar."

"Aww, relax, Faaris, I'm just playing," said Sanjar. He grinned, admiring the blade shining in the sunlight that was peeking through the glass.

"He's right," said Mehrzad. "Conceal it."

"I'll be king soon, you know," said Sanjar. "You can't tell me what to do."

"Ah, but you're not king yet," said Mehrzad. "Now, come with me."

Mehrzad took both Sanjar and Faaris by the arms and escorted them down the hall. "Now," he said, "I'm first and foremost deeply sorry for the loss of your mother and father. Your father was a great friend of mine and you should know that it breaks my heart as much as it does yours. But we are strong. And so, we will carry on as the leaders that we are. As the eldest, Sanjar will take the throne as king. Of course, he will need to marry soon so that

Pernia will have a queen. And that is another thing."

Sanjar grinned. "Please, I don't need a queen."

Mehrzad laughed to himself. "Ah, but you do, Sanjar. It is the law. Now, there are many scrolls to be signed, your parents' possessions to be discussed, and so forth. But you must be crowned soon, or else Pernia will be without a leader. You should be happy, my boy. It is a great honor and responsibility."

"No, no, I'm happy," Sanjar said. "Please, where do we begin?"

"We will honor the king and queen with a memorial, but first and foremost, we must crown our new king," said Mehrzad, opening the curtains to the Great Hall. "I know it's short notice, but your coronation must take place tonight."

Sanjar and Faaris followed him across the room, which seemed even larger without all of the guests and musicians buzzing around it. Servants were already busy preparing the Great Hall for the coronation. Faaris was careful to dodge several long tables as they were pulled one-by-one into the room. He glanced to the head of the room, where the two stairwells met, the last place he'd seen his mother and father. His mind was stirring, his heart burning with sadness, and his spirit aching to be anywhere but there in the Great Hall.

AT THE PEAK OF SUNSET, FAARIS FOUND HIMSELF standing as still as a statue inside his own chamber, waiting for the servants to put the final touches on his clothes. He sighed, staring at his reflection in the tall mirror in front of him. The gold-studded robe over his shoulders was only brought out a few times a year, usually only for celebrations, feasts, or ceremonies.

"When you're finished, I beg for just one moment alone," he said, watching the servants smooth every last curl into place. "I need to prepare myself."

"As you wish, Majesty ," they said with a bow, reaching for his gold crown. They laid it on his head and made their way out of the chamber.

"Baraz will come to escort you to the ceremony when the time comes, Majesty ," one of them said before closing the doors.

"Thank you," Faaris said, readjusting his crown to make it more comfortable.

When he was sure every servant was at least several steps into the hall, he sprang for the doors to conceal himself inside his chamber. With a deep breath, he darted for the balcony. He threw the silky red curtains back and broke into the cool twilight air, nearly collapsing over the edge of the balcony. For a moment, he closed his eyes and let the soft evening winds ease his mind. The sun was sinking lower and lower by the minute. He glanced up to the sky, hoping to see several stars, though the sun was still out.

"My love, my life, how can this be? Tell me that it's just a dream," he wailed to Setareh. Tears of resentment swelled in his eyes but wouldn't fall. "Tell me it's not happening," he choked.

He was so overcome with emotion that he couldn't manage to think clearly enough to come up with another rhyme. Whether Setareh even heard him or not didn't matter. What he needed more than anything was to free his heart of these bitter feelings.

"Why?" he said, shaking his head. "How can this be? What will happen when he's king?"

Just as he thought of leaving, Setareh's reply trickled down to him. "Fear not, dear stargazer. Do not cry. Sometimes we do not know the whys. But I do not like to hear you this way. What can I say to make you stay?"

"You see me, love," he said, almost laughing to himself. "You see me through. How I wish you truly knew. I'd tell you more, but I must go. Tomorrow I will let you know."

"Another promise I know you'll keep. Farewell for now and happy sleep."

Faaris smiled to himself. He kissed his fingers and reached up to her as he always did before leaving. Two solid knocks on the door and Faaris' heart jumped.

"Ready or not," Razi called from the other side of the door.

Faaris took a deep breath and glanced once more at Setareh. He was anything but ready.

The Great Hall was filled with people, even more people than the night before. Sanjar looked regal and more polished than ever. A silky, gold robe, far more extravagant than the one Faaris wore, hung over his shoulders. His long, jet-black hair was slicked away from his face with oils, and the facial hair along his jawline was cut into a design only a master craftsman could have created. He and Mehrzad were seated at the top of the stairwells, watching the guests settle into stillness. Razi followed Faaris up one of the stairwells to join them. Every member of the court was seated there. From the top, Faaris looked out at the crowd. The entire Great Hall was set for a celebration, complete with musicians, banquet tables, and even a snake charmer. Faaris took a deep breath at the sight of the snake. It was a king cobra, as sleek and dark as Sanjar's oiled hair. Faaris hated snakes; one wrong move was all it took to set them off.

Mehrzad stepped forward and cleared his throat. "People of Pernia. It is a great honor and privilege to welcome you here tonight. Within a matter of moments, Pernia will have a new king."

The people cheered and shouted, creating a near-deafening sound.

"So, without further ado, ladies and gentlemen I give you, Prince Sanjar Husrav Kir Kaspar Aghasi, son of the late King Azad Hormisdas Aghasi and Queen Soraya Vassy Aghasi, to be crowned the new King of Pernia."

The crowd roared again, whistling and cheering as Sanjar stepped forward. Mehrzad escorted him down the stairs to the throne, where he would be crowned. The crowd applauded the entire time, growing louder as they came closer to the bottom of the stairs. Faaris couldn't take his eyes off of the snake. It was contained by the charmer, but he couldn't help but notice how it wriggled at the sound of the crowd.

Faaris smiled and leaned down to Razi. "If I should I ever be crowned king, you won't find a snake at my ceremony."

Razi laughed. "That's Sanjar for you. He ordered it, you know. He's not afraid of anything. He said it's a symbol of his strength."

Faaris rolled his eyes. "I find it hard to believe Mehrzad allowed such a thing."

"He's the boss now," Razi shrugged. "Mehrzad can only say so much."

Faaris crossed his arms and shook his head, looking down

at Sanjar who was kneeling to be crowned. Mehrzad raised his already booming voice. "I now pronounce you, King of Pernia."

The crowd cheered even louder than all the times before. Faaris' head was spinning.

Just as the gold crown was laid over Sanjar's head, the snake slipped out of the charmer's trance. It opened its mouth to reveal its deadly fangs and charged straight for Sanjar's left forearm. Sanjar's eyes widened the second he heard its deadly hiss, and he looked up to see the snake slithering toward his arm. Before he could react, the cobra sank its fangs into his arm, nearly to the bone, as if it sought great revenge on him. The sound rang throughout the entire palace, causing everyone to stir. Mehrzad drew his sword and sliced the cobra in half, several times until he was sure it was dead. Sanjar managed to rip the snake off of his own arm but crumbled to the ground from the venom's sting. Mehrzad held his arms out wide over Sanjar, motioning for everyone to stay back.

Razi and Faaris rushed down the stairs. On his way, Faaris reached for a pitcher of water from one of the banquet tables. He carried it to Sanjar and knelt beside him. He tore a small piece of his sleeve off and dipped it in the water.

"Here," he said to Sanjar, "give me your arm."

Sanjar's eyes were tightly closed, sweat began to drip from his brow. Faaris slid Sanjar's arm out of the sleeve of his robe and laid the wet cloth over it, feeling his entire body trembling. A snarl curled in the corner of Sanjar's mouth as if he were resisting Faaris' help. Faaris took a deep breath and lowered his mouth to the wound, prepared to suck out as much of the poison as he could.

"Sanjar, it's alright."

"Good heavens, Faaris no," Mehrzad shouted and pulled Faaris away just before his mouth could make contact with the wound.

"Leave this to me," Mehrzad said. "We cannot put your life at risk too. Not the prince, heavens no. Fear not, we have other remedies."

Several guards knelt beside Mehrzad and began tending to the wound. Faaris sighed and stood. Razi took his arm and drew him back.

"Will he be alright?" Faaris asked.

"No worries," Razi said. "He'll live. We caught it in time. But any longer and he might not have. Those ones are deadly."

"*Why* is all I ask myself," Faaris mumbled. "Why on earth would he choose to have a snake at his coronation?"

6

SETAREH, PLEASE HEAR ME, I FEEL SO lost. I see all things come with a cost. Why must our love be star-crossed?"

Ariette sighed as she received the wish.

"Why such sadness, why such fear? These days despair is all I hear. I mean not to offend you, I only care. I wish your world I could repair. You are not hopeless, that I know. I wish I could convince you so. And I feel I've waited for so long. May I offer you another song?"

Faaris was quick to respond, as usual. "Of course, my love, please sing to me," he said. "Take away my memory."

"What is it now, has something else happened? A life on Earth I can't imagine," Ariette replied.

"Another day, another fight. My brother suffered a serpent's bite," said Faaris. "They're creatures that kill if you're not careful. My brother thinks not of these perils."

Ariette's heart sank. "The night, it isn't very long, so let me sing to you my song."

She sang to him. This time it was a new song. She didn't want him to get bored, and she had thousands of songs inside of her. For what seemed like forever, she lost herself in another melody, letting each word come from deep inside. She never planned the lyrics. She just let her thoughts and feelings inspire her. It never failed. As Ariette sang, her own brightness increased, but only a little. Aelius noticed from across the air. He grinned and threw a blorba at her.

"*Move*," he shouted.

Ariette stumbled a little and stopped singing.

"My mouth is moving, and my heart is beating," she called. "Is that not enough?"

"Not even close." Aelius called back.

"Now you're just picking on me," Ariette called. "This is the brightest I've ever been."

"I know," he called. "It's good, but it's still not enough. Just watch me and try to follow along. Then maybe I won't have to worry about you."

Ariette rolled her eyes as another wish came back to her.

"The sound of you, it soothes my soul," said Faaris. "I forget my pain with every note. You've stopped this moment here in time, with the power of your rhyme."

Ariette smiled. Her heart leaped inside of her as she watched the words diffuse into the air. "I'm glad you like it, truly I am. I'd do anything for such a friend," she answered so Aelius wouldn't hear.

"I wish to meet you face-to-face," said Faaris. "I pray someday I'll find a way. Impossible it seems to be. If only I could set you free."

"Please believe I feel the same," said Ariette. "Surely there must be a way. And free I am, but not at heart. I'm lonelier than you by far. You have your family and your friends. On only you I can depend."

"Are you happy where you are? What is it like to be a star?" he replied through another wish.

Ariette's heart sank as she received it. "I am happy, I suppose. But lonely still, and no one knows," she answered.

"Such sadness, Setareh, I hate to hear. Can I make it disappear?" he wished. "Truly, I wish to set you free. After all, you sang for me."

"Only if you can change the law," said Ariette. "But if you could, I'd be in awe. Granting wishes is forbidden. Even you I must keep hidden."

"Trust me, my love, we'll find a way," said Faaris. "We'll be together soon, I pray."

Ariette smiled and hugged herself. She had almost as much hope as she did doubt.

7

"WELL, I THINK THIS IS A CAUSE for a celebration of colossal proportions," Sanjar announced while lying still in the comfort of his own bed, preparing for the servants to finally remove his bandages.

Mehrzad arrived at the door along with two servants. "Good morning, Majesty ."

The servants went to his bedside and began to unwrap his arm.

"How are you feeling?" asked Mehrzad. "You're unusually quiet today."

Sanjar examined the wound as the servants removed the last of the bandages. Where he had last seen a bloody mess, there was now a long thin scar on the inside of his forearm beginning at the crease of his elbow and ending at his wrist. It almost resembled a snake.

"How nice," he said with a scratchy voice.

"My," said Mehrzad, "it looks even better than I thought it would."

"Ah, it's perfect," said Sanjar, smiling at the scar. "You know, to be honest, I was expecting worse."

Mehrzad nodded. "So was I. I don't mean to frighten you, but many of us believed you wouldn't survive. This is some sort of miracle."

"Well," Sanjar said with a sigh of relief, "you know me. I never surrender. It feels like it's been ages since I've left the palace."

The servants discarded the bandages and placed a bronze jar of ointment into Mehrzad's hands as they left the room.

"I feel fine," said Sanjar with a charming grin. "You know how nothing lifts my spirits more than a good party."

Mehrzad shook his head and placed an empty bronze jar of ointment on his bedside table. "Aye, Sanjar. That's quite enough parties, but I'm glad to hear that you're feeling better. There are far more important items of business that need your attention."

"Your king is alive." Sanjar cried. "Do you insult me by denying that there is reason to celebrate?"

Mehrzad sighed. "You mustn't say such things, Highness. We've done everything we can to help you. Need I remind you that it was your brother who tried to save you? You owe him much gratitude. He nearly risked his life on your behalf."

"Believe me, I shall reward him," said Sanjar, examining the wound. "Speaking of which, I crave a word with him. Where is he?"

Sanjar struggled out of bed and threw a red robe over his bare chest. He moaned the moment he moved his arm.

Mehrzad quickly reached for him. "Careful, my boy. You're still weak. Please, allow me to call him for you."

Sanjar rolled his eyes and swatted at the air. "I'm fine. Look at me. You know I wasn't going to let that serpent have his way." Clutching his wounded arm, he stormed out, still moaning from the pain.

"Aye," Mehrzad sighed, shaking his head.

Sanjar found Faaris in the place he knew he could always find him, at the foot of the lemon tree in the menagerie cradling a book and scribbling in his notebook. Faaris glanced up when he saw Sanjar at the doors, which were usually unlocked during the day.

"Sanjar," Faaris smiled and closed the book while rising to his feet.

"That's right, I survived," Sanjar said with a grin. "Care to see my scar?" Sanjar slid his sleeve up to reveal the thin snake-like scar.

Faaris raised his eyebrows. "That's um…it's healed quickly hasn't it?"

"I know, it's a miracle," Sanjar said with a laugh, letting his sleeve fall back over his arm. "I've come to thank you actually, as much as it pains my pride."

"Really?" Faaris smiled. "Perhaps it was a blessing in disguise. It sounds like you've found some humility."

Sanjar grunted. "Well, aren't you a champion. That must have been a feast for your ego."

"Believe me, it had nothing to do with ego," said Faaris. "Only love. You are my brother after all. We don't always agree, but when reality strikes like that, I'll always love you."

Sanjar rolled his eyes. "Actually, I'm impressed. I didn't think you had it in you."

"Perhaps there's more to me than you thought," Faaris said.

"Perhaps," Sanjar grinned, stroking his bearded chin. "Which makes me think…I have a favor to ask."

"Another one?" Faaris teased, raising an eyebrow.

"Oh," Sanjar said slapping his hand over his heart. "Forgive me. I still owe you for saving me. Whatever you want, it shall be yours. Just name your request."

Faaris lit up. "How about you return my gift to me?"

Sanjar thought for a moment. "Why not? But let's see how you handle this first. I need you to fetch something for me."

Faaris almost laughed. "Another favor?"

Sanjar clutched his wounded arm. "Well, if I weren't in this condition, I'd do it myself. You could say it's dangerous for someone like you."

Faaris frowned. "Someone like me?"

"You know," said Sanjar. "It's a little outside of the lines for someone who's used to reading and wishing on stars."

Faaris crossed his arms. "In books there is knowledge you know. And in stars…divine wisdom. I'm sure I can handle it."

"Well then," said Sanjar. "It appears it's time to find out if that's true. Go into the bazaar. Find the snake charmer and tell him I wish to have him executed for failing to contain the serpent unless he can give me a refund." Faaris' heart jumped inside of him. He gulped and scanned the ground at a loss for words. "What?" Sanjar laughed. "Not up for the task?"

Faaris shook his head. "Sanjar…it was an accident. You can't punish a man for something he didn't do."

Sanjar rolled his eyes. "The king can do as he pleases, Faaris."

Faaris gulped. "I—I can't, I…"

"Can't handle it?" Sanjar teased. "I thought so. I guess I'll just keep the bottle then and our little trade agreement is off."

"I suppose I could ask for a refund," Faaris said, rubbing the back of his neck.

"That's more like it. But if he refuses to give you the money," Sanjar swiped his hand across his neck, making an execution motion.

Faaris gulped. "I'll see what I can do."

"Good boy," Sanjar smiled, patting Faaris on the back.

FAARIS LEFT THE PALACE WITH RAZI BY HIS SIDE, both wearing dark cloaks that brushed the floor when they walked, and covered all but their eyes. If anyone in the bazaar knew he was the prince, there would surely be trouble. At the gate of the palace, Faaris shook his head and stared out at the sun-glazed bazaar before him. "Father would hate this."

Razi shrugged. "At least you get to get out of the palace for a while."

"Frankly, this isn't my idea of an outing," Faaris sighed.

After a quick walk down from the hilltop that the palace rested on, they arrived into the midst of the busy bazaar. The heat from the sun seemed much stronger than it was at the palace, and dust rose from every step they took. Faaris hadn't seen this many people since the last celebration. Trinkets, ornate rugs, dishware, food, jewelry, teas, and spices of all kinds filled the streets more with every step they took further into the marketplace.

"Where do you suppose a snake charmer would be at this hour?" Faaris asked, squinting at Razi in the light of the mid-day sun, trying to make his voice loud enough to be heard over the noise of the crowd.

"Snake charmers always set up where the most people are," said Razi. "You know, to make the most money."

"Lead the way," said Faaris. "You know this place better than I do. It's been so long since I've been out of the palace."

The sun cast his midday heat over the buy streets, reflecting off of the sand and the trinkets that filled the bazaar. The air was still, and the sun gave a certain warmth to the scent of perfumes and incense that danced through the air. As they walked deeper into the streets, Faaris noticed several beggars taking refuge in the shade of several jewelry stands. There were even small children who looked every bit as hungry as they were. The weary looks in their eyes cut straight to Faaris' heart. He could hardly look at them. The midday heat seemed to have sapped their energy and left them with no other choice but to sit in the shade until the sun began to fall. Sweat and dirt were smudged across their faces, but as bad as it was, their condition had not yet stolen the sparkle from their eyes. This was what hurt Faaris even more.

"Have things always been like this?" Faaris asked, looking at the people.

"There's always going to be poor people, Faaris," said Razi.

"But I have to say I haven't seen things this bad in a long time. If you ask me, Sanjar's been a lousy king. Sad, but what are you going to do, you know?"

"What *can* we do?" Faaris asked, following Razi to the center of the bazaar.

"Nothing." Razi laughed. "Nothing without Sanjar's permission."

Faaris smiled to himself. "Maybe that will be my reward. I'll ask for improvements to be made around here. He owes me two favors now after all."

The snake charmer was found at the centermost point of the bazaar, sitting on the ledge of a big water fountain with his legs folded and his eyes closed as if he were engaged in a meditation of some sort. The noise and chaos of the people around him seemed to dissolve around the edges of the fountain. No one bothered to come close to him. His skin was dark and glistening with sweat from the heat of the sun, which didn't seem to bother him even the slightest. He was wrapped in a long, white robe and matching hat and wore no shoes. The snakes were hidden inside a wicker basket on the ground beside him.

Faaris took a deep breath and approached the man. "Excuse me," he said.

The snake charmer opened one eye and scanned Faaris from head-to-toe. "May I help you, son?"

"Forgive me for interrupting," said Faaris, folding his hands. "I bring news from the palace."

The snake charmer opened both eyes and took a closer look at Faaris. "Your Highness," he gasped and dropped instantly to his knees to bow. "My apologies. What news have you?"

Faaris took a deep breath. People were beginning to stare as soon as they recognized him. "The king has sent me with a request but allow me to warn you that he's also told me of a terrible consequence for your disobedience. So, please bear with me."

"Anything, Majesty, anything," the man said.

"Well first of all, I apologize on behalf of the guards for killing your snake. We had to save the king," said Faaris.

"Certainly," said the man. "Think nothing of it. I have dozens more."

Faaris looked at the basket, imagining dozens of deadly snakes slithering inside. A chill crept down his spine. The snake charmer noticed Faaris' uneasy expression and laughed to himself. "The king is lucky it was only a king cobra and not this one," he said pulling a slender black snake out of the basket. "The dark cobra. It's one of a kind, you know. There's not another snake in the world like this one. He's more deadly than even the black mamba. One bite is the kiss of death."

Razi and Faaris took a step backward. Faaris gulped and tried to be still, watching the snake coil itself around the man's wooden staff.

The man laughed again and stroked the snake. "He paralyzes his victims instantly, leaving them dead in less than half an hour. Would you care to pet him?"

Razi lit up. "I would."

Razi started toward the snake. Faaris held his arm in front of him to stop him. "Razi." he scolded.

"Is this really the dark cobra?" said Faaris. "Like the serpent from the Legend of the Sima Bird? I thought it was only a myth."

The man shrugged. "He's named after that one at least. Then again, he *is* the only one of his kind, isn't he? That's why I keep him safe with me. I would therefore hold a piece of a very legend right here in my basket, wouldn't I? Just between us."

"You have my word. Although from what I understand, you and I would be in the minority of believers. So, this would mean the legend is real, then, no?" said Faaris with sudden excitement, running his hands through his hair. "I knew it. All these years I…this just makes so much…I mean you have no idea how long I…I mean of course it's—"

"Ah, I never said that," the man said with a smile. "Your guess is as good as mine. I've always believed it to be true, however. I'd be one of few as well as yourself I see."

The snake's tongue slipped in and out of its mouth. Faaris could feel its bright green eyes watching his every move.

A nerve-induced half-smile curled in the corner of Faaris' lip. "Sir," he said. "I've come to bring some important news to you from the palace, but first I'm going to have to ask you to conceal this creature before I come any closer. Please."

The snake charmer laughed to himself and guided the snake around the staff. "Ah, easy Highness. He can sense your fear."

Faaris grinned and let out a blunt laugh. "Well, he's dead on."

The man smiled and stroked the snake's small, sleek head as it curled its tongue with a hiss. "Sometimes the only way to conquer your fear is to befriend it. The less control you have, the more you truly have. This fellow could bite me at any moment, but I know that he never will. Do you know why? Because I'm in control. I once was afraid of him, but now the tables have turned. I know something he doesn't."

Faaris smiled. "And what is that?"

"I know his weakness," said the man. "Even the deadliest of enemies has a weakness. You just have to know how to find it. The moment I realize when to let go," he said removing his hand from the snake, "is the moment I have the most control."

"Inspiring, truly," said Faaris.

The snake hissed at Faaris. The snake charmer laughed again to himself and guided the dark cobra back into the basket. "You don't trust him, eh?"

"My brother trusted the king cobra, apparently," said Faaris.

The man laughed and stroked the snake's back. "I guess the snake didn't trust him," he said. "They always trust me."

"Please, sir," said Faaris. "I admire your mastery, but I'm terribly afraid of snakes. Especially after what happened to my brother. I order you to conceal the snake, or I won't come any closer."

"Very well," said the man. "Now what is this news you bring?"

"King Sanjar has asked to be refunded for your services at his coronation," Faaris said, almost feeling himself blushing. "I'm sorry."

The man began to sweat. "The king, he um…I'm afraid he paid me too generously, and I'm afraid I've already spent more than I can refund. I'm sorry, Highness. I will have to give you everything I have to equal it."

Faaris closed his eyes and took a deep breath. He rattled with several thoughts for a moment before speaking. "No," he said. "That won't be necessary. But I…" Faaris sighed again and looked at the ground. It was more than he could bear. He leaned closer to the man. "I have to warn you that he's threatened to have you executed for failing to oblige. Please, sir. I promise I will try everything I can to repay you, but I wish for you to live."

"Oh, Majesty," the man said. "How will I survive without any money?"

"Do you trust me?" Faaris said, looking into the man's weary eyes.

"I suppose," said the man. "I certainly want to live. But how can I be certain that you'll keep your word?"

Faaris smiled. "Believe me, I could never live with myself otherwise."

The man handed Faaris a small sack of coins. The look in his eyes was broken. Faaris could hardly look him in the face as he took the bag.

"Condolences, friend," said Faaris. "This isn't my doing."

The snake charmer scoffed, which cut Faaris' heart even deeper than it already was. Faaris shot a quick glance back at the snake charmer and leaned down to Razi's ear level. "Make sure he doesn't release the snake."

Razi patted Faaris on the back as they turned back toward the palace. "Ah, don't worry about it Faaris," he said. "You did the right thing."

"I suppose." Faaris sighed. "That all depends on what the right thing truly is. I feel as if I've just committed a crime."

"Nah, you're just following orders," Razi reassured him.

"Things will get better. You'll see."

SANJAR WAS WAITING IN THE GREAT HALL
as soon as they entered the palace. It was empty during the day
which made it seem even larger than it did during celebrations
and feasts. A long, red rug laid over the slick marble floors,
stretching all the way from the front doors to the throne at the
crown of the room. Tall marble pillars arose from the perimeters
of the room. At the back of the room were two winding staircases
that lead to the balcony which overlooked the entire room.

"Ah, welcome back, dear brother," Sanjar called from across
the room. "Do my eyes deceive me, or is that a bag I see in your
hand?"

Faaris tossed the bag at Sanjar's feet.

"Indeed, it is," Faaris said.

Sanjar grinned and laughed under his breath. "Well done,
Faaris. I have to say, I'm quite impressed."

"Well, I hope you're satisfied," Faaris said with a glare. "This
was all he had."

Sanjar drew a long sword out of his belt and slashed the bag
open. The coins came spilling out at his feet. "Aww," he whined,
looking down at the coins. "Not even a full refund. What a
shame. Looks like I'm going to have to raise the taxes again."
Faaris was burning with anger inside but stopped himself from
saying anything. "Now," said Sanjar. "Don't think I've forgotten
about your reward."

"The reward, yes," said Faaris. "Well, I've changed my mind."

Sanjar smiled and raised an eyebrow. "Really? No bottle?"

"Ah, not so fast," said Faaris. "You owe me two rewards now. One for saving you and one for doing this favor. For saving you, I ask to have my bottle back, and for collecting your refund I ask that you put every effort toward improving the lives of our people. I hadn't realized that so many were nearly in poverty. There must be something we can do."

Sanjar thought for a moment. "How about this?" he said. "I have another favor to ask. This one is very simple. Do as I ask, and I will entertain both of your requests."

"Only if you keep your word," said Faaris.

Sanjar closed his eyes and put his hands on his heart. "May I be banished to exile otherwise."

Faaris sighed. "Alright. What is it this time?"

"Go to the outermost part of the city," said Sanjar. "There will be a caravan arriving today. All you need to do is pick up my order."

"Shouldn't you ask the guards to do something like this?" asked Faaris.

"Never mind them," Sanjar said. "They have enough work to do around here. Look at it this way, you're doing them a favor as well. That should please you."

"Hardly," Faaris mumbled.

Sanjar squinted at him. "What was that?"

"I'll be back before sunset," Faaris said with a straight face. "Come on, Razi."

"Aye," Razi grumbled to himself. "Take it easy, Sanjar."

"Of course." Sanjar grinned placing his hand over the wound. "And you'll want to hurry back. I'm having a feast tonight in your honor, Faaris. You wouldn't want to miss that."

"There's no need to honor me. Really." Faaris called from the doors. "Just keep your word on my rewards, and I'll be happy."

"You're too modest," Sanjar called back.

8

THE SUN WAS AT ITS BRIGHTEST BY the time Faaris and Razi reached the outskirts of the city. The busyness of the bazaar subsided as the streets faded to sand. Here, the air was clearer, giving way to the beautiful blue sky that waited beyond the heights of the buildings. Faaris squinted, trying to spot the caravan across the empty sand dunes. "Where do you suppose we meet them?" he asked Razi.

"Usually here," Razi answered. "You know, they could be late. Sometimes deliveries are delayed for a couple of hours if they ran into a storm or something."

"Oh, wonderful," Faaris mumbled with a grin. "Well, I'll give them two more hours. Otherwise, I'm heading back to the palace. There's no sense in waiting all day for what may not show up until tomorrow."

"I couldn't agree more," said Razi with a laugh. "But what would Sanjar do if we showed up empty-handed?"

Faaris smiled. "Probably kill us."

"Nah," Razi said, swatting at the air. "We're better use to him alive."

Faaris grinned and returned his gaze to the horizon. Just as he did, a caravan of camels and horses appeared in the distance.

"Ah, perfect timing," said Faaris. "Let's get this over with."

Razi stretched his arms out in front of him and cracked his knuckles. "I'm right behind you."

They scurried across the last patches of grass before the ground turned completely to sand. The caravan was moving fast, coming closer to them with every second.

"Keep your eyes peeled," said Razi. "There could be a cobra hiding anywhere around here. You don't want to end up like Sanjar do you?"

"Noted," said Faaris, carefully watching his steps.

They met the caravan halfway between the city limits and the peak of the dunes. Every rider wore a pitch-black cloak over his shoulders. Their faces were like stone. The rider leading them dismounted his horse and drew his sword, removing the hood from over his head. Razi and Faaris held their hands up. The man towered over both Faaris and Razi as he stood before them. His eyes narrowed as he took a closer look at Faaris.

"Who goes there?" he said aiming his sword under Faaris' chin.

"I am Prince Faaris Aghasi, and this is my bodyguard, Baraz Azim. We've come to collect an order sent out by King Sanjar. Please, we mean no harm."

The man tucked his sword back into his belt and bowed. "Highness, forgive me, I didn't recognize you. I was expecting your brother. I can't imagine why he would send anyone else for such a… private order."

Razi and Faaris exchanged glances, looking slightly confused.

"He's recovering from a snake bite," said Faaris.

"Oh, how unfortunate," the man said, walking to unstrap a big, wooden chest from the back of one of the camels. He handed the chest to Faaris. Its weight dragged him down a little the moment it fell into his arms. "Well, send my condolences to Sanjar, and don't let anyone see you with this bag on your way back. I can't believe he would trust anyone else with this."

"Ha," Razi bellowed aiming his thumb at Faaris. "He's as official as they come. I don't think we have anything to worry about."

Faaris grinned and adjusted the chest into a more manageable position, noticing that it was bound by a lock. "Forgive me but, why the warning?" Faaris asked. "This is normal protocol isn't it?"

"You are aware of what's inside, are you not?" said the man.

"Regrettably," Faaris blushed. "I have no idea."

The man leaned closer. "Riches from the East, Highness," he whispered. "Worth more than you can imagine. Run into the wrong person and you're in trouble."

Faaris looked at the chest in his hands and then over at Razi. Razi shrugged. Faaris gripped the sides with both hands and looked up at the man. "I suppose we'll be on our way then."

Faaris hoisted the heavy chest onto his shoulder and took a deep breath, looking out at the city, which was now glowing in the late afternoon sun.

"We carry this in shifts, alright?" said Faaris looking down at Razi.

"You got it, Highness," Razi said, dragging his feet through the sands.

"Why don't you take the first shift?" Faaris grunted. "My shoes are challenging enough."

Razi laughed. "As you wish."

Faaris handed the chest to Razi and took a sigh of relief.

FAARIS BROKE THROUGH THE PALACE DOORS just as the sun was beginning to set. A rainbow of rich aromas filled the air, and the grand hall was buzzing with the sound of hundreds of guests as it always did during feasts. Everyone was poised and dressed in their finest clothes, as usual, waiting for the king's invitation for them to sit. A long dining table covered in a long red tablecloth was set with the feast of a lifetime. Fruits of all kinds adorned golden platters scattered around plates of steaming meats, vegetables, breads, and any and all delicacies that one could possibly imagine.

"Sanjar wasn't joking about the feast," Faaris laughed, peeking through the curtains into the grand hall to see an overwhelming amount of people, food, aromas, and sounds all lingering around the long table.

"Alright, give me the chest," Faaris whispered.

Razi handed the chest to Faaris, who was taken down slightly from its weight.

"I'm starving," Razi grumbled. "Sanjar may be a pain

sometimes, but what can I say, the man knows how to throw a feast."

Razi burst into the grand hall and marched toward his place like the regular that he was.

"Razi. Wait." Faaris winced, trying to stop him. He gulped and slipped into the dining room, cradling the chest. As he entered, Sanjar's eyes shot straight toward him.

"Ah… There he is," Sanjar announced.

Faaris smiled and carried the bag to him.

"You know, I didn't think you were serious about the feast." Faaris laughed. "You didn't have to do all this."

"Ah, you know me," Sanjar said. "There's always a reason to celebrate. Now, what's this in your hands?"

Sanjar snatched the chest and placed it on the table. He held his arms out, motioning for everyone standing around the long, colorful banquet to be seated.

"Ah, good and faithful subjects," Sanjar announced, turning all eyes in his direction. "I'm sure you're all curious as to why I've called you all here tonight to join me for this glorious feast. My first reason is to honor well…my survival. Obviously." He laughed along with everyone at the table. "But there is another reason," he went on. "As much as it grieves me, I feel a responsibility as king to do what is best for the kingdom, and so I call you here to make it known that there has been a crime among us."

The crowd gasped.

"I know, I know," Sanjar said, laying his hand over his heart. "And even worse, from one of our own." He reached toward the table and held the chest up over his head for all to see.

"My brother, and your own prince, Faaris, along with his bodyguard, Baraz, have been caught this evening engaging in the crime of thievery."

The crowd began to whisper. All eyes turned to Faaris.

Faaris' heart nearly stopped. He was sure he was going to die right then and there. All at once, he broke into a cold sweat, and his heart rate grew faster. He looked at Sanjar with sudden confusion.

Sanjar drew his sword and slashed the lock apart. He opened the lid with his sword and turned the chest onto its side, spilling the thousands of gold coins onto the table, looking down at Faaris with a scolding grimace. "Did you, or did you not return from the bazaar this evening with this unauthorized chest of gold?" he asked, loudly so that everyone could hear.

Faaris frowned. "I—I did, but I was only…"

"Ah-ha," Sanjar roared. "Ladies and gentlemen, do you know what the penalty is for stealing?" The crowd began to whisper amongst themselves. Faaris closed his eyes, clenching his jaw to contain his anger. "The penalty, as we all know," said Sanjar, "is death."

The crowd grew louder. Sounds of shock and sorrow began to emerge.

"However," said Sanjar. "May it be known that I am not a king of wrath. For a noble to commit such crime, the punishment is less severe. With great sorrow, I hereby summon Prince Faaris to either renounce his title or spend the rest of his life in prison as punishment for stealing."

The crowd gasped again and looked at Faaris.

Sanjar bowed his head and placed his hand over his heart. "Understand that I have spared him greatly where the laws would have otherwise had him put to death. He is my brother after all. But as for Baraz, I'm afraid the law still applies. Unfortunately, he must be put to death...tonight."

Sanjar pointed at two guards from across the room and snapped his fingers. The guards stood from the table and locked their hands around Razi's arms, lifting him off of the ground.

"What?" Razi bellowed, his face fervent with anger. "Hey, come on, Sanjar."

Sanjar shrugged. "It is the law, my friend. And what kind of king would I be if I didn't uphold the law. Let him be made into an example for all of you and for anyone who so much as thinks about stealing."

Faaris frowned. His eyes were on fire and his heart was pounding. Mehrzad looked at Faaris with disgust, a look Faaris had never seen from him. Faaris tried to shake his head to tell him otherwise, but Mehrzad lowered his head and looked away.

Faaris took a deep breath and rose to his feet. "No," he said. "This isn't right."

"How dare you argue with your king," Sanjar said. "I banish you to your chamber for the evening. I mean, it makes me sick to think that I should have to eat next to a criminal and my own brother. You should be ashamed of yourself." Sanjar whipped his hand across Faaris' cheek.

Faaris fled for his chamber, fighting to hold his tears back.

Sanjar turned and made a quick head motion at several guards, signaling for them to follow Faaris to his room.

"Excuse me ladies and gentlemen," said Sanjar, turning back toward the crowd. "Tough love, tough love. Now, shall we carry on? There's no sense in letting all this go to waste."

Faaris broke into a run as he burst through the crimson curtains. The cool, still air of the empty corridor was quick to greet him, giving him relief from the excitement of the feast. He was overcome with anger, so much that he could hardly let his tears fall. His heart was racing faster than his thoughts. Not once did he stop to notice that he was being followed. The guards caught up with him and grabbed him by the wrists.

"Leave me alone," Faaris shouted, trying to scramble out of their grip. "I order you."

"Sorry, Highness," one of them said, taking a strong hold over him. "We're just following orders."

"No," said Faaris. "Please. You don't understand. It was a trick. It wasn't my fault."

The guards ignored him.

"Unhand me, please," Faaris shouted as the dragged him up the stairs. "You don't understand."

Despite their silence, Faaris protested all the way to his chamber. His strength could not compare to theirs.

9

ARIETTE WATCHED FOR A twinkling wish to float up to her as it always did this time of night. Each wish told her a different story; a new insight into the mysterious life of her beloved stargazer.

"Will tonight be the night you finally shine, star?" Aelius called as the night began.

Ariette crossed her arms. "I am a disappointment to you, aren't I?" she called back.

"You don't have to be," Aelius called.

"Someday, you'll see," Ariette said to herself. She thought for a moment. "Aelius," she called across the air.

"Yes?" Aelius answered.

"How does one travel to Earth?" Ariette asked.

"No, no, no," said Aelius. "Don't even think about it, Ariette."

"I am only asking," Ariette called.

"I don't think you're strong enough anyway, so forget it," said Aelius. "It takes a tremendous amount of stardust. I doubt you'd make it halfway before burning out."

"Please, Aelius," said Ariette. "Will you help me? I need to save him."

"No, I won't do it," said Aelius. "It's too dangerous. Only the strongest stars have enough energy to shoot all the way there and all the way back in one piece. Believe me, I've tried it, and don't even think about asking me to do it again."

"But what if I am strong enough?" Ariette said, trying to sound sure of herself.

"But I know you're not," said Aelius. "You need a lot of stardust. More than you realize. It's a lot farther than you think."

Ariette looked worried. "How far?"

"Pretty far," said Aelius. "And trust me, you're not ready."

Ariette crossed her arms. "Well, how do I become ready?"

Aelius laughed. "That's a good question," he said.

Ariette sighed. "Won't you help me?"

Aelius shook his head. "I'm not going to be the one responsible for losing you to Earth forever. If that's where you'd rather be, then you're on your own."

Ariette took a deep breath. "I don't want to cause you any pain. I only want to save my friend."

"Then stay," said Aelius.

Ariette's eyebrows turned upward with concern. "I...I don't want to betray you, any star, the moon or the sun, but I need to save him. Please. I've never felt so strongly about anything."

"Look," said Aelius. "You don't know what Earth is like. Trust me, I've been, and I almost lost everything. It's full of traps. If the humans find out you're a star, you'll be exploited without a doubt. They're all greedy. If they find a star, they'll only want your power."

Ariette was quiet.

"Stay?" Aelius nudged.

"I…I can't," Ariette said. "My heart will be broken forever if I don't try."

"Ariette, look," he said.

"No," said Ariette. "I have to go. I promise I will return as soon as I'm finished. I promise."

Aelius smirked. "If you don't lose all of your stardust first," he said. "It only takes three days to lose all of it."

"I won't," Ariette said. "I will be very careful."

"You *think* you will," said Aelius.

"I *know* I will," said Ariette.

Like a soft rain shower in reverse, several drops of wishes began to rise from different spots of the earth. Ariette's big eager eyes scanned from one to the next, searching for her stargazer's. The wish she awaited practically had her name on it. Each wish was addressed by color to each constellation and was sorted by the leader once they'd all been collected. But since the law had changed, Aelius just dismissed any wishes with a swipe of the finger, sending them into the darkest, emptiest parts of space. These days, Ariette had to make sure to catch her wishes before they got to Aelius. All of a sudden, there it was, flickering like a precious gem. Ariette pulled it toward herself and cradled it in her hands. Her excitement faded the moment it reached her. She always knew what kind of wish it was by its appearance. This one would be sorrowful.

"Setareh...please...please hear me this time," said Faaris. "Forgive me if it doesn't rhyme. I need you now ever more. I feel so desperate, my heart is sore. No more of this I can take. I've made a terrible mistake. My greatest friend is set to die, and I am living in a lie. But if I try to do what's right, there's a chance that I could die tonight. What shall I do? What shall I do? Please hear me, my love. I need you."

His words were shaky. Ariette could hear his tears in every breath. Just as she was about to answer him, Aelius caught her. An angry blorba shot her way and severed the wish out of her hand.

"No," she cried, watching it trickle to pieces beneath her.

"That's it, Ariette," Aelius scolded. "No more."

"You cannot prevent me from listening to my own wishes. They are meant for me," Ariette called.

"Just watch me," said Aelius. "I'm closing our portal so wishes can't even get in."

"Aelius, please," Ariette cried.

"No," he said. "It's for your own good. I don't want to see you fade away. Now, you have no choice. You have to move like the rest of us. My constellation isn't going to fail because of your selfishness."

Tears began to fill Ariette's eyes. She turned her back to him and squeezed her arms tightly around herself. "It's for the best," said Aelius. Ariette's tears spilled harder and she couldn't manage to conceal them. Her light grew nearly three shades dimmer. "Aw, don't do that," Aelius whined. "Come on, I'll show you that you don't need wishes to be happy."

"But I do need love," Ariette mumbled.

"I can make you brighter if you'll just take my advice," Aelius said, flying to her side. "What do you say?"

Ariette sniffled and turned away from him. "Go away."

"Aw, don't be like that, little star," he said. "Come on, there's more to life than one lovesick human. Trust me."

Ariette turned to face him. "But he's in trouble."

"Ha. No kidding," Aelius laughed. "Look, they're all in trouble down there. You're better off up here with us. This is where you belong. You just need to learn the ropes a little better. Will you at least give it a chance?"

Ariette looked at Earth with heavy eyes. "But…he needs help."

Aelius laughed. "Like I said, they all do."

"Please, Aelius," said Ariette. "He could die soon if I don't help him."

"What do I care?" Aelius said. "Humans die all the time. Why is this one any different?"

"Because I…" said Ariette, tucking her hair behind her ear. "Well…I love him."

Aelius frowned. "You're a star, Ariette. You don't even know what love is."

"How can you be so heartless?" Ariette cried, tears beginning to swell in her eyes again.

"Because I'm a star," said Aelius. "I don't have a heart and neither do you."

Ariette closed her eyes and clenched her teeth. "You're… impossible."

"Hey, I'm not the bad guy," Aelius said. "I'm trying to protect you. You should thank me, but no, you're still ungrateful. I think it's time for you to grow up and separate fantasy from reality."

Ariette's tears spilled, pouring down her cheeks. "Leave me alone."

"Ah, you'll get over it," Aelius mumbled, floating back to his usual spot.

Ariette hugged her knees and let her tears flow until every last bit of sadness had been drained from inside of her.

10

FAARIS WAS TREMBLING ALL over. He took a deep breath and locked his gaze on Setareh as he sent his wish up into the cool, starry sky.

"My love, my life I call to thee. To spare a wish to set you free. With all my heart and all my life, I wish to have the world made right. This broken land has failed to see, it's far from what it used to be. The king has turned our days to night and left the kingdom far from sight. He reigns for power and lives for greed, it's his own might that is his king. So, Setareh, please with all thy light, I wish to have thy ears tonight. It is a change of fate I seek, to free us from our misery. I wish for the truth to be revealed, so that our kingdom can be healed."

Faaris closed his eyes and took a deep breath.

"But even more it is my plea, for you to be on Earth with me.

I love you more than you'll ever know. I cannot bear to let you go. My greatest wish will always be that you my love are truly free."

He held his breath as he watched the words float up into the sky.

"Please, Setareh," he whispered. "Please. I don't know what else to do. Please answer me before I do something foolish."

Faaris waited several minutes, staring up at the stars with every last bit of hope pulsing through his veins. After an hour had gone by, he looked up at Setareh again. "My love, have I offended you?" he said. "I wish not in vain, only for truth." Faaris waited for several minutes. Still, nothing. He clenched his teeth and drew in a deep breath. "Love is patient, but time is short."

He could only imagine Razi, being locked away in the cold, dimly lit dungeon, forced to rattle with the thought of his own execution. His heart was burning with anger. He hated the feeling. Something had to be done tonight. It was only a matter of time before the feast played out and Sanjar began carrying out his plans.

Faaris slipped out of his chamber, gathering every bit of strength he had on his way. The halls were empty while everyone was downstairs, but he knew the feast wouldn't last much longer. If he was lucky, it would carry on through midnight, though feasts rarely did. He scurried around several corners and down several halls until arriving at the door to Sanjar's chamber. The hall was as still and quiet as ever. Faaris slid his hand around the shiny, gold doorknob, praying that Sanjar was still downstairs. He held his breath and turned the knob, pushing the door open carefully.

He heaved a sigh of relief. The room was empty. His heart was racing, and his body was trembling now more than ever. He gulped and scanned the room. His mind was set on one thing—the bottle, which he knew Sanjar would have hidden well. Faaris closed his eyes and took a deep breath. As soon as he opened them, he spotted it, sitting on top of a big satin pillow in place of Sanjar's crown.

"Hello, old friend," he said, sliding his fingers beneath the cool, purple glass.

He snatched it and scurried out of the room as fast as he could. He flew into the hallway and nearly ran back to his chamber. Once inside, he locked the doors and slid to his knees to catch his breath. His mind was racing even faster than his heart.

The lanterns in his chamber were beginning to die out, making the room seem haunting, or perhaps it was his guilt. He clutched the glass bottle with both hands and closed his eyes. He tore the lid off. In a matter of seconds, the bottle began to shake at the base. It filled with a soft, misty light that grew into little spurts of mist, oozing from the lit. The familiar sound of the woman's humming began to fill the room. Faaris took a deep breath. Sweat began to settle on his brow, and his stomach churned. He closed his eyes and began preparing his wish.

The genie floated out of the bottle, bringing the vague echoes of her voice to full volume. She opened her eyes like a ghost who had risen from the dead. The way she was looking at him was every bit as evil as he'd remembered. Then came the song just as before.

"Hear this song and you will see,
The magic that's inside of me.
My voice, my magic melody,
Listen well, it is the key.

Close your eyes and dreams ascend,
Wish and you can capture them.
Anything your heart can find,
Sing to me in perfect rhyme.

Soft as dust, pure as the day,
This song will take your pain away.
Sing to me, your heart's desire,
Take this chance, lest it expire.

But when this song comes to an end,
This magic chance you will have spent.
Only thrice I'll sing for thee,
So, choose your wishes carefully.

You must speak now, this is the time,
Until my silence, I am thine.

Any wish you shall receive,
If your heart truly believes.
Limitations, there are some,
I cannot change the setting sun.

I cannot force the moon to rise,
Or take the stars out of the sky.
I cannot change what has been done,
But I can reverse what has just begun.

The natural laws I cannot change,
But only slightly rearrange.
So, if you wish to change your fate,
You must be wise and unafraid.

Your choice of words will be the key,
To any possibility.

She hummed the same tune for several more seconds for him to make a wish. Faaris gulped and took a deep breath.

"Genie, a wish to spare my lot,
To free me from my pain.
My lucky star has heard me not,
Please, let me explain.

Banish the king far from these lands,
Until there's not a trace.
And leave for me the golden crown,
So I can take his place.

I know not of the price I'll pay,
And I have much to learn.

But if you will grant this wish for me,
I'll free you in return."

A smile peaked in the corners of the genie's mouth. "Oh," she cooed, "you're too kind."

A chill ran down Faaris' spine. The genie gathered a small ball of glittering dust between her hands and smashed them together, letting it burst into a thousand sparks. Faaris had never seen such a thing. The glow of the dust danced across his awe-stricken eyes. Even the wildest fire couldn't have been this bright. As the last of the sparks trickled to the floor, the genie fell to the ground. Her luminescence had faded slightly, and her tail of mist had turned to legs. She began to rise as the room returned to darkness.

"So…it's done?" said Faaris.

The genie uttered a deep, raspy laugh. "So it is."

"Thank you," Faaris said with a slight bow.

"Silly boy," the genie laughed. "Don't thank me yet. You'll see tomorrow."

Faaris grinned.

"May I show you out?" he said, stumbling toward the door.

"I think I can handle myself," said the genie.

"You know, you'll be in trouble if anyone sees you out there," said Faaris taking a quick glance outside. "The world isn't kind to such creatures."

"What, I can't pass for a human?" the genie grinned, putting her hands on her hips. "This world doesn't know what's coming for it."

"Please, let me help you. It's the least I could do," said Faaris, opening the door. "I owe you the world for what you've done for me. What may I call you?"

"You can call me Roksana," the woman said.

"Roksana," Faaris repeated.

"Don't get used to it," Roksana laughed. "I don't think we'll be seeing each other again. Trust me, I'm no one you'll want to keep around. But while we're getting to know each other, what do they call a charming thing like yourself?"

"My name is Faaris. Prince Faaris, that is."

Roksana swiped her long, black-stained fingernail across the tip of Faaris' nose. "Well, enjoy your wish, Faaris. Or should I say, King Faaris."

Roksana walked across the room and out onto the balcony where she threw herself into the air and disappeared in flight. Faaris raced after her only to find himself speechless. He searched all angles of the ground, but there was no trace of her. He glanced up at the stars to see Setareh.

"What have I done?" he whispered. "Setareh, please forgive me."

Faaris grabbed the bottle and fled for the bazaar. He had to get rid of it. He slipped along the walls of the palace, hoping to make it outside without being seen. He stole a quick peak at the Grand Hall to see that the feast was coming to an end. His heart was racing. He turned and ran toward the menagerie to cut through and avoid being seen. By the time he broke into the night air, the moon was bright and full as it always was at midnight. He drew in a deep breath, watching it drift away into a cool mist.

The bazaar was easy to maneuver at night when it was quiet, lifeless even. Lights were almost all out, and all doors were closed. He knew he would have to be careful not to be seen, which was easy at midnight. Rather than sneaking straight through the middle of the bazaar, he scaled the perimeter. He knew he would reach the desert with either route.

An hour had passed by the time he finally reached his destination. It was a longer trip than he'd expected, but he knew it would be worth it. At the edge of the city, there was a long stream that flowed off toward the distance, separating the city from the desert. Without giving it another thought, he tossed the bottle toward the water, watching it disappear downstream.

FAARIS PRESSED HIS HANDS AGAINST THE HEAVY doors and held his breath as he pushed them open, doing everything in his power to remain silent as he entered the palace. The Great Hall was vacant and dark, lit by only the dying lanterns on the surrounding walls. He took a deep breath and started toward his chamber.

"Where have you been?" came a voice, echoing across the empty floor.

Faaris' heart jumped and started racing even faster than his mind. He sprung for the nearest wall and ripped one of the lanterns from it, holding it out into the darkness to shed light on the owner of the voice.

"Who's there?"

"Who's there?" the voice mocked as a hand reached to snatch the lantern from Faaris' hand.

"Sanjar." Faaris sighed and pressed his hand against his heart as soon as he saw Sanjar's grinning face glowing in the bronzy light of the flame. "It's you. Are you trying to kill me? You know I hate these kinds of surprises."

Sanjar laughed and adopted a relaxed stance, folding his arms with the lantern still in his hand. "So, what are you doing out this late?"

Faaris frowned and started walking toward his chamber. "Why should it concern you?"

Sanjar grabbed Faaris by the shoulder and pulled him back toward him. "I thought you might be up to no good, and as king I deserve to know."

Faaris wrestled himself free of Sanjar's grip and turned toward his chamber once again. "Me? You should know me better than that by now."

"So, tell me then," said Sanjar. "Where were you?"

"Out," said Faaris.

"You don't say," said Sanjar. "Where were you?"

"I went for a walk in the bazaar," said Faaris.

"What were you doing there?" asked Sanjar with a grin. "Stealing again?"

"I just needed some air," said Faaris. "Now leave me alone. And I never stole intentionally. You put me up to it. Now, where is Mehrzad. I need to speak with him."

Sanjar folded his hands. "Well, unfortunately, he's been sentenced to prison while you were away."

Faaris turned toward Sanjar with a raging fear in his eyes. "Mehrzad? Prison? Wha...why?"

"We had a little disagreement," said Sanjar. "That's all. I mean, I can't have someone constantly telling me what to do now that I'm king."

"But that's his job," said Faaris. "He's your advisor. He was Father's most trusted advisor. It's been this way for years. You can't just throw him in prison."

"I can do whatever I want, Faaris," said Sanjar. "Now, get back to your chamber unless you want the same fate."

Faaris stared at Sanjar with a burning fury in his eyes, his breathing increasing. For a moment he didn't move.

"Go on," Sanjar said.

Faaris took a deep breath. "Father would be disappointed."

"Perhaps," said Sanjar. "If he were here."

Faaris clenched his jaw, still glaring at Sanjar. "You're angry. I understand. I am too. But you shouldn't take it out on innocent people. Mehrzad only has our best interests at heart... not to mention the entire kingdom's. You can't just..."

"Get out of my sight, rat," said Sanjar. "We'll discuss this tomorrow. I'm going to bed."

With a deep breath, Faaris turned toward his chamber, too infuriated to let any tears fall, or worse to give Sanjar even the slightest chance to see them. Sanjar turned and trudged off to his chamber.

When Faaris was sure he was out of Sanjar's sight, he made a sharp turn toward the prison chamber below the palace. It was a place he had never been. It waited deep below the palace, hiding criminals of all kinds under careful watch by dozens of guards.

The armed guards saluted Faaris as he continued further into the prison chamber. The air was cool and thin, filled with the smell of sweat and armor. Faaris hardly breathed. He couldn't bring himself to look at the prisoners, though he could hardly contain his curiosity. He could feel their scornful eyes on him with every step that he took.

"Faaris," came the defeated voice of Mehrzad. "Faaris, is that you?"

Faaris turned in the direction of his voice. "Mehrzad."

He followed the voice further toward the back of the chamber to find Mehrzad sitting at the back of one of the cells, hands bound by two iron shackles like a bear in a cage, stripped of its strength and intimidation. He stood and made his way toward the bars to meet Faaris.

Faaris looked at him with a heavy sorrow in his eyes as he gripped the bars. "What happened? Sanjar said there was a disagreement."

Mehrzad shook his head. "I was ready for this the moment the crown was placed on his head. I'm the only thing standing between him and sovereignty. He just needed a believable excuse."

Faaris rolled his eyes. "A disagreement hardly qualifies in my opinion." He sighed and looked at his feet for a moment. "There's something I have to tell you. On the night of my birthday, my parents came to me with their gift and told Sanjar and I that it was against their wishes for Sanjar to take the throne. They wanted me to be king." Mehrzad's eyes widened. Faaris sighed once more. "I'm not sure if it's recorded in their will but..."

"We must find the documents," said Mehrzad. "Why didn't you tell me sooner?"

"I tried," said Faaris. "I was afraid. Sanjar threatened to kill me if I said anything to anyone."

Mehrzad came closer and gripped the bars. "Threatened to kill you? What's gotten into him? Faaris, listen to me. Go to your father's office. There is a safe hidden beneath a tile that contains all of the palace's most sacred documents. Find their will. If I know Azad, he would have recorded something like that far beforehand. I want you to find it and present it to the counsel."

"Only after I release you," said Faaris.

"Never mind me," said Mehrzad. "First, the documents. The sooner the better. We must pray that the writing is there."

Faaris nodded. "I'll do my best...er, which tile?"

Mehrzad glanced to make sure no one was near enough to hear. "The least of your expectations," he whispered. "You can do it, I know you can. Quietly, my boy. Do you have a key?"

Faaris nodded and slipped the necklace that held an array of keys from behind his collar. "Sanjar just went to bed," said Faaris. "This will be my only chance."

"Hurry," said Mehrzad.

Faaris nodded and scurried out of the chamber, heart pounding in his chest. The palace was quiet and vacant as it always was. Being seen or heard didn't concern him in the least. He slipped the key from the necklace and wiggled it into the lock. He took a glance over his shoulder and slid into the office, careful to keep the door from creaking as he pulled it open.

The moon shone through a large window at the back of the room, leaving him with just enough light. He scanned the floor in search of the loose tile. *In plain sight*, he thought. There had to have been hundreds of them. If he knew his father as he thought he did, it would have been the least suspecting one. He glanced down at the one beneath his feet and knelt to make his first guess. The tile moved a little. Faaris gulped and continued to tug at it until it loosened enough to remove. Faaris smiled when he saw the safe tucked tightly into the hole.

"And on the first guess," he said to himself as he lifted it out of the hole. The safe was just big enough to hold the papers, made of bronze engraved with a fine floral motif. He secured the tile back into place and hugged the safe close to his chest as he stood and made his way back to the door, feeling as if the moon and all the stars were watching his every move.

"MEHRZAD," HE SAID IN THE BREATHS HE COULD manage between panting, "I found it."

"Ah, I had no doubt," said Mehrzad. "Now let's hope it's intact."

Faaris slid the safe between the bars and into Mehrzad's hands, watching carefully as Mehrzad opened it. Inside were several rows of neatly rolled scrolls.

"It's this one I believe," said Mehrzad, pulling one of the scrolls out.

"What happens if it isn't in writing?" asked Faaris, watching Mehrzad uncurl the scroll. "My word is hardly enough for anyone besides you to believe. Sanjar would find a way to deny it, I'm sure."

"That's why we're praying for a miracle," said Mehrzad, eyes scanning the document. "Patience. I'm sure it's here."

Faaris held his breath as Mehrzad paused at a section in the document.

"Yes," he muttered, bringing his finger to the parchment. The corner of his mouth stretched into a smile.

Faaris couldn't help but smile too. "Well, is it?"

Mehrzad glanced back up at Faaris and passed the document to him to take a look. "Sure enough."

Faaris took the scroll into his hands to see his father's words etched perfectly in permanent ink. Faaris almost yelped for joy before Mehrzad raised his hand to his lips. "*Shh.*"

Faaris gulped and pressed his hand over his mouth. "Forgive me," he whispered. He took a deep breath and examined the document. There were hints of stardust around the words. Faaris lowered the document and cast his eyes up toward a small window at the top of Mehrzad's cell, where the stars were in perfect view.

"Will wonders never cease?"

Mehrzad chuckled, tears beginning to pool in his eyes as his cheeks beamed with a smile. Faaris released a heavy sigh and passed the scroll back to Mehrzad.

"Now to get you out of here," said Faaris. "Has Sanjar taken the key?"

"I don't know," said Mehrzad. "But the guards can't say no to the rightful king, now, can they? Ask. Go on. We have all the proof we need right here."

Faaris grinned and took the scroll. With a deep breath he took several steps toward the nearest guard. "Sir," he said. "I order you to release Mehrzad."

"Ah, forgive me Highness, but I must follow the king's orders.

He's not to be released," said the guard.

Faaris held up the scroll and pointed to the inscription. "There's been a mistake, apparently. It is I who should be king."

The guard frowned in disbelief as he read the inscription. "Why has no one done anything about this?"

Faaris shrugged. "We found out too late."

The guard took a quick glance over his shoulder. "Better late than never. What a glorious night."

Faaris grinned. "Release him, by order of the rightful king."

The guard returned his smile. "Yes, Majesty ."

Faaris kept a slight distance as the guard unlocked Mehrzad's cell. "Now to have a word with that boy," said Mehrzad, dusting off his robe.

Faaris handed the scroll back to Mehrzad. "I'll leave this with you."

"Ah, it's better that you take it," said Mehrzad. "You have greater authority than I do."

"Right," said Faaris. "Well, I'm going to my chamber for the night. It's been a long night."

"Yes," said Mehrzad. "I'll alert the counsel immediately, and we'll see to this business first thing in the morning. There's no way he's getting away with anymore of this nonsense."

11

FAARIS HARDLY SLEPT. THE FEW hours he had managed to doze off were filled with raging nightmares, as had been a regular occurrence for the last several nights. At sunrise, he lay sprawled across the edge of his bed, still rattling with nightmares. Three loud knocks came from the door. Faaris jolted awake.

"Faaris," came Sanjar's angry voice from behind the door.

"One moment," Faaris called.

He opened the door to reveal a very angry Sanjar, who was still a little groggy as if he'd just jumped out of bed in panic. The look in his eyes was like a starving wolf, ready to destroy the next living thing in sight. His red and gold robe hung limp over his bare chest and baggy pajama pants. He wasn't even wearing shoes. His usual gold earrings, rings and necklaces caught the light from the balcony as the door opened wider. Without saying a word, he slapped Faaris across the face and dragged him into the hall, gripping the edges of his collar.

"Where is the bottle?"

"Lost it, have you?" Faaris managed to say.

"Don't pretend like you had nothing to do with it," said Sanjar. "Where is it?"

Mehrzad appeared at the end of the hallway, the members of the counsel following close behind, marching toward them like a well-seasoned army. Sanjar released his grip, leaving Faaris a little off-balance.

"Sanjar," Mehrzad scolded, rushing toward them, looking angrier than Faaris had ever seen him, like a big grizzly bear hungry for justice.

Sanjar's eyes widened. "What is he doing here?" He turned away from Faaris as if nothing had happened and looked at Mehrzad with anger and surprise. "Who released you? I demand to know. He will be the next to die. Now, what is so urgent that you must come to your king so unannounced?"

Mehrzad stood over Sanjar with eyes of contempt and a face of stone. "I've received some urgent news regarding the two of you," Mehrzad said, looking from Sanjar to Faaris.

Faaris gulped.

"Well, on with it, then," Sanjar demanded. "I have a busy day ahead of me, starting with the execution of my unfaithful servant, Baraz."

"There will be no execution," Mehrzad said. "I've received word that there has been a mistake in regard to who the rightful heir to the throne is." Sanjar's expression faded and his eyes widened with fear. "We were searching the king and queen's documents and came upon another part of their will," Mehrzad went on, pulling a large scroll out of his vest and uncurling it. "It says here that their wishes were for their son Faaris to take the throne rather than the eldest son, Sanjar."

"Let me see that," Sanjar said, swiping the scroll from Mehrzad's hands. "There must be some mistake."

"Believe me, there is no error," said Mehrzad. "Only my own for failing to search these documents more thoroughly."

Faaris was nearly in shock.

"And there is one other document I want to discuss," Mehrzad said, looking at Sanjar. He pulled a smaller scroll out of his vest and opened it so that Faaris and Sanjar could read it.

"This is a letter to thieves from the East, is it not?" said Mehrzad. Sanjar gulped. "It is an order of gold which was stolen from the East. An illegal trade agreement signed, 'King Sanjar Aghasi'," Mehrzad said, looking at Sanjar. "And this was only the most recent one. I've received nearly dozens more like it this morning all with your name on it. Apparently, you've been in contact with these thieves for quite some time."

"What?" Sanjar said. "That's…that's ridiculous. Absurd. What about Faaris? He stole gold from a caravan last night."

"Yes, under your orders," Faaris said.

"Now, listen, my boys," said Mehrzad. "It is very clear to me that a crime has taken place, and I'm afraid the law must be followed."

Sanjar's eyes widened. "What does this mean? You can't

banish me."

Mehrzad shrugged and folded his hands. "It's either banishment or death, I'm afraid. I'm sorry, but it is the law. I do recall you said so yourself last night at the banquet. The guards will come for you tomorrow. Until then, you must wait in prison."

Faaris was stricken with sadness, a bittersweet variation. He glanced at Sanjar with loving eyes and placed his hand on his shoulder. Sanjar dismissed the gesture with a smirk. Mehrzad took Sanjar by the arm and locked two bronze shackles around each of his wrists.

"You're going to pay for this, rat," Sanjar mumbled to Faaris as Mehrzad led him away. "Even if they ship me to the ends of the earth, I will find you and see to it that you get what you deserve. This is far from over. In fact, it's only the beginning."

"We'll see about that," said Faaris with a straight face.

Faaris couldn't watch. He told himself it was for the best, trying not to think about what Sanjar's life in exile would be like.

AFTER WAITING SEVERAL HOURS IN HIS CHAMBER, Faaris heard the knock on the door from Mehrzad. He opened it and threw his arms around Mehrzad.

Mehrzad smiled and looked down at Faaris, bracing him by the shoulders.

"Thank heavens," said Mehrzad.

Faaris grinned with the most earnest look in his eyes. "Mehrzad, what about Razi?"

Mehrzad smiled. "Not to worry, my boy. We've already released him."

Faaris took a sigh of relief and pressed his forehead into Mehrzad's chest. "That's music to my ears. The thought's been killing me. You have no idea."

"Fear not," said Mehrzad, taking Faaris by the shoulders. "Now, I believe we have a ceremony to consolidate."

"And one with no serpents," Faaris said with a grin, following Mehrzad into the hall. "Birds, perhaps. Peacocks. White ones, like the Sima Bird."

Mehrzad laughed. "Indeed. Ah. You shall have that and more. You don't know how long I've waited for this day."

"Really?" Faaris beamed.

Mehrzad stopped and braced Faaris by the shoulders. "Oh, Faaris, you're going to make a fine king. I've always believed so if you were ever given such a chance."

Faaris smiled. "Truly?"

Mehrzad nodded. "Truly. I haven't a doubt in my mind."

THE BANQUETS WERE SET MORE LAVISHLY THAN ever. Faaris had ordered that everyone in the kingdom be invited, and nearly everyone who could travel in time to be there came. Nobles, merchants, farmers, peasants, and even beggars spilled into the Great Hall, which couldn't possibly hold them all. Faaris couldn't manage to steady his racing thoughts as he stood before them at the top of the stairs. It was the last place he'd seen his father. His mind went instantly back to that horrible night as if it were yesterday. His heart began beating faster at the thought. He thought of the future of the kingdom and what his father would have wanted for it. It was now all resting in his hands. He gulped and tried to look strong for the people, *his* people.

Razi carried a purple silk pillow with the golden crown resting on top toward Mehrzad, who stood beside Faaris.

"Ladies and gentlemen," Mehrzad announced, "recently, it has been revealed to me that King Sanjar has been caught in many crimes, not only in the last few days, but in the last several years, in fact."

The crowd gasped and stirred, whispering amongst one another.

"Rather than sentence him to death as the law would have it, he will face banishment. Our kingdom will no longer be in the hands of a criminal." The crowd cheered. "And so, his brother, the rightful heir, will take his place as king. It was discovered recently in the will of our late king and queen that Prince Faaris take the throne upon their death, and so it shall be honored. People of Pernia, it gives me great joy to present to you your newest king. I give you, Prince Faaris Arash Nima Cyrus Aghasi, son of the late King Azad Hormisdas Aghasi and Queen Soraya Vassy Aghasi, and brother of the renounced King Sanjar Husrav Kir Kaspar Aghasi to be crowned King of Pernia."

The crowd cheered and shouted so loudly that Faaris was sure he felt his heart skip a beat. He drew in a deep breath and lowered to one knee as Mehrzad lifted the crown from the pillow.

Faaris closed his eyes as the heavy gold was laid over his soft, shiny curls in unison with the roar of the crowd. It was a moment that would be sealed into his memory forever.

"Behold," Mehrzad announced, "the new King of Pernia."

Faaris rose and stepped forward to brace the edge of the

balcony where he could oversee the entire grand hall full of eager, smiling faces and many teary eyes. It was a moment he would never forget. Somehow, he had expected to feel free at last, but his mind kept going back to Setareh, wondering if he'd lost her forever. Everything he could possibly wish for was right before him. His kingdom would thrive once again and his best friend would live, but his heart was full of regret. Still, he was not satisfied.

12

ARIETTE WAS STIRRING INSIDE. SHE hadn't stopped thinking about her stargazer, wondering if the night had gone in his favor or not. She knew she had to do something soon. He had to live. She glanced at Aelius, only to find him going about his usual business, shining as brightly as ever and keeping a close eye on the Lux, which to her dismay, meant her. She drew every bit of stardust she could handle into her hands, creating the most energized blorba she had ever made. It had to have enough power to carry her all the way to Earth. If not, she risked dying out.

The chances of Aelius stopping her were always high. She would have to be fast and careful, especially careful, Aelius noticed everything. Fortunately, he was always busiest at this time of the orbit. She hoped he would be too busy to notice.

This would be her best chance. Still, a flaming white star shooting across the galaxy would be hard to miss.

Ariette drew in a deep breath and then another. She felt as confident as a baby bird taking its first leap from its mother's nest. She clutched the blorba firmly and closed her eyes.

"Please," she whispered to it, "if you can be as strong as my love, then perhaps I can do this. Love is the strongest force in the universe, so it is stronger than fear. From now on, I will lead with love." She took another deep breath, frozen by her own words. "I will lead with love."

She lifted herself out of her spot in the Lux. The feeling was strange. Every speck of stardust that kept her magnetized peeled away, leaving her feeling freer than ever before. She felt suddenly more weightless. The air around her seemed warmer and she had barely made it out of the Lux. She knew Earth would seem like a whole new world.

Ariette squeezed her eyes shut. She felt the energy of a thousand stars racing through her body. Stardust was racing through her, burning across her skin as if she were in a wild snowstorm. She couldn't imagine the amount of force it would take to shoot all the way to Earth. She caught onto a sudden current and in the blink of an eye she was off. She glanced back just as Aelius caught sight of her.

"Ariette," Aelius shouted.

Ariette turned and locked her sights, hopes and energy on Earth and the enormous kingdom that her stargazer called home. The sweetness of meeting him face-to-face would surely surpass any doubts she was having. Aelius took a deep breath and watched Ariette twinkle further into the distance.

"You're going to get yourself killed, Ariette," he shouted. "Don't make me come after you." He huffed and crossed his arms, watching her go. "Because believe me, I will if I have to."

As Ariette broke into Earth's atmosphere, she began flying faster as if she were suddenly being pulled toward the ground. The most weightless feeling of freedom came over her. All at once it seemed as if her life as a star were lightyears away from her. She was free. Free to go her own way. Fear consumed her, but somehow, she was more afraid of what would happen if she had stayed. One thing was certain—she had never felt more vulnerable.

A part of her knew it would be impossible to find one person. *There must be billions of them on such a big planet*, she thought. As she flew closer to the land, the space around her began to fill with light. She had never seen anything so unfamiliar. Specks of stardust began flying off of her as she soared toward the ground. She was moving faster than she ever had—too fast to notice anything other than streaks of moist, creamy clouds and bright lights in every color.

The air around her was getting warmer and thicker by the second. The usual cold, thin space that had once been so familiar suddenly seemed like exile compared to this, and she loved it. She wanted to belong here.

She was stopped by a strange force around her. She closed her eyes and was still for a moment, scanning the land to find her destination.

"Please lead me to him," she prayed.

She opened her eyes and took a deep breath. Earth was even more beautiful this close. Greens and blues of all kinds were more vibrant now that she was passed the clouds.

Its beauty enchanted her. The misty air welcomed her as if she already belonged. It was like something out of a dream. What had always seemed so mysterious and out of reach was suddenly right before her.

As she came nearer to the ground, signs of motion began to catch her eye, gliding across the land and flying the way stars did. But these creatures were not stars. They carried themselves on wings like she always imagined an angel's might be. Soft, and feathered, more delicate than even the smallest of stars. There was nothing like them in her world. For a second, she was breathless, just watching them.

She lowered herself closer to the ground. Her stargazer had always spoken of his kingdom's vastness in some of his wishes. Looking for the largest kingdom on Earth was her mission. It was the only clue she had. Fortunately, it stood out. There was no other kingdom on Earth that could compare. Still, finding one person in a land this big was starting to seem impossible.

With a big breath, she flew straight in its direction, praying to land in the right spot. Her speed was increasing the closer she fell to the ground. Her thoughts were racing. Focus, she told herself, trying not to lose control over the strength of her speed. She had never known anything so fast. She was sure it defied all laws of nature.

Her flight pattern suddenly seemed less like flying and more like falling, plummeting uncontrollably into largely spread sheets of sand. She tried to slow herself, but the force around was too great for her strength. She closed her eyes and prepared for the worst. Not far from the ground, something star-like caught her eye. It was a small object caught in the banks of a stream near the desert. It shone the way stars did in the moonlight. Her curiosity couldn't keep her from it. As she fell nearer to it, a magnetic force seemed to be luring her toward it. Her big, glossy eyes were fixated on it. Not even hearing her stargazer's call could have stolen her attention.

Like a small firefly, she flittered her way toward the strange, shiny object. It was the color of her eyes, maybe a few shades darker, and it glistened like the waters that flowed by the banks around it. Carefully, she reached out to touch it. Her translucent, stardust-covered fingers slid across the slick glass. It was cold and pleasant.

She swam around it, her trail of stardust illuminating the curvatures of the glass with her every move. Her heart was racing. As she came closer to the top of it, she noticed that it was sealed with a golden lid. She couldn't help but wonder what was hiding in such a beautiful object. She gulped and wrapped her arms around the golden lid. With all the strength she could manage, she tugged it off, watching the lid plummet into the waters of the stream. She peered inside, seeing only darkness through the opening. It was like a long, empty tunnel leading to a treasure that would surely be out of this world, or even her celestial world.

Smoke began to ooze from the top, bringing a strong pulling force with it. Suddenly, Ariette found herself gripping the rim of the bottle, struggling to keep from being sucked into it. The current was only growing stronger. She gasped and panicked, trying her hardest to fly away, but its strength was too great. Within seconds, she found herself swallowed by it, spiraling down its long neck and into the belly of the beautiful, glass bottle. The lid drew itself out of the water and bolted over the top, closing her into the darkness.

As soon as she hit the ground, she vaporized completely into thousands of specks of stardust, but she hadn't disappeared. She was new.

A rich, purple sheet of silky fabric draped over her new body, which was curled up, trembling in the center of the bottle's floor. Her heart had never beat this fast. She knew that eventually she had to emerge from beneath the sheet. Fear kept her still.

After several moments, she took a deep breath and slowly began to rise. As she did, she carefully unfolded the draping silk from over her head and gazed above to the long neck of the bottle that now imprisoned her. She released a soft, quivery breath and froze as the tunnel overhead echoed her own sound back to her. As she stood, ripples of the silky, purple sheet spilled around her to form an ornate, flowy dress adorning her from head-to-toe with ornamental jewels and beads.

The minute she tried to hold herself in a standing position, her knees buckled, and she crumbled back to the floor, watching her skirt whirl around her. She looked down at her new body. She barely recognized herself. Her flesh was soft and pale, unlike its usual celestial shade of lavender. Her hair, which had once been translucent, was now pigmented, still pale but slightly more golden. A star-like luminescence still lingered over her, but she looked mostly human.

She glanced around at her new surroundings to find the space empty. The walls around her were solid glass. They were such a deep purple that at night, they almost seemed solid. Through their ripples, she could see her own reflection. A ring of shock rang throughout her body.

Is this what stars always looked like? No. It couldn't be, she thought.

She was different. She could feel it.

She crawled across the open space to see herself more clearly through the glass. She touched the reflection she saw through it, sliding her fingertips across her face. She recognized her own eyes, face, and features, but something was different. She looked more like a human than before.

Her heart fluttered. Was she one of them? Would she belong here?

She gripped the wall and tried to rise to her feet. The light, weightless feeling she'd always had was gone. She was going to have to relearn everything she thought she knew about balance. With a deep breath, she steadied her focus on her feet. She scanned up through her legs and torso, trying to reestablish her sense of control. When she was sure she'd found a sense of strength, she pressed herself away from the wall and tried to stand for a solid three seconds. She drew in another deep breath and closed her eyes, somehow convincing herself that she wouldn't fall. She released her breath and opened her eyes. She glanced down at her feet. She was stable. She turned back to face the center of the floor and took a step.

Then another.

Then another.

She looked up into the dark, empty neck of the bottle. She was trapped.

"No," she whispered.

Her voice echoed around her, making the empty space seem even more haunting.

She jumped, trying to launch into flight, but instead of floating, she fell back to the ground. She swallowed hard. Tears began to pool in her eyes. The second she blinked they slid onto her cheeks and didn't stop all through the night until she couldn't keep her eyes open any longer.

Soft beams of sunlight streaked through the bottle when Ariette awoke. Her eyes burned from last night's tears. She pressed herself into a seated position and looked around at her surroundings. The space seemed much less frightening now that it was filled with sunlight. The edges of the bottle which had once seemed dark and mysterious were now visible, making the bottle seem much smaller. She glanced up toward the neck of the bottle. It was the darkest part of the space, even with the sun's light. She had only one thing on her mind. Escape.

If I can get myself into this, I can get myself out, she thought, glaring up at the top of the beautiful object that had gone from being an enchanting gem to a prison in only a matter of seconds. Suddenly, she loathed it, wanting nothing more than to be free. Her determination to escape was greater than her fear of facing the new world. Her mind was stirring with ideas of how she would escape. She wouldn't allow herself to believe that it was impossible, despite the doubts that began to sneak in.

She closed her eyes and focused all her strength on forming a blorba. Her heart began to panic. Something was missing. She tried again, but nothing happened, not even a spark. The usual sizzling rush of energy that rang through her wasn't there.

"No," she whispered, eyes glancing from one hand to the other.

The evil object had stolen her stardust, she was sure of it.

She took a deep breath and tried again. Stardust was a part of her. It was her strength, her energy. It wasn't possible for her to lose it so suddenly. It was there. It had to be.

She took another deep breath and tried to be as still as possible. Deep inside of herself, she imagined the feeling of creating a blorba. It always came from her center, a special kind of energy where her mind, body and soul seemed to unite. She locked her focus on her hands as if trying to force a blorba to appear. A small spark burst between her hands. She jumped a little inside and watched the spark fade. She tried to repeat it again, this time making a slightly larger spark.

A smile peaked in her eyes.

When she tried again, the feeling came back to her. A blorba in its fullest glow appeared between her hands. While she had it under control, she flung it to the top, hoping it would blast the lid off. To her dismay, when it reached the top, it weakened and faded to smoke.

Ariette sighed and looked up at the lid. She would have to be creative.

Flying wasn't her specialty. Stars usually weren't allowed to fly, so she didn't have much practice, but she knew she had it in her, all stars did. She wasn't used to the feeling of being on her feet anyway. Flying would be much more comfortable.

Using the same energy that she used to make a blorba, she lifted herself off of her feet, connecting to the air around her. She swam to the top, almost holding her breath. If she lost her focus, it would be a long fall to the bottom with nothing to break it but cold, hard glass. As she neared the top, she hovered, and made a blorba. Blorbas were unique as far as stardust went. They could be both hot and cold all at once. At their strongest, they could be powerful enough to penetrate glass.

She held the glowing stardust up to the lid, the flames casting swirls of light across her eyes. She guided the blorba toward the lid. Her hands were shaking. As it touched the lid, it dissolved into smoke. She lost her balance and lowered. Fortunately, she had maintained her flight. As soon as the smoke cleared, she rose again toward the lid. She pressed her hands against the cold, smooth lid and pushed with all the force she could manage. Still, it wouldn't move. She sighed and hugged herself, fighting with the bitter thought of being trapped forever. Soft tears began to fill her eyes.

I should have known, she thought, letting herself sink back to the floor.

Still, she wouldn't let herself believe that she was never going to be free, or that she would never see the outside world again or see anything again. Anything other than this dark, purple glass.

She swallowed hard. Her heart felt as empty as the space around her.

She sank to the floor. Everything she wanted most seemed so far away. She would have given anything to be a star again. Just to hear another wish from her stargazer would have been enough to revive her hope. She prayed things had gone well for him since they'd spoken last. She prayed he was still alive. She prayed that she would find him in time. She prayed for a miracle.

13

FAARIS OPENED HIS EYES JUST AS the sun began to break through the curtains leading out to his balcony. A stillness lingered in the air that almost offered a warning. Faaris rose and threw his red satin robe over his bare chest. As he made his way toward the balcony, he slid his feet into his usual day slippers. He pulled back the curtains with a certain hesitation and made his way into the cool morning air. He folded his hands and rested his elbows over the ledge. This was the moment when he usually saw Setareh for the last time before the sunrise concealed her. He couldn't bring himself to look at her this time.

Without looking up he said, "With all my heart I hope you're there, but I cannot wait a thousand years. I love you and I always will, but I cannot let my hours be still. One more time I call, my love, praying for signs from above. Signs that you hear me and that you're well. I fear now only time will tell. One more chance I give to you, to show me that your love is true. Speak to me, my love divine. I long to hear you one more time."

Faaris closed his eyes and waited. A gentle wave of cool autumn air swept across the balcony as his own lack of patience began to taunt his eager heart. Faaris took a big breath and cast his eyes toward Setareh. For a split second, his heart stopped. She was gone. Anger burned in his heart as tears filled his eyes.

"Curse love," he said. "Curse hope, curse heaven, beauty, the sun, the moon, the stars, and all things worth living for. I'm finished. Come what may."

He closed his eyes and pressed himself away from the balcony and toward the exit to his bedroom.

Mehrzad caught him by the shoulders just as he burst through the doors. Faaris was quick to smile.

"Faaris," said Mehrzad. "Thank heavens you're awake."

"Like always," said Faaris, still smiling.

"My," said Mehrzad. "I must say it's good to see you smiling."

"Tell me," said Faaris, "tell me one good reason I have not to smile."

Mehrzad smiled and patted Faaris on the back. "Well, I'm glad to see this sort of attitude. I assumed you'd be moping around for weeks."

Faaris shook his head at the ground. "I am king now after all. I must be strong. For Pernia."

Mehrzad raised his chin and gave him a knowing grin. "That's my Faaris. Now, come with me. This would be a good time to discuss several things on our to-do list. Perhaps over breakfast. What do you say?"

"Certainly," said Faaris.

Faaris followed Mehrzad down several long corridors, a few flights of stairs and more empty hallways until they arrived just outside of the Great Hall. Mehrzad made a left turn, leading Faaris outside toward the patio.

"It's far too lovely out to waste another minute indoors don't you think?" said Mehrzad as they broke into the cool morning air once again.

"I couldn't agree more," said Faaris.

The patio was spacious and empty, featuring several clear pools and greenery designed to feel like an oasis. Birds glided over the trees in sync with the waves of the breeze. Faaris and Mehrzad sat at a small table in the shade overlooking the pools as servants brought out a tea tray and began setting the table with baskets of freshly baked flatbreads, fig jam, fruits of all kinds, eggs, and cheeses.

"Now," said Mehrzad. "First and foremost, I want to know how you are. Your smile doesn't fool me, Faaris. You are only human after all. I want you to know that I understand and that it is completely acceptable to grieve."

"Thank you," Faaris nodded to one of the servants as they poured freshly brewed chai into his teacup. He turned back toward Mehrzad. "Sorry. Yes, and thank you as well for understanding. Your compassion has always impressed me, truly."

"Faaris," said Mehrzad. "Listen to me. I want you to know that I loved your parents as I love you. I understand what you must be feeling. And I'm happy to know that you feel ready to be strong for Pernia's sake. I admire your selflessness. Great kings are often made from acts of sacrifice."

Faaris managed a half-smile and raised his teacup to his mouth.

"Now," said Mehrzad. "The main thing I want to discuss with you is the subject of marriage."

Faaris almost choked on his tea. He cleared his throat and placed his hand over his chest before reaching for a napkin. "Marriage?" he said, still choking as he wiped his mouth.

"Yes," said Mehrzad. "I wasn't sure how you'd take it, but it is something that must be discussed. As you know, it is the law that the king must have a queen."

"Yes, of course," said Faaris. "I just…I seem to have forgotten."

"No worries," said Mehrzad. "I've done all I can to make this as painless as possible for you."

"What do you mean?" Faaris said with a grin. "It is my right to choose my own bride is it not?"

"Of course," said Mehrzad. "As long as she is of noble blood. Which is why I've taken it upon myself to find princesses from every neighboring kingdom for you to choose from."

Faaris smiled and shook his head, looking down at his lap. "You know when I was a child, I used to find it relieving that I wasn't the firstborn. I always felt that Sanjar wanted the throne more than I did anyway. He wouldn't have cared about who he married as long as she was beautiful and didn't give him too much trouble."

Mehrzad laughed. "Yes, indeed."

"But I…" said Faaris, shaking his head, "frankly I would rather marry a woman I truly love than rule a kingdom. It's not that I don't love Pernia, I do, it's just…"

Mehrzad nodded. "I understand."

Faaris looked up at him. "You do?"

Mehrzad laughed. "I've known you since the day you were born, Faaris. I know what's in your heart. I can see it in your eyes."

Faaris smiled. "Then won't you grant me some mercy on this one?"

Mehrzad smiled. "I would grant you the world if I could. Unfortunately, the law must be honored. I'm sorry, dear boy."

"No," said Faaris. "There's no need to apologize. It's not your fault."

For a moment there was silence.

"Mehrzad," said Faaris. "You don't suppose I could change that law. As king I should have the power, shouldn't I?"

Mehrzad sighed. "That is an excellent question, and I'm afraid I'm not sure of the answer. That law has been in place for centuries. But I can assure you that hope is not lost. There are many wonderful young ladies out there…princesses, that is. Your father met your mother in the very same way, and you and I both know they had a love like no other."

"Yes," Faaris nodded. "So they did. It was what inspired me to find such love. I thought even if I searched the ends of the earth, the heavens even, still I would never be so lucky as to find what I saw in them."

"Fear not," said Mehrzad. "Life often has a mysterious way of surprising us when were at our lowest point. I have no doubt that your best days are soon to come."

"Really?" said Faaris.

"Absolutely," said Mehrzad. "There's not a doubt in my mind. Now, come, we mustn't let all of this go cold."

"Yes," Faaris nodded, trying to snap himself out of the bitterness that was beginning to settle into his heart. "There's nothing in the world that could compare to fresh bread and a sunrise like this." He reached for a flatbread and tore off a piece, admiring the swirls of steam as they rose into the air. "I could right endless love poems about it, truly."

Mehrzad laughed.

Still chewing, Faaris grabbed his teacup and raised it for a toast. "Here's to new beginnings."

Mehrzad smiled and did the same. "To new beginnings."

Faaris swallowed as their teacups clinked against one another. "Cheers."

"Now," said Mehrzad after taking a sip of tea. "I've selected twelve young ladies from nearby kingdoms from which you will make your choice."

Faaris nearly choked on his tea for the second time. "Careful, Mehrzad, or I'll never live to meet them." He reached once again for the napkin to wipe his mouth.

"Yes, well, I think you'll find that this is the best arrangement," said Mehrzad.

"Perhaps, but only twelve?" said Faaris. "That narrows the odds a bit doesn't it? How can I expect to find someone I genuinely love from such a small selection?"

Mehrzad shrugged. "Your father chose from only seven.

Consider this a privilege."

"You're right," said Faaris, glancing down into his lap. "Forgive me. How can I be so selfish after everything you've done for me? I've lived my whole life trying to please others and so I shall continue, it seems, until the day I die. This time is no different. It's just another obligation I must fulfill."

Mehrzad smiled. "Fear not, Faaris. You may be surprised to find this experience quite enjoyable. After all, you've never been in love before, have you? Who's to say you won't find it in one of these princesses?"

"Perhaps you're right," said Faaris. "Perhaps I really know nothing about love."

"Love has a special way of working these things out I believe," said Mehrzad. "If in your heart, you are truly seeking it, it will find you."

Faaris almost laughed to himself. "You're saying all I have to do is say my prayers, sit back and wait for my miracle?"

Mehrzad shrugged and gazed out at the patio as the sun began to grow brighter. "I'm saying it would be unwise of you to give up so quickly. I believe this is only the beginning for you."

Faaris gulped and squinted out at the sun. "Really?"

Mehrzad nodded and took another sip of tea.

Faaris took a deep breath and reached for a small red grape. "I find that hard to believe somehow."

"Has your smile faded already?" Mehrzad said with a grin. "You seemed quite resolved this morning."

Faaris glanced down at the grape and began fidgeting with it, deep in thought. "There's not a man alive who wouldn't trade everything to be in my position right now, yet why do I feel as though I've lost everything? What's going to happen to me, Mehrzad?"

Mehrzad smiled at him and set his teacup onto the table. "Well, you're going to take life one day at a time. You're going to meet a wonderful woman, get married, and continue to lead our kingdom like the true king I know you are. Now, don't tell me you've lost hope already?"

Faaris took a deep breath and smiled up at Mehrzad.

Mehrzad nodded. "There it is."

"I suppose we carry on," said Faaris. "Don't we?"

"Indeed," said Mehrzad.

Faaris stood and tossed the grape into his mouth. "Don't worry. Even if I must be at a loss, I'll be sure that Pernia won't be. When do I meet the princesses?"

"Whenever you're ready," said Mehrzad. "Are there any special requests or requirements I can offer you on the matter?"

Faaris sighed at the ground. "See to it that I meet each of them one-on-one."

"As you wish," said Mehrzad.

"That way I can be sure I make the best decision," said Faaris. "How soon am I required to make my choice?"

"As soon as possible, preferably," said Mehrzad. "But to be fair, the court and I have decided to give you one-thousand days."

Faaris almost laughed. "That's an awfully specific value."

Mehrzad folded his hands. "That's more than enough time if you ask me. It was enough time for the king to fall in love with Scheherazade."

Faaris nodded. "Yes, but that was only a story, Mehrzad."

Mehrzad shrugged again and grinned. "You were always fond of stories. Consider it your own fairytale."

"As long as I can count on a happy ending, I suppose it will have to do," said Faaris. "Fair enough. It's a deal. What is life but a vapor anyway. At least I'll die knowing I did the right thing."

14

OR THE NEXT THOUSAND AND one nights, Ariette waited. Every time the moon rose, she thought of her stargazer until the pain of being without his wishes had consumed her. She couldn't help him. She was stuck, trapped inside the lonely bottle with nothing but her songs to keep her from losing hope.

As she lay on the cold floor, looking up into the mystery of the long, dark neck of the bottle, fear began to settle in. The thought had been haunting her for several months and was beginning to seem more real now. She sent a rush of stardust to her fingers and carved another line onto the glass floor, marking another day of confinement.

Ariette sighed as she let the stardust burn across the surface. "One thousand and one."

She would never be free. The lonely, empty, beautiful bottle would be her world for the rest of her life. She closed her eyes and drew in a deep breath at the thought. *No.*

For the next several months, she tried to escape, but it was no use. Not even her stardust was strong enough. Each day had been like the one before it. In between singing, thinking, walking, pacing, and testing the capabilities of her stardust, she watched the sun rise and fall. Aside from singing, watching the seasons change was the only thing that gave her joy. In all the time that had passed, she had become an even better singer than she was before. There was freedom in solitude, she had to admit. There was no one to hear her if she made a mistake, no one to judge her for trying.

Each night, she waited to hear a wish from her beloved stargazer, only to find herself disappointed night-after-night. Somehow, she believed he was still out there, waiting for her. He had to be.

Ariette sighed and pressed her hand against the side of the bottle. Autumn had arrived. She could tell by the way the glass felt. The summer's heat had faded, and it was slightly cooler to the touch.

She paced along the edges of the bottle, letting her fingers slide across the glass as she sang her stargazer's favorite lullaby. He had been on her mind lately.

The walls of the bottle began to shake. Ariette tumbled to her knees, struggling to hold her ground as the motion tossed her across the floor. A loud gaping echo came from the top of the bottle and sunlight flooded the empty space. Swirls of smooth, misty smoke began to slither around her feet. A strong current rushed through the bottle as if a hurricane were stirring inside, spinning her around in all directions. Sparks of what looked like stardust intertwined with the smoke and lifted her off of her feet. The smoke spiraled around her legs and carried her toward the top of the bottle in one sweeping motion. As she rose, she felt a sudden prick deep inside of her. An enchanting melody filled her from head to toe and she began to hum in perfect harmony with it. The higher she rose, the louder it became. The lyrics were written across her heart in an instant, as if she'd known them all her life.

She shielded her head as she broke through the lid along with all the smoke and stardust that had built up inside the bottle. The warm sun welcomed her once again into the glorious daylight she thought she would never see again. She emerged in song as if rejoicing to be free once again.

The words flowed out of her so easily as if she'd sung them a thousand times.

The bottle had been rescued from the stream since she'd fallen into it. It now lay in a small nest in the soft, flowery branches of a small tree. It was the only tree within sight, depending only on the waters of the stream to survive. Sheets of smooth sand stretched majestically into the horizon in all directions. It was a wonder that the tree was alive in such a place. It was some sort of oasis, far away from any civilization, but it was lush, nonetheless. It was the most wonderful thing she'd ever seen.

She glanced around for signs of life and noticed an exotic white bird with enormous silvery wings perched on the branch beside the nest.

Ariette smiled at the creature and sang.

"Hear this song and you will see,
The magic that's inside of me.
My voice, my magic melody,
Listen well, it is the key.

Close your eyes and dreams ascend,
Wish and you can capture them.
Anything your heart can find,
Sing to me in perfect rhyme.

Soft as dust, pure as the day,
This song will take your pain away,
Sing to me, your heart's desire,
Take this chance, lest it expire.

But when this song comes to an end,
This magic chance you will have spent.
Only thrice I'll sing for thee,
So, choose your wishes carefully.

You must speak now, this is the time,
Until my silence, I am thine.

Any wish you shall receive,
If your heart truly believes.

Limitations, there are some,
I cannot change the setting sun.

I cannot force the moon to rise,
Or take the stars out of the sky.
I cannot change what has been done,
But I can reverse what has just begun.

The natural laws I cannot change,
But only slightly rearrange.
So, if you wish to change your fate,
You must be wise and unafraid.

Your choice of words will be the key,
To any possibility."

As she sang, the bird chirped in tune with her. To Ariette's surprise, it was a wish, a wish like the ones stars received.

"Oh, precious one, what gift of mine,
Shall I require to turn back time?
Nothing more and nothing less,
I wish an egg into my nest."

Ariette couldn't have stopped singing if she had wanted to. When the last of the lyrics made their way out of her, she made a small blorba as she would to grant a wish if she were a star. The blorba drew the bird's sounds into it like a vacuum. It grew warmer in Ariette's hands as it filled with the bird's wish. The specks of stardust that danced throughout it began moving as Ariette prepared to grant the wish.

The moment Ariette stopped singing, the blorba exploded in her hands, leaving the remaining stardust to trickle to the ground. A sharp, icy pain pricked her wrist. She glanced at her hands and watched as a shimmery symbol appeared across her left wrist, twisting and curling into an ornate design. As each line appeared, the stinging sensation burned her skin like the coldest of ice. "Ah," she cried and almost slipped a tear. She squeezed her eyes and clenched her teeth, trusting that the feeling would pass. She opened her eyes and looked at the finished mark, winding its way across her wrist. The wish had been granted.

Ariette glanced to the nest, hoping to see an egg. Sure enough, there it was. As pure and perfect as any wish could be. It wasn't any ordinary egg by the look of it. It was celestial. It was without a doubt a gift. Before Ariette could even finish admiring her work, a strong force sucked her back into the bottle. Once again, she found herself in the center of the floor surrounded by emptiness.

"Please, free me again, dear winged creature," she said.

Her mind was stirring with thoughts of escaping. She wanted nothing more. Not even being a star was this confining. She stood and walked closer to the edge of the bottle. She touched the glass and moved closer hoping to see outside. Vaguely, she could see the bird's silhouette sitting in the nest beside the new egg.

"Please," Ariette whispered, "please wish again. I want nothing more."

The sharp hissing sound of a snake crept around the bottle.

Ariette watched as the bird fled her nest. The shadow of a snake coiled around the bottle and two hands closed in around the bottle's neck. The walls shook around Ariette as the hands lifted it out of the branches of the tree that it so safely rested in.

The voice of a man made its way through the glass. "It must be my lucky day." The voice was muffled. Ariette's heart started racing. "How on earth did you get there?" the man said to himself. "I mean, what are the odds? I've waited too long for this. At last, I finally get what I deserve."

Ariette didn't flinch. The voice was strange and unfamiliar.

The lid burst off, and Ariette found herself surrounded by mist and stardust once again. She closed her eyes as every bit of stardust that was inside of her filled with song—the same song as before. Her own echoes surrounded her as the stardust carried her to the top. She had transformed again into a wish-granting slave.

As she erupted into the daylight, her eyes arrived at the face of the mysterious voice, only to find it concealed completely by a black mask. Two snake-like eyes were the only visible features, staring at her with the sharpest intentions. A black beard as long as a serpent hung from his chin, braided and tied at every inch with small, gold ornaments. The man only listened, remaining still as she sang.

Ariette couldn't have stopped singing if she'd wanted to. It was the strangest feeling. It was almost as if she were a puppet, and an outside force was pulling the words out of her mouth in perfect harmony as before, as if it were a performance.

"Hear this song and you will see,
The magic that's inside of me.
My voice, my magic melody,
Listen well, it is the key.

Close your eyes and dreams ascend,
Wish and you can capture them.
Anything your heart can find,
Sing to me in perfect rhyme.

Soft as dust, pure as the day,
This song will take your pain away.
Sing to me, your heart's desire,
Take this chance, lest it expire.

But when this song comes to an end,
This magic chance you will have spent.
Only thrice I'll sing for thee,
So, choose your wishes carefully.

You must speak now, this is the time,
Until my silence, I am thine.

Any wish you shall receive,
If your heart truly believes.
Limitations, there are some,
I cannot change the setting sun.

I cannot force the moon to rise,
Or take the stars out of the sky.
I cannot change what has been done,
But I can reverse what has just begun.

The natural laws I cannot change,
But only slightly rearrange.
So, if you wish to change your fate,
You must be wise and unafraid.

Your choice of words will be the key,
To any possibility."

The man in black cleared his throat, keeping his eyes locked on hers. Without any motion or expression, he said,

"For just three days, I wish you free,
But only temporarily.

Not as my genie, but my slave,
You'll do exactly as I say.

Oblige and freedom you shall earn,
Fail and to your bottle you shall return."

A smile spread across Ariette's face and lit her eyes with the purest joy. The wish was quaking in her hands in the form of a blorba like the time before, burning with his words. She glanced at the man with a look of gratitude. She had never been so eager to grant a wish. With a deep breath she let the blorba burst, with it destroying all she would ever see of such confinement again. The second it burst, her tail of mist and stardust turned back to legs and she fell to the sand. She felt the familiar prick on her wrist as the time before. "Ah," she cried again as she had granting the previous wish. She clutched her wrist as if to stop the pain. Another silvery mark twisted its way across her skin, creating a new design next to the previous one.

She glanced to the bottle, which rested in the man's hands. It seemed much smaller now. She gulped and dug her fingers into the sand beneath her, grabbing a handful and letting it slip delicately between her fingers.

"I...I don't believe it," she gasped, almost in shock. "I'm free?"

The man in black knelt and took her by the arms to help her up. "That's right," he said. "Consider me your rescuer, but don't thank me yet. I'm not finished with you."

She looked into his piercing eyes as he pulled her to her feet, almost taken aback by their unusual color. "Who are you?"

"They call me Kobra," he said, bowing to kiss her hand. "Dark Kobra."

"Dark Kobra," said Ariette, staring at him. She had never seen anything like him. He was a human—a *real* human. He was tall and lean, and smelled of sweat and cologne. "Please, may I see your face?"

The man laughed. "I'm afraid that would defeat the purpose of the mask, wouldn't it? You wouldn't want to see my face anyway, I'm quite hideous." He started pacing around her. "The request

I ask is simple. You will travel to the palace and find the king. When you do, you will kill him, however you'd like to really. Be creative. Although, I will offer you a suggestion." He slid a small sharp blade out of his sleeve and laid it into Ariette's hands.

Ariette gasped and dropped it into the sand at her feet. "No. I...I couldn't."

Kobra laughed. "I don't believe the choice is yours, genie. My wish is your command." He kicked at the sands and swept the blade up into his hand.

"Now," he said, gripping the blade in his right hand, pointed outward. "You'll want to hold it like this, see."

Ariette gulped. She could feel the stardust stirring within her in a sickening way.

Kobra aimed the blade at his own chest and made an upward motion. "Now, I won't...you know, but you want to pierce him right were the ribs part. Any higher, and you'll run into his breastbone. Any lower, and you'll miss his heart. Place the tip of the blade here," he said pointing it precisely where his ribs parted.

"You're..." Ariette stuttered, shaking her head. "You're crazy if you think I'll be killing anyone."

Kobra laughed and took a step toward her, hovering over her in a terrifying way. "You're crazy if you think you have the choice."

Ariette's entire body began to tremble. "I'm not afraid of you."

Kobra grabbed her cold, trembling hand. The stardust was stirring wildly inside of her. It was a feeling she had never felt before.

"Consider the consequences," he said laying the blade back into her hands, more firmly this time. "For your freedom's sake.

Once he's dead, I will claim my second wish and use my third wish to set you free. You have my word. Remember, it's either this or back to your bottle to be my genie forever."

Ariette glared up at him as the cold blade met her hands.

Kobra positioned the blade in the position he had shown her and aimed it at his own chest, right where his ribs parted. "Like this," he said. "One upward motion. And I want you to give it all you've got. He may try to fight you. Try to catch him in his sleep, that might be easier."

Kobra took her by the shoulders and turned her in the direction of the palace.

"Follow the stream that way," he said. "You should reach the palace by tonight. Then it's just a matter of finding the king. And I wouldn't waste any time if I were you. Three nights will quickly pass you by. You should be able to catch him by then. It's easy, Pigeon. Just don't be seen. You seem like a clever girl, I'm sure you can handle it."

He struck a devilish smile and winked in a way that was actually a little charming, though Ariette wouldn't have dared to admit it.

"And trust me," said Kobra, "you won't want to disappoint me."

Ariette gulped and looked at the blade. She couldn't manage any words.

"A word of advice," said Kobra. "Get him to trust you. That way, he'll never see it coming."

Kobra drew a small object out of his sleeve. All in one swift motion, he smashed it onto the ground, sending an enormous cloud of thick smoke around the tree. Ariette shielded her eyes and coughed, trying to escape the smoke. When it cleared, she scanned the oasis. Dark Kobra was nowhere in sight. Neither was the bottle. She dropped the dagger onto the ground and crumbled to her knees, watching the tears that she had been fighting to hold back fall onto the sand. She buried her face in her hands and let every last tear pour out until her eyes couldn't produce any more. For a moment, she was still, letting the warm desert air sweep the tears off of her face. She opened her eyes and looked up at the sun. She took another deep breath and looked down at the silver dagger resting in the sand beside her. Ariette slid her fingers underneath its cold metal surface and lifted it out of the sand.

"So, this is what it takes to be free?" she said to herself, looking back to the sun.

15

AARIS," SAID MEHRZAD AS HE dragged Faaris out into the dim hallway. "I'll have no more of this childish behavior. What's gotten into you?"

"I can't do this any longer, Mehrzad," said Faaris freeing himself from Mehrzad's grip. "I don't even want to be king if this is what it takes."

"Now don't try to scare Emira off too, I beg you, lest I take it upon myself to force you to marry her," said Mehrzad. "Your time is up. You've seen twelve worthy princesses and somehow managed to repulse all but this one."

"I know," said Faaris. "Believe me, you have no reason to worry. It's impossible to make her believe I'm anything less than a god. She worships the ground I walk on. I'm convinced there's nothing I could say now to convince her that what I feel is far from true love."

Mehrzad sighed and took Faaris by the shoulders. "Now Faaris, be reasonable. What would your father say? I knew him well enough to know that neither he nor your mother would be pleased with you. Now, for the sake of the kingdom, I beg you, don't ruin your chances with this one. I think it could turn out quite well."

"Impossible," said Faaris, shaking his head at the ground.

Mehrzad sighed. "Now Faaris, listen to me, I..."

"No," said Faaris with a fiery frown. "In all my life I can assure you I've never felt more like a prisoner."

"I told you from the beginning," said Mehrzad. "Great kings must often make great sacrifices."

"I fear this one is too great, Mehrzad," said Faaris. "I ought to have some say in the matter."

"Need I remind you that we had a deal," said Mehrzad.

Faaris gulped. For a moment there was silence.

"Faaris," said Mehrzad. "Pernia has never been stronger than it is today, and it's all because of you. At last, our kingdom is thriving once again. You should be proud, my boy. You've done well. How dare you be selfish enough to complain? You have everything any man could ever dream of and more, and you're not yet twenty-one. Emira is no exception. I've seen nothing but good come of her, and that's not to mention her remarkable reputation. She's a lovely girl."

"Then perhaps *you* should marry her," said Faaris as he turned and started down the hall.

"Faaris," Mehrzad scolded following after him.

Faaris glanced over his shoulder to see Mehrzad hurrying behind him. With a deep breath, Faaris started into a run, watching the sun begin to fall through the tall, open windows that lined the walls.

"Faaris," Mehrzad shouted, struggling to keep up with him. "Come back here this instant. I order you."

"You can't order me," Faaris called back. "I make the orders."

"Faaris, enough of this childish nonsense," Mehrzad called. "You're behaving like your brother."

Faaris stopped just as he'd reached the end of the hall and turned back toward Mehrzad. "I resent that."

"Then come back here and prove to me that you're a true king," said Mehrzad.

"Please forgive me," Faaris called. "But there's something I must do. I promise I will return shortly."

"Where are you going?" Mehrzad called.

Faaris disappeared around the corner and made his way outside as fast as he could. The air around him was growing cooler as the sun was sinking lower.

"Faaris," Mehrzad's voice echoed down the hall as Faaris flew out into the evening air.

Faaris closed his eyes and drew in a deep breath. He was moving as fast as his feet would carry him, and his heart was racing even faster. He made a sharp turn and darted across the patio toward the front gates. Faster than the sinking sun, he ran into the bazaar not paying any mind to the kind of looks he was getting from the people. Without stopping, he continued toward his destination. Just as twilight began to settle in, he arrived at the darkest, most desolate part of the bazaar. It was a place that many Pernians hardly knew, or if they did, they spoke nothing but terror about it. The stands nearby looked as if not a soul had attended them in centuries. Tattered fabrics and old dusty rugs hung gauntly from the tops of the buildings, and the streets were covered in dust and broken glass. A trail of burning incense swirled through the air, coming from a tattered tent hidden deep within the slums.

Faaris slowed his pace as he approached the tent's entrance. He pulled back the hanging fabric of the entrance and did his best to remain quiet as he stepped into the darkness. He coughed and fanned at the air which was thick with incense and cigar smoke.

"*Salaam*," he whispered, squinting in the vague light that came from an array of multi-colored lanterns hanging over a small table to the side of the space.

"Who goes there," came a woman's raspy voice from the shadows.

"It's me," said Faaris.

The woman laughed. "Faaris. Back so soon?"

"Yes," said Faaris, making his way toward the table.

"Something wrong, Highness?" said the woman.

"Yes," Faaris said again. "I have a favor to ask of you."

The woman stepped into the light to reveal none other than Roksana. On her pale angular face was a smile of intrigue. Shiny locks of long hair as dark as the night fell down the sides of her face beneath a dark blue headscarf and down her sides until reaching their end at her hips. Two large silver hoops hung from

146

each of her ears. A long dark blue dress hung just shy of her ankles, revealing her bare feet and black-stained toenails. A black anklet hung around her left ankle. She was as beautiful as he'd remembered.

"Like I said," said Roksana. "It seems I owe you."

"I want to revoke my wish," said Faaris.

Roksana laughed.

"Please tell me it's possible," said Faaris.

Roksana kept laughing. "I knew you'd come crawling back."

Faaris stepped closer and rested his hands on the table. "How dare you mock my misery."

Roksana went on laughing. "I thought this was what you wanted, love."

"It…" Faaris paused. "It was. But I was young and foolish then. It was impulsive of me and I've regretted it ever since. I'm a prisoner to my everyday life, and now I must marry someone that I'll never have even the slightest of feelings for."

"Poor Faaris," said Roksana with a grin.

Faaris frowned. "What? You will help me, won't you?"

Roksana sighed and sat on the table so he could see her face more clearly in the light of the lanterns. "Unfortunately, I'm powerless now."

Faaris swallowed hard.

Roksana grinned and crossed her legs, wrapping her hands around her knee. "The only way I can give you what you want is if you'll return me to my bottle."

Faaris clenched his jaw and closed his eyes. "Impossible."

Roksana's smile faded. "What do you mean?"

Faaris opened his eyes. "I threw it into the river several years ago. Surely it could never be found now."

Roksana slapped her hand to her forehead. "You did *what?* Faaris, I really thought you were smarter than that."

"S-sorry," Faaris mumbled.

Roksana paused in thought. "Alright, I'll make you a deal. If you can find the bottle and bring it to me, I'll grant your second wish, but you must leave the third wish for me."

"Deal," said Faaris. "I'll try, but I can't assure you I'll find it."

Roksana leaned in closer and ran her fingers down the short goatee on his chin. "I have faith in you, Faaris. It appears neither of us have much to lose."

"Only my life perhaps, for searching the ends of the earth," said Faaris with a straight face.

"I thought maybe you'd rather die anyway than go on in this miserable new life of yours," said Roksana. "That you'd find the odds to be worth the risk." Faaris was silent. "Come now," said Roksana. "It can't hurt to try."

Faaris closed his eyes. "Alright."

Roksana lit up. "We have a deal?"

"So we do," said Faaris. "I'll leave tomorrow as soon as I can. You have my word."

16

THE BIRD HADN'T RETURNED SINCE Kobra had scared her off. Ariette glanced at the egg, which was still resting in the nest, wondering what would happen to it if the bird never returned. She bit the tip of her fingernail and stood to walk closer to it. She tucked the dagger into her dress and lifted the egg gently out of the branches, admiring how it fit perfectly in her two hands. There was no other egg on Earth that could compare to it. In the light of the sun, it sparkled like stardust, swirling with a different color every time it moved. It faintly even had the cool, starry scent that was all too familiar to her. Across its surface were several intricate markings like the one's on her wrist. Assuming the winged creature would possibly never return, she tucked the egg away. She knew she couldn't stay there under the tree and hide from the dreaded third night, no matter how much she wanted to. Wishes were powerful. It was sure to happen and she knew it. That was what hurt the most.

As she started toward the city, the winged creature swooped back into the nest.

"It's you." Ariette gasped.

The winged creature let out a loud sound and flew onto Ariette's head, dropping the egg back into her hands.

Ariette giggled and caught it. "You don't want it anymore?"

The creature cooed and wrapped her wings over Ariette's shoulders.

Ariette stroked the creature's silky feathers. "I have to say, it's nice to see you again, but I can't stay, unless you want another wish."

The winged creature flew off.

"Wait," Ariette called after her.

She leaped across the stream that ran beside the tree and stumbled into the desert sands. The winged creature was a speck in the distance.

"Wait," Ariette called again and started running after her. Sand began to fill her slippers as she ran deeper into the desert. "Wait," she cried again, watching the creature disappear into the sun. "Come back," she wailed, dragging her feet across the sand. She stopped to catch her breath. She couldn't even see the city over the dunes. There was nothing but sand as far as she could see. "This is impossible," she said to herself.

She lifted off her feet and into the air, carried with the strength of her stardust. As she ascended into flight, she gasped and looked down at the dunes below her.

She smiled and let out a celebratory shout. "I'm…I'm flying."

The second she stopped to think, she lost her sense of flight and plummeted into the thick sands followed by a cloud of dust. Fortunately, they were soft enough to take the edge off of the fall. She sighed and brushed several long hairs out of her face. A strong, sandy gust of wind tossed her hair in all directions and nudged her forward. She stumbled a little, but as soon as the warm desert air filled her lungs, her spirit was renewed. She pulled each of her shoes off and dumped the sand out of them. She stood and brushed the sand off of her dress. She took a deep breath, letting the warm desert air revive her. She kicked at the sand and followed the horizon closer toward the city.

Just as the sun began to set, she noticed a caravan peaking over a nearby sand dune. She lifted the ends of her dress and ran toward them.

"Hello," she called, waving her arms above her head. She prayed that her voice would be loud enough to reach them. It usually didn't have much power.

To her surprise, the camels and their riders began moving in her direction. There must have been at least thirty camels, each carrying bags of merchandise on their sides. Their riders were all dressed in white cloaks covering all but their eyes. At a distant glance, their white cloaks almost looked ghastly against the glow of the ever-sinking sun as the wind swept across them.

"Are you lost, miss?" the leader of the caravan asked. "What's a pretty thing like you doing out here?"

Ariette stopped. She noticed several weapons tucked into the saddles of their camels. "I…," she stuttered. "I'm making my way to the city. I've been lost…very lost, actually."

"I can see that," the man said. "What a coincidence, we're on our way to the city to celebrate the king's birthday…oh, and his wedding. Wouldn't want to miss this one."

Ariette bit her lip. "I'm not so sure I wish to see the king, actually."

"Oh, you'll change your mind once you meet him." One of them laughed. "Every girl in the kingdom's in love with him."

Ariette rolled her eyes. "Meet him? No. Please, I'm…looking for someone else."

The man jumped off of his camel and walked toward Ariette.

"Oh," said the man. "Who, may I ask?"

"Well," said Ariette, looking several inches down at him. To her surprise, there was a slight height difference now that they were both on their feet. "He was my stargazer."

The man squinted. "Stargazer, eh?"

Ariette gulped. "He um…he loved wishing on stars. He would always tell me his wishes. We sort of had a long-distance relationship."

"Does he have a name?" the man said with a grin. "Besides 'stargazer'."

Ariette sighed. "I'm sure, but if he does, he never told me. I only wish I would have asked. We sort of forgot that part. We just had this…this instant connection. It was like I'd known him forever. I guess it's my fault."

The man laughed. "Well, that's unfortunate," he said. "The thing is, I know just about everyone in the kingdom. If I had a name, I could probably take you right to him."

With a quick nod, he motioned for the camel to sit. All at once the camel dropped onto its hind legs as they folded, followed by its front legs. The ground seemed to rumble, and a cloud of smoke arose as its body met the sand. The man took Ariette by the waist and lifted her onto its back. The camel growled and a glop of spit oozed out of its mouth. Ariette's heart jumped a little.

The man laughed. "Don't worry, she won't hurt you." Ariette smiled and tucked her hair behind her ear, still looking at the camel with fear-stricken eyes. "It's a short ride," the man reassured her, patting the camel on the neck. "The city's just over that dune. I'm Baraz by the way, but my friends call me Razi."

Ariette smiled. She stroked the camel's side as it began carrying her through the sand.

"Um… have any of you seen a beautiful, white creature with huge wings by any chance?" she asked.

Razi laughed. "You mean the Sima Bird?"

"Sima Bird?" said Ariette, squinting in the light of the sun.

Razi grinned. "You're not from here are you?"

Ariette blushed and tucked her hair behind her ear. "Not exactly."

"Well, everyone in the kingdom knows that legend," he said.

Ariette squinted again. "Legend?"

"Looks like it's story time," said Razi, smiling off into the horizon. "Well, once upon a time, there may or may not have been a wise, magical creature called the Sima Bird. The legend says whoever her shadow passes over is sure to be king, but she flies so high that no one's ever seen her."

"Oh," Ariette mumbled, looking disappointed.

"But if anyone were to see her," said Razi, "they were guaranteed a lifetime of happiness. But if anyone were to kill her, they would die in forty days."

"Is it true?" Ariette asked.

Razi shrugged. "Who knows? I've certainly never seen her."

"So, if it is true," said Ariette, "how powerful is she? If she can make anyone king, surely, she would have the power to save anyone from a terrible fate, wouldn't she?"

Razi laughed. "We're all looking for miracles, aren't we?"

Ariette rolled her eyes. "I'm only asking. And it's not for me, it's for someone else."

"A lover, I assume?" Razi said with a grin.

Ariette frowned. "Yes. Why is that so funny?"

"Nah, forget about it," said Razi, swatting at the air. "You just reminded me of a friend of mine."

"Oh," said Ariette, looking down at her lap. "Who?"

"The king, in fact," said Razi. "Until now, I haven't met anyone who's more concerned with love than he is."

Ariette smiled. "He sounds like a very wise king, to me. Love has to be the greatest treasure in the universe."

"Yeah," said Razi, "but heartbreak's no fun. I'd rather be alone forever than suffer like he has. After he lost his true love, he's never been the same. I told him not to believe in silly things."

Ariette frowned. "Love is not silly. Not when it's true."

"No," said Razi, "just disappointing. True love is just another myth, but hey, to each his own."

Ariette took a deep breath. "A myth? No. Is Earth not full of love?"

Razi shrugged. "I'll let you be the judge of that. Seems like only a few are lucky enough to find it."

Ariette sighed. "So, if the legend of the Sima Bird were true, could she help me find it?"

Razi laughed. "I guess. Why not? She sounds pretty powerful to me."

When the men weren't looking, Ariette pulled the dagger out of her dress and tucked it into the camel's saddle. "You can't force me to do anything, Dark Kobra," she whispered to herself.

The rider in front of her turned. "Did you say...Dark Kobra?"

"Dark Kobra?" the men chorused, all turning to face Ariette.

Ariette blushed, the second she saw all of their eyes staring back at her.

"You know Dark Kobra?" Razi asked. "You're not one of his spies, are you?"

Ariette gulped. "Um..."

"Do you have any idea who that man is?" said Razi. Ariette shook her head. "He's the most ruthless killer in the East," said Razi. "He killed the king and queen several years ago. And they don't call him Kobra for nothing. He's so swift, they say you won't even hear him coming before he strikes. The entire kingdom wants him dead. He's the worst thing that's ever happened to Pernia. If you ever hear that name again, run...and if you're working for him, you can find the city on your own."

"Well, I...," Ariette stuttered, "thank you for your warning, but please believe I mean no harm."

Razi smiled and crossed his arms. "So, what are you, then? A princess?"

Ariette lowered her head and tucked her hair behind her ear. "I...I'd rather you didn't know."

"Off to seek your fortune in the city, I assume?" Razi smiled. "Steal the king's heart like all the other maidens who've tried?"

"Not exactly," said Ariette.

"So, you're a dancer, then?" said Razi. "A fortune-teller? You have to be something more than a peasant by the way you're dressed."

Ariette sighed. "I am Ariette. And that is all you need to know."

AS THE CARAVAN REACHED THE TOP OF THE DUNE, greenery began to appear as they left the desert behind. The riders brought their camels to a sudden halt and looked out at the city that awaited. Ariette looked to see the palace glittering in the distance at the highest point of the entire city which was spread out in the valley below it. Mountains erupted at the horizon, enclosing the palace from the ocean that waited several miles beyond it. A clear river weaved around the perimeter of the city and into the desert. Greenery began to appear further toward the heart of the valley, giving life to the barren desert around it. Homes were spread here and there around the grand bazaar, leading up to the palace. The sun peeked through the mountains, making the city seem like a golden oasis.

"Breathtaking, isn't it?" Razi said.

Ariette smiled, her eyes aflame with enchantment, "I've never seen anything like it."

"Well, allow me to be the first to welcome you to the greatest kingdom in the world," said Razi.

Ariette was in awe, letting the cool evening breeze dance through her hair and carry her fears away. Razi walked toward her and lifted her out of the saddle, waking her from her daydream.

"Well, here we are, Miss Ariette," Razi grunted, setting her on her feet. "Are you coming with us or not?"

"To the palace?" Ariette asked. "Um… no. I…I'll be fine on my own, but thank you. Razi, right?"

Razi nodded with a wink. "That's right."

Ariette bit her lip and drew out the dagger. Carrying it flat across her palms, she walked toward Razi.

"Please…take this," she said. "It is my gift to you. For taking me to the city."

"Where did you get this?" Razi marveled as Ariette laid the dagger across his palms. "This is a work of art. You sure you'll be alright without it? The city is full of thieves. The streets are pretty dangerous, especially after dark."

Ariette bowed and smiled. "I'll take my chances."

"Suit yourself," Razi said tucking the dagger into his belt. "Well, it was a pleasure to meet you, Ariette. Good luck finding true love."

Ariette smiled. "Thank you, but I don't need luck. I have something better."

She folded her hands behind her back and watched the caravan descend into the city. A cool, sandy breeze swept across her ankles as twilight closed in over the sands. She was happy to be rid of the dagger. Ariette took a deep breath. The sun had almost set. She closed her eyes and focused on flying again.

Stardust filled every part of her being and steadily lifted her feet out of the sand. She focused, trying to stay calm as it carried her several feet into the air. With a gentle burst, she leapt further into the air. Her entire body glowed with its familiar shade of periwinkle, streaking across the city like a shooting star. She smiled, relishing in the feeling of being one with the air.

As she was approaching the palace, she began to lose momentum. Her stardust was getting weaker already. Suddenly, the fear of losing it forever crept into her mind, destroying her flight pattern. Instantly, she fell to the ground. She tried to burst into flight again before hitting the ground but was too late and crashed roughly into a stand full of big silk carpets and rugs. As soon as she landed, she felt a jolt as her head slammed against a wooden beam, and she fell unconscious on top of a tall stack of rugs. There wasn't a soul in sight to see or hear her.

17

ARIETTE OPENED HER EYES. FOR A moment, it almost seemed like she was back in the bottle. She blinked several times to rid herself of the sudden shock that had come over her. She had awakened in a dark tent, lit faintly with lanterns of every color. The air was hazy with incense and cigar smoke, making the tent seem even darker. She found herself sitting on a silk pillow at a table below a canopy of lanterns. A woman's silhouette crept around her.

"Well, well," came a raspy voice from behind. "You're a long way from home, aren't you?"

"Who's there?" Ariette managed to say, searching the shadows for signs of motion. The woman came around to sit across from her at the table, revealing herself in the light of the lanterns. She slammed her hands on the table.

"They call me Roksana Estera," she said, rolling her tongue. "But I believe the better question is, who are you?"

"I...I am Ariette," she said. "Please, where am I?"

Roksana laughed and tapped her long, black-stained fingernails on the table. She pressed herself away from the table and drew a long, slender cigar out of her pocket. She reached into one of the lanterns, letting the tip of the cigar catch the flame. The beads and jewels that covered her from head to toe clinked together with her every move like chimes.

"You're in my tent, darling," she said blowing a puff of smoke into the air. Ariette coughed and fanned it away from her. Still, she couldn't escape the unpleasant aroma, the entire tent was infused with it. "Come all this way and seen nothing but that pretty, purple bottle, have you?" said Roksana.

Ariette's heart jumped inside of her.

Roksana laughed. "That's right, genie. I know everything about you. We're the same you know."

Ariette smiled and shook her head. "We are nothing alike, I promise you. You don't know anything about me."

"I was a star once," said Roksana.

Ariette felt a lump in her throat. The stardust inside of her electrified and began racing through her.

"You're...you're the star," Ariette stuttered. "But, how did you...?"

Roksana laughed to herself. "I was so bright I made even Aelius jealous. You should have seen it. Surely he told you the stories about me."

Ariette gulped and hugged herself. "Yes. They sounded more

like warnings to me."

"Warnings." Roksana laughed. "So, if you've been warned, why is it that you've come to Earth anyway? Must be very important. Won't you tell me?"

Ariette tucked her hair behind her ear and lowered her head.

"Don't be shy," said Roksana. "Your secrets are safe with me."

"Well," said Ariette. "I believe in…" She swallowed hard again. Somehow it was difficult to say. Ariette closed her eyes and drew in a deep breath. "I believe in love."

Roksana rolled her eyes. "Ha. Believe me, it doesn't get any easier here. The stars are right, love really is only a myth."

Ariette shook her head. "But it can't be. Not when I can feel it."

Roksana grinned. "How precious. You know, I hate to be the one to break the bad news to you, but stars feel nothing and are therefore incapable of feeling love."

"You're wrong," Ariette said. "I have too much proof. Since I was very young, I received wishes from my stargazer. My only stargazer. I was so small that no one but him would ever have thought to cast their wishes to me. But…" Ariette paused and looked down at her hands. "But he saw me," she said. "He saw me when no one else did. He believed in my power. He believed in me. Every night, he called to me, until it was forbidden. The last time I heard from him, he told me that he was in danger, and he wished for help. So, here I am. Aelius warned me of the dangers of coming to Earth, but that is true love, is it not? To love someone enough to risk your life to save them. What I wouldn't give to see him face-to-face…to know that he's safe."

A sly grin curled in the corners of Roksana's mouth. "What you wouldn't give, you say?"

"I would give anything to see him," said Ariette.

Roksana cast a sly look at Ariette. "Anything, you say? Well, what if I told you that I can make this possible for you?"

Ariette froze. "You mean, he's...he's alive?"

Roksana crossed her arms and nodded. "That's right, Angel. He's alive, and he's here in Pernia. Now wouldn't you like to see him?"

Ariette was speechless. Every ounce of stardust inside of her started racing through her faster than the speed of light. She stood and spun in a circle.

"I...I don't believe it." She gasped, pressing her hands over her heart. "He's alive."

Roksana laughed to herself.

Ariette gulped and looked up at Roksana, heart still racing, "Will you take me to him?"

"Oh yes," said Roksana. "Anything your heart desires. I only ask for one thing in return."

"Well..." said Ariette, "what is it?"

Roksana grinned. "We each want what the other has, you see. All I ask is for a simple trade. I want my stardust again, and you want to be a human. You'll give me your stardust, and I'll take you to your love where you can live happily ever after. What do you say?"

Ariette stopped for a minute. She glanced down at the markings on her wrists. "It sounds wonderful, but..."

"But?" Roksana laughed. "There's nothing to dispute. We

both get what we want. This is the greatest bargain you're going to find."

"But without my stardust, how will I grant my stargazer's wish?" said Ariette.

Roksana's expression hardened. "Don't be stupid, girl."

Roksana grabbed Ariette by the wrist and pulled her closer. "Do you know what these are?" Roksana said, looking at the markings on Ariette's wrist.

"I..." Ariette stuttered.

"These are your fate if you stay here," Roksana said with such an anger that Ariette started shaking from head to toe.

Ariette gulped and looked nervously at her wrists. "My fate?"

Roksana released her and ripped the long, black cloak off of her shoulders, revealing the unthinkable. Ariette gasped as a ring of shock electrified every nerve in her body. Nearly every inch of Roksana's skin was tattooed with the markings from the neck down. Only a few had made their way onto her face.

"No," Ariette whispered to herself.

"A lifetime of wishes is what's in store, genie," Roksana said. "You become theirs. You vanish beneath all of their selfish requests. Save yourself while you still can."

Ariette looked at the meager two markings on her own wrists and then back at Roksana. She couldn't manage to speak.

"Now," said Roksana, "I happen to know this love of yours. Rest assured he is alive. You'll be pleased to know that he still speaks of you often. The smallest star in the night sky, his one and only lullaby."

Ariette stood. "He's alive?"

Roksana laughed. "That's right. Now, how about our deal? I know you're dying to see him."

"Well, yes," said Ariette, "but what about the wishes I must grant?"

Roksana rolled her eyes. "Don't worry about it. A wish once granted will always come true. Unless that is, someone sets you free first, but I doubt you'll find such an offer."

Ariette stopped. The king would die because of her if she didn't try to stop it, but at the same time, she wanted nothing more than to finally meet her stargazer.

"It's really a small price to pay," said Roksana, "and you'll be with your true love forever. It's give and take, you see. That's life. Get used to it."

Ariette took a deep breath. "The thing is…I haven't granted the one I've wanted to grant the most yet."

Roksana stood and began pacing. "Give, give, give," she said, lurking through the shadows. "You know all about that, don't you? Wouldn't you like to take for once in your sad, lonely little life?"

"Please," said Ariette, "will you at least tell me the name of my stargazer?"

Roksana threw her head back laughing. "Ha. Silly star, that's not how this works. A deal is a deal. Now do we have one or not?"

Ariette gulped and gripped the tablecloth. "I am not silly," she said. "And I know a trap when I see one."

With a big breath, Ariette grabbed the ends of the tablecloth and swashed it across the lanterns, extinguishing the flames and turning the tent to complete darkness. She burst into flight, skating her way out of the tent and back into the bazaar. Once free, she didn't even stop to glance back at the tent. She stumbled out of her flight and onto her feet where she started into a run toward the palace. Roksana raced after her, stopping outside the tent. With a devilish smile on her face, she watched Ariette run for the palace. "Fine. If you want to make a game out of it, let's play. You can't escape me, little star."

Tears began to fill Ariette's eyes with every stride. As they fell, they streaked across her cheekbones and into the air behind her. She couldn't run as fast as she wanted to, she was still getting used to the feeling of being on her feet, but nothing could have stopped her from moving forward.

The palace was the last place she wanted to be, but at least she could try to offer the king some type of warning before the wish came true. The moonlight illuminated the streets, paving the way for her as if to lead her into the deepest part of her worst nightmare.

She scurried through the empty bazaar, not stopping to notice anything around her. When she arrived at the palace gates, she stopped, immediately awestricken at its impressive size and splendor. Tall, white stone walls rose up around the gates, towering over her. Vines of rare, night-blooming jasmine hung from the top and grew up from the ground, curling through the bars of the gate. As the golden sky faded to night, the white flowers began to reveal themselves along with their enchanting fragrance. The scent was as beautiful as the plant was mysterious. The mystery of what was beyond the gates was even more so. Ariette gently lifted herself into flight and rose above the palace to catch a glimpse of the entire thing. Complete with several gardens, fountains and towering six stories, it was even more magnificent than it looked from the ground. She had never seen anything so grand. Not even the entire cosmos could have compared. A round blue dome caught her attention, hidden in the center of the courtyard. She lowered toward it. It seemed like the safest place to hide.

Just as she came close to it, she lost control of her flight and tumbled toward it, gathering more speed with every second. She let out a scream as she crashed through the stained glass and into the menagerie where she landed in a large fountain, spilling water over the edges. Fortunately, it was just deep enough to break her fall. The garden was dark. Only the moonlight shone through the large hole that was now in the glass. She splashed around, trying to find something to grab on to. She wasn't used to water, but she hated it already.

She swam across the rippling water, leaping for the edge. As soon as she grabbed it, she pulled herself into a seated position, her feet still dangling in the water. She squeezed her hair to ring the water out and flipped it over her shoulder. She glanced at the markings on her wrists and plunged them into the water, anxiously trying to scrub them away. No matter how hard she tried, she couldn't get rid of them.

The moon was big and bright overhead. She took a deep breath and lifted her head toward the sky, amazed by how a world that she thought she knew so well suddenly seemed so far away. From Earth, there were even more stars than she'd imagined. The first to catch her eye was Aelius. She now saw the difference in size among the stars. Aelius was by far the brightest aside from the moon.

"Do you see me?" she whispered, gazing up at her home. "Would you hear me if I sent a wish?"

She hesitated. Deep inside, she wouldn't have dared to wish. If Aelius were to know her true wishes, he would know the kind of trouble she was in and shoot to Earth in a second to bring her home.

She slid her feet out of the water and swung them around to the other side. She braced the edges of the ledge and looked around. It was too dark to see anything, but she could tell there were plants all around the garden. She stood and walked into the brush to hide for the night. She walked as far away from the doors as possible and slid her back along the trunk of a lemon tree into a seated position. With a deep breath, she curled her knees to her chest and admired the beauty of the stars until she fell asleep.

18

$\mathcal{J}$UST AS THE SUN BEGAN TO RISE, A gentle, feathery brush swept across Ariette's nose, waking her. When she opened her eyes, she was greeted by the sounds of trickling fountains and the light of the sun. A soft, misty scent lingered through the air like an ocean breeze, mixed with the sweet smell of citrus from the lemons that had fallen around her. Fruit trees of all kinds filled the garden along with a rainbow of exotic flowers and marble statues of the Sima Bird. There was a tile path winding through the plants that was painted blue to look like a river. The air was clear yet moist, as if a rainforest had been captured inside the dome.

Ariette took a deep breath, letting the feeling of the new place wash over her. She smiled and looked up at the sun who was showering his rays down into the garden. She felt the prick of talons creep across her lap. An elegant white bird crawled across her legs, fluttering her feathers across Ariette's face. Ariette scrambled to her feet to find that there were ten more just like it surrounding her, each one pecking at fruits that had fallen from the tree. She was careful not to step on any of their long, delicate feathers. A smile came across her face as she watched them make their way around the garden. They reminded her of the bird from the oasis. She remembered the egg, which was still in her pocket, and drew it out to examine it again. Sliding her fingers across its smooth, glossy surface, she wondered if the bird would be mad that she had taken it. She tried to convince herself that she was helping a friend by protecting it for her while she was away. A part of her hoped the bird would come for it soon so she could see her again.

The doors to the menagerie began to rustle at the sound of the keys wiggling into the lock. Ariette turned toward the doors. Her heart started racing, and her eyes searched for the best place to hide. She tucked the egg back into her dress.

The doors opened. Ariette scurried as quickly as she could to hide behind a tall statue of the Sima Bird, which was as far away from the doors as possible. She held her breath, peaking over her shoulder to see who had entered the garden. A tall, olive-skinned young man walked in, running his hands through the thick brown waves of his hair that had fallen around his face.

He guided the beautiful princess Emira behind him, their hands interlaced. Her dark brown hair was intricately braided and tied at the back of her neck with a sheer, pink sash. Her long, dark tresses it rippled down her shimmering pink dress. The dress was more beautiful than any garmet Ariette had ever seen since being on Earth. With every step she took, the dress glimmered in the light that cast into the menagerie from the glass dome above.

He smiled and said something to her, but Ariette couldn't make out his words. The princess smiled in return and lifted the ends of her dress to take a step forward. As they walked deeper into the menagerie, Ariette was able to hear them more clearly.

"They're beautiful, Faaris," the princess said to him, looking around at the eleven white peacocks at their feet. "Have you named them?"

"Of course," Faaris answered. "Every one of them."

"How charming," said the princess, sliding her hand onto his shoulder.

Faaris reached for a silk bag that was hanging beside the door and drew out several dried dates. "Would you like to feed them?" he asked, handing one to her.

The princess smiled and plucked the date from his hand. She crouched a little and held her hand out to one of the birds. "Ow," she screeched and pulled her hand away. "I think it bit me."

Faaris laughed and knelt to the bird. "Aphrodite, behave yourself."

He turned back toward the princess. "My apologies. If only I could teach them to behave as nicely as they look."

The princess took a deep breath and smoothed her dress. "I had no idea they were so aggressive."

"Only sometimes," Faaris said with a smile. "Usually, they're quite calm. Although, at their worst they can be deafening. They've been my greatest joy for many years. I've learned to forgive their flaws. I mean, I'm not perfect either."

Faaris took her hands and led her over several birds. "Watch your step."

The princess smiled. "You know, Faaris, the more I get to know you, the more I like you. You say you're not perfect, but I believe you are the most perfect man in the world."

Faaris laughed. "I assure you, I'm far from perfection. I certainly try, though. Although, I'll warn you, I'm not easily understood and I'm very stubborn. Actually, I'm surprised you have such affection for me. Most people find me strange."

"Not strange," said the princess. "Rare. I ask myself every day how I got so lucky. Don't you feel the same?"

Faaris smiled. "Well, I'm glad I was able to charm you. I hope you won't find me too delusional." The princess smiled and rolled her eyes. "I mean, sometimes, I can't even stand to be with myself," said Faaris with a shrug. "I'm insane, I assure you. I often get these strange thoughts, you know, like nightmares. Do you? I don't know where they come from, but they scare the life out of me. I wouldn't blame you if you wanted to walk away from this engagement right now."

"Oh, Faaris," said the princess with a playful nudge. "There is nothing you could say to make me fall out of love with you. I mean, only a fool would walk away from the chance to be the Queen of Pernia."

"Really," said Faaris looking disappointed, "you're that sure?"

The princess nudged him again. "Don't be silly, Faaris. Of course, I am."

"Well that's good, then." Faaris smiled half-heartedly. He took a deep breath and glanced up at the sun. "Welcome to the rest of your life."

Faaris walked toward the big fountain at the center of the garden and dipped his hands into the dancing waters. He sighed and glanced upward to greet the sunrise, only to notice the gaping hole in the glass. His expression changed.

Ariette bit her lip and turned away from them, pressing her back against the statue. She stumbled a little but managed to keep quiet. She held her breath and gazed up at the sun. Several of the birds began to appear in front of her, one-by-one until there were at least six of them creeping around the statue.

"No," she whispered in their language, shooing at them. "Go away. Please go away."

"What have you got there?" Faaris laughed, following the peacocks toward the statue.

Ariette bit her lip and closed her eyes. She melted to the ground as Faaris came closer, praying that he wouldn't find her.

"Hello?" said Faaris. "Is someone there?"

Ariette stood and braced the sides of the statue, wanting nothing more than to disappear. She closed her eyes and filled her spirit with stardust, letting it cover every inch of her. She held her breath, just waiting for Faaris to turn and see her. Just as Faaris came around the statue, Ariette managed to dissolve herself into thin air. She couldn't stay hidden for long without reappearing, but she had spared herself a few seconds.

Faaris scratched the back of his neck, arriving to see only the birds pecking at the ground. "I'm warning you," he said to them, "I'm not in the mood for games."

Ariette focused on reappearing on the other side of the door, but she had never tried anything like that before. When she couldn't maintaining her control any longer, she fell to the ground and crashed onto the floor in a cloud of stardust.

Faaris turned and drew a sword from his belt, aiming it right at her. His shoulders dropped the moment he saw her. "Be still, my beating heart," he breathed, lowering his sword.

Ariette gasped and hurried to her feet. "No. Please."

The princess gasped and grabbed Faaris' arm. Her eyes scanned Ariette from head-to-toe. Her eyes were wide with shock. "Faaris, who is this girl?"

"I can assure you I have no idea," Faaris said, his eyes still set on Ariette.

The princess grabbed Faaris by the shoulders and turned him so that they were face-to-face. "How dare you lie to me? I am your fiancé. Surely she didn't just fall out of the sky."

"Emira, please," said Faaris taking her by the hands. "I have never seen this girl in my life. Believe me."

"Of course," Emira scoffed, rolling her eyes. "I knew you were strange."

"Please, let me explain," Faaris said, tucking his sword away.

"There's nothing to explain," said Emira. "I've seen enough. There's nothing you could say now that could convince me otherwise."

Emira turned and pushed Faaris into the fountain. "Goodbye, Faaris," she called, rushing for the doors. "I hope you two are very happy together." She slammed the doors, leaving Faaris and Ariette alone in silence.

Faaris groaned and ran his hands through his wet curls as he emerged from the water. He stood, soaked from head-to-toe, and turned to see Ariette standing with fear in her big, glossy eyes.

"I…I'm sorry," said Ariette, not hesitating to run toward the exit as fast as she could.

"Wait. Stop," Faaris said, sloshing through the knee-deep waters. "Don't go. It's…it's alright."

Ariette stopped and took a deep breath before turning back toward Faaris. "Please," she said, "I mean no harm. Release me and I will be out of your sight. I promise."

"Not so fast," Faaris said, wagging his finger at her with a grin. "I can't let you leave until I know who you are first. Otherwise, I have to assume you're an intruder."

"No," Ariette said, holding her hands in front of her.

Faaris climbed over the fountain's ledge and slipped his gold vest, which was heavy with water, off of his shoulders. He let it splatter onto the floor with a sigh of relief and rung the water out of his shirt.

"Who…um…how did you get in here?" Faaris asked, scratching the back of his neck.

Ariette bit her lip. "It was an accident. I know I'm not supposed to be here, but if you'd just let me explain…"

Faaris grinned and opened his arms in a negotiable way. "Well, frankly I'm hoping it has something to do with the giant hole in my roof." Ariette glanced up at the top of the dome, seeing the broken glass. Faaris crossed his arms. "I mean, I can only assume that was you, unless some kids in the bazaar got carried away in a game of catch. Care to explain?"

Ariette smiled. "Well, I...I fell."

Faaris looked puzzled. "Fell?" he said, almost laughing. "Fell from where? I don't suppose you were flying."

Ariette smiled and fidgeted with her fingers. "Well...it was an accident."

"It's alright," said Faaris. "It can be repaired. I'm just glad it was you and not a thief or a spy or something like that," he said, a slight suspicion hiding in his tone. "I mean, sneaking through the roof strikes me as something only a thief would need to do. Wouldn't you agree?"

Ariette huffed and put her hands on her hips. "I am not a thief."

"Alright," said Faaris crossing his arms, "then what are you, if you don't mind my asking?"

"Please believe I mean you no harm," said Ariette. "I will gladly leave if you wish me gone."

"Not until you explain yourself," said Faaris. "Forgive me, but until I know why you're here I have to assume the worst. Unless you want to spare us both the trouble and tell me now."

"Please," Ariette said, trying to catch her breath. "I...I've come to warn you."

Faaris sighed. "Oh. Forgive me, you must understand, there is a criminal who's out to kill me at the moment. It's not exactly the most pleasant thing to have in the back of your mind, and sneaking into my home like this doesn't exactly hold you in my favor."

"Oh," said Ariette, taking a softer tone. "Why would anyone want to kill you?"

Faaris lowered his head and wiped several drops of water off of his face. "That's an excellent question. I've been wondering that myself. Let's just say that I have an enemy who's a...a little jealous. I have to stay inside the palace at all times to protect myself until he's captured. And who knows when that day will come."

Ariette smiled to herself. "You are a prisoner."

Faaris smiled. "In a sense," he said. He paused and looked up at her, casting his warm, golden eyes up into hers. "What is your name?"

Ariette smiled. Faaris had the kindest face she had ever seen. His eyes were rich with wisdom for one so young, swimming with mystery and more curiosity than could possibly be satisfied in a lifetime. Drops of water were hanging from several wet curls around his face and from the short hairs on his chin, dripping onto his face and down his nose.

Ariette looked down and tucked her hair behind her ear. "I am Ariette."

Faaris smiled. "Ariette," he said, studying her face. "Such a name. I must say, I've never heard anything like it. Where did you say you were from?"

Ariette smiled. "I'm from a place very far away from here. Somewhere I'm sure you've never been."

"Don't take this the wrong way," said Faaris, "but at first I thought you were some sort of peri. Either that or a very confused princess."

"Peri?" Ariette said.

Faaris grinned. "You really aren't from here, are you?" he said.

Ariette shook her head.

"Well, in Pernia, we have many legends about mythical creatures and, you know, supernatural beings, that sort of thing. These creatures are featured in many of my poetry books. I'm sure you have stories like these where you're from as well."

Ariette shook her head again.

"No?" Faaris laughed. "I must say that comes as a bit of a surprise to me. Well, according to the stories, the peri are magical creatures renowned for their…their beauty." He blushed. "Despite having evil hearts, that is. They are sort of like genies but without the wishes. They have other talents."

"Like what?" Ariette asked.

Faaris laughed. "Like stealing the souls of mankind. Then again, don't buy into it too much, they're only stories."

Ariette smiled. "Well you will be glad to know that I am not one of them."

"You must be an angel then," said Faaris. "Sent from Heaven to save me from marrying someone I don't love."

"Not exactly," Ariette smiled.

"But you are lost, I assume," said Faaris.

"Well, actually, I came looking for someone," Ariette said, hugging herself. "But I do not think I will find him now. Please, where can I find the king? I need to tell him something."

Faaris smiled and lowered his head. He spread his arms and bowed. "At your service. What can I do for you?"

Ariette felt her mouth open a little. "You…you are the king?"

"Is that so hard to believe?" Faaris laughed.

"No," Ariette said. "It's just that I…well, I wasn't expecting to find you in this part of the palace."

Faaris shrugged and looked around the garden. "I'm always in here actually. Ask anyone."

"Please," Ariette smiled, "what is your name?"

"Faaris," he said, still smiling at her with his kind eyes.

"King Faaris," Ariette repeated, matching his face with his name in her memory.

Faaris laughed. "Yes, but please, just call me Faaris."

"Faaris," Ariette repeated. "I…well, I've come to warn you, actually."

Faaris' smile melted. "Warn me? Of course, what is it? Tell me, please."

"Well…there is someone who wishes something terrible upon you," Ariette said.

Faaris stopped for a moment to collect his thoughts. "Who sent you?"

Ariette gulped. "It was a…an acquaintance of mine whose name should not concern you, but please believe I've come to save you."

"As the king I believe it is my right to know who sent you," said Faaris. "Please. I must know. Otherwise the suspicion might kill me before my enemy does."

Ariette squinted. "Enemy?"

Faaris shrugged. "It's the way it is for any king. Fortunately, there are people like you who are kind enough to warn me of such dangers."

Ariette gulped and managed to smile.

"Alright," Faaris sighed taking her by the arms. "Well, thank you for warning me. A thousand times, thank you. I'll alert the guards immediately." Ariette let out a sigh of relief as Faaris turned for the doors. "And if you ever decide to share with me the name of this acquaintance of yours, I'd be happy to know," said Faaris turning back toward her. "Until then, please, come with me."

"Oh, no," Ariette said, shaking her head. "I shouldn't be here. I've delivered my message, and I think it's best that I be on my way, but thank you."

Faaris smiled. "Don't be afraid. You're safe here. I promise. There's someone I want to introduce you to."

Ariette shook her head. "No. I'm not safe here and neither are you."

Faaris squinted and crossed his arms. "Don't worry, we're going to figure all of this out."

Ariette gulped and glanced up at him with her big beady eyes. "Um…"

Faaris smiled. "It's alright," he said. "Please, join me for dinner tonight. I must repay you for saving me. It's the least I could do."

Ariette hesitated but felt herself nod. "By the way," she said. "I'm sorry for chasing your fiancé away. I can bring her back to you if you wish."

Faaris grinned. "It's alright," he said. "I believe everything happens for a reason. I should thank you, really."

Ariette smiled and squinted. "And why is that?"

Faaris smiled at the ground and then back at her. "You've done me a favor. I didn't want to marry her anyway," he said.

Ariette smiled.

Faaris cleared his throat. "Please, come with me," he said as he held his hand out to her. Ariette hesitated. "It's alright, I promise," said Faaris. Ariette nodded and slid her hand into his.

Faaris guided her across the garden and opened the doors. "So, if you're not a peri, where are you from?"

Ariette shook her head. "I am very far from home. A place I'm sure you've never been."

"How far?" Faaris asked.

Ariette's eyes widened. "Far."

Faaris laughed. "And you've come all this way to bring this news to me?"

Ariette smiled and nodded.

"Will it be a difficult journey home?" Faaris asked.

Ariette lowered her head. "Very difficult. Impossible, actually."

"Oh," said Faaris, a little surprised. "Well, we have the finest carriages in the world. It would be my honor to assist you."

Ariette shook her head. "I'm sure my brother will come for me if I'm not back in a few more days. He's very…"

"Protective?" Faaris smiled.

Ariette let out a quick laugh. "That would be an understatement."

"I see," said Faaris. "It's none of my business, but if he's that worried, why wouldn't he come with you?"

"It was a dangerous journey," said Ariette.

Faaris grinned. "Yet, here you are."

Ariette bit her lip. "The truth is, I left without him knowing. I had to."

"It sounds to me like you ran away," said Faaris.

Ariette blushed and looked at the ground, tucking her hair behind her ear. "You could say that."

Faaris smiled and looked straight into her eyes. "Well, I'm glad you did."

19

"FAARIS," CAME MEHRZAD'S ANGRY voice from the end of the hall.

Faaris' heart jumped at the sound, and he turned to take Ariette by the shoulders. "Wait here for a moment, alright?" he said, leaving her by the doors.

Ariette shook her head, watching him run off to meet Mehrzad down the hall.

"I can explain," said Faaris holding his hands in front of his chest.

"Have you lost your mind?" said Mehrzad, bracing Faaris by the shoulders. He pulled his hands away and shook the water off. "Good heavens, my boy, you're soaking wet."

"Trust me, you don't know the whole story," said Faaris.

"Listen to me," Mehrzad scolded. "I am utterly appalled. I

might have expected this sort of behavior from your brother, but never from you."

"Believe me," said Faaris, "you've heard wrong."

Mehrzad crossed his arms. "Alright, then explain to me this instant what another girl was doing inside the menagerie. I know you're not fond of the idea of getting married so soon, but this is no time for this kind of nonsense. Do you understand?"

"Mehrzad, please," Faaris said. "It isn't what you think. Yes, there was a girl in there, but I can assure you I've never seen her in my life. And I wasn't going to marry Emira anyway. You and I both know that. I've told you a thousand times, I'll have Setareh or I'll rule alone."

"How can you be so selfish, boy?" Mehrzad scolded. "As the king, it is your responsibility to your people to take a wife—a human wife. I don't want to hear another word about this Setareh. It's nothing more than childish fantasy, and I think it's best that you put it behind you. Pernia must have a queen. It is the law."

"Well then perhaps I should change that law," Faaris said, looking seriously into Mehrzad's eyes. "I am the king after all. Setareh is real. I assure you, I haven't lost my mind."

"What would your father think?" Mehrzad said under his breath. "That law has been in place for centuries."

Faaris swallowed hard and looked at the ground. "I should hope to think he would support my decision. He loved the kingdom as much as I do, but I still think he would want me to be happy. I am more than just a king, after all. Do I not deserve true love as much as anyone else?"

"Listen, my boy," Mehrzad said. "You will learn to love Emira.

Trust me. These things take time."

"Then tell me why it is that I've known her for almost two years and felt absolutely nothing," said Faaris. "I think I've actually fallen out of love with her with each day that's passed. She's not the one for me. I'm sure of it."

"Well, then we'll find another princess for you to marry," said Mehrzad.

"No," said Faaris. "I've made my choice."

Faaris sighed and looked up at Mehrzad. "Please, Mehrzad," he said. "Let me trust my heart. I beg you."

Mehrzad sighed and closed his eyes, pinching the bridge of his nose as if he had a headache. "Oh, Faaris," he said. "Don't do this to me, I'm old."

Faaris gulped. "Now let me explain the girl."

Mehrzad sighed and followed Faaris toward the menagerie. "I certainly wish you would."

When Faaris opened the doors to the menagerie he glanced around only to find her gone. The several peacocks which had come out of hiding were the only signs of life to be found as they made their way around the garden. It was as still and tranquil as ever.

"She was here a minute ago, I promise," said Faaris. "Ariette," he called.

Mehrzad crossed his arms. "I hope you've been honest with me about this girl, Faaris. I would hate to think you've made up this story to save yourself from the truth."

"Don't you trust me?" Faaris asked, looking offended.

Mehrzad sighed and closed his eyes. "Of course I do, my boy.

Forgive me."

"Then you'll not say another word about it," said Faaris.

Ariette peaked out from behind one of the statues. Faaris smiled and jogged toward her, leaving Mehrzad to catch up with him.

"It's alright, don't be afraid," said Faaris, reaching out his hand to Ariette, who smiled and let him lead her out into the hall. She bowed as soon as she saw Mehrzad towering over her.

"What is your name, my dear?" Mehrzad asked.

"I am Ariette," she said. "I have only come to bring you a warning. There is someone who wishes the king dead soon…very soon."

"Indeed, there is," said Mehrzad. "We've been searching for him for three years now. Even better would be if you can tell us of his whereabouts."

Ariette bit her lip. "All I can offer you is my warning. I do not know of his location, but I'm sure he is not far."

Faaris and Mehrzad exchanged looks.

"Very well," said Mehrzad. "Young lady, do you have a place to stay?"

Faaris looked at Mehrzad with lowered eyebrows.

Ariette shook her head. "It is very kind of you, but I will be alright on my own. I must return home soon, anyway."

Mehrzad smiled. "Will you at least allow us to escort you home safely?"

Ariette smiled and lowered her head. "I'm afraid my home is too far for any of your chariots, but thank you."

"Ah, well, you must stay until Faaris' birthday celebration, then," said Mehrzad. "I insist. You will be our guest of honor."

Ariette blushed. "Oh, no, I...I couldn't."

"Nonsense," said Mehrzad, winking at Faaris. "Come with me."

The soft pitter-patter of small footsteps crept around the corner. A small round face peeked out from behind a tall red curtain near the end of the hallway.

"Faaris," came the sound of a little girl's voice.

Faaris turned toward the curtains. "Excuse me," he said to Mehrzad and Ariette, jogging toward the little girl.

"Parisa," he said, kneeling to greet her face-to-face, "have you been spying on us?"

"Emira said you made her really mad," Parisa mumbled.

Faaris smiled and tucked several loose strands of dark brown hair away from her face. "It's alright, Mushroom. I'll explain everything to you later."

"But why did she leave?" Parisa asked. "Is she coming back?"

Faaris laughed to himself and shook his head. "No, I don't think she'll be coming back. She's...she's not my true love."

"Oh," Parisa whispered. "Who's that?" she asked, pointing to Ariette.

Faaris smiled. "Her name is Ariette, but she's a stranger, so I want you to stay away from her, alright? She's going to stay here for a while so we can keep an eye on her."

"Are you going to marry her now?" Parisa asked.

Faaris laughed. "What's gotten into you, Mushroom? Besides, I think we both know you're the only girl for me."

Parisa blushed and giggled. "Good. I don't want you to

get married. If you get married, then we won't be able to play together anymore. I miss you. Ever since you became the king, you never have time to play with me anymore."

Faaris smiled and wrapped his arms around her. "Ah. Believe me, I feel the same. Don't worry, once things settle down, I'll have all the time in the world for you, I promise. Why don't you go find Razi for me? I need to talk to him."

Parisa nodded and ran off.

Faaris turned back toward Mehrzad and Ariette. "Forgive me," he said. "It was just Parisa."

"She saw Emira storm out," Mehrzad said crossing his arms.

"She'll understand someday," said Faaris, scratching the back of his neck.

Mehrzad shook his head. "She also heard Emira say she wants nothing to do with you."

"I'll send her a letter of apology explaining everything, don't worry. Believe me, I couldn't live with myself otherwise," said Faaris. "All I can do then is hope she believes my story and pray that Parisa doesn't think I'm a monster."

Razi slipped out from behind the curtain. "Psst. Faaris," he said. Faaris turned.

Ariette's heart jumped as soon as she saw Razi. "You," she whispered.

"Well, what do you know?" said Razi, putting his hands on his hips. "I thought you'd be with the love of your life by now. How did you end up here?"

Ariette smiled and shook her head. "It's a long story."

"Ah, you'll find him," Razi said with a wink. "These things can take some time, you know. You seem like the type that doesn't give up easily."

"Excuse me," said Faaris. "You…you know each other?"

"Yeah, I know Ariette," said Razi.

Ariette just smiled.

"Ah," said Faaris, stroking his chin. "Um… Mehrzad, will you please escort Miss Ariette to her room while I have a talk with Razi?" He turned to Ariette. "We'll meet again soon."

"Certainly," Mehrzad bowed. "Come with me, my dear," he said kindly to Ariette, leading her toward the nearest stairwell.

Mehrzad leaned into Faaris' ear, making sure that Ariette didn't hear him. "We need to keep an eye on her," he whispered. "Make sure she is who she says she is. Now, leave it to me. I want you to stay away from her."

"I'm way ahead of you," Faaris whispered.

Mehrzad nodded, and he and Ariette disappeared behind the curtains.

"Well, you bounce back fast," Razi laughed, giving Faaris a playful nudge.

"Not so fast," said Faaris. "How do you know her? What can you tell me about her?"

Razi grinned and crossed his arms. "I found her wandering around in the desert on my way back into the city yesterday. She said she was lost, looking for some long-lost lover or something, so I took her to the city."

"Believe it or not, but I think she's a genie," said Faaris in a whisper.

"Whoa, Faaris," Razi grunted. "I'm starting to worry about

188

you. I think all the stress is messing with your head. A genie? You need to stop reading all those stories. They aren't real."

"Don't worry," said Faaris. "I'm going to set her free as soon as I can. The last thing the world needs is more evil."

"Oh, and then you're going to marry her?" Razi teased. "I saw that look on your face."

Faaris laughed. "Easy, Razi," he said. "I never said anything about that. I've told you already, it's Setareh or no one. You and I both know I wouldn't be caught dead with a genie. She scares me."

"Her?" Razi said with a laugh. "She's like…like an angel or something."

Faaris crossed his arms. "Probably a strategy to allure fools into taking their chances with wishes."

"Always something with you," Razi said, shaking his head. "Let me tell you something, Faaris. You need to stop pushing people away. There was nothing wrong with Emira. She was pretty, smart, funny, and she made a mean baklava. Man, I'm going to miss that. Oh, and she was, you know, a human. And Ariette is not a genie. She's a poor girl who's heartbroken and lost and we should do the right thing and help her. The last thing she needs is for us to push her away or make her feel like some sort of monster. You need to get your priorities straight and get your head out of the clouds."

"Look, Emira was a nice girl," said Faaris, "but I can't help it if I wasn't in love with her. I owe it to myself to be happy with who I choose, don't I?"

Razi sighed. "Nah, you just need to open your eyes a little.

Get out of your own head. Setareh's not real, but Pernia is, and it needs a queen."

Faaris frowned. "I truly believe that Setareh's still out there and that someday, fate is going to bring us together."

Razi rolled his eyes. "Fate? You know, for your sake I hope you find her, but in the meantime, good luck chasing that goose, and don't say I didn't warn you."

Faaris smiled at the ground. "Go on, laugh at me like everyone else."

Razi patted Faaris on the chest. "Keep dreaming."

Faaris sighed and ran his hands through his hair.

"Is Ariette coming to dinner tonight?" Razi asked.

"I don't see why not," said Faaris. "She is our guest after all. It might be a good chance to find out more about her. Find out if she's working for Kobra. I admit, I have a slight suspicion. He seems like the sort of man who would do anything to get his hands on a source of power... genies included."

"Come on, Faaris," said Razi, clasping his hands together.

"Have I ever been wrong about these kinds of things?" Faaris said spreading his arms.

"Alright, you've got a point there," said Razi, scratching his chin, watching Ariette gracefully talking to Mehrzad, "but what are the odds? I mean...*her*? She seems so nice. I mean look at her. She's too...."

"Beautiful," Faaris said with a clever grin. "Exactly. It's always the unassuming ones that prove to be the most dangerous. You can never be too careful."

"Alright," Razi laughed, "well since you've sworn out of love, you think I've got a shot with her?"

Faaris smiled. "Be my guest. Just be careful, and please, for the love of peace, behave yourself. And if I hear one more word about marriage, I think I'm actually going to lose my mind."

20

ARIETTE SAT IN THE WINDOW frame of her room, hugging her knees and gazing up at the starry sky. She sighed as a cool, evening breeze brushed across her face. In these quiet moments, she could almost trick herself into believing that it was all a dream and that she would wake up soon and be a star again. Three soft knocks came from the door. Ariette's heart jumped a little. She unfolded herself and let her feet slip onto the marble floor. She walked toward the door. Three more knocks came from the door. Ariette stood in silence beside it, almost holding her breath. She slid her fingers onto the bronze doorknob.

"It's alright," came the familiar sound of Faaris' voice from the other side of the door, "it's just me."

Ariette pulled the door open, peaking through to see Faaris

smiling at her along with Razi. Both were dressed in their finest clothes, shimmering from head to toe in silk and jewels.

"Are you hungry at all?" Faaris asked.

Ariette looked confused. "Hungry?"

"You must be," said Faaris. "It sounds like you've come a long way to bring your warning to me. It would be my honor if you'd join us for dinner tonight. If you'd like to, that is. I can't force you to do anything if you don't want to. I just thought it would be..."

"Alright," said Ariette. "I will join you."

Faaris smiled and let out a sigh. "Excellent. Please, come with me."

Ariette returned his smile and followed him into the hall. "Faaris," she said.

"Yes," said Faaris.

"What is dinner?" Ariette asked. "Is it a custom of yours?"

Razi grunted a laugh. "It's only the best thing in the world... well one of the best things. It's definitely at the top of my list."

Faaris laughed a little to himself. "I must admit, I'm becoming more and more interested in learning about this country of yours. Where exactly are you from?"

Ariette blushed and tucked her hair behind her ear. "Well, our customs are...not like yours."

"Ah," said Faaris stroking his chin. "I must say, it surprises me that your customs don't include dinner."

Ariette shook her head.

Faaris smiled. "Well, I think you'll be pleasantly surprised then," he said.

Ariette smiled and followed them to the dining hall.

The banquet was set as it always was. Small trays of dates and figs scattered the table from end-to-end and golden goblets were filled with wine. Bowls of spiced rice and vegetables were placed evenly across the spread alongside plates of fish, roasted squab, and baskets of bread. Fruits of all colors were arranged as if they were flowers in big, bronze bowls. The dining room itself was exquisite. The chandeliers that hung over the table were lit one by one, the flames dancing across the gold and bronze dishware. A servant stood still at every torch that lined the walls of the dining hall. A trio of musicians were seated on tall chairs toward the back of the room, one tapping on a set of drums, another plucking strings on a sitar, and another strumming the strings of an oud. Razi and the members of the court stood over the chairs at their usual places. Faaris was the last to arrive at his seat, like always, this time with Ariette by his side. He led Ariette to the head of the table and offered her the seat beside his. He took the top of the chair and pulled it out from beneath the table.

"Will this be alright?" Faaris asked motioning for her to sit. Ariette smiled and nodded, overwhelmed by the splendor of the banquet. She had never seen anything like it. Faaris stood over his chair and held out his arms, motioning for everyone to sit.

Conversation began to fill the room and became so loud that Ariette knew her soft voice would be impossible to be heard over it. She noticed numerous lemon slices garnishing several of the platters. The smell reminded her of the menagerie. She reached for one. Faaris glanced up after taking a sip of water with a look of confusion on his face. Ariette took a bite of the lemon, only to find that it didn't taste at all like she'd imagined, but she liked it. She had never eaten before. Stars didn't need food. She took another lemon and dipped it into a small dish filled with a silky, golden liquid. The taste was sweet.

Faaris was struggling to contain his laughter as he took a sip of water. Razi snorted a quick laugh and continued to dig his fork into a plate of roasted squab.

"Come on, Faaris," Razi laughed, jabbing his elbow against Faaris' arm, "have some real food. You don't know what you're missing."

Faaris smiled to himself. "Ah, Razi, you know I don't eat those things. You know what squab is, don't you?"

"You bet I do," said Razi. "It's delicious is what it is."

"It's pigeon," said Faaris. "I'll never eat a bird as long as I live. They're too special to me, any kind."

Ariette smiled up at him. "Please," Ariette said, leaning over to Faaris. "What are these called?"

"Lemons," said Faaris with a smile. "Do you like them?"

Ariette nodded. "They're wonderful. Although not as sweet as they smell. Does all food here taste this way?"

Faaris smiled and plucked a dried fig from the table. "Here," he said handing it to her, his kind eyes glistening in the candlelight. "Try this."

Ariette bit her lip and took a bite. She was surprised at the taste. It was nothing like the lemon, to say the least.

"How do you like it?" Faaris asked.

Ariette nodded. "It's nothing like the lemon."

"So, tell me my dear," said Mehrzad from across the table.

"Where have you come from?"

"She's from a place quite far," Faaris cut in. "Much farther than we could imagine." He glanced at Ariette with a smile and a subtle nod.

Ariette smiled at him as if to thank him for sparing her from the agony of trying to explain herself.

"Will it be a difficult journey home?" Mehrzad asked.

Ariette nodded. "Impossible, actually. I'm afraid I've come too far."

"Oh," said Mehrzad. "Have you come alone?" Ariette nodded. "I'm quite impressed," Mehrzad said with a smile, slicing his knife through a roasted squash. "You're brave for coming so far on your own. I have no doubt you can survive anywhere."

Ariette beamed. She hadn't thought of herself in that way at all. Then again, she had come this far. "Well," Ariette said, still smiling, "it has not been so easy. This is my first time away from home."

"What is your age, if you don't mind my asking?" said Mehrzad.

"Do you wish to know in Earth years?" Ariette asked.

Mehrzad laughed to himself. "Why of course, my dear. What other kind of years are there?"

Ariette smiled and fidgeted with her fingers, "Well, it could be Earth years, lightyears…decades, months, days, hours, minutes, seconds…whatever you prefer."

Mehrzad smiled, "Very well, why not Earth years then."

Ariette gulped. "Well, the earth has passed around the sun nineteen times since I was born. So, I am nineteen years old. I was born in the middle of July."

A sudden interest sparked in Faaris and he looked at her with intrigue. "Ah, it sounds like you've studied astronomy."

Mehrzad smiled at Ariette from across the table. "I used to be an astronomer, you know. Before I became the palace's full-time advisor, that is."

"Have you ever charted stars?" Faaris asked.

"Charted?" said Ariette.

"You know, mapping out constellations…that sort of thing," said Faaris.

Ariette glanced at her hands in her lap. "I haven't. I mean I know where every star is, but I have never needed a map. Have you ever charted stars?"

Faaris furrowed his brows with a strong amount of certainty. "Oh, absolutely. I've always been fascinated with stars. I've been charting them for as long as I can remember. When I was a child, I used to lie out in the garden on clear nights wondering where it all came from. I was completely taken with the idea of there being something so much greater than us. I wanted to make a connection to prove to myself that we really weren't very different from the stars. All of the stories I've read always said to make a wish."

Ariette smiled and rested her chin in her hands. "Did you?"

Faaris laughed to himself. "I made many wishes, actually."

Ariette bit her lip, a look of concern looming in her eyes. "Do you still?"

Faaris' eyebrows shot up. "Wish?" He shook his head. "No, not anymore. I suppose it really is all just fantasy. Then again, anything is possible, isn't it?"

"Absolutely," Ariette cooed, hope reawakening in her eyes. "Anything is possible if you truly believe it is."

Faaris gulped and looked down at his plate.

Ariette touched his hand. "Perhaps you should start again," she said.

Faaris looked up at her and smiled. "Perhaps."

Ariette glanced up to see the moon peeking through a tall open window. "It's getting late."

"So it is," said Faaris. "You're not thinking of leaving already, are you? Won't you stay a little longer?"

Ariette started to shake her head. Faaris felt a slight tug at his arm. He glanced to his side to find Parisa, clinging to his sleeve. She wore a silky, pink dress that almost met the floor, and her head was covered by a silk hood in a darker shade of pink.

"Hello, there," Faaris smiled, turning to take her hands. "Bored already, huh?"

Parisa yawned. "I'm sleepy."

"I can see that," said Faaris with a grin, scooping her up and setting her on his knee. "We haven't even had dessert yet. This isn't like you. I must say, I'm quite concerned."

Parisa giggled and flopped her head against his chest. With another yawn, she cast her round brown eyes up at his. "Can we play our song again?"

"I thought you were too sleepy," Faaris said laying his hand on her head.

"Not anymore," Parisa said with a yawn.

"Why don't I sing you to sleep, hmm?" Faaris whispered. He hummed a light melody to her.

Parisa giggled and put her small hand over his mouth. "Shh… not yet, Faaris."

Ariette suddenly lit up. "You like to sing?"

Faaris beamed. "Occasionally. I don't much anymore. It's been a while."

Ariette sighed. "Oh. Well I'm sorry to hear that. I love to sing."

Faaris smiled to himself.

"Is that so?" Mehrzad said, folding his hands.

"It's my greatest joy," said Ariette.

"Well, my dear, you are welcome to sing for us," said Mehrzad.

Ariette blushed and tucked her hair behind her ear.

Parisa gasped. "Yes. Please?" She tugged on Faaris' robe again, gazing up at him with deep sparkling eyes, her innocence slicing straight through to his soul.

Faaris laughed to himself and shook his head at her. "You can't look at me like that, Mushroom."

"Pleeeeease," Parisa begged.

Faaris sighed and rolled his eyes. He stood from the table, walked toward the musicians, and held his hand out to the one playing the small string instrument. "May I?"

The musician bowed and handed him the instrument. "Certainly, Your Highness."

The room fell silent as Faaris plucked the first note. He continued strumming as he made his way back to his seat. Every head turned in his direction and followed him all the way across the room. As he passed his friends, he nodded and returned their smiles. Ariette stood and let the soft melody trickle into her heart.

She closed her eyes as a smile came across her face. Faaris hummed softly as he closed his eyes and slipped into the melody. His voice was gentle and soothing, traveling quietly around the room with every step that he took. The sound poured through Ariette's heart like the steam from freshly brewed tea. Suddenly, she saw him differently. Any coldness or hostility that she'd suspected in him seemed to melt away. No one with a voice so warm could ever be cold. Her eyes followed his fingers carefully as they plucked each string. His hands were so elegant. Ariette drew in a deep breath and rested her head in her hand, still mesmerized by watching his hands work with the instrument so precisely. She wanted nothing more than to join him. Faaris stopped playing and the crowd clapped, all wearing smiles on their faces. He smiled and bowed, tucking the string instrument behind his back.

Ariette cleared her throat, then began singing, letting the lyrics come freely from her heart. Those were the best ones. Deciding to trust her heart, she sang the song she had last sung to her stargazer to cheer him up. Faaris' expression changed as soon as he heard her voice. It was all too familiar to him. The lyrics were telling him stories of his past, stories that had begun to fade from his memory. When he'd gathered his courage, he joined her in song. Ariette's heart started racing. In that moment, she and Faaris exchanged glances, sharing the same look as if they had known each other forever.

The entire room was excited. Not a soul had ever seen Faaris this ecstatic.

The musicians assisted them by adding drums, chimes, flutes, and more strings until the entire room was filled with energy and every guest was on their feet. Mehrzad smiled and clapped along. Parisa grabbed a small tambourine and played beside Ariette. When the song reached its end, the guests clapped and cheered. Ariette and Faaris smiled at one another, hearts still racing.

"Whoop, whoop," Razi shouted.

Faaris cleared his throat and held out his hand to Ariette. When she took it, he held it high above their heads and they both took a bow.

Mehrzad was almost crying tears of joy. "Why, Faaris, I haven't seen you this happy in years."

Faaris smiled. "I don't know what's come over me," he said, pressing his hand against his racing heart. "It's some kind of illness, I'm sure of it."

Razi was grinning and shaking his head.

Faaris set the instrument beside his chair and sat down to rest. Parisa came to his side and began tugging on his sleeve. Faaris knelt to listen to her. "What is it, Mushroom?"

"I'm sleepy," Parisa said rubbing her eyes.

Faaris smiled and lifted her into his arms. "Already?"

Parisa nodded.

"Fair enough," Faaris said, tucking her hair away from her face.

Mehrzad smiled up at them. "Off to bed already?"

Faaris smiled. "It's been a long day." He touched Ariette on the shoulder on his way out, "I'll catch up with you later, I promise." Ariette smiled and nodded.

Parisa, who was nearly falling asleep on Faaris' shoulder, whispered, "Can Ariette come too?"

"I think it's best if we leave her here," Faaris whispered.

"Please?" Parisa begged, looking at him in the same heart-melting way that she always did.

"Don't do this to me," Faaris whispered. "She's a stranger, remember? I can't trust her yet."

"Razi can come with us," Parisa whispered. "Please."

Faaris sighed and rolled his eyes. He took several steps toward the table and leaned closer to Ariette's ear. "Ariette," he whispered. Ariette turned toward him, looking hopeful. Faaris cleared his throat. "Care to join us?"

Mehrzad made a quick head gesture at Razi, motioning for him to follow them.

Razi coughed and threw his napkin on the table. "I'm coming, I'm coming. You don't have to tell me twice."

21

ARIETTE FOLLOWED FAARIS INTO
Parisa's room, leaving the door halfway open. Her eyes
explored the quiet room, which was dark aside from the light of
the moon and two lanterns at the sides of the bed. Ariette hugged
herself and stepped further into the room. It was fairly small and
simple, but still decorated as lavishly as any other room in the
palace with silk sheets and pillows, artwork featuring the Sima
Bird, ornate carpets, and several gold-framed mirrors. A small
dish of incense rested on a table beside the window. Ariette was
mesmerized watching the delicate swirls of smoke dance into the
air.

Razi cleared his throat. "I'll uh…guard the door."

Faaris nodded and left the door halfway open.

Ariette followed the moonlight toward the window and lifted

her skirt to sit on the edge. Seeing the stars gave her a sense of peace. Faaris carried Parisa into the room and laid her softly onto her bed. Faaris glanced to see Ariette gazing out at the stars. He smiled and sat on the end of Parisa's bed. "Stargazing?"

Ariette was a little startled. She turned and tucked her hair behind her ear. "They're so beautiful from here."

Faaris smiled. "Indeed, they are."

He picked up the string instrument from the floor and ran his hand across the strings. The sound drifted into the air and blended with the rhythm of the incense.

Parisa yawned. "Faaris."

Faaris laid his hand over the strings to silence their vibrations. "What is it?"

"Tell me a story," said Parisa.

Faaris smiled. "Hm...alright. First, close your eyes."

Ariette turned toward them and hugged her knees to listen.

"Once upon a time," said Faaris, plucking several of the strings, "there was a young prince. He had everything he could ever wish for, but his heart was empty. One summer night, he found himself alone outside in the garden, gazing up at the glorious stars, wondering what could possibly be more enchanting."

Ariette beamed.

"It was then that he decided to make a wish," said Faaris.

"What did he wish for?" Parisa asked.

Faaris smiled. "Love, of course. What else could satisfy an empty heart? He waited several more nights to see if it came true, and it wasn't until the third night that he received an answer. It floated down into his hands in the form of a bright light. He was completely astonished. He had never seen anything like it before."

Ariette uncurled herself.

"When it fell into his hands, it burst into a thousand pieces and let out the words of a star," said Faaris. "His heart was warm with joy, and from then on, he wished upon her every night with ballads confessing his love for her. One night, he came to find that he had fallen in love with her, but it wasn't long before he realized what a terrible mistake he'd made. As it turned out, their love was star-crossed. Each knew that they could never be together."

Parisa gently touched Faaris' arm. "Faaris, does this story have a happy ending?"

Faaris sighed. "I hope so."

Parisa giggled and hugged her pillow. "Faaris. It has to have a happy ending. The star's supposed to come to Earth so they can get married and live happily ever after."

Faaris smiled and stroked her head. "Life doesn't always have happily-ever-after's, you know."

"Well, my story can," said Parisa.

Faaris grinned. "Alright, why don't you tell the rest, then."

Ariette stood and came to sit on the bed beside Parisa, the golden candlelight catching the jewels on her dress and the sparkle in her eyes. "I will finish the story."

Parisa smiled. Faaris bowed his head and glanced back up at Ariette.

"The star was so in love that she defied the laws of the Earth and sky and fell from the heavens to find her love," said Ariette. "But it was not so easy. She traveled the lands in search of him, but because she was not a human, she was not strong enough to continue her journey in this strange land. With each day, she became weaker as her stardust nearly flickered out inside of her."

Parisa gasped. "No."

"Shh…" Ariette hushed, raising her finger to her lips. "It has a happy ending, I promise."

"Okay," Parisa whispered.

"One magical day, fate stepped in," said Ariette. "And she stumbled upon her true love. He filled her lonely heart with love and gave her strength again."

"How did she know it was her true love?" Parisa asked.

Ariette smiled, looking across the bed at Faaris. "She just knew. There was a song. It was her favorite lullaby. They were the only two to ever hear it. One magical night, he sang it to her, and in that moment, she knew in the same way that a bird always remembers where her nest is even after flying all over the world. He was her sanctuary."

Faaris returned her smile and for a moment they were silent. He shook his head as if to snap himself out of a trance. "Well, I think that's enough for tonight."

"Wait." Parisa whispered, tugging on his arm. "They have to get married and live happily-ever-after. Faaris. How did the prince know it was her?"

Faaris grinned at Ariette so charmingly that it was as if every inch of her had liquified. "He knew the minute he heard her voice."

Ariette swallowed hard and tried to steady her racing heart.

"Then one night," Faaris went on, "the prince took her outside to the place where he had first laid his eyes on her and pulled a special ring out of his pocket. And you can guess what happened next."

"He asked her to marry him." Parisa gasped.

Faaris turned to Parisa with a smile. "And she said…"

Parisa smiled and yawned. "Yes."

Faaris pulled the sheets up over Parisa. "And they lived…"

"Happily-ever-after," Parisa whispered with another yawn, letting her heavy eyelids fall shut.

Faaris smiled and leaned in to kiss her forehead. "Goodnight, my love."

He blew out the candle beside her bed and stood, returning the string instrument to its place beside the bed. Ariette stood and followed him out. "Goodnight, Parisa," she whispered.

Faaris took Ariette by the hand and led her into the hall, closing the doors behind them.

Razi met them in the hall and leaned into Faaris' ear. "Uh, Faaris," he whispered, "I can't believe I'm saying this, but I'm actually starting to believe your little fairytale. I think we both know she's all yours."

Faaris smiled.

"Congratulations," said Razi. "Now don't blow this one."

Faaris smiled and turned toward Ariette. "Please, allow me to escort you back to your room."

Ariette felt herself nod. Her hand felt so safe inside his that she never wanted to let go. The warmth of his hand was comforting to her cold fingers. It was a feeling she had never had before.

Razi grinned. "I'll uh… be in the dining room if you need

me." He gave Ariette a quick salute. "Keep a good eye on him, alright?"

Faaris grinned and gave Razi the usual salute of departure.

To Ariette's dismay, Faaris released her hand as they came around the next corner. After climbing two stairwells, they arrived at the floor where Ariette's room was. As they walked down the hall, Faaris' eyes were set far into the distance as if he were lost in thought.

"I must say, you're a wonderful storyteller," he said. "That was very endearing."

Ariette smiled. "Well, you did the hard part for me. I was only finishing what you started." The hall was so quiet, she was almost whispering. "And I don't think I could make such lovely sounds with the strings and tell a story at the same time. What do you call the wooden instrument?"

"It's called an oud," said Faaris. "My mother taught me how to play."

Ariette lowered her head. "It's beautiful."

She folded her hands behind her back as she continued down the hall. "Faaris," she said. "I'm very sorry that you lost her. And your father."

Faaris looked down at her with a wild look of suspicion in his eyes. "How did you know?"

A ring of shock came over Ariette and her eyes grew as big as the moon.

"I...," she took a deep breath, "I just knew. I can sense these things, I guess."

"Ah, so you are a witch," Faaris grinned, returning his gaze to the distance.

Ariette smiled and tucked her hair behind her ear. "You must not joke about such things. Please believe I am no such thing. And please don't ever call me that again."

Faaris smiled. "I was only joking. Will you ever forgive me?"

"Perhaps," said Ariette.

"Oh, don't do this to me, I beg you," said Faaris. "I need a yes or I'll never sleep tonight."

"Alright...yes," said Ariette, crossing her arms. "You are forgiven."

"Thank you," said Faaris with a bow.

When they arrived at Ariette's door, Faaris pushed it open and scanned the room. He opened it wider and held his hand out to invite her in.

"Well, Ariette," he said standing at the door. "As I said, my home is yours. Don't let anyone stop you from exploring as you wish. If anyone tries, tell them I gave you permission."

Ariette smiled, and turned back toward him, moving closer to the doorframe. "Faaris."

"Yes," Faaris answered, eager to listen.

"You've been more kind to me than any human I've ever met," said Ariette, studying the gentle expression on his face. "I just wanted to say thank you."

Faaris smiled at her with a gentle nod. "I believe it's you who deserves the thanks."

Ariette frowned and turned her head to the side. "For what?"

"For coming here," said Faaris. Ariette smiled. "Now, all I ask is one favor," said Faaris. "Please don't run off tonight. I want to see you again."

Ariette smiled and laid her hands on the door, ready to close it. "I can't make any promises." Faaris cast a feeble smile at the ground. Ariette put her fingertips under his chin and drew his eyes back to hers. "But I have no intention of going anywhere. As long as you can promise me that I will be safe here."

"Rest assured," Faaris whispered. "There are guards everywhere." He glanced quickly over his shoulder. "They're probably watching us right now. Which is why I can't stay much longer. I'll return for you in the morning. I promise."

"Faaris," Ariette whispered, sliding the bird's egg out of her pocket.

Faaris' eyes grew wider as soon as he saw it. "Will wonders never cease? You must tell me where you found this."

Ariette smiled. "It's from a very special friend of mine. I want you to have it. I know you love birds so much and you've been so kind to me. In case I don't see you again, I want you to keep it safe for me."

"It would be my honor," Faaris said, taking it from her.

"Faaris," Ariette whispered. "One more question."

Faaris leaned closer, still bracing the door. "Of course."

Ariette took a deep breath and gazed up at Faaris. "You're the prince in your story, aren't you?"

Faaris smiled and lowered his head. "Was it that obvious?"

Ariette smiled. "Is it true? Are you in love with a star?"

"Go ahead," said Faaris, rolling his eyes, "laugh like everyone else."

Ariette shook her head. "I might. Except, I believe you."

"Really?" said Faaris. "Well, you're the first."

"Faaris," said Ariette. "When was the last time you made a wish?"

Faaris took a deep breath. "It's…it's been a while."

Ariette looked at him with concern. "Why did you stop?"

Faaris swallowed hard and looked down at the ground. "I lost her."

"Your star?" said Ariette.

"Yes," said Faaris. "She was the one star that I always sent my wishes to. She was my best friend. She saw me through many trials as I grew up. She heard it all. Somehow, I wasn't afraid to tell her anything. She listened like no one on Earth ever had. As time passed, I started to fall in love with her. It's strange I know. Then again, love is strange. All I knew her by was her words, and still there was no girl on Earth who could have possibly compared to her. Then one night, all of a sudden, she stopped returning my wishes. I tried again the next night, but still I heard nothing in return. So, I lost faith in her and gave up on stars completely." Faaris looked down at his hands, twisting a gold ring on one of his fingers. "I promised myself I would never fall in love again."

Ariette lowered her head. "Oh."

Faaris managed a weak smile. "It's alright. Don't worry about me. I suppose there's a reason for everything. Perhaps with a little time it will all make sense someday. Still, I'll never forgive her for the heartache she's caused me."

Ariette smiled. "Anything is possible, is it not?"

Faaris crossed his arms and gave her a wise grin. "Let me ask you this then. Do you believe in wishes?"

Ariette laughed to herself. "Of course."

Faaris stole a quick glance over his shoulder to see two guards coming down the hall in the distance. He slipped into the room and closed the door. Ariette followed him out to the balcony.

"If you could have one wish right now," said Faaris, gazing up at the moon. "What would it be?"

Ariette smiled to herself and rested her elbows on the ledge of the balcony. "No one's ever asked me that before. One wish?"

"Anything at all," said Faaris, the night air tossing his perfectly groomed waves out of place.

Ariette sighed. "Well, that is a very big decision. What would you wish for?"

Faaris laughed to himself. "I'd wish you would have asked me that sooner."

Ariette smiled. "Why is that?"

"Well," said Faaris, "because yesterday, I would have wished to have my true love here with me, but now I suppose I would wish to spare my life."

Ariette's smile faded. "One wish and you would wish for love?"

Faaris folded his hands and played with one of the gold rings on his fingers. "It's the most powerful thing in the world, and I truly believe it's powerful enough to save me from even the worst of fates."

Ariette looked up at him with concern. "You're that sure?"

Faaris sighed and looked up at the stars. "I have to be. All I know is that if I can find her, I can stop all of this."

Ariette lit up as a long-lost sense of hope started to return to her. "How?"

Faaris smiled, still looking up at the stars. "One wish."

22

ARIETTE TOOK A DEEP BREATH AND hugged herself. "One wish?"

Faaris shrugged. "I think it's enough to save me...to save Pernia. The problem is that I don't think I'll ever find her. The last time I spoke to her, she didn't answer me. I was desperately in trouble, so I handed it to a genie instead."

"A genie?" Ariette whispered.

"Regrettably," said Faaris with a smile. "She was the closest thing to evil that I've ever seen. Sometimes, I think I would have been better off to let fate have its way. Then again, my best friend would have died that night if I hadn't. I had no choice."

Ariette closed her eyes. Nothing could have been more painful than hearing those words. She opened her eyes again and searched the sky. "Show her to me, Faaris. Show me your star."

214

Faaris shook his head and slid off of the ledge. "It's no use. She's gone. I came back the next night to see her, but she wasn't there. It's been three long years since I saw her last, yet, somehow, I believe she's still out there. She was always right there among the brightest stars though she was surely the smallest of all stars."

Ariette took a deep breath, trying to stop her heart from beating so fast. The place he was pointing to was her place.

"I…I am very sorry you lost her," said Ariette. "Truly. I hope you find her someday."

A gust of wind sent a chill across the balcony. Ariette hugged herself and started walking back inside. "Thank you again for being so kind to me."

Faaris nodded and followed after her. "And you." He paused at the door and gave her another smile. "I'll return in the morning, I promise. Please don't go anywhere."

Ariette smiled and braced the door, looking into his eyes, praying for him to see the truth in them. "A lovely soul I'm glad to meet. Farewell for now and happy sleep."

Faaris smiled down at her with a straight face. He nodded and took her hand, drawing it to his mouth. "Goodnight," he said and kissed her hand. "Put your mind at ease and sleep well. Everything's going to be alright, I promise."

Ariette smiled and closed the door a little further, peaking up at Faaris through the crack that remained. "I don't sleep actually but thank you."

Faaris laughed to himself. "You don't sleep, and you don't eat, and yet somehow, you're still alive."

Ariette smiled and shrugged. "Here I am."

Faaris bowed, still smiling. "Well, whatever suits you then. Until tomorrow, Ariette."

With a deep breath, Ariette nodded and closed the door. The moment she was alone, she hurried out to the balcony. A gust of cool, night wind caught her as she braced the stone ledge of the balcony. She closed her eyes and drew in another deep breath. As she reopened them, she locked her focus on Aelius, praying for him to hear her.

"Aelius, please, hear my call," she said. "I beg of you, please lift the law. I've found my love, I can attest. I need this wish to do the rest. I know this wish you will receive. If you wish me well, please answer me." She watched her words drift into the air, disappearing in the moonlight. She closed her eyes and waited. The feeling was agony. Aelius flickered in the sky. Ariette's heart started racing. A part of her didn't believe what she saw. Then all in one motion, Aelius shot across the sky like a bolt of lightning on a clear path toward her.

A small tear of joy glistened in her eye as she watched him. In the blink of an eye, he tumbled onto the balcony in a whirlwind of light and stardust. The moment he hit the ground he transformed into a more human-like form like hers. It had seemed like ages since Ariette had seen him. He was as tall and muscular as ever, even in human form, and was dressed in a Pernian-style suit in the color of stardust. His translucent, twinkling hair had turned to an icy blonde much like hers had and his skin was soft and pale. His eyes remained their usual shade of cold grey.

Ariette hurried to his side to pull him to his feet.

"Aelius." She gasped, throwing her arms around him.

"Easy," said Aelius, brushing stardust off of his arms. "I haven't come to grant your wish."

"Wait," said Ariette. "I don't understand. You've broken the law?"

Aelius rolled his eyes and crossed his arms. "Ariette, I made that law. All this time, I thought you were dead."

Ariette gulped.

"I came looking for you three days after you left, and there was no sign of you anywhere," said Aelius. "So, I assumed you were dead. For three years, I came back every full moon to look for you but never found even a clue. And I said I would come for you if things got bad, so here I am. Now, let's go home. Time costs stardust, and I won't be wasting any more of it."

"Bad? No. Aelius, I found him," Ariette said squeezing both of his hands. "I found my stargazer. I'm sure of it. But he's in danger, and I need to save him. Please. I… I love him, and I…I wish to stay here with him."

Aelius was burning with anger. "Ariette, I've come here with one intention and that is to bring you home safely before you get into any real danger."

"No," said Ariette, several tears slipping from her eyes. "I won't. I've come too far. I can't leave now that I've found him. I won't lose him again. Aelius, please."

Aelius grabbed her by the arm. "Trust me, it's for your own good. The Lux needs you, Ariette, and I won't let you fade away. Not when I can stop it."

"No," Ariette cried, dropping to her knees as more tears poured from her eyes. "If you truly care about me, you'll let me stay. I want nothing more."

"Look," said Aelius taking her by the shoulders. "If you truly wish to be with him, there's only one way for you to do that and it's to become human forever. You can't have both. It's him or your stardust. And heed my warning, if you choose him, you will never be able to return to us."

A cold wind brushed across the balcony, sweeping Ariette's tears across her face. She closed her eyes and wrapped her arms tightly around Aelius, burying her face in his strong chest. Aelius took a deep breath and squeezed her in return. Feeling the chill of his stardust revived her a little. She hadn't realized how much she had already lost.

"What was that for?" asked Aelius.

Ariette took a deep breath and looked into his eyes. "In case I never see you again. I'm sorry, but I can't go with you."

Aelius swallowed hard. "You're already weaker, Ariette. I can feel it." He took her by the wrists and unraveled her hug. The silvery markings caught his eye. He frowned and gave her his worst scolding look. "What is this?"

"I…" Ariette stuttered. "It was an accident."

"You're trapped, aren't you?" Aelius scolded.

Ariette sighed and closed her eyes. "I…I fell into a…"

"A bottle, I know," said Aelius. "It's happened before to many stars. I warned you of things like this, Ariette. You've been exploited for your power and now you're a slave. I knew this would happen. You've brought shame upon your brother and shame upon all the stars and the entire heavens."

Another tear slid down Ariette's cheek. "Aelius, please don't say that. It was a mistake. I didn't mean to cause any trouble. I was only trying to make things right. I love my stargazer, and my feelings for him haven't changed. I want nothing more than to stay here with him. Won't you help me?"

"I can't," said Aelius. "I don't have the power. Only a human can do that if it's what you truly want. But I hope that you'll agree to return with me immediately. I can't let you fade away. Not when I can stop it."

"There's nothing you can do," said Ariette. "I'm bound to the wish. I can't return until I'm free. It's the only way to break it, but I need the bottle to do that, and I don't have it. Only a human's wish can set me free. Give me one more chance, Aelius. Please. I will find the bottle and free myself. Then, I promise, I will return with you."

Aelius closed his eyes and rested his head in his hand.

"Please," Ariette whispered. "I haven't come all this way to just go right back to where I started."

Aelius sighed and looked down at her. "So, you say you've found true love?"

Ariette nodded, eyes stricken with fear.

"And you truly love him?" said Aelius.

"More than anything," said Ariette. "I don't even care if I run out of stardust, if it means I can live here with him forever."

"You'll care when you start to fade away," said Aelius. "A star can't survive here for more than three days. End of story. You'd be dead by now if you hadn't gotten stuck in that bottle."

"Aelius," Ariette said. "There must be a way for me to stay here. I know there is. You're hiding it from me, aren't you?"

Aelius sighed and held his hands in front of him. "There is, but I… I want you back with us."

Ariette bit her lip. "What is it?"

Aelius closed his eyes and shook his head. "I fear if I tell you, I'll never see you again."

Ariette lowered her head with a sigh. "If you truly care about me, you will allow me to be happy."

"You don't know what's best for you, Ariette," said Aelius. "Trust me."

"You can't possibly know my heart," said Ariette.

Aelius' glow dimmed. He took a deep breath and looked into Ariette's eyes. "Find your bottle, and get out of this mess. I'll return tomorrow night to bring you home. I'm not taking any more chances. And in the meantime, stay away from that human of yours."

Ariette looked confused. "Why?"

Aelius rolled his eyes. "Just…whatever you do, don't kiss him."

"Kiss?" said Ariette, perplexed. "What is kiss?"

Aelius sighed and scratched the back of his neck. "It's a… it's a human thing. It's when…well, how do I explain it? Their lips touch. It's how they show affection. The moment your lips meet the lips of a human, you will become human too, and then it's too late, you'll be stuck here. Your fate is sealed. You'll never have your stardust again. I'm serious. Promise me you'll stay away from him. And promise you'll return with me as soon as you free yourself." Ariette nodded. "Promise me," Aelius said, burning her heart with his silvery eyes.

Ariette closed her eyes. "I promise."

"That's my little star," said Aelius. "Now, in the meantime, remember, no kissing, no running off, and no dying. Got it?" Ariette nodded. "Be safe," said Aelius. "I'll see you tomorrow night."

He ignited himself into a flame of stardust and darted back toward the moon, leaving behind a glittering trail. Broken hearted, Ariette watched as he reappeared beside the moon in his usual place. She crumbled to her knees, and her remaining tears flooded the ground in a symphony of endless sobbing. When she was drained from sorrow, she pulled herself to her feet and took a deep breath. She made her way across the dark bedroom and sat on the edge of the bed. She looked at the markings on her wrists with disgust. They almost glowed in the darkness. She was ashamed, heartbroken, and hopeless, but she was anything but finished. Faaris had to know the truth. The night was at its darkest, which meant the moon was at her brightest. Ariette stood and quietly made her way out of the bedroom and into the hall. Her heart was heavy with more emotions than she could possibly juggle at once, but something was pulling her. It was the feeling she always got when someone was sending her a wish.

23

FAARIS FOLDED HIS HANDS AND rested his elbows on the ledge of the balcony as he did every night, hoping that one night he would see Setareh again. His eyes were damp, but not heavy enough to produce any tears. He sighed and ran his fingers through his hair, clearing several strands away from his face.

"My love, my light, please forgive me. Things aren't the way they used to be," he said. With another deep breath, he ran his fingers across his chin, twisting the hairs as his fingers brushed by them. "You are my day, you are my night, my life is dark without your light. Every hour I think of you, but now I don't know what to do. My love goes on, I can't ignore, and every day I love you more. Every night I cannot rest, my heart still aches, I must confess. To hear your voice would be so sweet, still nothing cures my memories. The emptiness, I cannot take. Surely, soon my heart with break. No girl on Earth could match your light, my heart grows colder every night. Though I see you not, you're my best friend, and I fear I'll never love again. Just one word is all I need, to cure me of this bitter grief. Please tell me, love, that you're alive, so I can find some peace of mind. I long to look upon your face, to finally feel your sweet embrace. Come to Earth, please come to me. I want nothing more, please hear my plea. Nothing more and nothing less. I love you still, I must confess. I'd rather die than be alone. Life without you is life unknown. I'm sad inside and full of grief. In only you I've found relief. Your song is like the air I breathe, it heals me from my suffering. I'm sorry for how long it's been, but I long to hear your voice again. Hear me love, please hear my plea. Nothing else will comfort me."

Faaris took another deep breath and buried his face into his hands, letting his words twinkle into the air. Something was different this time. Rather than floating to the stars, they floated over his head, leading his eyes toward the bedroom. Through the darkness, a soft light flickered from inside the room, and Setareh's soft, breathy voice drifted through the air like mist. "Fear not, my love, I am alive. Your empty heart I shall revive. Now I know just who you are. Please believe, I am not far."

Faaris' heart was pricked instantly. He laid his hand over his chest as if to steady his pulse. Behind him was the voice that had always soothed him, the voice that he'd known all along. Ariette stepped out of the shadows, glowing with the kind of radiance that only true love can bestow. Still cradling the blorba, she looked at Faaris. "I should have told you when we met, my name is really…"

"Ariette," they chorused, as Faaris turned to see her.

Faaris' eyes were glistening with unfallen tears in the moonlight. He let out a gentle sigh as a soft smile fell upon his face.

"I knew it was you," he whispered and made his way toward her.

Ariette returned his smile and stepped closer to him, the cool night breeze sweeping her hair behind her. When they were face-to-face, she paused to let the blorba burst, spilling specks of stardust at their feet.

Faaris gulped and ran his hand down her hair, looking down at her as if she were the greatest treasure in the universe. "How long I've waited for this moment. My Setareh. Why didn't you tell me sooner?"

"I…" Ariette stuttered, "I was afraid. I was afraid you wouldn't believe me."

Faaris smiled and shook his head. "Don't be afraid. There's no longer a need to fear. We can conquer anything now that we're together. Like I said, love is the most powerful thing in the world…in the universe for that matter."

Ariette smiled as Faaris leaned in so that their noses almost met. He cast his golden eyes down at her. "Follow me," he said.

Ariette smiled up at him and felt him squeeze her hand more tightly before starting for the hall.

"Where are we going?" she asked.

Faaris smiled. "You'll see."

He checked to make sure no guards were around and started

into a run, leading Ariette behind him. Ariette stumbled over the ends of her dress a little, causing Faaris to lose his balance slightly.

Faaris smiled back at her. "Are you alright?"

"I'm not very good at running," said Ariette, gathering her skirt in her hand so that her feet were free. "The feeling of having my feet on the ground is still very strange to me."

"I'm afraid we'll be seen if we walk," Faaris whispered. "It's only a few more stairs. Can you manage?"

Ariette smiled. "I'll try."

"Just follow my lead," said Faaris, squeezing her hand more tightly. "I won't let you fall. I promise."

He led her past several guards and up several dimly lit stairwells until they'd arrived at the top story of the palace. Their hearts were racing more with every step. Faaris led her carefully through a narrow, winding stairwell leading to the highest tower in the palace. Ariette braced the walls of the tunnel as they made their way to the top, surrounded by nothing but darkness.

"Faaris," said Ariette, her voice echoing through the tunnel. "I can't see."

Faaris squeezed her hand a little tighter. "It's alright. We're almost there. Just follow my voice."

Ariette took a deep breath and lifted the ends of her dress to slide her foot onto the next step. "Faaris. You should know that I think Parisa is a very special girl. She is…your sister?"

Faaris smiled to himself. "Not exactly. Her mother died the day she was born. Her father was a servant at the palace, but there was a terrible siege here several years ago, and he was one of the many who lost their lives to Dark Kobra. We were both orphaned that day. She was only a baby at the time. I've cared for her ever since."

Ariette looked at him. "I'm...I'm so sorry. It's terrible to have lost someone you loved."

"That's the way it is, I suppose," said Faaris, climbing several more steps. "I'll never forgive Dark Kobra for the hole in my heart."

"We must learn to forgive everyone," said Ariette. "Even our enemies."

Faaris paused and looked down at her, despite the darkness. "You've humiliated me terribly, my love."

"Why is that?" Ariette asked, smiling to herself.

"Because you're right," said Faaris. "I hope you will forgive me for being so resentful."

Ariette smiled up at him. "You're forgiven. Anyone has the right to feel that way after losing someone they loved."

Faaris laughed under his breath. "I suppose we must learn to love the enemy and hate the crime."

"Exactly," said Ariette. "Even though it's difficult sometimes."

"Well, only a fool assumes life is easy," said Faaris.

"Life is not easy?" Ariette asked, looking suddenly bewildered.

"Well, it's as easy as you perceive it to be," said Faaris. "I can't promise you a life on Earth will be perfect if you chose to stay, which I hope you will, but perhaps that's the beauty of it."

"I want to stay more than anything," said Ariette. "If it's Earth or Mars, I want to be wherever you are."

When they reached the top of the stairwell, Faaris slipped the necklace off and selected a small gold key from it. He slid the key into the lock and lifted a small trap door overhead. He guided Ariette through it, taking each of her hands to pull her up behind him. They were greeted kindly by the cool night winds and the moonlight as they stepped into the small circular space. A thick, marble ledge was the only thing closing them in, the rest was open space. It was as if they were at the highest point of a mountain, leaving the rest of the world below.

"Oh," Ariette breathed, seeing the spectacle of stars above her. This was the clearest she had seen them since she'd been on Earth. There were no trees or rooftops to stand between her and the sky. It had to be the best view on Earth.

Faaris smiled and crossed his arms, raising his eyes toward the sky. "Breathtaking, isn't it?"

Ariette walked to the edge of the balcony and rested her hands on the ledge beside a long gold telescope. From here she could see more stars than she even knew existed.

Faaris closed the trap door. "Look down."

Ariette turned and glanced down at her feet to see a detailed chart of stars covering every inch of the sleek blue marble surface. Lines were drawn to connect the constellations, scratched neatly in a shimmery gold paint. It was a work of art.

"Oh," Ariette gasped, kneeling to run her fingers along the smooth surface. "You did all of this?"

Faaris examined the chart, rubbing his chin with a smile. "Yes. It's not finished yet. Then again, I'm not sure something so infinite will ever be finished... at least not in my lifetime. There are thousands of stars. It's almost impossible."

Ariette smiled up at him. "I thought anything was possible."

Faaris laughed. "Well, not anything, I suppose," he said, "just, most things. We've found each other, haven't we?"

Ariette smiled. "Perhaps when you truly want something, you'll find a way to make it yours."

Faaris returned her smile. "Perhaps. Or perhaps it was destiny all along. Destiny has a way of calling us like that. Yet, at the same time, it's ours to choose. We can choose our own path, or we can walk the one that was chosen for us. I've always tried to choose the path that leads me away from the darkness and toward the light. And so, I've chosen you."

Ariette beamed. She was overcome with happiness, sadness, and love all in one intoxicating mixture of emotion that she'd never known before. Every loose end seemed to have come together all at once, as if her journey had at last met its end.

24

DARK KOBRA SLID ALONG THE outside of the tower, gripping the stone with two metal spikes, listening carefully to every word. He crept over the ledge and slithered onto the floor beside Ariette and Faaris.

"Faaris," said Ariette. "Do you trust me?"

Faaris smiled and took her hands. "Of course. Should I not? I must admit, it hurts me that you feel the need to ask."

Ariette took a deep breath. "There's something I need to tell you, but I'm going to need you to trust me."

"Anything, my love," said Faaris. "From now on, there will be no secrets between us."

Ariette closed her eyes. "On my way to Earth, I made a terrible mistake, and now I fear I will be a prisoner forever. You've saved me from a life trapped in the sky, but I'm not free yet. I'm not all that you believe I am, but I love you, and you deserve to know the truth. Would you believe me if I told you that..."

"That's she's really a genie," came the voice of Dark Kobra as he slithered onto the floor.

Faaris squinted at Ariette. "A genie?"

Ariette and Faaris turned to find Dark Kobra stepping toward them. Faaris drew his sword and threw his arm in front of Ariette to shield her.

Ariette grabbed Faaris' arm. "I...I can explain."

Dark Kobra drew a long, silver sword from his back and slammed it over the trap door, leaving them with no way of escape. He let out a deep laugh under his breath. "Ah. The look on your face was priceless, Your Highness. One for the records, truly. It was almost as good as the night I killed your parents."

"Ah, so I suppose you've come to kill me now too?" said Faaris with a steady glare.

Kobra laughed and leaned against his sword. "Actually, I've come for my genie, but who knows? Anything's possible."

Kobra slithered to the ground and flipped onto the ledge behind Ariette and Faaris. He curled his fingers around Ariette's shoulders and leaned close to her ear. "*Sssss*-urprised to see me, Pigeon?" he hissed into her ear, his tongue curling like a snake's. In one fluid motion, Kobra returned to his own sword, with Ariette by his side and Faaris' sword in his hand. His dexterity was like magic.

"I thought you weren't allowed to enter the city," Ariette whispered, struggling to free herself from Kobra's grip.

Kobra laughed to himself. "Do I really seem like the sort of man who follows the rules?"

"Release her," said Faaris. "I order you."

Kobra threw his head back laughing. "Ha. I only take orders from one man and that's me. You're nothing in my eyes."

"Nothing?" said Faaris. "Well, let me ask you this then. Why is it that you want me dead? What could you possibly achieve by killing me? If it's my wealth or my title, you're wrong, and you'll never have it. The people will never trust a man like you to be their king."

Kobra grinned and started pacing, still squeezing Ariette by the arm. "A man like me. You must think you're so clever, Highness."

Faaris gulped. "You're nothing but a murderous thief, a coward hiding behind a mask. My death won't make you any more of a man, and it won't crown you king, not in a thousand years. I'm not afraid of you."

Kobra glared at Faaris in such a way that it sent chills down his spine. "You should be. And I'd watch my mouth if I were you."

Ariette reached for Faaris' sword. She held her breath as she slid her fingers onto the cold metal. She locked her eyes on Faaris, hoping he would notice. Faaris caught her stare. Ariette didn't blink as she pulled Faaris' sword out from Kobra's belt. Kobra slashed his arm down in front of her, breaking her contact with the sword. He laughed and twirled her into a tight headlock. "I'll put you back in your bottle, Genie, I swear it," he hissed.

Ariette was trembling all over, surrounded by the strong, spicy scent of the cologne that clung to Kobra's sleeve. Catching her breath seemed impossible.

"Ariette," said Faaris, shaking his head. "Don't be afraid, he can't hurt you."

Kobra's eyes narrowed. "Just watch me."

"No," Faaris jumped, holding his hand out in front of him.

Kobra laughed and pulled Ariette toward the ledge. "No," Kobra sneered, mocking Faaris. He stomped one foot on the ledge and drew the spikes he used for climbing out of his sleeves. "Do you honestly think I'd bring harm to such an exquisite creature," he said, stroking Ariette's cheek.

Ariette turned away.

A sly grin peaked in Kobra's eyes. "Aww, don't be like that, Pigeon," he said. "I'm doing you a favor, remember? In a matter of time, you'll be as free as a bird."

"A bird in a cage, maybe," Ariette mumbled.

Faaris shook his head to himself. He looked at Ariette with heavy, broken eyes. "So, you *are* working for him. I knew it. You're his genie and you're here to spy on me so you can catch me in the right moment and kill me yourself. You lied to me, and I fell for it. I was bewitched by your beauty like all the other fools who've wasted their time with such wicked creatures."

"No," said Ariette, tears filling her eyes. "I didn't have a choice. I'm a prisoner. I would never wish to harm you. Please. I'm telling the truth."

The look in her eyes was begging for mercy with the kind of innocence that only a child could possess. Faaris closed his eyes and clenched his jaw.

"Please," Ariette managed to say, her voice trembling as she struggled to hold her tears back. "Surely, you trust me."

Kobra smiled and turned his head toward Faaris with eager eyes. "Did you think she loved you?"

He turned to Ariette with a smile. "Well done, Pigeon. I must say, I'm impressed. It looks like you've discovered his weakness. You've stolen his heart and managed to break it even further."

Ariette closed her eyes, letting a tear slip onto her cheek. "Having a heart is not weakness. And love is no temptation when it's true."

Faaris gulped and frowned at Ariette. "Is it true? Have you tricked me? Who are you? Tell me the truth."

Another tear slipped onto Ariette's cheek. "I am Ariette. I am your star. I am the one you called Setareh for all those years. I would never wish to deceive you. I love you. I always have and I always will. Please believe me. Please."

Faaris closed his eyes. "I want to believe you, but answer me this. Are you a genie, and are you working for this man?"

Ariette closed her eyes, forcing another tear to fall. "I...I am. But it isn't what you think. I promise."

"Alright," Faaris scolded. "What is it then? Please, I have every right to know."

"You're right. You deserve to know the truth," said Ariette. "The night I came to Earth to find you, I fell into an enchanted bottle by mistake, and I've been trying to free myself ever since. This man has promised to free me if I grant his wish...but..."

Kobra laughed under his breath. "But I ask a high price. Isn't that right, Pigeon?"

Ariette glared at him. "I will never be free, will I? You've tricked me."

Kobra tilted his head and slid the back of his finger across her cheek. "Now is that any way to talk to your rescuer, genie? I have to hand it to you though, you're much smarter than I thought. Which makes me think…now would be an excellent time for a second wish. I'm in charge after all."

Ariette gulped. She closed her eyes and drew in a deep breath. "Whatever you wish, please, promise me that no harm will come to Faaris."

Kobra grinned through the mask. "Don't worry, I have something special in mind for him. But for now, it looks like I'll have to…revise my first wish a little. It seems to me that things have changed." He grabbed Ariette and slithered across the ledge, bending and twisting in remarkable, almost inhuman ways. "But that's alright, I'm flexible."

Faaris gulped and looked at Ariette. "Ariette, don't do this. You have the choice. Don't let him convince you otherwise."

"Actually, she doesn't," said Kobra. "She's mine." He turned to Ariette. "Unless, that is, she decides to grant my wish. Then she will be free, I give you my word. May I die a miserable death otherwise."

Still bracing Ariette, Kobra slipped the glittering purple bottle out of his pocket and raised it to his mouth to bite the lid off through the black fabric of his mask. He spit it onto the floor and tightened his grip on Ariette.

"Now, bear with me, Pigeon," said Kobra. "I've never been good with poetry."

Ariette tried to fight her way out of his grasp, but her strength was no match for his. Kobra laughed and only tightened his grip.

"Honestly, Pigeon, why bother?" he laughed. "There's nothing you can do now."

Ariette looked at Faaris with a raging fear in her eyes. Faaris kept a straight face and cast a subtle wink at her. Ariette's eyes widened. Faaris locked his eyes on hers and raised his finger to his lips, motioning for her to stay silent.

Kobra cleared his throat. "Since you're too clever to be trusted, my wish will have to be adjusted. It seems you run the risk of flight, back to your bottle for the night."

"No. Please," Ariette cried. A blorba appeared between her hands. No matter how she tried to resist it, the force was too strong.

Faaris shook his head as a cold wind swept his curls across his forehead. "Ariette, no. You have the choice. I know you do. Don't let him control you."

Kobra laughed. "Silly boy. That's not how this works."

The blorba was trembling in Ariette's hands. She closed her eyes, prepared for the worst. Faaris made his way toward her. Kobra drew his sword.

Faaris held his hands in front of his chest. "Easy. I just want to say goodbye before we part."

Kobra rolled his eyes and lowered his sword. "You're trying my patience, Highness. Just make it quick."

Faaris cleared several loose strands of hair away from Ariette's face. With his thumbs, he gently brushed her tears away and gave her his warmest smile. He leaned in closer to her, prepared to kiss her. When their noses met, he looked deeply into her fearful eyes.

"Do you trust me?"

Ariette nodded. Faaris smiled and leaned closer, bringing his lips toward hers. Kobra saw and grabbed Ariette around the waist and swung her aside, suspending her over the edge of the tower. The blorba was still burning in her hands. Kobra slipped a small blade from his sleeve and slashed Faaris across the side of his neck.

"Ah," Faaris cried, stumbling to the floor in an anxious attempt to escape.

He had managed to get away before Kobra could slit his throat, leaving only a small streak on the side of his neck. He pressed his hand to his heart as if to make sure he was still alive. He slid his hand up to the cut on his neck. He touched it and removed his hand to find it wet with fresh blood. With a sigh of relief, he steadily rose to his feet. Ariette watched in agony as several drops of blood slid from the cut and down his neck as he stood.

Kobra grunted a quick laugh, watching Faaris come to his full stature. "Don't underestimate what I'm capable of," said Kobra. "I've killed more people than you can imagine, and I'm not afraid of killing you right now."

"Please," Ariette cried. "Don't harm him. I...I will surrender."

"Alright," said Kobra. "Since you know how much I like making deals, how about this? Grant my wish, and I'll spare him this time."

The blorba was shaking. Ariette closed her eyes. Kobra shot his head toward her with a devilish frown. "Now, genie."

Ariette's heart jumped, and the blorba shattered. She melted from his grasp, dissolving into the air in a million specks of stardust, swirling around until finally succumbing to the bottle's powerful suction. As she fell into the bottle, the lid bolted back over the top, leaving her once again alone in the darkness that was all too familiar.

Faaris glared at Kobra with a look of disgust. He raised his sword and took a strong swing at Kobra who was quick to draw his own sword and break the swing with the loud sound of clashing metal. Still holding the bottle in one hand, Kobra took another aim at Faaris' throat.

"Now to finish that slit I started," Kobra grunted, taking more swings at Faaris. "I've never missed you know. I must say, it hasn't been my night."

"What a shame," Faaris said, panting. "I hate to destroy your ego, but you won't be cutting it any further tonight."

"We'll see about that," Kobra hissed through clenched teeth as the sound of cold metal sliced through the stillness of the night air. "It's been too long since my last assault. I'm hungry you know. Hungry for blood."

"Well it won't be mine that satisfies your nasty craving," said Faaris, dodging another swing. "I can't let you take away my love and my life in the same night. It just doesn't seem fair. Wouldn't you agree?"

"I never play fair," Kobra grinned, taking a smooth swipe across Faaris' head. He missed, and Faaris continued to defend himself.

"So, tell me," said Faaris, "if you've been so eager to kill me all this time, why has it taken you this long?"

"What an excellent question," Kobra hissed, twirling around

to dodge one of Faaris' swings. "I've been training, you see. The death of the king will surely be the highlight of my career. I wouldn't want to jeopardize my chances."

"Ah," said Faaris. "I understand. Well, I'm sorry to tell you, but I have every intention of ending your career before any of that happens. Which reminds me…any last words?"

Kobra's back suddenly hit the hard stone of the surrounding tower. A ring of shock came over him, and he glanced around to find himself pressed against the edge of the tower, only seconds away from plummeting to his death.

"Well, would you look at that," Kobra said. He laughed to himself, looking down at the ground far below. "How did I let this happen?"

"Distraction, perhaps," said Faaris.

"Distraction," Kobra laughed, looking at Faaris who had secured him against the edge. "I never lose focus. Besides, you wouldn't kill me if your life depended on it. I can see it in your eyes."

"You're probably right," said Faaris with an intense glare, a fierce look only his worst of enemies would ever see. "Then again, I've never been one to measure a man's value by the number of lives he's taken."

"I meant it when I said you're nothing in my eyes," Kobra snarled as sweat began to slide onto his face, smudging the black charcoal around his eyes.

Faaris shook his head, still wearing the glare. "No man is of any greater value than another. Physical strength only goes so far, in my experience. A man's true strength is measured by the strength of his heart, a muscle you've clearly neglected."

Kobra grunted and searched for a way out of Faaris' trap. He took a hard swing at Faaris using his elbow. Faaris ducked to the ground and scurried away from the ledge. Kobra drew his sword as Faaris was getting to his feet and slashed it in Faaris' direction in one sweeping motion. Faaris fumbled for his sword and managed to break the impact just in time, sending another loud clashing sound into the air. Kobra tucked his sword away and thrust himself high into the air, performing a smooth backflip onto the top of the ledge. With a sly grin, he hurled two star-shaped shuriken blades across the sides of each of Faaris' shoulders. In the blink of an eye, the weapons spun back into Kobra's hands, landing perfectly between two of his fingers.

Faaris paused to catch his breath. He glanced at each of his torn, bloodstained sleeves. It had happened so fast. He took a deep breath. The two scratches were dripping with blood. A cold sweat broke across his skin, and he looked up at Kobra with wide, fear-stricken eyes.

"Like I said." Kobra grinned, standing so still that he almost looked like a gargoyle on top of the tower. "I never play fair."

"You know, you say you've discovered my weakness," said Faaris. "Perhaps, I've discovered yours as well."

Kobra let a roaring laugh into the night sky. "I have no weakness, you fool. I'm invincible."

"And that's just it," said Faaris with a grin. "Everyone has a weakness."

Kobra crossed his arms and rolled his eyes. He jumped back onto the floor and began walking toward Faaris, scraping the ground with his heels. "So, if you're so clever, what is it then?"

Faaris smiled and shook his head. "You said it yourself. You believe you're invincible, but I know that you're only human. Your foolishness reveals everything."

Kobra laughed. "How brave of you to insult a man of my reputation," he said. "I ought to kill you right now."

Faaris opened his arms. "It certainly seems like you've been trying, doesn't it?"

Kobra laughed and shook his head, moving backward toward the balcony with his hand over his heart. "Oh, this was only my first strike. I have much bigger plans for you. The death of the king is worthy of a real show. Since you've been a such worthy opponent, I'll leave you with a scratch for now," he hissed and jumped into the air, flipping over the edge and disappearing in seconds.

Faaris ran after him, peering over the ledge only to find that he was nowhere in sight. He let out a long-awaited sigh of relief and sank to the ground, resting his back against the tower's wall. He smiled to himself and drew the glittering bottle out of his pocket.

"There's no need to fear, my love," Faaris whispered to the bottle.

25

FAARIS TOOK A DEEP BREATH AND plucked the lid off of the bottle. He squeezed the bottle more tightly as it began shaking. Soft, misty stardust steamed out as the familiar, enchanted melody danced through the air. Ariette's silky voice followed as the smoke grew higher.

Ariette emerged as she had all the times before, singing the same tired song that she knew all too well. Faaris watched with wide eyes as his beloved rose above him like a glowing ghost, carrying the song that had the power to grant any wish.

> *"Hear this song and you will see,*
> *The magic that's inside of me.*
> *My voice, my magic melody,*
> *Listen well, it is the key.*

Close your eyes and dreams ascend,
Wish and you can capture them.
Anything your heart can find,
Sing to me in perfect rhyme.

Soft as dust, pure as the day,
This song will take your pain away.
Sing to me, your heart's desire,
Take this chance, lest it expire.

But when this song comes to an end,
This magic chance you will have spent,
Only thrice I'll sing for thee,
So, choose your wishes carefully.

You must speak now this is the time,
Until my silence, I am thine.

Any wish you shall receive,
If your heart truly believes.
Limitations, there are some,
I cannot change the setting sun.

I cannot force the moon to rise,
Or take the stars out of the sky.
I cannot change what has been done,
But I can reverse what has just begun.

The natural laws I cannot change,
But only slightly rearrange.
So, if you wish to change your fate,
You must be wise and unafraid.

Your choice of words will be the key,
To any possibility."

Faaris couldn't help but smile. He was happy to see her again. What had only been several minutes had seemed like an eternity. He cleared his throat and rose to his feet as he sang.

"Your face again, so sweet to see,
If you only knew how you've rescued me.
I wish to do the same for you,
If indeed our love is true.

No longer will you be in darkness,
No longer captive to a man so heartless.
My love, my life, please hear my plea,
It is my wish to set you free."

A soft tear of joy slipped from Ariette's eye as she let a blorba form in her hands. She took a deep breath, staring at it with every hope imaginable.

She smiled, closed her eyes, and let it collapse. The moment it burst she fell to the floor surrounded by a cloud of stardust.

Her glow faded, and her misty lower body returned to legs.

Faaris rushed to her side and knelt to take her by the arms. "Are you alright?"

Another tear fell from Ariette's eye, and she threw her arms around Faaris, burying her face in the safety of his chest. "I'm... wonderful."

She couldn't help but cry. It seemed as if all of the tears she'd been holding back were suddenly free to spill out. She couldn't have stopped them if she tried.

Faaris returned the embrace and gently stroked the back of her head, letting her sob until she couldn't any longer. Softly, he took her face into his hands and brushed the tears away, giving her his warmest smile.

Ariette was quick to return his smile. "But what happens now?" she said. Her voice was still trembling.

Faaris shook his head. "I told you to trust me."

Ariette smiled and threw her arms around him once again. "I will never doubt you again, Faaris. Will you ever forgive me?"

Faaris stroked her hair. "Of course, I will."

Ariette glanced at her wrists to see if the markings were still there. To her surprise, they were gone. "I...I don't believe it," she gasped, unable to stop staring at her perfectly clean skin.

Faaris grinned. "You're back," he said.

"Faaris," Ariette breathed. "I...I love you."

Faaris smiled and took her hands, raising her to her feet as he stood. Once they were on their feet, Ariette wrapped her arms around him again.

"I love you too," Faaris whispered. "I always have and I always will. Just promise not to leave me again. My heart couldn't bear losing you."

Ariette shook her head. "There has to be a way for me to stay."

Faaris shrugged. "We've made it this far," he said. "I'm sure we can figure something out."

"Faaris," Ariette cooed. "I know you're afraid of wishes, but please don't be. I wish to repay you for saving me. May I offer you a wish?"

Faaris took Ariette's hand and knelt to the ground. He bowed and brought one hand over his heart. He gazed up at her, her face blending with the stars behind her, glowing in the moonlight as if she were an angel.

"Just one," Faaris whispered, eyes aflame, shining in the light of the moon. "My love, my light, on this beautiful night, I hope you know you are my life. Never was there a creature so fine, as my one and only love divine. Like the star that you are, you shine in my heart. Wherever I go, I will be where you are. You've awakened my heart after thousands of days. A deed a whole lifetime could never repay. The time since we parted has seemed so long. I've missed the sweet sound of your beautiful songs. I wish to grow old with you, just watching the stars. Wherever we go, if it's Venus or Mars. A life without you, I refuse to accept. For the rest of my days, I will be in your debt. You've rescued my heart from a world of despair and given me wings like the birds of the air. Fly with me, my love, and at last we'll be free. My only wish now is that you marry me."

Ariette caught herself holding her breath. She let out a big sigh and let every ounce of her fill with stardust. She released

Faaris' hand and formed a small blorba.

Faaris stood and touched her wrist, lowering the blorba. He smiled at Ariette and shook his head. "But only if you truly want to."

Ariette returned his smile and let the blorba dissolve, falling to her feet in a shower of stardust.

"At last, my love, you've set me free," she said. "A thousand thanks for saving me. True love in you, I truly see. There's nowhere else I'd rather be."

Faaris smiled and took her by the arms. "You bring to me the stars, the moon and the sun, and on the wings of love you and I will run. Softer than the dust and as pure as the day, I'd be forever yours if you'll promise to stay."

Ariette shook her head. "I promise I am yours, but I can't promise to stay. Though nothing in this world could ever keep me away. Our marriage, I accept, and I want nothing more. I give to you my vow, to love you and to be yours. But if I must return to the place I belong, you will always have my heart, my promise, and my song. Just look up to the sky, I am not that far. Wherever you go, I will be where you are."

Faaris smiled and let out a sigh of relief. He took her face into his hands, stroking her cheeks with his thumbs and looking at her with more love than could be imagined. He leaned in to kiss her.

Ariette closed her eyes. Just before their lips could meet, she lowered her head. "Faaris."

Faaris opened his eyes and moved away from her. "Yes?"

"I can't," she whispered. "Not yet."

Faaris nodded and looked at the ground. "Forgive me. I forgot."

Ariette smiled and brought her hand to his cheek. "Someday," she said.

Faaris smiled and drew her into a tight hug, wrapping one hand around her back and one hand safely over her head. For a moment, they were motionless, letting the cool night winds wash over them.

Faaris knelt and picked the bottle up from the ground. "Now," he said with a grin. "What shall we do with this? The last time I tried to dispose of it, it found its way back to me. Perhaps we should destroy it. Care to do the honors?"

Ariette took a deep breath as Faaris handed her the bottle. "Destroy it? No. I...I couldn't. I fear something terrible will happen if it let it go."

Faaris smiled and drew her chin up. "I fear something terrible will happen if you don't."

26

ARIETTE THOUGHT FOR A MOMENT, staring down at the glittering bottle in her hands. She took a deep breath and tucked it away into her dress. Somehow, she couldn't bring herself to destroy it. The palace was quiet and lifeless as Faaris led Ariette back to her room for the night. There were only a few more hours left before sunrise, and the night was at its darkest.

Faaris took Ariette's hands as they stopped at her door. "I can't wait to tell Mehrzad about our engagement. I've never been happier, truly. He'll arrange a wedding as soon as possible, I'm sure. He's been urging me to marry for several years now. He'll be delighted."

He leaned closer and laid a tender kiss upon her cheek. "Until tomorrow."

Ariette's eyes lit up, and she brought her fingertips to the place where Faaris had kissed her. Until now, she had never known such a feeling. Faaris smiled at her and slipped away.

Ariette smiled and closed the door. She hugged herself and hummed Faaris' favorite lullaby, dancing out onto the balcony. She sat on the ledge and looked up at Aelius who was twinkling beside the moon in his usual spot.

"I've made a promise that I cannot keep. Please understand, I'm in love too deep. I wish to stay on Earth with Faaris. And I will tomorrow when we share our first kiss. This is my life. This is my choice. Finally, I have found my voice. There's nothing you can do or say. I have made up my mind. I choose to stay."

She took a deep breath and watched the wind carry her words up to the stars. She stood and smoothed her skirt. She didn't care if Aelius responded or not. It didn't matter. Her mind was made up.

A blorba shot down and exploded onto the balcony beside her.

"I knew your promise couldn't be trusted. Once again, I'm disgusted. Come back home, I order you. Don't make me come again for you."

Ariette took a deep, fervent breath and made another blorba. "Please, Aelius, don't take me away. Tomorrow is my wedding day. This love in me, you can't defeat. For once, I feel I am complete. At last, I've finally found my way. You must believe, I wish to stay."

With a grunt, she fired the blorba toward Aelius with all her strength, letting her anger send it racing into the night. Tears that had been waiting to fall began to fill her eyes. She sighed and turned back toward her room. Aelius didn't respond.

Ariette opened the curtains to enter the bedroom, leaving them open as she always did so she could see the moon. She arrived to find what appeared to be a dark figure seated on the bed with such stillness, Ariette was almost sure it was only her tear-drenched eyes playing tricks on her. She froze. In that moment, her heart seemed to have stopped. Thoughts began to spill into her mind, trying to uncover the mystery of what waited before her.

"I have your stargazer," came a raspy voice that could be no other than Roksana Estera.

Ariette gasped and took a step backward. "Who's there?"

"Why it's me, darling," said Roksana. "Don't you remember?"

"What have you done to him?" Ariette whispered.

Roksana laughed to herself. "Rest assured, he's alive…for now. Would you like to see him?"

"Please," said Ariette, "don't harm him. I'll do anything."

Roksana grinned. "I was hoping you'd say that. Come now. We must reunite our lovers."

Roksana nodded, and the hiss of Dark Kobra sliced through the silence as his shadow appeared behind her. Before Ariette could realize what was happening, she felt Kobra's arms coil around her waist as he lifted her up and swung her over his shoulder. No matter how hard she tried to fight him, her strength could not compete with his.

"Faaris," Ariette cried as loud as she possibly could.

Kobra laughed and gripped a long rope, overlooking the city from the edge of the balcony. "He can't save you now, Pigeon. It looks like I'm going to have to teach him a lesson for stealing you away from me like that. And I suggest you save your breath." He glanced over at Roksana with a sly wink, and then turned back to Ariette. "You're going to need it. I might just want another wish."

Roksana cackled and followed Kobra as he jumped over the edge and slid down the rope. The second his feet hit the grass, he broke into a run, eager to escape the palace. Roksana removed the rope from the balcony and was quick to follow, covering their tracks.

They soon arrived at Roksana's dark, hazy tent, a place Ariette never wanted to see again. She could hardly make out her surroundings in the little light that the multi-colored hanging lanterns offered. Echoes and whispers rang through the air as if the tent itself contained a cosmos of secrets. Kobra swung the entrance open and set Ariette on the rug-covered ground, maintaining a firm grip on her wrists. He slipped two gold shackles out of his vest and locked them around each of her wrists, binding her hands behind her back. Roksana entered and sealed the entrance shut, closing them into the darkness.

Ariette released her breath as soon as she realized she had been holding it. She coughed after taking in a breath of thick, sweet-smelling incense. In the light of the colored lanterns, she saw Faaris tied to a chair across the table. The way he was looking at her was enough to make her heart stop.

Roksana walked toward the table and plucked a long cigar from a hanging lantern. She took one puff and blew the smoke into Faaris' face. Faaris was quick to turn away, despite coughing a little.

Kobra picked Ariette up and slithered toward the table, seating her across from Faaris. He pulled a long rope from the ground and tied her to the chair as he'd done to Faaris. When the rope was secure, he slid to Roksana's side and lowered his head to meet hers. He slipped his mask down to reveal his mouth and pulled her into a passionate kiss.

Kobra grinned and pulled the mask back over his mouth. "Victory is *sssss*-weet."

Ariette and Faaris exchanged wide-eyed glances.

Roksana laughed and stood behind Faaris, looking Ariette dead in the eyes. "So, you thought you could escape me, little star? Cute."

Ariette took a deep breath.

Kobra shuffled toward Ariette. "You know, I should have known you wouldn't come through on your end of the deal. Which is why I suppose I'm going to end it right now, assuming that you've surrendered. Surely, you remember the consequences of disobeying me."

Ariette's breathing grew faster. She looked across the table at Faaris, her eyes pleading for help.

"And speaking of deals," said Roksana, eyes darting toward Faaris. "It seems you've decided to keep her to yourself."

Faaris took a deep breath. "I can explain."

"Alright," said Roksana. "Explain to me what is so difficult about keeping your word. I'm surprised at you, Faaris. I assumed you to be a man of virtue. Perhaps I was wrong."

Faaris closed his eyes. "Things are different now. I...I couldn't..."

"Couldn't what?" said Roksana. "Couldn't give her up?"

"I couldn't bring myself to put her in danger," said Faaris. "I'm sorry."

Kobra grinned and slipped the bottle out of his vest and laid it on the table in front of Ariette, whose eyes widened. She hadn't even seen him steal it from her pocket.

"How sneaky of you. I can't believe I let you get away with stealing my bottle," said Kobra. "Now, unless you tell me now that you'll fulfill your end of the deal in due time, say hello to your eternal destiny."

Ariette was trembling from head-to-toe just staring at the bottle. "No," she whispered. "Please."

"Perhaps," said Faaris, "perhaps some sort of agreement could be reached?"

Kobra's snake eyes darted toward Faaris. "Agreement?" He crossed his arms and stood a little taller. "Like what?"

Faaris shrugged. "A fair trade, perhaps. Surely a man as wise as you should know that a genie is no treasure. Not when you could have something like this." He fidgeted against the rope and struggled to reach into his pocket.

"Something like what?" Kobra said, stroking his chin.

"Well," Faaris grunted with a slight laugh. "I'm dying to show you, truly. If only I could get my hands free, I could retrieve it."

Kobra glanced at Roksana. "Where is it?" Roksana asked. "Kobra, can't you see that he cannot be trusted."

"I'm afraid it's hidden too well," said Faaris. "You couldn't find if you tried, I'm sure. Besides it's extremely delicate. I wouldn't want you to break it. But it would be my pleasure if you would allow me to redeem myself and prove to you that I am in fact a man of my word."

"Try me," Kobra laughed.

Faaris shrugged. "Alright, but don't say I didn't warn you. One wrong move and you'll shatter it completely. Then you'll never have its power."

Kobra took a deep breath. "You're too clever, but not clever enough to fool me." He slid a small blade out of his sleeve and slashed the rope that was holding Faaris to the chair. Kobra grabbed the back of his neck and held the blade to the side of his jaw. Faaris took a deep breath and reached into his vest to pull out the egg. Kobra tightened his grip on Faaris' neck. "I don't have time for these games."

"Patience," said Faaris, taking the egg into both hands. "It's no ordinary egg."

"You should hope so," Kobra grunted. "Your life is depending on it."

"Oh, I'm sure of it," said Faaris. "This is the egg of the legendary Sima Bird. Surely, you're familiar with the story. Every Pernian knows it."

Kobra scratched his chin. "I have no patience for stories."

"Trust me," said Faaris. "I think you'll like this one."

Kobra sighed and rolled his eyes. "Put the egg on the table."

Faaris reached out to lay the egg safely on the silky tablecloth. As soon as he did, Kobra retied the rope around Faaris' chest.

Kobra stepped forward to face Faaris and tucked the knife

away. He put his arm on the table and leaned into a more comfortable slouch. "Enlighten me."

"Well," said Faaris, talking with his hands despite being tied up, "in short, this creature, this Sima Bird, has the power to bestow kingship upon anyone." As he spoke, he slipped a small knife out from the side of his belt, watching Kobra to make sure he didn't notice. He began sawing at the rope from behind his back. "She's more powerful than any genie, I'm sure. The one to behold her has surely found the greatest treasure in the world."

"Really?" Kobra said, a sudden spark of interest alive in his snake-like eyes.

Faaris nodded. "All I ask in return is simple. Release us, and all of this power shall be yours to cherish for the rest of your life. And you'll give me your word that you'll leave us in peace and bring no more treachery upon this kingdom, or any other for that matter, unless you wish to spend the rest of your life in prison. It's an offer you won't find anywhere else, believe me. You'd be a fool not to accept it. Understand that I've spared you greatly where the laws would have otherwise had you put to death."

Kobra scratched his chin, eyes focused on the egg.

"Wait," Roksana hissed. "Under one condition. Our little star here has something I desire. Something I'm sure she'll have no further need for if she wishes to stay on Earth forever." Ariette closed her eyes. "That's right, angel," said Roksana. "I still want your stardust. And you can be sure that you won't be released until it's mine. Surrender it to me now, and freedom is yours. I'll leave you with one warning, however. Whatever you do, you must never destroy that bottle. Do you understand?"

Ariette gulped. "Is...is the egg not enough?"

Roksana grinned and looked straight into Ariette's eyes. "Not even close, darling. Faaris has given us the egg. Now it's your turn."

Ariette took a deep breath. "I...I..."

"Ariette, go on," said Faaris with a deep, knowing look, "it's a fair trade. Give her what she's asked for."

Ariette looked surprised at him.

Faaris winked and gave her his usual wise grin. "It's alright. Clearly, Kobra's deal with her wasn't enough."

Roksana turned toward Faaris with a hint of loathing in her eyes. "What?"

Faaris shrugged. "Surely, there's been some sort of agreement between you two. I can't imagine why else a star would give up her stardust...her freedom."

Roksana glared at Kobra. "He made me an offer only a fool would refuse."

Kobra crossed his arms and laughed to himself, placing his hands firmly over her shoulders from behind. "I made you an offer only a fool would accept, my love. It was you who was kind enough to fall for it."

Roksana turned and glared back at him, swatting his hands off of her shoulders. "I had no choice. When Faaris released me from the bottle, I soon realized that freedom for a genie appears to be a death sentence if you're not wise. My stardust was preserved inside the bottle. I began losing it within seconds of my release. If I hadn't met this devil of a man in the bazaar that night, I would have died. Kobra swore he'd kiss me and save me from my inevitable death if I would agree to help him get what he wanted. Now, is it really too much for me to want my stardust again? This way everybody wins…well, he and I do at least."

Roksana laughed and folded her hands over the table.

Faaris shrugged. "Well, what are we waiting for? Ariette, go on."

Ariette took a deep breath and looked from Faaris to Roksana. "I can't make a blorba when my hands are tied."

Roksana rolled her eyes and took a deep breath. She looked at Kobra with a quick head gesture. Kobra moved toward Ariette and slashed the rope around her. Ariette took a sigh of relief, not realizing how tight the rope had been. Kobra pulled a small blade out of his sleeve and held it to her chin. He turned to Roksana, cutting his eyes toward the bottle and gave her a quick wink. The corner of Roksana's lip curled with delight.

"Now, on with it, star," Roksana demanded. "I've never been very patient."

Ariette took a deep breath and looked once again at Faaris, who nodded with approval. Ariette closed her eyes and let every part of her fill with stardust. Faaris severed the rope around him and let it fall slowly to the floor. He gripped his knife and slipped into the shadows. A small prick of light began to form in Ariette's hands. Roksana smiled.

As the blorba grew, Faaris made his way carefully around the walls, using the darkness to his advantage. He dragged the fallen rope off of the ground and moved closer to Ariette, still staying hidden in the smoke and darkness. Faaris reached for a hanging dish of burning incense and threw the smoke into Kobra's eyes.

Kobra screamed. Faaris scooped Ariette into his arms and fled the tent.

Roksana turned angrily toward Kobra. "Stop them. Don't just stand there. It's only smoke. You're not defeated."

"I can't bloody see, you witch," Kobra snarled, still rubbing at his eyes. "Now, make yourself useful and get me some water. Now."

Roksana walked to the back of the tent to grab a tall pitcher. As soon as she turned, she threw the water in Kobra's face, dropping the empty pitcher to her side. Kobra grunted, wiping his eyes with his sleeves, smudging the dark charcoal that was always painted around his eyes.

"Now," said Roksana, "what are you waiting for? After them."

"Not so fast," Kobra said. He grinned, running his hand down his masked face to clear the remaining water. "We had a deal."

27

STILL CARRYING ARIETTE, FAARIS ran across the dusty ground and through the empty bazaar as fast as he could, not stopping to look back. Even carrying her, he was faster than she was if she were on her feet. Ariette locked her arms around his neck and looked back at the tent. There was no sign of Roksana or Kobra. Ariette took a deep breath and steadied her focus on Faaris' quickening pulse which she felt from his neck, watching as they passed through the lifeless bazaar. Rugs and trinkets hung over the tall beams overhead, casting shadows across their fear-stricken faces as they raced for the palace. Ariette closed her eyes and let the sounds of Faaris' footsteps on the dirt soothe her racing thoughts.

Ariette took a deep sigh. "Faaris." Faaris, still running, managed a quick glance back at her. "I never wish to leave you," she said.

"I'd do anything to keep you here, believe me," Faaris panted, "and safe. I have a feeling this isn't over. They'll surely return for us. It's only a matter of time. We just have to be prepared for when they do."

Faaris set Ariette onto her feet as they arrived at the tall palace gates. The majestic height of the palace towered over them, making Ariette suddenly feel small. A full moon hung overhead, casting her light through the vines of the flowering night-blooming jasmine that surrounded the gates. Ariette clung close to Faaris' side as if he were her lifeline, praying for the moon not to see her. Faaris swung the necklace over his head and selected the key. Ariette was careful to watch for Roksana or Kobra as Faaris unlocked the gates.

"Don't worry," Faaris whispered, opening the gates just wide enough for the two of them to slip through. "I think we've lost them for now."

Ariette grabbed the back of Faaris' shoulder and moved closer to him, still looking back into the bazaar. "I don't trust them."

"And you shouldn't," Faaris said leading her through the gates.

They entered the courtyard to the sounds of trickling fountains dancing in the light of several torches. An array of citrus trees and flowers bloomed throughout the courtyard, all swaying in the night wind which was growing cooler by the hour.

"Watch your step," said Faaris, guiding Ariette through the darkness and across the brush.

Ariette glanced up at the enormous palace towering over them. The palace itself almost seemed like a city all its own.

Music was spilling out faintly from inside. The usual sounds of drums, chimes, strings, and flutes floated out into the courtyard. Faaris took Ariette by the hand, interlacing his fingers with hers as they made their way through the courtyard.

"Tomorrow couldn't come soon enough," Faaris said.

Ariette smiled and looked up at Faaris, halfheartedly as a cool gust of wind swept through the courtyard.

Faaris looked uneasy. "Is something wrong?"

Ariette shook her head at the ground. "I'm afraid my brother will come to take me back."

"Once you become human, it will be impossible, right?" said Faaris.

Ariette smiled. "Yes. We just need to get married as soon as possible. I've promised my brother not to kiss you otherwise."

"Tomorrow is the soonest possible," said Faaris. "And a kiss is a part of the ritual. He'll have to understand." Ariette smiled.

Faaris led Ariette deeper into the brush, where they would be hidden in the trees. He crouched at the foot of a lemon tree and rested his head against the trunk, casting his eyes up at the moon, which was big and bright. Ariette sat beside him, letting her head rest in the curve of his neck.

"Faaris," she said, looking up at the moon, "are there any more wishes you would like before I give up my stardust?"

Faaris smiled and sighed. "I no longer have the need for wishes. I've already been given everything I could ever need and more. Besides, I think the world is better off without such magic. Life already has magic of its own."

"Like what?"

Faaris smiled down at her. "Like this. This moment here. Love and all its beauty. Sunrises, sunsets, harvest moons, eclipses. Everything is by design. I think its best when we leave it that way instead of always trying to change its course. That's when we truly see its beauty. Now. Whatever still troubles you, I want you to forget about all of it. I want you to trust me when I say that there's no need to fear. Everything will be alright. I promise."

Ariette glanced up at him. "But...I..." Faaris smiled, as if to stop her from saying anything further. Ariette took a deep breath and rested her head against his chest. "I trust you."

For a moment, they were silent, letting the beauty of the night surround them. The darkest hour of the night was upon them and the moon was at her brightest. The fresh, sweet smell of the lemon blossoms filled the air as several small flowers showered over them.

After falling asleep for a while, Faaris opened his eyes to find that Ariette hadn't slept a wink. Her eyes were wide open, staring up at the stars deep in thought.

Faaris took a deep breath and looked up. "Still awake I see."

Ariette smiled. "I don't sleep, remember."

"Ah, that's right," said Faaris. "So, what's it really like up there?"

Ariette sighed. "Dark. Cold. Lonely. It's nothing like Earth. It's beautiful, but much less exciting."

Faaris grinned. "Well, which do you prefer?"

Ariette laughed to herself, "I think I prefer to live here. It's exciting and wonderful and there's so much to explore. I'll never be bored. I'm sure of it."

"Right you are," said Faaris. "You'll be pleased to know that there's more to the world than can ever be explored in a lifetime. I for one am content where I am, but if it makes you happy, I'd love to show you all that I can of this world before our lives here must come to an end."

"End?" Ariette said.

Faaris laughed to himself. "Well, nothing goes on forever, not even stars. That's life. We must make wise use of our time while we're here, so that we can live forever. Lesson number one on navigating a life on Earth."

Ariette smiled. "I couldn't have wished for a better human to lead me through this life. Stars don't live forever. That's another reason I want to become a human. You have the chance to go on. When a star dies, it vanishes completely. It no longer exists. It's rare that one does, but I guess when time comes to an end, so will the stars."

There was a deep look in Faaris' eyes as he looked over at her, deeper than his usual. "Well," he said, "in that case, I believe the answer to your earlier question is no. No, you are most definitely not wrong for coming to Earth. You couldn't be more right, in fact."

Ariette smiled and closed her eyes. "I have no doubt that this is where I'm meant to belong."

"Ariette," said Faaris. "Do you remember my last wish?"

Ariette nodded. "I remember all of your wishes. All four-thousand three hundred and eighty-one of them."

Faaris grinned. "You said, 'Trust me, my love, we'll find a way. We'll be together soon, I pray."

Ariette smiled. "And now I see that I can truly trust you."

"No," said Faaris. "My last wish was to free you of your life as a star and bring you here. I knew that's what you wanted."

Ariette frowned and shook her head. "I don't remember that wish. You must have sent if after my brother cut off all of my wishes."

"Oh," Faaris breathed. "All this time, I thought you'd abandoned me."

Ariette bit her lip and shook her head. "Oh, Faaris. I'm so sorry. Will you ever forgive me?"

"Of course, I will," said Faaris. "It's just that perhaps if you had heard it, things would have been different."

"Perhaps this was the way things were meant to be," said Ariette. "It wasn't the course we expected, but we have reached the outcome we were searching for, haven't we? I think it was worth waiting for. Maybe a change of fate was our true fate after all."

Faaris smiled. "Fate is mysterious. Something I'll never understand. Perhaps, we're not meant to."

"Why search for an answer that's not meant to be found?" said Ariette. "That seems like a waste of time to me."

"Right you are," said Faaris. "But sometimes, I can't help myself. My mind likes to explore these things."

Ariette giggled. "Mine too. Perhaps that's why I'm here…and why I still don't understand how I've succeeded."

"In my experience, when you truly set your mind on something, you'll find a way to make it yours," said Faaris. "I can almost guarantee it."

"So, I see," said Ariette. "And so, I conclude that life is strange."

264

Faaris laughed to himself. "Now you're starting to sound like a real human. It's alright, not one of us understands life. We just live and learn as we go. It's troubling, I admit, when you're the sort of person who likes predictability, but I love life in spite of how harsh it's seemed at times."

"All that time, I never knew you were a prince, let alone a king," said Ariette.

Faaris smiled. "I was a prince all the time you spoke to me. My brother was king at the time, remember?"

"Oh," said Ariette. "The one with the snake bite?"

"Yes," said Faaris. "But wrongfully so. I should have been the king."

Ariette was surprised. "What?"

Faaris closed his eyes. "I never told you this, but I used the genie to wish the crown upon myself. My brother was a terrible king, and the kingdom was suffering because of him. I knew I had to do something to make things right. I was desperate. The moment I made the wish, he was exiled, and I never saw him again. The guards searched the entire kingdom and found no trace of him. Nothing but this…"

Faaris slipped one of the gold rings off of one of his fingers and held it in the moonlight. "They found it in the sands. It could only mean one thing. No one can survive out there for very long."

"I'm sorry you've lost your family," said Ariette.

"It's alright," said Faaris. "That's the way life is, I suppose. But I have you now. Perhaps, someday we'll have a new family."

Ariette smiled. "Perhaps."

A cool breeze tossed at their hair and infiltrated the garden with its chill, sweeping mist from the fountains across their skin.

Ariette paused. "Faaris." Faaris turned with an attentive look. "How did you find the bottle?"

Faaris gulped and looked down at his hands as he interlaced his fingers. Ariette caught a tear in one of his eyes, on the peak of falling. Faaris gulped again. "It was given to me."

Ariette reached to lay her fingers over his. "By who?"

As Faaris looked up at her, he blinked, and the tear fell onto his cheek. "My parents."

Ariette blinked twice and looked at the ground, still touching Faaris' hand. "Oh," she breathed, wearing a look of confusion. "I don't know what it's like to lose someone you love. Stars die very rarely, and still, I hardly knew any of them enough to love them the way you loved your parents. But I'm sorry. Very sorry. It sounds awful."

Faaris' face wrinkled, as if he were trying his hardest to fight the deep sadness within him. The feeling overcame him, and more tears spilled down his face. "I miss them," he choked.

Ariette's eyes filled with tears. Seeing him this way severed her heart in two, as if the sharpest blade had been driven through the deepest part of it. She touched the side of Faaris' face, trying to draw his weary eyes to hers. "Faaris," she said, shaking her head. "It makes me sad to see you this way. Please...please don't..."

Faaris shook his head and looked up at the moon. "I hate that bottle more than hell itself. The moment I saw it I knew no good could come of it. It turns out I was right. I lost everything that day."

Ariette paused. "I came of it."

"Not you," said Faaris. "That's different. You didn't choose it. I did. And I've regretted it ever since."

Ariette winced. "Why? It has brought us together, hasn't it?"

Faaris shook his head. "It was a desperate last resort. All I wanted was to make things right. Now that I look back, I'm sure there must have been another way to get what I wanted. One that didn't involve magic."

Ariette bit her lip and looked down at the ground. "But perhaps it was meant to be. Without the bottle, we never would have met."

Faaris smiled. "I guess in the end, I suppose I would rather tolerate a little regret if it means I get to have you."

Ariette shrugged. "Nothing in life is free. Everything is a compromise, isn't it?"

Faaris smiled at the ground. "It would seem so, wouldn't it? Does it scare you at all?"

Ariette frowned. "What?"

Faaris looked up at her. "Life. Does it scare you?"

Ariette blinked at the ground and hugged herself. "I…maybe a little. Does it scare you?"

Faaris nodded. "Sometimes. But then I think, there's so much it has to offer beyond those fears. So much that's worth the risks. I've come to the conclusion that in the end, there are very few things worth worrying about."

Ariette rested her head in the curve of Faaris' neck and clutched his arm as if he were the only thing keeping her safe.

"Faaris," Ariette whispered. Faaris turned his head down

toward her to listen. "I feel so safe when I'm with you," she said, closing her eyes. "I never wish to be apart."

Faaris smiled and glanced down to admire her face. "The feeling is mutual, believe me."

"I wish time would stop right now so we could stay in this moment forever," Ariette said opening her eyes to look up at the glittering night sky. "I would give anything."

Faaris smiled. "Why wish for one moment when I can give you a lifetime of moments just like this one...or even better?"

Ariette smiled at the thought. "Alright," she said. "You've convinced me, but you must keep your word, Faaris."

"Don't worry," said Faaris. "I always keep my word. Ask anyone."

"Good," said Ariette. "Now I can't wait for the rest of my life."

28

FAARIS OPENED HIS EYES JUST AS the sun began to rise over the horizon. The air was clear, and the sky was the soft color of Ariette's eyes, which were still wide open, as they'd been the entire night. For the first time, she had watched the night fade into day. She watched hummingbirds bounce from flower-to-flower, birds dip their feathers into the fountains, and butterflies dance on the morning breeze. The fresh scent of lemon mixed with the aromas of all kinds of flowers swam across her nose. As the sun rose higher, the usual heat began to settle in. Faaris smiled down at Ariette. He stretched his arms high above his head and ran his fingers through his hair before rising to his feet. He dusted his pants and held his hand out to Ariette to help her up.

"Let's go find Mehrzad," said Faaris. "He's the only one who knows about us."

Staying close by his side, Ariette followed Faaris across the back of the garden and through a small entrance that was free of guards. Carefully, they made their way through the empty halls.

As they approached the Great Hall, Razi came flying toward them. "Faaris," he panted. "Faaris, you're never going to believe this."

"Razi," said Faaris, bracing him by the shoulders. "Is everything alright?"

"Where have you been all night?" said Razi. "I've been looking everywhere for you."

Faaris' eyes widened. "How did you know we were here?"

"Faaris, I'm your bodyguard," said Razi. "I've got eyes in the back of my head. You're lucky I'm on your side on this one."

Faaris smiled. "Good. So, what am I not going to believe, then?"

"Ah, yes, the news," said Razi. "Now, try not to let this kill you, but your brother, Sanjar…well, he's…he's back."

Faaris' heart suddenly jumped inside of him. "You're joking. I don't believe this."

"I told you," said Razi. "He's in the Great Hall. Care to see him?"

Faaris put his hand over his heart. "I…of course I would."

They entered the big, vacant Great Hall, to find Sanjar standing beside Mehrzad, with his hands folded behind his back near one of the tall marble pillars at the side of the room. Sanjar wore a long green robe, looking cleaner and more polished than ever before. His short beard, which fell just below his chin was neatly groomed into a small patch of hair and his head was covered with a hood which flowed down the sides of his face. Rays of sunlight cast through the windows that lined the walls, catching the sheen of the silk on Sanjar's robe.

Faaris gulped as soon as Sanjar turned to face him. The entire room was silent as Faaris walked across the floor.

Sanjar crossed his arms and smiled at Faaris. "Surprised to see me?"

"I'm in shock actually," said Faaris. "How…how are you?"

"Peachy." Sanjar grinned. "Just peachy. In case you're wondering what I've been up to, I've been crawling my way across Asia in search of the greatest of treasures."

"Have you?" Faaris smiled. "And what is that may I ask?"

Sanjar lowered his head and laid his hand over his heart. "My heart."

Faaris raised his eyebrows. "Oh. And have you found it?"

"Indeed, he has," said Mehrzad. "He comes to us a changed man, and I couldn't be more grateful."

Sanjar smiled. "I should thank you, Faaris. Exile was the best thing that's ever happened to me. I met a man in Japan, who changed my life completely. Thanks to him I've uncovered the truth that lies deep inside of my soul and realized what a selfish man I had become. My only hope now is that you'll forgive me for the way I treated you before."

A small tear swelled in Faaris' eyes. "Will wonders never cease? Of course, I'll forgive you."

Sanjar opened his arms toward Faaris for the first time ever and welcomed him into a hug.

"I'm so proud of you, Sanjar," said Faaris, patting Sanjar on the back. "Truly."

"Thank you, dear brother," said Sanjar. "I am eternally in your debt."

"Think nothing of it," said Faaris. "I'm just happy you're alive."

Sanjar laughed. "As am I. Oh, I have so many stories to tell you."

Faaris grinned and raised an eyebrow as he slid out of the hug. "Yes, I'm sure. I'd love to hear them."

"So, Mehrzad tells me you're engaged," said Sanjar. "Congratulations."

"Oh, yes," said Faaris, turning toward Ariette. "Allow me to introduce my fiancé. This is Ariette."

Sanjar grinned at her and raised her hand to his lips. "Beautiful. Hello, Ariette. It's a pleasure to meet you. Faaris where did you find her?"

Faaris laughed to himself. "Believe me, I've searched the entire universe. It seems fate wouldn't have had it any other way."

"How romantic," said Sanjar. "Well, it sounds like you got everything you've ever wanted."

Faaris smiled and nodded. "It would seem so. I'm quite happy. Happier than I've ever been, in fact. And you?"

Sanjar grinned from ear-to-ear, in a cat-like way. "Like I said… peachy. Just peachy. And you should know that I haven't come to steal the throne, even though it is rightfully mine. I come in peace. To make amends, dear brother. I've come to a place where I've accepted Father's law as it is, and therefore, I accept living peacefully under your reign. I ask forgiveness from all of you, from all of Pernia, for that matter. From now on, I will strive to live more like you, Faaris. I'm humbled, honestly. I was wrong."

"Truly, the change in you is overwhelming," said Faaris, running his hand across the hairs on his chin. "But I couldn't be more pleased."

"Well, enough about me," said Sanjar placing his hand over his chest. "This is your day, isn't it? You and your bride to be, that is."

Faaris smiled at Ariette. "Indeed, it is. I must say, at last I finally feel that things are in harmony. I can't imagine life getting any better than this."

Mehrzad smiled. "Neither can I. I never thought this day would come."

Sanjar bowed to Ariette. "My dear, it would be my honor to escort you to your groom tonight, if you will allow me to. I believe my title is suitable."

"Ah, what a splendid idea, Sanjar," said Mehrzad. "Yes, we will make arrangements promptly."

"So, your adventures in Asia," said Faaris, turning to Sanjar. "You must tell me everything."

"Of course," said Sanjar. "I'll warn you, there's much to tell."

Faaris smiled. "I'm patient," he said. "I'm curious to know what you've learned, and may God bless the man who's responsible for this change in you."

Sanjar closed his eyes and lowered his head. "That man is me, Faaris. One can be given instruction, but it is his choice whether or not he will act upon it, isn't it?"

Faaris smiled and shrugged. "Right again."

Mehrzad turned to Ariette with folded hands. "Come with me, my dear. I want to have a word with you before the ceremony tonight."

"Yes," said Ariette, a little surprised. "Of course."

29

ARIETTE FOLLOWED MEHRZAD into a part of the palace that she'd never been before. Mehrzad closed the door as soon as they'd entered the room. Ariette stepped inside to find countless shelves full of books surrounding a big circular table in the middle of the room. A chart of stars like the one Faaris had created was drawn on the table, covered slightly by several maps and a big globe. Sunlight spilled into the room through tall open windows that lined the circular room. A candle chandelier hung high over the table from the arched ceiling which was covered with a chart like the one on the table.

Ariette touched the chart on the table. "Faaris showed me a chart like this last night. I didn't know you charted stars too."

"As I said before, I was once an astronomer," said Mehrzad.

"I've studied the stars for many years. You sounded like quite the expert at dinner. Of course, that isn't why I've brought you here. First and foremost, I want to discuss your marriage."

Mehrzad walked toward a table in the back of the room and picked up a tea kettle. He arranged two small teacups, both painted with a beautiful intricate design, onto the forefront of the table and poured a steaming, golden liquid into each of them. He smiled and walked toward Ariette, placing one of the teacups gently in front of her, his aged hand slightly shaking as he laid it on the table.

"Be careful, it's very hot," said Mehrzad.

Ariette smiled and rose the cup to her nose to take in the delightful smell of cinnamon, orange, and spiced chai. "Thank you," she said, holding the small cup with both hands.

"You know," said Mehrzad, "Faaris is like a son to me. I've seen nearly every minute of his life as his caregiver and now his vizier, and I don't recall ever seeing him as happy as he's been since you arrived."

Ariette blushed and smiled, tucking her hair behind her ear. "I too have never been this happy. Love is..." She bit her lip and set the teacup on the table, staring at the rising swirls of steam. "Love is magic."

Mehrzad smiled, the wrinkles around his eyes turning upward. "Indeed, it is. And speaking of magic..." He walked toward the bookshelf and pulled a big blue book out. Intricate gold and silver swirls and stars covered its exterior, twinkling as Mehrzad carried it past one of the windows. He laid it on the table in front of Ariette. "I thought you might appreciate this," he said.

276

Ariette hesitated to open it. She looked up at Mehrzad like a child, as if to ask him if it was alright. "Go on, my dear," Mehrzad smiled. "Have a look."

Ariette peeled the book open, revealing thousands of thick pages covered with writing in a language she had never seen before. She flipped through several more pages until arriving at a page with pictures.

"Since you will be my beloved Faaris' bride, I'd like to take this time to learn more about you," said Mehrzad.

Ariette smiled and turned another page. "What do you wish to know?"

Mehrzad stroked his beard. "All I have are two simple questions, if you don't mind," he said.

Ariette looked up at him, ready to answer.

Mehrzad smiled, wearing a wise look in his old eyes. "Where have you come from, and where are you going?"

Ariette's heart started racing. Deep inside, she knew he would never believe her if she told him the truth. She paused and took a deep breath.

"As I said, I've come from a place very far from here," said Ariette, fidgeting with her fingers underneath the table. "So far that you couldn't have possibly traveled there. And where am I going? I can't possibly know the future, but with hope, I'll follow my heart wherever it leads me. I know now that I can trust it. It's taken me this far, and wonderful things have happened."

Mehrzad smiled and crossed his arms. He extended his arm toward a map on the table. "My dear, what is the name of your country?"

"Country?" Ariette asked, eyes going to the map. "I…"

Ariette squeezed her eyes shut and bit her lip. "I fear you wouldn't believe me if I told you the truth."

"My dear," Mehrzad smiled. "I ask for nothing more. If I may be honest, I've had a strange suspicion about you since I first saw you."

"Suspicion?" Ariette managed to say.

Mehrzad crossed his arms again and smiled down at her in a fatherly way. "I know what you are."

Ariette gulped, took a deep breath, and stood. "You do?"

"In recent years, I've noticed some inconsistencies among the stars," said Mehrzad, placing his hand onto the place in the chart where she had always been. "Two of them seem to have gone missing."

"Oh," said Ariette, casting her eyes at the chart where his hand was.

"The color of your eyes is unlike any other that I've seen," said Mehrzad. "Your knowledge and that soft glow around you that only the keenest of eyes could see all reveal everything."

Ariette gulped. "And what is that?"

"You come from a place quite far indeed," said Mehrzad. "You come from the heavens." Ariette took a deep breath. "You are a star," said Mehrzad. "Are you not?"

Ariette closed her eyes as a rush of fear fell over her. Aelius' words played back suddenly in her mind.s *"If the humans find out you're a star, you'll be exploited without a doubt. They're all greedy. If they find a star, they'll only want your power."*

"Don't be afraid, my dear," Mehrzad smiled. "You can trust

me. You're safe here."

Ariette took a deep breath and rose from the table. "What you say is true. I just…I didn't want the world to know my secret. I was warned of the danger that would come to me if anyone found out what I really am, and so I've tried to hide it all this time. Faaris is the only other one who knows."

Mehrzad placed his hand over his heart and bowed his head. "I will make sure that no harm comes to you. It will be my honor to protect such a special creature."

Ariette smiled, feeling the weight of her fears lift off of her heart. "The moment I kiss Faaris, I will no longer be a star. I can't wait for that moment to come. Then I will be free."

"Ah," Mehrzad smiled. "I've never known that about stars."

Ariette smiled. "There is much you don't know."

"Well, now that you'll be staying here, you will have plenty of time to share your stories with us, won't you?" said Mehrzad. "If you so choose, that is. I have great respect for your world. More than you realize, in fact. I would never wish to disrupt it or to exploit you. As an astronomer, I'm only curious. You must understand."

Ariette started pacing alongside the table, letting her fingers slide gently across the surface, running past the constellations that had been etched onto the chart. "Of course. I'm just as curious about this world as you are about mine."

"Tell me," said Mehrzad. "Was it your curiosity that brought you here?"

Ariette smiled. "Not exactly. I came here looking for love."

"Well, may I say congratulations," said Mehrzad, smiling. "I believe you have succeeded."

"It would seem so," said Ariette. "Love is better in your world, stronger it seems. I felt like I was the only star who felt such things. So, I believed with all of my heart that I was destined to be on Earth. I believed that it was the only way for me to be truly happy, to feel complete inside."

"Ah," said Mehrzad, "but completeness does not exist, I'm afraid. Not even here. No journey is ever completed. Even life itself never really ends. It orbits just like the things of your world. Earth is full of cycles and patterns, rises and falls. We are, in fact, more similar than you think."

"Are you saying I will be disappointed here?" Ariette asked.

"Not at all," said Mehrzad. "I'm only preparing you, because I care for you. I want you to understand that you won't find happiness in the things of this world, just as you weren't able to find it in the things of your world. What you truly seek is found within. It is something you must learn to carry with you wherever life takes you."

Ariette smiled and lowered her head. "I'm very sure of my decision."

"I love Faaris deeply, you know," said Mehrzad, placing his hand over his heart. "More than you know. He's like a son to me. I couldn't bear to see him hurt. I only want him to be happy. He's seen enough pain to last a lifetime. He's suffered enough loss. Whatever you do, please don't hurt him. Never break his heart, never cause him grief. That's all I ask."

"I only wish to love him," said Ariette. "I promise. I've spent a long time searching for him, and now that I've found him, I could never let him go."

Mehrzad closed his eyes and bowed his head. "I'll take your word for it."

He took her hand and raised it to his mouth to kiss the top of her wrist. His rough, grey beard tickled her skin like moss.

"I will be happy to share the secrets with you," said Ariette. "The secrets of the stars, although, they're not really secrets. There's nothing that will bring danger to your world for knowing. Perhaps I could even be of assistance to you."

Mehrzad raised his eyebrows. "I'd be delighted to know."

Ariette cleared her throat and leaned in -to whisper. "Your chart is wrong by the way."

Mehrzad let out a jolly laugh. "I have no doubt it is. And how grateful I am to have you to shed some light on it."

Ariette bowed. "I'll do what I can to share with you all that I know."

"My thanks, truly." Mehrzad bowed.

"It's the least I could do," said Ariette. "You have all been so kind to me."

"Now," said Mehrzad, "a marriage is a sacred thing, you know. It is something that must never be broken. It unifies two souls forever. You must let nothing come between that bond. Do you understand?"

Ariette nodded. "I will spend the rest of my life trying to protect it, believe me. Love is the greatest power of this world and mine. If I have love, I feel I have everything."

"Right you are," Mehrzad smiled, lifting her chin with his fingertips. "And what a marvelous queen you're sure to be."

Ariette's smile faded.

"Queen," she whispered. She gulped and blushed. Of all the thoughts that had crossed her mind, she hadn't considered that.

"Now, my dear," said Mehrzad. "What is your full name? We'll need to know for the ceremony."

"My full name?" Ariette said, looking down at her hands.

"Your first and last names, or more have you any," said Mehrzad. "What shall we call you?"

Ariette took a deep breath, "I am Ariette. Ariette Setareh."

30

THE COURTYARD WAS FILLED WITH sunlight and soft morning air. A breeze created ripples across the surface of the tea, which filled the cups on the table. The courtyard was empty, and the waters of the pools were so still they almost blended with the stone floors around them.

"Incredible." Faaris grinned, setting his teacup back on the table. "So, what did he say when you finally surrendered?"

Sanjar threw his head back and rolled his eyes. "Ah. That old man? He said, 'I believe you're beginning to understand the true meaning of patience.'"

Faaris laughed. "And that's where it all began."

Sanjar laughed, raising his teacup to his mouth. "Apparently. He said, 'I always welcome a good challenge, and you, my friend, are the greatest challenge of my career'. And I said, 'You have no idea, Sensei.' We grew together, you know. I sort of miss him."

Faaris nodded and laughed. "I still can't believe you survived that walk up the mountain. It must have been exhausting."

Sanjar took a deep breath. "By then, I was prepared, but otherwise…who knows? At that point, I wanted nothing more than to die anyway. I had nothing to lose. Speaking of death, he spent the longest time helping me to overcome my fear of snakes after what happened at my coronation. He taught me how to charm them in fact. Every day, I was forced to take a small bite from a snake." Sanjar grinned with pride and slid his left sleeve up to reveal the scar of a snake's fangs in the same place as his first bite.

Faaris' eyes widened. "And you survived?"

"It was only a small amount of venom," said Sanjar. "Just enough for me to acquire immunity. I can now survive any snake attack. Now, I shall never fear them again."

"Inspiring, truly," said Faaris.

Mehrzad walked into the Great Hall from behind the tall, red curtains.

"Gentlemen," said Mehrzad.

Faaris and Sanjar turned.

"I must say, it's wonderful to see you two finally getting along, but I'm afraid I must interrupt it for now," said Mehrzad. "The wedding preparations are almost complete, and the announcement has reached the farthest ends of the kingdom. It seems we're expecting a large turnout. I haven't seen so much excitement in all my years at the palace."

Faaris gulped and smiled, looking down at his hands.

Sanjar took a deep breath and put his hands over his knees to press himself to his feet. "Well, it sounds like you have a long day ahead of you, Faaris."

Faaris smiled and nodded. "It would seem so."

Sanjar nudged Faaris and slapped him on the shoulder. "I'll get out of your way and give you some room to breathe before things get crazy."

"A few deep breaths should suffice," said Faaris. "And I'm sure once I see Ariette again, I'll be as good as new. It's going to be a long day without her."

Sanjar smiled and nudged Faaris again. "I'm just teasing. Enjoy yourself tonight for once in your life, alright? I dare you. You deserve it."

Faaris frowned and smiled. "Thanks."

Sanjar grinned and threw his arm around Faaris' neck as they began walking. "Make every moment count. You only get married once. And after all, it is your last day before starting a new chapter. Savor it. Your life is about to change forever."

Faaris smiled. "So it is, and I couldn't be more ready."

"You're not the least bit nervous?" Sanjar asked, freeing Faaris from his grip. "I'm impressed. This isn't the Faaris I remember."

"Why should I be nervous?" said Faaris. "This is the day I've been waiting for nearly all my life. For once, I feel things are finally starting to go right. I couldn't be happier, in fact."

Sanjar laid his hand over his heart. "You really are in love, aren't you? Well, may I just say that your Ariette is the most beautiful girl I've ever seen. It will be my honor to escort her to you this evening. You're very fortunate. I mean you're the richest man in the world, you're the king of the greatest kingdom on Earth, and you have the most beautiful girl in the universe for your wife, and not to mention the best brother in the world," he said with a wink. "But that one's a given. I only wish that I could be so lucky someday. Perhaps, I'll have to start wishing on stars, eh?"

Faaris laughed. "You really think wishes are the reason for my fortune?"

Sanjar shrugged and stroked his chin. "What else could be?"

"I could think of a few things," Faaris smiled. "Perhaps it was just my destiny all along and wishes had nothing to do with it. I don't believe in luck."

"That's some good karma, then," said Sanjar. "You really know how to get what you want. I'm impressed. You'll have to teach me those mysterious ways of yours."

"It's no mystery, believe me." Faaris smiled.

Mehrzad folded his hands. "Come now my boys, we must get you cleaned up. The night will sneak up on us in no time."

"Of course," said Sanjar. "Oh, but first, I almost forgot. I have a wedding gift for each the bride and groom. Faaris, I'll present you with yours before we part ways until the ceremony."

Faaris smiled. "You didn't have to get me anything. How thoughtful."

Sanjar shrugged. "Think nothing of it. It cost me nothing." Sanjar reached deep into the pocket of his robe and pulled out a chain of black hair as long as a serpent, braided and tied with gold ornaments at every inch. Faaris' eyes widened. He couldn't bring himself to touch it.

"That's right," said Sanjar. "Behold, the beard of Dark Kobra. I've taken it upon myself to slay him, once and for all. At last, our kingdom will be safe."

Faaris was nearly in shock. He reached for the braid. "Sanjar, I…I don't believe this. How?"

Sanjar grinned, "It was simple, really. I stopped by a fortune-teller's tent on my way to the palace and to my surprise, Kobra himself was there. I recognized him the moment I saw his beard. There was only one other time I'd seen a beard like that, and it was that fateful night we lost our parents. Kobra was quick to recognize me as well, then again, who wouldn't? I was the king after all. We talked it over briefly and then I struck a deal. The witch was listening, and she offered to help us settle things once and for all. We put our weapons aside and sat face-to-face at the table. She placed a simple board game in front of us and stood over us holding a blade that had been freshly coated with the venom of a black mamba. We kept it very simple. Winner takes the blade, loser…tastes the blade."

"Good heavens," said Mehrzad. "How brave of you, Sanjar. What was the game, may I ask?"

"Backgammon," Sanjar said. "Kobra didn't know that I had spent nearly all twenty-six years of my life mastering it. Faaris knows."

"It's true," said Faaris. "Mother used to make us play it to settle an argument. You always complained, but I'm sure you feel differently now."

"I never thought it would save my life," said Sanjar.

Mehrzad bowed and braced Sanjar by the shoulders. "The

kingdom is truly in your debt, dear boy. You have no idea what this means."

"What does it mean?" Sanjar grinned, eyes wide with excitement.

"It means we can all sleep peacefully at night," said Mehrzad. "Praise God."

"How about, praise Sanjar," said Sanjar. He laughed and spread his arms open. "I was the one who had to get my hands dirty."

Faaris laughed to himself.

"Oh, and one more thing," said Sanjar, reaching into his pocket to draw out a handful of gold jewelry: two earrings, three rings, and a necklace. "What kind of victor would I be if I left all this gold on the dead body of a criminal? For you, Faaris. I wasn't sure how you'd feel about it, but it's yours if you want it."

"We'll share it," said Faaris. "After all, Kobra took something from both of us."

"How generous," said Sanjar. "Rings or earrings, for you?"

"Well, there are three rings and two earrings," said Faaris. "So, there are several ways we could divide it. I say whoever takes the earrings also gets the necklace, leaving the other with the three rings. Or we could split it as two rings and a necklace for one and two earrings and a ring for the other."

Sanjar scratched his chin. "It's your call, since it is my gift to you. Although, may I say I think you'll appreciate the rings," he winked.

"Why is that?" asked Faaris.

"You'll see," said Sanjar.

288

"Alright," said Faaris. "The earrings and the necklace for you, and three rings for me."

Sanjar smiled. "As you wish," he said, handing Faaris the rings.

Faaris examined them. One ring was in the shape of a serpent, meant to wrap around the entire finger, its head facing upward toward the wearer's fingernail. The second one was also a serpent, coiled more tightly in a horizontal direction. The last one was a wedding ring.

"Interesting," said Faaris.

"What?" said Sanjar, swinging the necklace around his neck and stringing the earrings through each of his ears.

"I didn't know he was married," said Faaris.

"Look again," said Sanjar.

"This one is a wedding ring," said Faaris, looking at it more closel. "A Pernian wedding ring."

"Ah, yes," said Sanjar. "That's an interesting story actually. I came to find out that it's Father's ring. Kobra stole it from him the night he killed him. Of course, he was so smooth that no one saw it."

Faaris gulped and slipped the ring onto his finger. "This one, I'll wear then, gladly. I'm not sure I can bring myself to wear the other two. I'll store them away, perhaps."

"Ah, they're just rings," said Sanjar, swatting at the air. "They don't mean anything."

"You're probably right," said Faaris. "But you know how I feel about things like that."

"We all know," Sanjar teased, his wide eyes staring at the

ground.

"Maybe someday I'll find the courage," Faaris smiled, tucking the rings into his pocket.

Parisa crept in from behind the curtain. "Faaris," she squealed. "Faaris. Guess what."

Faaris lit up as soon as he saw her. "What is it, Mushroom?"

Parisa leaped into Faaris' arms and locked her hands against the back of his neck. "Mehrzad said I can be in the wedding."

"Ah," Faaris smiled. "This day just keeps delivering more and more pleasant surprises."

"I saw Ariette's dress too," Parisa whispered. "It's the most beautiful dress I've ever seen. When I get married, I'm going to have one just like it."

"Are you, now?" Faaris grinned, bracing her by the waist. He set her onto her feet. "Listen, I have someone to introduce you to."

Parisa sighed and wiped a loose strand of hair away from her face. "Who?"

Faaris held his hand out toward Sanjar. "This is my older brother, Sanjar. He's been missing since you were a baby, and now he's returned to us."

"Oh," Parisa said, looking fearfully up at Sanjar.

"Hi there, cutie," Sanjar grinned, kneeling to meet her face-to-face. He pinched her nose and looked at her from eye-to-eye. "The last time I saw you, all you did was cry and scream my ears off."

"Well, I'm all grown up now," said Parisa, folding her hands behind her back. "I'm seven years old."

"I can see that." Sanjar grinned. "Mushroom, was it?"

Parisa giggled. "Parisa."

"Gorgeous," Sanjar said with a charming grin. "What a relief. For a second, I thought your name was actually Mushroom. I thought, what a hideous name for such a sweet little girl. You keep Faaris out of trouble, alright…Parisa?" Parisa nodded. Sanjar bowed and gave her a quick wink. "Goodbye for now, Princess. I'll see you tonight."

Razi entered the room and knelt beside Parisa. "Hey there," he said. "I believe miss Ariette needs some assistance with her dress if you want to do the honors."

Parisa gasped. "Yes."

Faaris grinned and motioned for Razi to walk with her.

"Come on," Razi said, motioning for her to follow him toward the stairs.

Mehrzad folded his hands and turned to Faaris and Sanjar. "Now, we must get the two of you ready."

Half an hour had passed, and Faaris stepped out of the bathroom, running his hands through his freshly washed hair, to find Sanjar and Mehrzad waiting for him in the hall.

"So," said Faaris, surprised to see Sanjar without the hood covering his head. His head was completely shaven. "I see you cut off all of your hair. I was wondering what you were hiding under the turban."

"Ah, it was protocol," said Sanjar, running his hand across his head. "It grew on me, what can I say."

"It's a good look for you." Faaris smiled, walking toward his chamber. "So, any advice for me? Any wisdom you can offer?"

"If you want my advice, it's like I said before," said Sanjar as they entered Faaris' chamber. "Enjoy your day, and savor the night. This happens once in a lifetime."

"He's right," said Mehrzad. "Allow yourself to enjoy the evening. Make the most of it. You deserve it."

Faaris ran his fingers through his damp hair, letting several drops of water fall onto the rug. "If I could just know that everything will be alright, I can relax. It's just...it's the fear."

Faaris reached for the first layer of his suit and stepped into it. He slipped his robe off from over his shoulders and folded it before tossing it on his bed.

"I'll admit, it's a little irrational," said Faaris. "Kobra's dead. It's impossible, but I have a strange feeling about tonight. He seems like the sort of man who would have a backup plan. I imagine he has some sort of alliance he's entrusted to carry out his plans. You can call me insane, but he said he always gets what he wants, and he wanted nothing more than for me to die. I'm afraid he might have arranged something, you know?"

Sanjar shrugged, "You're not insane. But you are clever, I must say. That's the reason you're still alive, assuming this man must have made many precious attempts at achieving your execution."

Faaris took a breath and shook his head at the ground. "Indeed, he did. I appreciate your sympathy, truly. I've been on edge in fear of my life far too many days since his first attack."

Sanjar shrugged. "Who could blame you? I mean, I'd feel the same if I knew someone was out to murder me."

Mehrzad laughed to himself. "He's absolutely right. Well spoken, Sanjar."

"Of course, I'm right," Sanjar smiled, pulling his shirt off and dropping it onto the floor. His chest, shoulders and arms were covered in dark tattoos and were more muscular than Faaris remembered.

"Good heavens," said Mehrzad. "Even in all my days of reading, I've never seen so much ink."

Faaris turned to see, taken aback at the sight of them. He crossed his arms and raised an eyebrow at Sanjar with a slight smile. "I assume this happened in Asia?"

Sanjar grinned and slid his finger across the ink on his chest. "These are the marks of a true master. They're symbols of my eternal strength and resilience, and now I shall wear them forever. They are my badges of honor, gentlemen. I wouldn't dare insult them if I were you."

"I thought your changed heart was all you needed to symbolize your journey," Faaris teased.

"So why are you wearing that piece of gold around your finger, then?" said Sanjar, pulling each of his slippers off. "Is the love in your heart not enough to prove your feelings?"

"I don't want to argue, Sanjar," said Faaris. "I was just starting to believe we'd finally outgrown that. I was only curious. Was it painful?"

Sanjar rolled his eyes. "I'm still alive, aren't I? By the time I got the first one, I had already trained my mind well enough that I felt almost nothing. The last one was like the brush of a feather. I dare say I even enjoy that kind of pain now."

Faaris nodded. "Right," he sai "So, I would assume your entire belief system has changed as well, then?"

"I'm practically a new man," said Sanjar. "It's for the better."

Mehrzad lifted a white and gold suit off Faaris' bed. "Now gentlemen, let's maintain the peace between the two of you. Especially tonight. I don't want to hear any arguing, is that understood?"

"Of course," said Faaris. "Forgive me."

"My apologies," said Sanjar with a nod. "To each his own."

Faaris looked at the suit with amazement. "I can see why you wanted to start dressing this early. There has to be at least six layers to all of that."

"It isn't much different from your coronation suit," Mehrzad reassured him.

The fabric was thick on its own and was even heavier with the jewels. Faaris was surprised to find that it wasn't as uncomfortable as he'd imagined when seeing it on the head of his father. He stood in front of a tall, narrow mirror, admiring himself. A smile came across his face.

"What do you think?" Mehrzad asked.

"It's nice," Faaris said.

"Look," said Sanjar. "Don't worry about Kobra. He wanted me dead too you know. I'll watch your back and you'll watch mine. As brothers should."

Faaris smiled and took a deep breath. "Sounds like a plan."

Sanjar smiled and rolled his eyes, spreading his arms, inviting Faaris into an embrace. Faaris hesitated but moved into his arms. Sanjar gave him a firm pat on the back as he always did.

"You bring tears to my old eyes, boys," said Mehrzad. "I never thought I'd live to see such a thing."

294

Sanjar shrugged, coming out of the embrace. "We're a team. Faaris the wit and I the strength. As it should have been all along. Besides, there are guards at every turn."

"That didn't stop him last time," said Faaris.

"True," said Sanjar, "but you didn't have me looking out for you that time. I was selfish, remember? Nothing can stop us now."

Faaris smiled and smoothed his robe over his chest. "I'm going to take your word for it, mostly because it is my wedding night after all, and I don't want to lose the whole evening to fear."

Mehrzad laughed to himself. "Good idea."

Sanjar's suit was a rich blue, with hints of gold running along the edges and through the intricate pattern of the silky fabric.

Sanjar grinned "Now, be honest," he said, moving Faaris aside so that he could see himself in the mirror. "Have I ever looked this good?"

"Perhaps it's that new heart of yours," said Faaris. "It has a way of changing a person."

"Perhaps," said Sanjar. "Although I'm almost certain it's my hair, or lack thereof. Ha."

Faaris smiled and rolled his eyes, glancing over at Mehrzad. "Some things never change."

"Improvement is all we can ask for," said Mehrzad under his breath.

Sanjar walked across the room to the door. "Well, if you'll excuse me, I'm going to go fetch the bride. I haven't given her my gift yet."

Faaris and Mehrzad exchanged surprised glances.

"How thoughtful of you, Sanjar," said Mehrzad. "I'm sure

she'll be delighted."

"I know, I know," said Sanjar not bothering to look back as he made his way out, "I'm full of surprises."

31

ARIETTE SQUEEZED THE WATER OUT of her long, silky hair as she sat on the side of the enormous pool of water, still waiting for the maid who had promised to come for her. An enormous, white silk robe spilled down from her shoulders, nearly swallowing her long, slender frame beneath it. If her imagination had its way, she could have very well been the beautiful winged creature sitting beside the stream. The bird would have almost escaped from her memory, had it not been for the robe and the bathing pool which, like the robe, was probably much bigger than it needed to be.

The bathroom was dim and tranquil, rich with the golden glow and the scent of candles that were all around. Ariette watched the flames dance across the ripples of the water as she moved her fingers across the glossy surface. Two kind, older women entered the bathroom, each wearing loving smiles.

"Come my dear," one of them said.

Ariette smiled and got to her feet, careful not to slip on the marble floors. She followed the maids back into her chamber to find a long, flowing gown laid across her bed.

"Oh," she breathed, shoulders falling.

Parisa was standing beside the bed, grinning as if trying to contain her excitement.

"I..." Ariette stuttered, clutching the robe tightly around her. "It's beautiful."

The sun was beginning to fall in the window beside the bed, casting his golden glow into the room. The delicate jewels and pearls that studded the dress glittered like fresh snow in the sunlight. In no time, Ariette found herself wearing it, standing before a tall, narrow mirror.

"So fair," one of the maids said, running her hand along Ariette's long, almost white hair. "Like an angel."

Ariette smiled as the maid fastened two long, delicate earrings into each of her ears. The dress flowed far past her feet. The fabric was soft and light against her skin. The long sleeves were sheer like the dress she'd worn before, studded with small pearls and jewels. White floral designs curled across the entire gown, reminding her of the times she'd spent in the garden. Her long hair was pulled back neatly at the front, left to fall as it always did down her back. A small jewel dropped down the middle of her forehead, making its way back into her hair in a long, delicate chain of gold.

"Have you ever seen anything more beautiful?" one of the maids said, stepping back to admire her work.

"I can't say that I have," said the other with a smile.

Parisa was smiling the whole time. "Ariette," said Parisa. "When…when I get married, I'm going to have a dress like yours."

"Are you?" Ariette smiled. "No, you'll have a better one I'm sure."

Parisa nodded.

"Well, I think your dress is lovely too," said Ariette. "Thank you for helping us tonight."

Parisa smiled. "You're welcome."

The maids smiled and made their way to the door.

"You are beautiful, my dear," one of them said. "Faaris is very fortunate."

"Do I have to leave too?" Parisa asked. "I want to stay with Ariette."

"Whatever you wish, Parisa," said one of the maids. "You may stay until Prince Sanjar comes for Miss Ariette, alright?"

"Alright." Parisa smiled.

The maids closed the doors behind them.

Parisa squealed and flopped onto the bed. "It's going to be the most magical night ever."

Ariette giggled and sat on the edge of the bed beside her. Parisa sat up and crawled onto Ariette's lap. Ariette smiled and welcomed her into her arms. With a deep breath, Ariette gazed out at the sunset. In the back of her mind, she was just waiting for Aelius to come for her.

"I want to thank you for being so kind to me," said Ariette, still staring at the sun.

Parisa sighed. "Faaris always said I was the only girl for him."

"Oh." Ariette smiled. "Well, we're very much in love. I hope you can forgive me."

Parisa smiled. "It's alright. If he has to marry someone, I'm really happy it's you."

Ariette's heart nearly liquified inside of her. She smiled and pulled one of the jewel-studded pins out of her hair. She wove it through several locks of Parisa's hair. "There. Now you don't have to wait until your wedding to feel like a princess."

Parisa smiled and touched the jewel. She wrapped her arms around Ariette's waist and buried her face into her chest. Three strong knocks came from the door. Parisa shot up.

"It's alright." Ariette smiled. "Come in."

The doors opened to reveal Sanjar, hands folded behind his back.

"Hello, ladies," he said. "I hope I'm not interrupting anything."

Ariette smiled and glanced at the sun to find that darkness had begun to settle in. "Not at all. Is it time already?"

"Ready or not?" Sanjar grinned.

"Ariette, is it time for me to go?" Parisa whispered.

Ariette nodded and stroked the side of Parisa's smooth, brown hair. "I'll see you downstairs very soon."

Parisa nodded and made her way past Sanjar.

Sanjar laughed and spread his arms as he watched her run off. "Nice to see you too, cutie."

Parisa smiled back at him and kept walking. Sanjar closed the doors behind him. He turned toward Ariette with his hands pressed over his heart and his head tilted. "Ah. What a vision you are in white," he said.

Ariette smiled and tucked her hair behind her ear, causing

one of the jewels to slip out of her hair. Sanjar slid to her side to catch it quickly before it could hit the floor. The sudden motion startled Ariette a little.

Sanjar smiled and tucked the pin back into her hair. "Careful, there. You're a clumsy little thing, aren't you?"

Ariette blushed. "I…well, I…yes."

Sanjar grinned and finished fastening the jewel into place. "How adorable."

Ariette smiled and lowered her head. Sanjar raised his chin and took each of her hands, drawing her eyes back to his. "Before we go, I have something for you."

"That's very kind of you," said Ariette. "You didn't have to…."

"Ah, it's only fair," Sanjar shrugged. "I wasn't going to bring something for Faaris and leave you out."

Sanjar grinned and pulled out the glittering purple bottle from behind his back. "A gift for the bride."

Ariette lowered her head and smiled at the ground as Sanjar laid it in her hands. A cold rush of what was left of her stardust rang throughout her body as her fingers met the smooth glass.

Arictte gulped. "It's…"

"Beautiful, isn't it?" said Sanjar.

"It is," Ariette said. "Where did you find it?"

"It's no ordinary bottle, you know," said Sanjar.

"Oh?" Ariette nearly chocked.

"This is a genie," said Sanjar. "It has the power to grant any three wishes. I suggest you choose wisely."

"Oh, I…" Ariette stuttered. "I already have all of my wishes."

Sanjar nodded and started pacing, hands folded behind his

back. "I know what you are, you know," he said.

Ariette gulped and squinted at him more closely, unable to speak.

"Faaris always spoke of his 'lucky star'…Setareh, I recall," said Sanjar. "He always said that he would have her or no one. And if I know one thing about my brother, it's that he never goes back on his word."

Ariette was still. "You may have fooled everyone else, but you have not fooled me. I know who you are."

"Oh, do you?" Sanjar said with a smile. "You've got me all figured out?"

Ariette took a deep breath and clenched her jaw, glaring into his eyes with the utmost confidence. "You're Dark Kobra."

Sanjar laughed to himself as his expression faded to a sly grin. "*Sssss*-urprise," he hissed, curling his tongue in the same snake-like way that Kobra always did. "Smart girl. Now, swear you'll say nothing to anyone, or I might just have to kill you."

"You killed your parents so you could be king, and you have wished to do the same to Faaris," said Ariette. "You used the disguise because you knew that no one would trust you to rule if they knew what kind of man you really were."

"You must think you've succeeded," said Sanjar, grinning at her. "How precious. I told you, Pigeon I always get what I want. And speaking of which, I believe I still have a third wish."

"A wish you'll never have," said Ariette. "You lied. You lied to all of us. You've deceived me and betrayed Faaris, Mehrzad, and all of Pernia. And you will never succeed."

"I already have," said Sanjar. "It's only a matter of time now.

302

The moment my wish comes true, Faaris will be dead, and I as the rightful heir will reclaim my place as king. I should thank you, really. You did all it all for me. All I have to do now is sit back and watch." His mouth curled into a grin and he laughed in a mocking way, a way that made Ariette feel sick inside. "You will return to your bottle where you will be my genie for all eternity. No power on Earth can stop me."

"You're wrong," Ariette said. "Faaris will not die tonight."

Sanjar kept laughing. "It seems you've forgotten my wish."

"Your wishes no longer exist," said Ariette. "I am no longer a genie."

She pushed her sleeves up and held out her wrists which were free of the markings.

"Impossible," Sanjar snarled.

Ariette pushed her sleeves back down and dropped her arms to her sides. "Faaris has set me free."

Sanjar looked out at the moon. "I should have known."

"You must promise me that you will not harm Faaris," said Ariette, her gentle voice shaking. "Otherwise, please believe I'll tell the guards, and you'll return to your punishment, or worse. I'm not afraid of you."

Sanjar frowned and shot his snake-like eyes back at her. "You should be," he said.

Ariette gulped.

Sanjar grinned and held his arm up for her to take it. "Come now. Wouldn't want to be late to your own wedding," he said.

Ariette glared up at him. She refused to take his arm. Instead, she hurried to the door.

Sanjar was quick to catch her by the arm and pull her roughly to his side. "Eager, are we?"

Ariette's heart started racing. Her hands grew cold and began to shake as Sanjar lead her steadily into the hall. The night had cast its darkness into every corridor, leaving only the light of the lanterns to guide them.

"I'll admit," said Sanjar, "I underestimated you. A mistake I won't be making again."

Ariette was silent, keeping her eyes on her feet.

"I should thank you, however," said Sanjar. "I wouldn't be here tonight if it weren't for you."

Ariette didn't say a word. She didn't dare to look at him, either.

"You got me thinking, you know," said Sanjar. "Who needs genies, anyway? Stars must be much more powerful. I mean, who wouldn't want unlimited wishes? With a genie, you only get three chances to get what you want. Perhaps all this time I should have been wishing on stars. It's too bad you'll be back in your bottle soon. I might have to keep you around after all."

Ariette turned her head away from him.

"Faaris is too clever," said Sanjar. "I can't believe I didn't think of this. He doesn't love you, Pigeon. He's only using you for your power. Don't be fooled."

"You're wrong," Ariette muttered. "When he kisses me tonight, I will be powerless forever. He loves me for who I am, not because of my power."

Sanjar laughed and rolled his eyes. "Do you believe everything he tells you? I'm sure he has a few more wishes up his sleeves. He's just waiting for the right moment. Trust me. He isn't who you think. He's stolen gold from a caravan, lied before the king, and stolen my throne. He's a thief, and this is just another one of his tricks to get what he wants."

"I don't believe what you say," said Ariette. "Faaris isn't like you."

"Maybe you're right," said Sanjar. "He's worse."

"There's nothing you can say that will change my mind," said Ariette. "There is no darkness in anyone that will not come to the surface sooner or later. It's only a matter of time before all of Pernia knows what you've done."

Sanjar grinned, staring forward with a cool look in his eyes and shook his head as if teasing the thought. "Three years and I've never been caught. I doubt tonight will be any different."

"Don't be so sure," said Ariette.

Sanjar slowed his walking pace and turned toward her with a wide-eyed smile. "Are you threatening me?"

Ariette gulped and clenched her jaw, glaring up into his icy eyes.

"I must say, I've never seen you like this, Pigeon," he said. "You're incredibly charming when you're angry, you know. Perhaps I'll have to make you my queen, rather than my genie. I had promised Roksana I would marry her, but what is my promise worth anyway? She should have seen it coming. What do you think about that?"

"I think you're disgusting," Ariette mumbled. "You're a coward and a snake, and I will never trust you."

"Ah, you'll change your mind," Sanjar grinned. "I'm really not so bad once you get to know me. After all, no one's perfect. Not even Faaris. At least I know I'm not perfect. That's the difference between us. I'm smart. I'm skilled beyond belief. Stronger and faster than any man you'll ever meet. And I've never lost a battle."

"Well, I believe that's about to change," said Ariette.

"Again," Sanjar teased, "you, my dear, are wrong. But don't let me destroy your precious hopes, please. The last thing everyone wants to see is a hopeless bride."

Ariette lost her balance, as she stumbled onto an unexpected set of stairs. Sanjar was quick to catch her and pull her back to her feet.

"Better be careful," said Sanjar, pulling her back closely to his side. "Might I suggest that you do us all a favor and stay off of the dancefloor tonight."

"If I live that long," said Ariette.

Sanjar laughed. "Oh, you're just like Faaris," he said. "Watching him dance, or shall I say try to dance, makes me wish I was dead. You should dance with me. I can teach you how to control that terrible balance of yours. How about it?"

"Not even in your dreams," Ariette said, turning her head away from him.

Sanjar closed his eyes with a sarcastic smile and placed his hand over his heart. "I'm hurt. Honestly. I believe this is the first time a woman has ever rejected me."

"Surely, it won't be the last," said Ariette.

Sanjar grunted, returning his gaze forward. "You won't be so brave after tonight. I guarantee it."

"Please," said Ariette, "how will you kill Faaris? You don't have a sword, and I don't have your blade any longer or your wish to grant. It's forbidden to have weapons at a wedding ceremony. Is it not?"

Sanjar grinned. "I have my ways. I've always felt an exemption from those rules. As the king I was used to always making the rules. I never followed them. This conversation will be between the two of us, do I make myself clear? Now, swear you'll say nothing of our little talk, or I may just have to kill you too."

Ariette gulped. "You wouldn't kill me. You need me."

Sanjar tapped his chin. "Actually, since you'll soon be powerless, it seems you are of no further use to me, doesn't it? The only thing you'd still be good for is being my queen."

"I will never be your queen," said Ariette.

"I take it you'd rather die then?" said Sanjar.

Ariette glared up at him. "No, but at least then I would be with Faaris forever instead of with you."

Sanjar returned her glare. "Unless you choose not to kiss him, however, I have no problem putting you back in your bottle. Surely, you'd prefer that to death."

Ariette frowned and locked her eyes once again on the ground. She wanted nothing more than to be free of his grasp, to see Faaris and tell him everything.

32

AS THEY CAME DOWN THE remaining steps, Ariette could see the tall, red curtains at the end of the hall. The moonlight cast through the tall windows and into the dim, candle-lit hallway. The sounds of string instruments began to seep through the curtains. The sound was so enchanting, Ariette was almost able to find a sense of peace.

Sanjar was unusually quiet as they approached the curtains, eerily wearing the same sly smile in his eyes as if it were set in stone. Ariette's heart was racing faster than ever, her mind even faster. No amount of deep breaths could soothe her.

Sanjar pulled the curtains back to reveal more people than Ariette had ever seen in one room before. All at once, they rose to their feet as she entered the room. They were all looking up at her with smiles, some even had tears in their eyes.

The air was cooler and crisper as the curtains closed behind her, filled with the pleasant aroma of flowers and incense. The Great Hall had completely transformed into the most beautiful scene Ariette had yet seen on Earth. The entire room was lined with white and gold candles of all shapes and sizes, twinkling like stars and filling the room, making her forget it was night. All of the chandeliers and lanterns were lit, making the room glow even more. Ariette glanced to the glass ceiling high above to see the moon and all the stars. A soft sadness pricked her heart. She wished her family could be with her for this moment.

Sanjar continued to lead her across a long, cleared pathway toward the stairwell on the right as Parisa tossed the last of her rose petals onto the carpet. Ariette gulped and glanced around, letting the beauty of the Great Hall take her mind away from all of her racing thoughts and fears. Perfectly arranged bouquets seemed to be at every glance. Silk draperies spilled from the tall ceilings like liquid gold. Two white peacocks from Faaris' sanctuary rested like live statues atop two tall white pillars at the foot of each of the two adjoining stairwells. Flowers and drapes flowed from the balcony at the top of the two stairwells, the place where Faaris had stood for his coronation. It was the highest point of the Great Hall, overlooking the entire room. The musicians were filling the room with their soft, harmonious song.

Ariette took a deep breath as Sanjar led her forward. The bitter words of his every threat were spinning through her mind. Every step forward was agony. She couldn't wait to meet Faaris at the top of the stairs and tell him everything.

"You seem a bit uneasy, Pigeon," Sanjar whispered with a grin as they came closer to the foot of the stairs.

"You promised no one would get hurt," Ariette whispered.

"I never promised anything," Sanjar snarled, still smiling. "Besides, my promise is as good as nothing. You should know that by now."

Faaris was waiting for Ariette at the foot of the stairwell on the left. He glanced across the room at her in such a way that all of their surroundings seemed to vanish. Ariette's heart was at ease as a certain strength filled her spirit. Faaris' smile was enough to ease her heart for a moment. Ariette looked at Faaris, trying to warn him with the look on her face. Faaris frowned and shook his head with a smile as if to say, 'what is it? I don't understand'. Ariette's eyes were pleading with agony. She tried to cast her eyes at Sanjar, hoping that Faaris could read her mind. Faaris looked at her, still confused.

Sanjar released her, leaving her with a long walk up the stairs by herself. She took a sigh of relief as Sanjar stepped aside. Her next challenge would be making it gracefully to the top without falling. Her balance was still unsteady. She lifted the ends of her dress and locked her focus on her feet as she took each step up. She glanced across at Faaris, who was climbing the stairs on the other side of the room. He smiled and slowed his pace to match hers. Ariette laughed to herself and returned his smile, although embarrassed. She stumbled a little as she neared the top, hoping that no one had noticed. With a deep breath, she regained her focus and managed to clear the last two steps.

As she reached top of the stairs, she met Faaris in the middle of the balcony. Faaris took her by the arms and leaned in closer to her face, stroking her wrists with his thumbs. There they were alone at the top of the balcony. As Ariette's eyes met Faaris', the hundreds of guests below them suddenly seemed to fade away.

Faaris smile faded as soon as he saw the fear in her. "Something troubles you, my love," Faaris said.

Ariette took a deep breath. "Something terrible is about to happen."

Faaris smiled at her and squeezed her hand. "Something wonderful is about to happen."

Ariette shook her head. "You're not safe tonight," she managed to whisper.

Faaris smiled. "It's alright, remember? There's no need to fear."

Ariette's heart was racing. "He's here."

Faaris gulped and shook his head. "I don't understand. It's impossible. He's dead."

Ariette bit her lip and shook her head as Mehrzad stepped forward from behind.

Ariette heard the faint hiss of a snake and glanced around to convince herself that it was only her nerves playing tricks on her. "Did you hear that?" Ariette whispered to Faaris.

Faaris shook his head. "Hear what?"

Mehrzad opened his arms wide over the crowd as the last note of the musicians' song faded. "People of Pernia," he said, bringing his voice to a powerful tone. "Greetings to all of you most respectful guests. Today is the first of October. It shall be remembered as a day of celebration of the union of our beloved King Faaris and his new queen, the lovely Ariette Setareh."

Faaris smiled and stroked her wrist again. "Ease your mind," he whispered. "Trust me."

Ariette smiled in return and released a soft sigh. She stole another glance at the moon through a window at the entrance across the room. No matter what she did, she wasn't able to settle her thoughts.

"Ariette," Faaris whispered, drawing her eyes back to his. "Focus." Ariette closed her eyes and nodded.

"The sun, the moon and the stars in heaven indeed shine brighter tonight," Mehrzad began. "We could not have wished for a more beautiful night to gather together to witness the union of this man and this woman in marriage. Although it is a day of joy and love, we are often called to remember the ones that could not be here with us tonight on such an occasion. It is my only wish that the late King Azad and Queen Soraya could be here to witness such a special moment in the life of their son and our beloved king, Faaris.

"With deepest sorrow, we mourn their loss, though all is not lost, for in eternity, love goes on, and love they had indeed. As a close friend of theirs, I know they wanted that same love and more for their own son and his bride someday. I've known Faaris since the day he was born, and not a moment has gone by that hasn't been filled with love and virtue because of him. As his caregiver and appointed vizier, it is my great honor to ordain this momentous event in his life. I have every confidence that he will be a great and noble husband as he has been a king. His beloved reigns from the heavens as a true gift from above. I don't recall ever seeing my dear Faaris happier than he has been since this young woman stumbled unexpectedly into our kingdom.

Often, it is destiny that calls two people together in mysterious ways. And on the rare occasion that such a two find each other, naturally, they ask to be married as soon as possible. And so, it is that King Faaris Arash Nima Cyrus Aghasi and Ariette Setareh present themselves before all of Pernia on this beautiful night to be united in the sacred bond of marriage."

Ariette and Faaris were lost in one another's eyes, smiling as if they had forgotten every fear.

Mehrzad cleared his throat. "Before I proceed with the vows, if anyone objects to this union, I ask that you speak now or forever hold your peace."

A small blade spiraled across every candle in the room. The flames died in the blink of an eye, leaving the room dim with only the lanterns and the moonlight casting through the glass above. The crowd gasped and began to stir. The hiss of a snake sliced through the darkness for a second time.

"Did you hear it this time?" Ariette whispered.

Faaris grabbed Ariette and held her closer to him as if to shield her. "Yes."

Another blade flew across the balcony, slicing across the throats of each of the standing guards with a deadly precision. One-by-one they melted to the ground. Ariette watched in horror and turned to Faaris with wide eyes. Faaris gulped and took a deep, nervous breath. Just as the blade flew toward Mehrzad, he ducked and fled the balcony to direct the guests to safety. No one hesitated to escape, leaving a buzzing swarm of people running for the exits. Faaris glanced to the floor below and nodded at Razi, who then grabbed Parisa and lifted her onto his shoulder to carry her to safety. Faaris pulled Ariette to the ground to avoid any flying daggers, remembering what had happened during the last siege.

"Faaris," Ariette whispered amidst the noise of the crowd. "We have to get out of here."

"Shh…" Faaris whispered, interlacing his fingers with hers, "follow me." His eyes were dead set on the exit, which was just a few steps away.

The hiss of a snake rang through the air again. A slender, black snake slithered beside Faaris, weaving his way toward his arm, curling its tongue with every hiss. Its mouth was open wide and ready to strike. As Faaris turned to see the snake's open mouth driving toward his left forearm, it dove forward and sank its fangs into his skin. Faaris screamed as the unexpected sting began to fill his blood with the black cobra's deadly venom.

Ariette turned to see the snake's mouth clenched tightly around Faaris' lower arm. "Faaris."

The tall, dark figure of Dark Kobra jumped onto the floor in front of them and summoned the snake back toward him.

"I object," said Kobra, kneeling to guide the snake back into his sleeve. The snake released its grip and slithered back toward him. Faaris moaned and clutched his bleeding arm, looking up at Kobra.

"*Sssss*-alâm," Kobra hissed as the snake slithered back into his sleeve and up through his collar, its head peeking out beside Kobra's. "I told you I wasn't finished with you."

Faaris froze with an angry glare, trying his best to keep his composure. "I must say, I've never seen a two-headed snake before."

Ariette took Faaris and held him close, trying to take his mind off of the pain. She managed a quick glance over her shoulder to find that the floor below the balcony was empty. It had only taken a few seconds for the guests to disappear—every guest except one.

"Patience, Kobra," came the voice of Roksana Estera from the floor below.

With what little strength he had, Faaris turned to see Roksana standing in the back of the room with her arms crossed and a devilish grin on her face. She blended with any other guest, dressed elegantly from head-to-toe in jewels and beads all hanging gauntly from the long dark-green dress that she wore. She began making her way toward the stairs.

Roksana smiled and lifted the ends of her dress to take her first step onto the stairs. "Kill the king but leave the genie to me."

"Oh, I already have." Kobra laughed, letting the snake slide out from his sleeve once again. "It's only a matter of time. I had some assistance this time. I didn't even have to get my hands dirty."

Roksana glanced at the snake with a smile. "Cute."

"I stole him from my last victim," said Kobra with a laugh. "The poor fool didn't stand a chance. I pity anyone who dares to pick a fight with me. I now hold the one and only black kobra, the world's deadliest snake—well second deadliest that is. You know, aside from yours truly."

Roksana laughed. "You devil."

Kobra bowed.

Mehrzad came up the stairs gripping a long, sharp sword in his hand. His face was fiercer than a lion's, full of anger and loathe as he crept toward Kobra. Kobra noticed and cut his eyes toward Mehrzad as he slipped a small dagger out of his sleeve and twirled it between his fingers. "Take another step, old man, and join your king in death."

Mehrzad gulped and froze in his tracks and held his hands up. "Kobra," he said. "You know very well that you are not welcome here. I order you to leave at once."

"Not until I get what I've come for," Kobra hissed.

Ariette took a deep, quivery breath and held Faaris' face between her hands, looking into his weary eyes. Her heart had never beat this fast. Faaris grabbed onto one of the balcony's beams and tried to get to his feet. Kobra laughed. A wave of dizziness caught Faaris the moment he rose, and he stumbled a little. He pressed his hand over his racing heart as he struggled to get a deep breath. He made his way toward Mehrzad and stole his sword.

"Faaris," Mehrzad scolded.

The moment it was secure in his hand, Faaris threw a fierce swing toward Kobra. Kobra drew a long staff from his back and broke Faaris' swing. Faaris stumbled to his feet and took another swing.

"Faaris," Mehrzad scolded again, rushing to pull him back. "Have you lost your mind? You must be still."

"No," Faaris panted, still swinging. "I have to settle this. I can take no more of it."

"Please," said Mehrzad. "For the sake of your life. Put down

316

the sword and be still."

"Not until I finish this," Faaris said with more anger in his tone than ever before.

"It's over, Faaris." Kobra laughed, dodging Faaris' swings which were getting weaker each time. "I've already won. In a matter of minutes, you'll be dead. Tell me, are you feeling weaker yet?"

"Not the slightest," Faaris grunted.

"If you were wise, you'd listen to the old man and surrender now," Kobra hissed with a smile in his eyes. "Or by all means keep fighting and die sooner. A snake like this only takes twenty minutes to kill. You can't win anyway. Your skills are no match for mine."

Kobra made a quick nod to Roksana, who scurried toward Ariette. Roksana slipped a small dagger out of the side of her shoe and grabbed Ariette, holding the dagger across her throat. "Hold still, angel, unless you wish to die too."

"Faaris," Ariette cried. Her heart was beating faster with every second. She couldn't take her eyes off Faaris.

As Faaris turned toward Ariette, another wave of dizziness swept over him and he dropped to his knees, coughing and struggling for breath.

"Faaris," Ariette cried again, a bitter tear slipping from her eye. She wanted nothing but to free herself of Roksana but couldn't bring herself to even flinch with the blade only millimeters from her throat.

Kobra laughed and tucked his staff away, shuffling his feet toward Ariette. "Now as for you, Genie. You've disobeyed me.

It seems to me that I have no choice but to put you back inside your bottle." Kobra drew the bottle out of his pocket.

Ariette gasped as another tear slipped from her eye. All this time she was sure it had been in her possesion.

Kobra laughed. "Surrender or die. It's either the bottle or death." Roksana gripped the blade more. Ariette held her breath.

A flaming spark of stardust flickered from above. Ariette recognized the sound and glanced above to find a shooting star, flying toward the palace. In a matter of seconds, the star crashed through the glass ceiling and onto the floor below the balcony. Ariette drew in a much-needed deep breath as she watched the star transform into Aelius, who lifted himself into the air and flew toward the balcony. Spirals of smoke and stardust faded softly around his human-like form, leaving him dressed in the same Pernian-style suit as before. His silvery eyes burned with a sense of vengeance. Mehrzad, Faaris, and even Kobra froze in amazement as the strange, glowing creature landed in a cloud of stardust on the ground in front of them. Aelius crossed his arms and whirled toward Ariette.

"Ariette," he scolded. "Time to go."

"No," Ariette cried, another tear falling from her eye. "I won't leave him this way."

Aelius glanced to see Roksana from the corner of his eye. As he took a closer look, his eyes widened with shock. "You? You're... alive?"

Roksana grinned. "Aelius. It's been at least a thousand years since I've seen you. You're looking well. And of course, I'm alive, you fool. This is Earth not a black hole."

"So," Aelius scolded, crossing his arms. "Got everything you ever wanted?"

Roksana tightened her grip on the blade and glared at him. "Almost."

"You thought you could stay here and keep all of your stardust, didn't you?" said Aelius. "You must be disappointed."

"Why should I be?" said Roksana. "All I need is a simple trade, and it will all be mine once again. I'm only a wish away. Now, it's time to put the genie back where she belongs."

Roksana released her grip on Ariette and shoved her into Kobra's strong grip.

"Ariette," Faaris panted from the floor, struggling to lift his head. "Go with your brother. It's alright."

"No," Ariette cried, another tear sliding down her cheek. "I won't leave you this way."

Aelius flew in front of Ariette and pointed at Kobra. "Stay away from my sister. If it's stardust you want, how about a trade? I'll give you some of mine, and we'll be on our way. That is what you want, isn't it?"

Roksana lowered her eyebrows and crossed her arms. "You're bluffing."

Aelius crossed his arms and shook his head. "No. I'm serious. I have plenty of it. My sister doesn't even have enough left to get herself back home. I doubt she even has enough for one more wish."

Roksana grinned. "You strike a tempting bargain, Aelius," she said. "I accept."

"Excellent," said Aelius. "Now release her, and it shall be

yours."

Kobra hesitated, then removed his arms from around Ariette.

"Now," said Roksana. "The stardust."

Aelius closed his eyes and made a small blorba.

"Aelius," Ariette cried, grabbing his arm from behind. "No. Please. You don't have to do this. She can have mine. I wish to stay on Earth anyway."

"You don't have enough, Ariette," Aelius scolded, swinging his arm away from her grip. "You'll fade away without it."

When the blorba had reached its full brightness, Aelius passed it to Roksana, who was eager to welcome it. The moment it met her hands, it flooded her body and returned her long-forgotten glow to her, leaving Aelius' glow slightly dimmer.

"Alright," said Aelius. "You have what you want, now let us go in peace. Come, Ariette."

Ariette closed her eyes. "Wait."

"Ariette," said Faaris. "Go. It's alright. Without me, there's nothing for you here. You'll be safer this way."

Ariette bit her lip and shook her head, crawling toward Faaris. She lifted his limp head onto her lap and stroked the side of his face. "I can't leave you."

Faaris smiled and touched her hand. "It's alright. Wherever you go, I will be where you are," he whispered.

A tear slid down Ariette's cheek. "No," she whispered.

"Now, my love, before I go," Faaris said, his eyes beginning the fall shut, "all I ask is for one last thing."

"Anything," Ariette said, shaking her head.

"My love...my life," Faaris breathed, with the last of his breath, "on this beautiful night. I...wish...for you...to save my life."

Ariette took a deep, shaky breath and closed her eyes, drawing every last spark of stardust she could manage from within her until a blorba appeared between her shaking hands. The feeling was different this time. It was as if a part of her died, but a part of her suddenly felt so alive all at one.

"Ariette," Aelius scolded. "You have no stardust left. You can't afford it. Humans die all the time. That's life. Now, let's go home so you can recover."

Ariette turned her head toward Aelius, the blorba burning in her hands. "But I love him."

"Ariette," Aelius said, "I'm warning you."

Ariette looked down at Faaris. His eyes were beginning to fall shut and he was quickly losing consciousness. She let the blorba burst, thousands of specks of stardust falling over Faaris' face as his eyes closed. Ariette felt a sudden weakness as the stardust left her body. Her glow faded and she crumbled to her hands and knees on the floor beside Faaris.

Kobra grinned. "Aww, too late, Pigeon. What a tragedy." He nodded quickly at Roksana and turned to leave. "Come now, my queen. Our work here is done."

Roksana laughed under her breath and turned to follow Kobra out. "Life's just not fair, is it?"

Aelius looked at Ariette. He shook his head and swallowed hard, watching her on the verge of fading out. "I...I tried to warn you, Ariette."

Ariette closed her eyes and took a deep breath. "I'm...I'm fine."

"No," said Aelius. "You're weak. I'll have to carry you home, now."

Aelius walked to Ariette's side and took her by the arm to drag her to her feet. "Alright," he said, "you've said your goodbyes."

"Wait," Ariette cried, trying to free herself from Aelius' hands.

"No, Ariette," said Aelius. "That's enough. We're going home."

Ariette panicked as Aelius pulled her away from Faaris. Another tear slipped from her eye. "I have to say goodbye."

Aelius frowned and took a deep breath. He released her. "Fine. Quickly. And then we leave."

Ariette turned toward him and nodded before rushing to Faaris' side.

Faaris' eyes began to open, and life began to return to his body. He took a big breath as another cool gust of wind washed over him and awoke, still feeling weak. He glanced down at his arm. The bleeding had stopped, and the stardust had washed all of the poison from his veins, leaving only the scar of the snake's fangs carved into his skin. He struggled to push himself up into a sitting position, to find Ariette sitting beside him.

"Faaris," Ariette gasped and wrapped her arms around him. "You're alive."

"Because of you," Faaris whispered into her ear, laying his hand around the back of her head and stroking her hair.

"I never wish to leave you again," Ariette whispered, holding him.

Faaris released her and let his hands slide down her arms and into his. They rose to their feet together, holding on to one another's hands.

Faaris looked up at Aelius. "Please," he begged. "Is there any way she can stay? You care about her, don't you?"

"Of course I do," said Aelius, kicking at the ground. "It's just… she'll die if she stays here any longer."

Faaris frowned at him. "She'll live if she becomes human."

Aelius made a quick sweeping motion with his arms. "No. We had a deal. She's coming with me. End of story. No more negotiations. She doesn't belong here, and she never will. She's not safe here, and I think you and I both know that. If you truly love her, you should want what's best for her."

Faaris sighed and looked at Ariette, stroking the side of her cheek with his finger. "Fine."

Ariette bit her lip and shook her head.

Faaris looked into Ariette's eyes. "He's right. You're not safe here, Ariette. I love you more than anything…and so I…I must let you go."

"I don't want to go," said Ariette turning toward Aelius. "Aelius, please. If you care about me, you'll let me stay."

Aelius frowned. "Is this really what you want, Ariette? A world of pain and sorrow and…death?"

Ariette looked back at Faaris and placed her hand on his cheek. "You forgot love. That is the reason I came, and it is the reason I choose to stay."

"No," said Aelius. "I forbid it. We had a deal."

"He's right," said Faaris.

Ariette looked at Faaris. "But…"

Faaris gulped and stroked her hair. "It's alright, Ariette. Love is patient. I've waited this long to have you. I can surely wait a little longer."

Ariette shook her head as tears began to fill her eyes. "Stars don't go on after this life, remember? If I leave, I'm afraid this is goodbye forever."

Tears began to swell in Faaris' eyes and he took her into a tight hug. "Now that I've found you, I don't know how I'm going to live without you."

Ariette released him and took his hands, looking into his kind, golden eyes. "I will always be a wish away, my beloved stargazer."

"Ariette," Aelius said. "Let's go. We're losing stardust with every minute."

Ariette was fighting to keep her tears from falling. "Faaris,"she said in a shaky voice. "I'm sorry for causing you any pain."

Faaris shook his head. "No. You've saved my life. Never feel the need to apologize. I wouldn't undo a single moment that I've spent with you."

Ariette's expression softened. "At least we got to have this adventure together. I got the chance to meet you face-to-face. I got to touch you, hold you. At least now I will no longer wonder. Soon, it will all seem like a dream."

Tears were swelling in Faaris'eyes, his throat stinging from trying to hold them back.

Ariette closed her eyes and lowered her head. "Goodbye, Faaris."

Faaris swallowed hard and drew her eyes back to his, struggling to keep his tears from falling. He studied her face to as if to etch it into his memory. "Goodbye, my love. My Setareh. My Ariette."

Faaris took Ariette's face between his hands and kissed her

forehead. They each closed their eyes and rested their foreheads against one another's, their noses brushing and their lips almost touching. Ariette took a deep, quivery sigh, wanting nothing more than to kiss him and stay with him forever.

"Kiss me, Faaris," she whispered, voice still shaking.

Faaris opened his eyes and looked into hers. "Believe me, I want nothing more," he whispered, "but…"

Kobra crept up the stairs behind Faaris, with a dagger in his hand. Ariette noticed out of the corner of her eye.

"Faaris," Ariette cried, pulling him aside just before Kobra could strike.

Faaris gasped and turned to find Kobra charging toward him. He glanced to his side and noticed his sword laying almost an arm's length from his grasp. With a deep breath, he dove toward it and secured it in his hand. Just as Kobra threw his first strike, Faaris managed to block the swing and began to defend himself as Kobra continued to strike.

"I've never lost a battle," Kobra hissed, "and I'm not about to lose again."

"I wouldn't be so sure," Faaris grunted, swinging fiercely at Kobra's sword.

Aelius grabbed Ariette and pulled her aside. "You should thank your lucky stars that he's alive, Ariette. Let's go."

"Wait," Ariette said.

"No," said Aelius. "I've had enough of your foolishness."

Ariette pulled herself out of Aelius' grasp with all of her strength and ran toward Kobra.

"Ariette," Faaris scolded, "stay away."

"No!" Ariette cried, leaping onto Kobra's back. "This man is not who he says he is."

"Aargh!" Kobra cried, squirming to try to get her off of his back. "Not now, Pigeon."

Ariette locked her arm around his neck and pulled the black mask off of his head, revealing the sweat-drenched face of Sanjar.

Sanjar grunted. "You wicked little…"

Faaris nearly lost his breath and stopped fighting. "Sanjar?"

A bright light broke through the broken glass above and suddenly everyone in the room was still, watching in awe as the entire Great Hall filled with light. A pair of enormous white wings burst through the remaining glass and the Sima Bird swooped in from above whipping the air around as if she'd brought a raging storm with her. She made her way around the Great Hall and toward Ariette and Faaris as if to defend them.

Ariette lit up from the inside. "It's you," she breathed watching the bird glide through the air.

Faaris' eyes widened, and a childlike smile spread across his face. "Will wonders never cease?"

Sanjar frowned, turning to see the enourmous heavenly creature flying over Ariette and Faaris' heads. He grinned and drew a blade from his sleeve. Just before the bird could land on top of Faaris' head, Sanjar threw the blade toward the bird.

"No," Ariette cried, watching in horror as the blade plunged into the heart of the Sima bird.

The bird let out a resounding cry as she fell to the ground below the balcony, her wings floating behind her as if she's fallen from the sun once again.

"Sanjar," Faaris cried, turning to Sanjar in horror, "what have you done."

"I'm the king," Sanjar roared, pointing toward his chest. "That stupid legend can die too."

"Have you forgotten the warning?" said Faaris.

"You think I actually listened to those ridiculous stories?" Sanjar smirked. "What warning?"

"The Curse of the Sima Bird," said Faaris. "Whoever kills her is fated to die."

Sanjar turned as pale as the moon. He looked down at his own hands and then back up at Faaris with a raging anger in his snake-like eyes. His sweat had smudged the black charcoal down from his eyes making him look as black-hearted on the outside as he was within. Sanjar drew another sword and swung it toward Faaris. "If I die, then you can die too. I never lose."

"You already have," Faaris said, slashing his sword against Sanjar's. "Legend has it."

"We'll see about that," Sanjar snarled, wiping sweat across his face. "Do you honestly think I'll die because of a stupid legend? Oh wait, you probably do. You believed that wishing on a star could make all of your little dreams come true, didn't you?"

"I think you're foolish for believing that you won't die," said Faaris. "You're afraid of the truth, and so you've refused to accept it and now your making jokes like you always do when you're afraid. If I may say so, it's a terrible mistake."

"What do *you* know?" Sanjar said, rolling his eyes and taking another hard swing toward Faaris.

"Perhaps more than you think," Faaris grunted, dodging the

swing. "Tell me, have you been Dark Kobra all this time?"

Sanjar grinned. "The one and only."

"So, you were Dark Kobra on the tower last night?" said Faaris.

"You're ridiculous, Faaris," said Sanjar. "Who else could match my skills?"

"You were Dark Kobra holding us captive in the bazaar that night," said Faaris. He paused and glared up at Sanjar. "And you were Dark Kobra on the night of the siege…"

Sanjar gulped and raised his chin.

Faaris took a deep breath and looked solemnly up at Sanjar. "You killed our parents so you could be king."

"Exactly," Sanjar said, twirling his small blade into his belt and drawing out a longer, sharper one from his back, "and I have no problem killing you too."

Sanjar thrust the sword toward Faaris' chest. Faaris grabbed onto the balcony's ledge and swung himself onto the stairwell beside it. His heart was racing, and his mind was still grappling with the fact that he'd just survived the jump. Still surprised at himself, Faaris looked down at the sword in his hand.

Mehrzad stepped in, wearing his worst scolding look. "Sanjar," he said, stepping forward. "Is this true?"

"How else was I going to get what I wanted?" said Sanjar creeping toward Faaris.

"You threatened to kill me that night if I said a word about your plan," said Faaris, making his way up the steps. "I'll never forget it. It was the moment I knew things were never going to be the same—the moment I knew I could never trust you again."

Sanjar grinned. "It doesn't matter now. I always win. This

time is no exception."

"You're wrong," said Faaris. "Whether I die or not, you will never be king. Not in a thousand years."

Sanjar rolled his eyes. "That's what you think."

He pulled the bottle out of his pocket and bit the lid off, spitting it onto the ground. "Genie, I order you, hear my plea. Meet your fate for disobeying me. Return to your bottle where you belong, and sing to me your magic song. With this wish, I seal your destiny as my genie for eternity."

Ariette was still as his words dissolved into the air.

Sanjar stared at her. "Now, genie. What are you waiting for? Grant my wish."

Ariette walked toward him. "I am no longer a genie. I am no longer your prisoner. You can't control me anymore. My stardust is mine to choose what I will do with it." She took a deep breath and grabbed the bottle from Sanjar's hand and held it high above her head. Tears of anger filled her eyes as she looked at Sanjar. "And I choose to be free."

With a deep breath, she threw the bottle to the ground, shattering it into a thousand pieces of shiny purple glass.

"No." Roksana gasped. "You stupid girl. What have you done?"

Mehrzad came up behind Sanjar while he was distracted and locked his hands behind his back with two iron shackles.

Sanjar hissed, trying to slither out of Mehrzad's strong grip. "Let go of me."

The moment the bottle shattered, Roksana, Aelius, and Ariette began to fade into thin air, their bodies returning to their glittering star form.

Faaris gasped running to take Ariette's fading hands. "Ariette. No. Please. Don't leave me."

"I'm sorry," Ariette whispered as her face began to fade into its old glowing shade of purple.

Faaris took a deep breath and took her face into his hands. A familiar rush of stardust flooded Ariette's body rising up from her toes and filling her body with stardust. She glanced down and watched with sorrow as she began to return to her original form. Faaris pulled her toward him, drawing her into a kiss. Ariette's eyes fell shut as their lips met and she felt herself dissolve into a thousand specks of stardust. All at once, she, Aelius, and Roksana faded away and floated up into the starry sky, the same way that they had flown to Earth.

Ariette and Faaris' lips parted as she disappeared. Faaris opened his eyes to find her gone, watching as several sparks of her stardust fell to his feet. He brought his fingertips to his lips to touch the last of the soft, electric stardust that still lingered on them. He raised his face up to the night sky, watching her fly away. "I love you."

Sanjar laughed, watching Faaris crumble to his knees in sorrow. "Looks like neither one of us gets what we want."

Faaris sank to his knees and lowered his forehead to the ground as tears began to fill his eyes.

"Oh, Faaris," Mehrzad sighed.

"Leave me alone," said Faaris.

"Faaris, my boy," Mehrzad said.

"Go," Faaris sobbed, looking up at them with red, wet eyes, tears sliding down his face. "All of you."

Mehrzad bowed and dragged Sanjar away to prison, where he would await his death.

"I loathe you, rat," Sanjar hissed as Mehrzad pulled him through the curtains. "I hope you die of heartbreak."

MEHRZAD WALKED INTO THE EMPTY GREAT HALL as sunlight began to fill the windows and shine down through the broken glass above. Faaris was frozen in the same position as when he'd left him. Mehrzad knelt beside Faaris and drew him to his feet.

"Have strength, my boy," said Mehrzad, his voice echoing through the empty Great Hall.

Faaris lifted his head to find Mehrzad kneeling beside him.

"Sanjar's been captured, and you are alive," said Mehrzad, bracing Faaris by the shoulders. "All is well."

"All is not well," Faaris mumbled, looking up at Mehrzad.

Mehrzad sighed and closed his eyes. "Now, Faaris. A love come and lost is best left alone. If it is truly a piece of your heart that she has, she will find a way to return it to you. Besides, you're so young. I would hate to see you give up so quickly."

"Love has forsaken me, Mehrzad," Faaris mumbled. "I've lost everything. I fear my heart will never heal now. It's…it's too much. I would have been better off dead if I would have known I was going to lose her anyway. I will surely never love again."

"Fear not, Faaris," said Mehrzad. "All is not lost. Now, I understand your sorrow, but all wounds will heal with time. You have your whole life ahead of you and an entire kingdom depending on you to lead them forward. I know your father would have wanted you to be strong, to rise and lead your people forward. Great kings must make sacrifices on behalf of their kingdom."

Faaris looked up at Mehrzad, eyes still damp.

Mehrzad sighed and took Faaris by the shoulder. "Life goes on, my boy. Everything will be alright in time. I promise. Now, come with me. We have a great deal of business to discuss regarding your future."

Faaris smiled and looked back at the ground.

"I know it may seem a bit soon," said Mehrzad. "But you are still required to marry, as I'm sure you're aware. It is the law, and it is what's best for the kingdom."

"I know," said Faaris. "I just…I need a moment alone. To clear my head before I make any decisions."

As Faaris turned to escape to his sanctuary, Mehrzad bowed and cleared his throat. "A moment, Faaris. Not an entire month."

Faaris smiled back at him. "You know me too well. Give me a week."

"Three days," Mehrzad said.

"My birthday is on the ninth," said Faaris. "That's seven days aside from this one. Until then, I ask to be left alone, please. I will see you all at the celebration. Notify everyone."

Mehrzad sighed and closed his eyes. "But Faaris…"

"That's an order," said Faaris with a straight face.

Mehrzad bowed. "Yes, Your Highness."

33

S AY SOMETHING, ARIETTE," SAID
Aelius.

Ariette couldn't look at him. Her heart was even emptier now than it was before. The cold, dark space that she never wanted to see again was all around her as if she had never left, as if nothing had changed.

"Look at you, star," said Aelius, trying to sound hopeful. "You're glowing. You're brighter than ever before. And now so is the Lux. We're brilliant."

"Then tell me why I feel so dark inside," Ariette said.

"Things are better this way, Ariette," said Aelius. "Trust me. This is the way it's meant to be. I told you, you never should have left."

Ariette hugged her knees. "I have finally found true love and then had it taken away from me faster than the speed of light. Tell me how I can ever be truly happy now?"

Aelius lowered his head.

Roksana glared at Ariette from across the sky. "Well, now no one's happy, and it's all because of you. I could have been the Queen of Pernia. It's a shame that humans are fools. Sanjar promised me everything I had ever wanted, and I was just one wish away… if he hadn't gotten himself cursed."

"We are no different," said Ariette. "I was a fool for thinking things would be better on Earth."

"You two should thank me for saving you," said Aelius. "At last, our world is in harmony…and more importantly, my world finally makes sense again."

"You don't know what it's like to love," said Ariette. "If you understood, you would allow me to return to Earth."

Aelius looked at her with a certain concern. Roksana rolled her eyes. "I'm going back."

"No," said Aelius. "You don't have enough stardust to even get halfway there anyway. Believe me, I made sure of that. You're stuck here until the end of time."

Roksana crossed her arms and tilted her head with a charming smile. "You think I'm going to let that stop me?"

"You've caused enough trouble, Roksana," said Aelius. "The last thing those poor humans need is more of your ridiculous games. You're staying right here, where you belong, both of you. You'll die if you try to leave without my help. Consider yourselves warned. End of story."

Ariette closed her eyes. "Aelius."

"End of story," said Aelius.

Wishes were still floating up as they always did. Ariette watched them pass over her head, trying not to let her tears fall.

"Aelius," Ariette said. Aelius turned toward her, still frowning. "I've done everything you've asked," said Ariette. "I have come home. Since I will never see Faaris again, will you at least allow me to hear his wishes?"

Aelius closed his eyes, resting for a moment in the arid stillness.

"Please," Ariette whispered, on the brink of tears.

Aelius opened his eyes and took a deep breath. "Fair enough."

Ariette smiled as he opened the portal with a wave of his hand. The moment it opened, the wish made its way softly into Ariette's hands.

FAARIS RESTED HIS ELBOWS OVER THE LEDGE of the tower in the same way that he always did when he spoke to her. The air was still, and the moon was full and bright. The Lux was more brilliant than it had ever been before and so was Ariette.

Faaris took a deep breath and turned to the chart at his feet. He knelt and touched the word 'Setareh' that he'd etched into the marble several years ago. He gulped and grabbed a golden stone that was on the floor beside him. With one stroke, he scratched a line across the letters. Above them, he began to carve an 'A', followed by an 'r', and then an 'i' until he'd finished spelling 'Ariette'. He brushed the golden dust away and rose to his feet, looking at her name. Faaris walked toward the ledge of the tower and returned to his usual position. A soft breeze caught his hair this time as he looked up at Ariette.

"My love, my light, by day, by night. I fear I'll never make things right. My only wish, my only plea, is for you to stay on Earth with me. I die inside with every breath. Each moment without you is worse than death. I wish for your happiness, my beloved star. Wherever you go, I will be where you are. Don't spend your life in sorrow like me. Do whatever it takes to be free. It didn't stop you then, and it won't stop you now. I believe there is still a way, somehow."

ARIETTE CLOSED HER EYES AND TOOK A DEEP breath as the last of Faaris' words vanished into the dark, empty space. Aelius glanced toward her and then away. Ariette was fighting back tears inside, clenching her jaw firmly. She glanced at Aelius just as he turned away from her.

"My love, how can you do this to me?" she whispered, forming a new wish. "You know I'd do anything to be free. To hear your voice and not see your face is worse than even the worst of fates. I, too, would rather fade away, than be without you another day. A life of sorrow, my life will be, until the day I am truly free. But don't let your sorrow darken your life. I wish for your happiness despite your strife."

FAARIS SIGHED AND CLOSED HIS EYES AS Ariette's words floated past his ears.

"Here, at least you'll have my words," said Faaris. "Here is the wish you never heard: My love, my life I call to thee, to spare a wish to set you free. With all my heart and all my life, I wish to have the world made right. This broken land has failed to see, it's far from what it used to be. The king has turned our days to night and left the kingdom far from sight. He reigns for power and lives for greed. It's his own strength that is his king. So, Setareh, please with all your light, I wish to have your ears tonight. It is a change of fate I seek, to free us from our misery. I wish for the truth to be revealed, so that our kingdom can be healed. But even more it is my plea, for you to be on Earth with me. I love you more than you'll ever know. I cannot bear to let you go. My greatest wish will always be that you, my love, are truly free."

ARIETTE SMILED, UNABLE TO STOP HER TEARS from falling, "It seems to me that there was no need. Your unheard wish has come true indeed. Sanjar has met his rightful fate and has been cursed because of hate. You have found your rightful home and claimed, at last, your rightful throne. Has the truth not been revealed? Has your kingdom not at last been healed?"

FAARIS SMILED AND SHOOK HIS HEAD. "BUT MY wish is not at all complete, and I fear that it will never be. More than all the things on Earth, that will fade to dust with time, I wish to save your perfect heart and keep it safe with mine."

ARIETTE TOOK A DEEP BREATH AND WATCHED the words dissolve into stardust and slip through her fingers. She caught Aelius looking at her again and decided not to send a reply until the next night.

FAARIS DRIFTED TO SLEEP ON THE BALCONY
until the sunrise peaked in the horizon and concealed Ariette
from his sight. Another day of moping in solitude had passed
him by.

"This has to be worse than before," he said to himself. "At least
then I had hope."

In the earliest hours of morning, when the palace was quiet
and lifeless, Faaris slipped away from his chamber only to steal
a pot of tea from the kitchen and get a breath of fresh air. On
his way back, he stopped by the menagerie to feed the birds, but
didn't stay with them as he usually did. Not even their company
was enough to console him. In fact, seeing them only reminded
him of his pain.

Once inside his chamber again, he set the teapot on his
desk and poured the steaming golden liquid into a small teacup.
He took a deep breath as the comforting scent of orange and
cinnamon filled his room. He carried the teacup out onto the
balcony to watch the sun climb to its greatest height and then
fall back beneath the horizon, giving way for the moon and the
precious stars.

Faaris sighed and gazed up at Ariette. "Forgive me, but I can't
forget my sorrow. I dread the hour the sun rises tomorrow. Each
day shall be as the one before, until I feel my heart no more.
It grows colder now, with every second, truly heartache is life's
deadliest weapon."

ARIETTE SIGHED. "I DO NOT WISH FOR YOU TO DIE. You must not let your life go by. Faaris, please save yourself. Such sorrow is not good for your health. I will not speak to you again, until you find your strength within. I challenge you to face the day, to think not of your heart that aches."

"FINE. MY LOVE, YOU SEE ME THROUGH," FAARIS said with a smile. "I'll collect myself if you wish me to. But please do not stop answering me. That would be worse than anything."

"FAARIS, HAVE YOU GIVEN UP?" ARIETTE ASKED. "IS the distance stronger than our love?"

"Of course, it's not, but my heart is sore," said Faaris. "I cannot take this anymore."

"Do not fear, you'd always say," said Ariette. "I still believe there is a way."

"A miracle it would take, for sure," said Faaris. "I can't imagine another cure."

"Do not lose hope, it's all we have," said Ariette. "This really isn't all so bad."

"Tell me, love, how is it not?" Faaris laughed. "Please don't tell me you forgot. The years before we spent apart. The pain inside your lonely heart."

"But then the days we were together," said Ariette. "I can't imagine what could be better. They would not have come without my risk, if it wasn't for your selfless wish."

"My wish was not selfless, Ariette," said Faaris. "But quite selfish, did you forget?"

Ariette laughed to herself. "Right you are. It was indeed. But it was for you and also for me."

"So, I'll wish again," said Faaris. "What should stop me? Even if we must repeat our history? In a second, I'd live it all again, if it means I'll have you in the end."

"No, you do not understand," said Ariette. "I cannot leave, it has been banned. Besides I'm sure I'll die for trying. I do not have enough stardust for flying."

"I'll think, and then I'll think some more," said Faaris. "There is a way, of that I'm sure."

"I hope you're right, but who really knows?" said Ariette. "This is our fate, and so it goes. We were star-crossed from the day we met. The hopeless Faaris and Ariette."

"Don't say such things," said Faaris. "They are not true. Hope is not lost for me or you. What hope did we have in the beginning? Do not believe our love is ending."

34

HREE LOUD KNOCKS ON THE
door startled Faaris.

"Faaris," Mehrzad called, still knocking on the door.

"I'm coming," said Faaris.

"Faaris," Mehrzad said the moment the door opened. "I'm sorry to trouble you so soon, but there is something important we must discuss. It's urgent."

Faaris joined him in the hall, looking concerned. "What is it?"

"Why don't we discuss it over breakfast, my boy?" said Mehrzad. "You haven't eaten in three days."

Faaris smiled. "I have no appetite, Mehrzad."

Mehrzad sighed and laid his hand over Faaris' shoulder. "At least come for a walk with me. It will be good for you to get out for a while."

Faaris smiled. "You're probably right."

"Excellent," said Mehrzad, nodding for Faaris to follow him out. Faaris sighed and closed the door behind them. They were silent for several steps.

"Are you feeling any better?" Mehrzad asked. Faaris shook his head. "Time is all you need," Mehrzad said.

"A lifetime, perhaps," Faaris mumbled.

"Your friends have missed you," said Mehrzad. "Parisa tells me that Razi isn't quite the storyteller that you are."

Faaris smiled at the ground. "One of these days she'll have to understand that I'm only human. I can't be strong all the time."

Mehrzad nodded and folded his hands. "As I said, these things will pass with time."

Faaris sighed. "Not this one," he said. "I'll never be the same again."

"At least try to overcome this," said Mehrzad. "Please. If you can't do it for yourself, think of the kingdom."

Faaris rolled his eyes and nodded. "You know my weakness."

Mehrzad stopped walking for a moment and crossed his arms, looking into Faaris' eyes. "I know your strength."

When they reached the lowest level of the palace, they walked out onto a large patio, which was still decorated for the wedding with candles and flowers all lining a big rectangular pool at the center of the open space. They sat at a small wooden table overlooking the pool. The sky was a soft lavender, tinting the waters of the pool, which were still and tranquil. The air was still and cool as it always was at this hour of the morning. Servants brought a tea tray along with a tray of flatbreads, fruit jams, honey, walnuts, eggs, cucumbers, cherry tomatoes, and grapes.

"Now," said Mehrzad, pouring sweet-smelling chai tea into each of the teacups, "what I want to discuss is in regard to not only your future, but also the future of the kingdom."

Faaris nodded. "Of course," he said, raising his teacup to his mouth to take a sip. "What is it?"

"Well," said Mehrzad. "You are still expected to marry. Pernia must have a queen."

Faaris' heart nearly stopped. He closed his eyes at the thought as the steaming hot tea slid down his throat.

Mehrzad took a deep breath, seeing the intensity in Faaris' face. "Faaris," he said. "Now, listen to me."

Faaris shook his head, staring at the floor. His blood was boiling inside of him. His thoughts were racing faster than ever. "No," he said.

Mehrzad sighed and set his teacup onto the table. Faaris frowned and looked up at Mehrzad, on the verge of tears. "How dare you come to me in such a time and tell me this. I'd rather die."

Mehrzad sighed. "Faaris," he said.

"I'll die, Mehrzad," said Faaris slamming his teacup onto the table. "I assure you."

"Now, Faaris, be reasonable," said Mehrzad.

Faaris took a deep breath as the strongest anger filled his soul. He couldn't contain it anymore.

"For the kingdom," Mehrzad said. Faaris ran his hand across his mouth and onto his chin, twisting the hairs on it. "Think of the people," said Mehrzad. "All great kings must make sacrifices."

Faaris closed his eyes and clenched his jaw. A small tear slid down his cheek.

"Faaris," Mehrzad said.

Faaris overturned the table, then turned toward the door from which they'd come. The metal trays slammed against the stone floor as the contents spilled onto the ground.

"Faaris," Mehrzad called, grabbing Faaris firmly by the arm.

Faaris forced himself free and continued walking. His heart was pounding, and his entire body was pulsing with fury.

"Faaris," Mehrzad called again, starting after him.

Faaris slammed the door before Mehrzad could reach him. By the time Mehrzad entered the hall, Faaris was already out of sight.

35

AS THE SEVENTH DAY OF FAARIS' solitude came closer, Ariette began to feel the pain in his heart. She found herself no longer able to be strong. Even her glow began to fade.

Aelius floated to her side and touched her shoulder. "Ariette," he said. Ariette turned, trying to hide the emptiness that was inside of her. "You must forget your sadness," said Aelius. "It's beginning to affect your brightness. You've faded a shade with every passing day. Don't think I haven't noticed."

Ariette rolled her eyes and hugged herself. "I can't overcome such sadness, Aelius. I've tried, but I... I can't. My heart is emptier with every orbit."

"Ariette," said Aelius, taking her by the shoulders. "You're stronger than this."

A small tear of stardust slid down her cheek. "I am not. I...I am nothing."

Aelius shook his head. "That's not true, star. If you weren't strong, you wouldn't have risked your life to save your human. I..." He sighed. "Not even I could have done that." Ariette turned toward him, a sudden spark of light in her eyes. Aelius sighed and closed his eyes. "I was wrong, Ariette." Ariette noticed the pain those words had caused him by the look in his eyes. They were the three words she thought he would never say until the end of time. "I was wrong about you," said Aelius, "and I was wrong about love. If it's strong enough to steal a star's brightness so quickly, I don't know of anything that could possibly be more powerful. Do you not see that it's killing you slowly?"

Ariette gulped and looked down at her hands. Until now, she hadn't noticed the drastic loss of brightness. She hadn't even felt it. She felt nothing, in fact, nothing but numb.

"I'm worried about you, Ariette," said Aelius. "What can I do to bring your brightness back?"

Ariette closed her eyes and turned away from him. "I believe you and I both know my answer to that."

Aelius sighed and closed his eyes, putting one hand on his hip and pinching the bridge of his nose with the other. "So, what's going to happen to you, star?"

"I don't know," said Ariette.

"Do you even care?" said Aelius. Ariette turned away from him. "Come on, Ariette," said Aelius. "You're stronger than this. I know you are."

Ariette shook her head. "I am not. Not anymore. My heart

was always my greatest strength. How can I be strong when half of it is on Earth?"

Aelius' shoulders lowered.

Ariette squeezed her eyes shut and lowered her head. "I will never be the same again."

Aelius took a deep breath. "Time will heal you if you let it, you know. Please let it, Ariette. For me. I hate to see you like this."

Ariette bit her lip. "Believe me, I've tried to be strong, but I feel I must try harder now that my heart is broken."

"I understand, Ariette," said Aelius, "but…"

"No," Ariette cried, turning suddenly toward him with tears dripping from her eyes. "You don't understand. You have never understood, and you will never understand. You don't have a heart, much less a drop of love inside your entire body, while the things I have felt run deeper than two hearts put together."

"Ariette," Aelius said.

Ariette pressed her hands against her heart as more tears continued to spill down her cheeks. "Please believe I will die, Aelius. I promise you."

Aelius took a big breath, trying to tame the anger within him. "Ariette, stop it. Stop being so dramatic."

"I won't," Ariette cried. "Not until you understand me. Although, I doubt that day will ever come."

"Ariette, stop," Aelius scolded.

"Leave me alone," Ariette mumbled.

"No," said Aelius. "I won't stand for this."

"Please," Ariette sobbed. "Just go."

Aelius sighed and floated back to his usual place.

A spark of light caught Ariette's attention. Night had come sooner than she realized. Another wish was floating up toward her. She opened it to let out Faaris' words.

"My love, these days are agony. Content I know I'll never be. My world is dark, it's falling apart. Only you can heal my broken heart. Forgive me for complaining, are you feeling better? Something tells me you won't be 'til we're together."

Ariette smiled. "Oh, Faaris, my stargazer, you know me so well. We're trapped under the same horrible spell. These days are painful since we've been apart. It seems like we've gone back to the start."

"I bring to you the most awful news," said Faaris. "I must marry soon, and it's not mine to choose. Mehrzad says that Pernia must still have a queen. Surely, this is the worst I have ever been."

Ariette's heart was racing as the words faded into the air. "No, Faaris, don't tell me such things. You must change the law, are you not the king?"

"You've made me smile, my star," said Faaris. "How I wish it were that easy. I feel that my heart is now broken completely. Come to me, my love. Come to me now. I believe there's still hope, somewhere, somehow."

"It is not in me, of that I'm sure," said Ariette. "I don't believe in love anymore. All it's done is cost me my heart, and even worse, it's torn yours apart."

"Your words may be true, but we must be patient," said Faaris. "We've gone through too much to be this complacent."

"Right you are, but I can see no end," said Ariette. "Love's cruelty I still do not understand."

"Your light has grown darker, I can see it from here," said Faaris. "Please don't tell me it means what I fear. I know your heart aches, but you must hold out. With hope we can solve this, I have no doubt. At the first sign of sunrise, I'll search every book I can find. Until my eyes can't stay open or until I go blind. Don't be afraid, soon enough you'll be here. I couldn't bear it if you disappear."

"So don't keep breaking my heart then, Faaris," said Ariette. "But please know that I will love you regardless. So, forget all of your books, you won't find a solution. We were doomed from the start…that is my conclusion."

"Just watch me, my love, I shall prove you wrong," said Faaris. "Perhaps I'll save you with your own song. Sing to me, my love. It has healed you before. Your voice has great power, of that I am sure."

"Maybe, if I had the strength within," said Ariette. "But without my whole heart, where do I begin? My songs always came from inside of my heart. I fear I can't sing now that we are apart."

"Then I'll sing your song to you, until you are strong," said Faaris. "Though, true love has more power than any song."

Faaris took a deep breath and closed his eyes, beginning to sing his favorite lullaby to her. Ariette closed her eyes as the song drifted up to her and danced across the dark starry space. For a moment, it was as if time itself stood still. As the song went on, Ariette couldn't help but feel the urge to sing with him. She would have given anything to relive the time they'd sung it together at the palace. She took a deep breath and began to hum. The feeling was sweet and as natural to her as breathing. She let it evolve into singing, as the rest of the universe slipped away. It had been too long since she'd last sung, and the return of the familiar feeling was complete bliss. When they reached the last note, Ariette felt much lighter inside, but her glow was still weak.

"Singing never fails to lift the spirits," said Faaris. "And if not singing itself, it's your beautiful lyrics. Sing to me a new song, your voice is unreal. Let it come from your heart, whatever you feel."

Ariette closed her eyes and drew in a deep breath. She began to sing to him. Words of love, sorrow, regret, and to her surprise, hope began to fill her heart. Stardust carried them down gently to Faaris who was all too ready to hear the sweet sound of her silky voice again. The song poured out of her as it always had, which was more proof to her that her gift of song would be something that she could never lose. No amount of sorrow was strong enough to take away what was—and always had been—hers. That thought lingered with her as she sang.

Faaris was hers.

When the last note had left her, she took a deep breath and rested in the silence that followed. Nothing was going to take him away from her. If she had to risk her life all over again, for him it would all be worth it. She no longer cared. A life without him would be far worse than any danger she would face for taking a chance.

Aelius floated to Ariette's side. "Ariette," he said. Ariette turned to see him looking at her with the sincerest sorrow she had ever seen in him. Aelius closed his eyes and took a heavy sigh. "Go."

Ariette's eyes widened as if she didn't believe what she had heard. "What?" she said.

"You heard me," said Aelius. "Go. Right now."

"Aelius," said Ariette. "But...how can I? Surely I'll fade out before I even get halfway there."

Aelius shook his head. "Not with my help."

Ariette's heart filled with delight, and she threw her arms around his neck.

"I love you," she whispered.

"I..." said Aelius, "I love you too. And so, I have decided to let you go."

Ariette smiled.

36

IT HAD RAINED ALL NIGHT, stormed in fact. It was the perfect match to Faaris' mood. Three loud knocks came from his bedroom door at twilight on the final day of his promise. His greatest wish was to make time stop. Not a single book in the greatest library in all of Pernia had given him even the slightest clue when it came to coping with an emptiness this intense. He had just finished dressing in his finest suit as usual, ready for a day of celebration, which he knew would feel more like torture this time. He had hardly slept. His eyes were still locked on the sky, savoring the final hours of night before it would fade into morning. He took a deep breath and let the cool morning breeze fill his lungs.

"Faaris," came Mehrzad's voice from the other side of the door, along with three more knocks.

Faaris sighed and made his way toward the door.

Mehrzad gave Faaris a warm smile as soon as the door opened. "May I be the first to wish you a happy birthday, my king?"

Faaris managed a half-smile.

"And also..." Mehrzad added, "...a happy engagement. Don't think I've forgotten about our deal."

Faaris sighed. "Oh, Mehrzad, isn't it bad enough that I'm another year older?"

Mehrzad smiled. "Ah, Faaris, it's for the good of the kingdom, we've been over this. I know you're stronger than these emotions which are soon to pass."

Faaris smiled at the ground. "I'm afraid I'm not, Mehrzad. Nothing on earth is stronger than love. From now on I'll be bitter until my last breath."

Mehrzad frowned and took Faaris by the arm. "Then you'll be bitter...and married. Your life will be as joyful as you choose. Come."

With a sense of anger, Mehrzad pulled Faaris into the hall.

"No," Faaris cried. "Mehrzad please. I am not capable of moving past this. I...I will renounce my title before I will marry someone that I don't love."

"Heaven forbid," Mehrzad scolded. "I just want you to know that Pernia has never had a king as great as you. To see you give that up would be the worst thing I've ever seen in my entire life, not to mention in all my years of faithful service to your father... and your father's father."

Faaris was quiet.

Mehrzad sighed. "I know these things are never easy, but

such is life."

"You will never understand the way that I feel," Faaris mumbled. "It's not possible. You've never been married or been in love."

"A life devoted to service is the life I chose, Faaris," said Mehrzad. "I have no need for those things, but I love you more than you realize. I loved your parents equally so, and I've vowed to do anything to protect you for as long as I live."

Faaris gulped and looked up at Mehrzad with sorrow in his eyes. "Really? Well, then if that's so, you'll let me do as I wish."

"I didn't say I wanted what you believe is best for you, my boy," said Mehrzad. "I want what I know is best for you, and trust me, this marriage is a good idea."

Faaris shook his head. "There is nothing you could ever say to convince me."

"Poverty," said Mehrzad. "War. The death of all Pernia as we know it. I always thought you valued protecting the kingdom from those things. Perhaps I was wrong."

Faaris looked up at Mehrzad. "Does my heart not have value?"

Mehrzad sighed and closed his eyes.

"Can I at least wait until sunrise?" Faaris begged.

"You will have many more nights to see the stars," said Mehrzad. "But your life is waiting for you downstairs. You've put the outside world on hold for long enough."

"I want to see Ariette before the sun rises," said Faaris. "Please. It is my birthday after all."

Mehrzad sighed and folded his arms. "Say your goodbyes and then promise me you will put all of this behind you and join us downstairs to begin a new chapter in your life. Have we got a deal?"

Faaris closed his eyes. He hadn't realized that he was clenching his jaw so tightly that he was beginning to get a headache. Faaris opened his eyes, a haunting mixture of anger and sorrow hiding in ripples of green, brown, and gold. "Fine."

Mehrzad nodded and continued down the hall, leaving Faaris beside the door.

Faaris was quick to rush back to the balcony. He took a deep breath the moment he reached the edge. He was too angry to let any tears fall. A strong gust of wind swept across the balcony as he looked up at the sky. The golden sunrise was beginning to stain the sky with soft pinks and purples. As the moon began to fade, Faaris looked to find Ariette. His heart nearly stopped. She was gone.

"No, Ariette." He gasped. "I know you're there. Please don't tell me you've disappeared. Do you hear me though I see you not? The pain I feel is worse than I thought. But, if I must marry, I must say goodbye. It will be harder to live now than to die. But I can't speak to you again, knowing that our love must end. I'm sorry, and it breaks my heart, but we were star-crossed from the start. I'm ready now to set you free, even if it's not with me. I'll love you always, though we must part. Forever I'll be in the dark." Faaris gulped and closed his eyes. The tears that had wanted so badly to fall finally slipped from his eyes. "Goodbye, my love," he said, voice shaking.

He wanted to die. In that moment, he wanted nothing more than to leave this life and all of its misery behind forever. No feeling on earth had ever been worse than this.

Just as the moon began to fade, a distant spark of stardust caught his eye. He gulped and rose to his feet, watching as the light came closer and closer toward him. The air grew warmer and the wind picked up as if another storm were coming. The sound of Ariette's voice began to echo on the breeze, filling the air around him with the sweet sound of his favorite lullaby. Faaris closed his eyes to take it all in as if it were the last time, he would ever hear it.

He looked up to see a blinding light filling the sky. There before his eyes was a glowing figure, floating toward him. For a second, he felt as if his wish to die had come true and an angel had come to escort him to paradise. He took a deep breath and pressed his hands over his chest to make sure that his heart was still beating. Faaris shielded his eyes as the light and sound came closer. The light shattered, and Ariette appeared beneath the brightness as a thousand specks of stardust showered to the ground, dressing her in a gown of stardust. Faaris uncovered his eyes to see her glittering in the open air, floating toward him. A soft smile came across his face and he opened his arms to her. Ariette floated into his arms, sliding further down until their noses met. Gravity caught her as soon as she met the ground and she fell into Faaris' arms.

"You know," Ariette whispered, smiling into each of his eyes, "if you catch a falling star, you should make a wish."

"You're back," Faaris whispered.

"And here to stay," said Ariette.

Faaris smiled and slid his hands gently down her arms until

their hands met. "In that case," he said, "I have nothing more to wish for."

Still holding her hands, he knelt and gazed up into her big, bright eyes. The sun had faded completely, leaving an enchanting, starry scene behind her.

"But I must ask you again," said Faaris with a smile. "My love, my light, you are my life. Do you still want to be my wife?"

Ariette smiled. "Of course I do."

Faaris smiled and rose to his feet to take her into a tight embrace.

"Promise me something, Ariette," Faaris whispered. "Now that you're here, promise that you'll never leave me again. I couldn't bear it."

Ariette giggled. "I left the heavens to be here with you in this brutal, yet beautiful place you call home. Do you think I would have left if not for love?"

Faaris released her and secured his hands around her ribcage. "I can't think of a better reason."

Ariette smiled and rested her forehead against his. Faaris leaned in to kiss her. Ariette opened her eyes just before their lips could meet. "Not yet," she whispered.

Faaris smiled. "Are you afraid?"

Ariette sighed and looked at the ground. She took a deep breath and hugged herself. "I... it's everything I've ever wanted, but it's also...a change. What if it's painful? What if I lose everything that has always been a part of me forever? What if I die here? What if you die and then I'm left here alone in a world that I don't understand? What if..."

Faaris shook his head and placed his hand on her cheek. "What if all of your dreams come true? What if everything you've ever wanted lies on the other side of those fears? Change, even good change, can feel scary at first, but I promise you, as sure as the sunrise, when the storm clears..." He took her by the shoulders and turned her attention to the dewy sky where a soft rainbow stretched across the morning clouds. "There is always a rainbow in its place."

Ariette smiled. A chill rang throughout her body as her eyes met the array of faded colors all blending seamlessly into one another. She had never seen anything like it.

Faaris took Ariette by the hand and led her downstairs where the celebration had already begun. Every eye in the room turned to Ariette the moment they entered the ballroom. She was glittering with stardust and glowing brighter than anything they had ever seen. An overwhelming mixture of shyness and nervousness suddenly came over her as she saw all of their eyes staring at her. Faaris smiled to the crowd and led Ariette gently toward Mehrzad.

"Faaris," Ariette whispered, gripping his hand more tightly. "I'm afraid."

"Don't be," said Faaris, smiling down at her. "They know who you are."

"I'm afraid for them to see me this way," Ariette said. "I...I don't belong. I'm not like them."

"Indeed, you're not," said Faaris. "But is that really such a bad thing? You're glowing."

Ariette smiled and lowered her head. "Soon I will belong."

Faaris returned her smile as Mehrzad approached them with a knowing look.

"Perhaps that will be the last time I deny you any ridiculous requests, Highness," said Mehrzad.

Faaris smiled and bowed. "My intuition has never failed me, Mehrzad. Why should this time have been any different?"

Mehrzard bowed. "Forgive me," he said. "I stand corrected."

Mehrzad turned to Ariette with a gentle smile. "How are you, my dear?"

"I'm wonderful," said Ariette. "I'm here to stay."

"She's right," said Faaris.

"Well, may I say I am delighted," said Mehrzad. "Perhaps your birthday hasn't turned out so bad after all, Faaris."

Faaris smiled at Ariette. "This is the greatest day of my life, in fact. And the greatest birthday gift I could ever wish for."

Ariette beamed.

"A wedding shall be arranged," said Mehrzad, "and then we will talk about a coronation ceremony for our new queen."

Ariette looked at Faaris. She had forgotten about that.

Faaris smiled. "Don't be afraid. There won't be any snakes this time."

"Ah, yes," said Mehrzad. "Speaking of snakes, Sanjar has been locked in prison and kept under constant watch. There's not a chance he could escape."

Faaris looked upset. "Will he really die, Mehrzad?"

Mehrzad shrugged. "Only time will tell. For every deed, whether good or evil, there is a consequence."

37

SEVERAL DAYS HAD PASSED AND the eve of the wedding ceremony was upon them. The fresh, crisp feeling of a new autumn filled the air with beauty and mystery as it always did. Ariette found herself once again dressed in white, this time even more beautiful than the first, sitting in the window frame of her room, gazing up at the stars which she was soon to leave forever. Stardust still covered her from head to toe as it would until her first kiss that night. A bright flame of stardust suddenly came flying out of the sky, shooting toward the balcony. Ariette glanced in its direction and in a matter of seconds, Aelius came crashing into her room in a whirlwind of stardust. He stumbled a little but managed to grab onto the side of the wall to catch his balance.

"Aelius," Ariette cried and ran to throw her arms around him.

"What are you doing here?"

"Easy there," said Aelius, brushing several specks of stardust off of his arms. "I've come to witness this special day of yours. Why else?"

Ariette smiled and hugged him again.

"And who knows," said Aelius, "perhaps I'll stay here too."

"Oh," Ariette gasped. "Aelius…"

"Hey," said Aelius pulling her off of him. "I said perhaps. But I must admit, in all my lightyears I've never seen anything like the way you two look at each other. It would be a shame to miss out on something so powerful."

"You really want to stay?" said Ariette.

"What can I say?" said Aelius, "I'm convinced."

Ariette smiled. "Besides," said Aelius, "Sirius always wanted to be the brightest star anyway." Ariette giggled and took his arm.

The Great Hall was decorated more beautifully than before. White peacocks rested elegantly on marble stands, white butterflies glided gracefully through the open air and moonlight spilled through the newly replaced glass ceiling. Aelius guided Ariette to the top of the stairs and delivered her to Faaris with a gentle bow. Faaris returned the gesture and took Ariette by the hands, squeezing them with confidence. His hands were warm and slightly moist. It was the familiar feeling that had comforted her many times before. At that moment, Ariette had never felt surer of herself, or of anything for that matter. The feeling was pure strength and she never wanted it to leave her. For once, she finally felt as if she was where she was destined to be. Her entire body was shaking as Mehrzad delivered the vows. Fortunately, 'yes' was all she could manage to say. Tears of stardust were just waiting to fall as she looked into Faaris' eyes and squeezed his hands. She could see that he was fighting to hold tears back too.

Faaris looked into her eyes as he slid the delicate, gold ring onto her finger. When the time came for her to do the same, her hand was shaking so much that she almost dropped his ring. Once each of the rings were secure on their fingers', they returned to the comfort of holding hands.

The moment was coming. The moment that would change her life forever. The kiss. Her heart beat faster and faster with every passing second. Once their lips met, there would be no turning back. Ever.

"By the power vested in me," said Mehrzad. "I now pronounce you husband and wife. Faaris, you may now kiss your bride."

Ariette took a deep breath. Her entire body of stardust was still shaking. Inside, she was saying her goodbyes to the fiery, icy feeling that would never be a part of her from this moment forward.

Faaris gulped and looked at her in the deep, warm way that he always did, the look she wanted to carve onto her heart forever.

"My Ariette," he whispered. "My beautiful Setareh."

Ariette smiled and blinked, causing several tears to fall. Her fears subsided, and butterflies filled her stomach. She was ready. Faaris tucked a strand of silky hair behind her ear and secured his hand around the back of her neck as he pulled her lips toward his. The stardust nearly burned his skin, but he didn't care. He knew that in a second it would turn to flesh. Ariette's eyes fell shut as her lips met Faaris'. For a second, she felt as if she had died and become new. The fiery, icy feeling left her, leaving her feeling lighter with every second. Warm blood began to fill her new heart and flood her new body with life. Faaris wouldn't release her until every last bit of stardust had vanished.

The crowd gasped and awed at such a beautiful sight. The room was glowing several shades lighter, and every star in the heavens seemed to shine brighter. The moon was big and bright, crying tears of moonlight over their heads.

The moment their lips parted, Ariette opened her eyes and drew in her first breath of life. The crisp autumn air filled her new lungs and revived her entire body. Her hands were steady now. The feeling was strange but wonderful. In fact, it was the best she had ever felt in her entire existence. Faaris was speechless as he looked at her, shaking his head in disbelief with the warmest smile on his face.

Ariette took another deep breath and managed a smile.

"You're…" Faaris breathed, "…you're beautiful."

He ran his hand through her real, white blonde hair which was softer and smoother than any stardust could ever be. He stroked her milky skin and slid his hand back into hers.

Ariette smiled down at their interlaced fingers. She was like him now. At last, she belonged. She was real. She was human. A soft, wet tear slid down her cheek. She brought her fingertips to her cheek to touch it. It was no stardust. It was better.

"May I be the first to welcome you to Earth, Ariette?" Faaris whispered.

Ariette smiled and blinked several more tears from her eyes. A tear slipped from Faaris' eye and he drew her into a tight embrace, firmly holding the back of her head.

"I love you," Faaris whispered.

"I love you too," said Ariette.

"I'm so proud of you," said Faaris.

Ariette smiled. Her new heart was beating faster. The real feeling felt so...unreal.

Mehrzad cleared his throat. "People of Pernia. It is my greatest delight to present to you for the first time, the king and queen of Pernia."

The crowd roared and cheered louder than Faaris had heard at any ceremony that had ever taken place there in the ballroom.

Faaris pulled Ariette out of the embrace and took her hands again. "Congratulations, by the way," he said.

Ariette smiled at him, confused.

Faaris smiled and looked into her big periwinkle eyes. "You're free."

Ariette smiled as more tears began to fill her eyes. "Truly free," she whispered.

Faaris pulled Ariette away from the crowd and ceremony, past the tall red curtains, and down the hallway until they arrived at the doors of the menagerie. When they arrived at the doors, Faaris slipped his necklace off and selected the key.

"I want to show you something," he said.

Ariette smiled and raised an eyebrow. "What is it?"

As he turned the lock, Faaris grinned over his shoulder at her. "I got you a wedding present."

Ariette stepped inside to see thousands of white butterflies dancing above the trees, floating in the air like flower petals shining in the light of the sun's rays that were beaming through the glass domed ceiling.

"Faaris," she gasped.

One of the butterflies landed on her head as several others danced around her.

"They're wonderful," Ariette cooed, completely mesmerized.

"You know, they remind me of you," Faaris said, admiring her as she twirled around like a child lost in wonder. "Every one of them started off crawling, and after enduring many days trapped inside a chrysalis, at last they were free to fly."

"You think I'm flying?" Ariette asked.

Faaris smiled. "Soaring."

THE WEDDING CELEBRATION HAD LASTED LONG past midnight. After returning to the Great Hall for several more hours of music and food, Faaris took Ariette by the hand and led her outside into the cool night air surrounding the big garden. Tree branches swayed over their heads and flower petals showered softly over them as they stepped into the beauty and serenity that was laid out before them. Ariette and Faaris each took a deep breath the moment they stepped into the night air.

"I saw that look on your face," said Faaris.

Ariette turned her head slightly. "What look?"

Faaris grinned. "You wanted to get away from the crowd as much as I did."

Ariette smiled. "You know me too well."

They sat on the ledge of the largest fountain in the garden and gazed up at the starry sky. Ariette took a deep breath of fresh, cool air and rested her head in the curve of Faaris' neck. They interlaced their fingers, resting in the serenity of the rippling water until the sun began to give light to the new day.

"Do you remember the last time we were out here, looking up at the stars like this?" said Ariette, watching as the sky began to fade to morning.

"Of course, I do," said Faaris. "It was a moment I prayed I'd never forget."

"I said I wished to stop time in that moment," said Ariette. "And you told me not to wish for such things because there would be moments even better to come. Now I see that you were right."

Faaris smiled and stood. "I have something else for you."

Intrigued, Ariette sat up suddenly and tucked her hair behind her ear.

"Faaris," she said. "I feel terrible. You've given me two gifts now, and I've given you nothing."

Faaris smiled as he walked toward a rose bush. "You've given me everything."

He reached into the leaves and pulled out the glittering egg that the Sima Bird had left behind.

"Oh," Ariette breathed, covering her mouth with her hands.

"She left it for us," said Faaris.

Ariette ran her long, slender fingers across the smooth surface of the pearl-like egg. "What should we do with it?" Ariette asked.

Faaris shrugged. "I suppose we protect it for her."

Ariette nodded. "It would be my honor. I...I miss her."

"Don't worry," said Faaris. "She's never gone. If the legend is true, she's sure to rise again just as the sun does each time it falls."

Ariette smiled.

As the sun replaced the night with morning, several delicate fractures began to crawl across the surface of the egg.

"Faaris," Ariette gasped. "Look."

Faaris smiled. "What did I tell you?"

The egg began to quiver as more, larger fractures began to break across the surface. A bright light began to seep through the cracks as the familiar silvery feathers began to burst from the surface. Ariette and Faaris quickly laid the egg on the ground and watched as a big, white bird with wings like an angel erupted from the egg. It was a sight that one was sure to never see in their lifetime. With eyes wide open, Ariette and Faaris watched as the new Sima Bird emerged into the air and took to the sky. Just as she had fallen, she rose, disappearing into the sun, leaving behind a trail of twinkling stardust.

"Faaris," said Ariette taking each of his hands.

"Yes," said Faaris softly, his golden eyes twinkling in the sunlight.

"I have to ask you something," said Ariette.

Faaris smiled. "Anything."

Ariette looked afraid. "Do you believe I have made the right decision?"

Faaris smiled at her. "Do you?"

Ariette sighed and ran her fingers through her hair. "At last, I've found you. I've succeeded. My journey has reached its end. You're alive. I'm alive. We're together. We're happy. We have true love. But something inside of me is missing, and I don't know why. Why do I feel this way if I've succeeded?"

"Ariette," said Faaris. "Perhaps you didn't come to find me."

Confused, Ariette looked at him.

Faaris smiled. "You came to find yourself."

A soft morning breeze washed over her. Ariette let her eyes fall shut. For a moment she was still, listening to the beating of her own heart.

"And let me ask you this," Faaris whispered. "Have you?"

A tear slipped from one of Ariette's eyes, which were still closed. She opened them and looked up at the sun. Tears began to fill her eyes. She was no longer able to look at the sun like she could before. The brightness was too great for her human eyes.

"What will become of me without my stardust?" Ariette whispered. "I'm…"

Tears choked the words out of her. She looked down at her hands—her *human* hands—covered in soft pale skin of her very own as a tear fell onto one of them.

"I'm no longer the same," Ariette whispered as another tear fell. "Will you still love me?"

Faaris smiled and stroked her hair, letting his finger slide onto her cheek to brush the tear away.

"I've fallen in love with you, Ariette," he said. "I loved you before I ever laid eyes on you, before I knew your name, before I held your hand, and before I kissed you. And I will love you always, for who you are inside. Whether you are Ariette, Setareh, a star, a genie, or a human, I will love you. And I will never stop loving you, even after death. And I want you to love yourself as I love you, no matter who you appear to be on the outside. There is something beyond all of that, and it lives inside of you."

Another tear fell onto Ariette's cheek.

Faaris gently lifted her chin to turn her face toward his. "And it is beautiful," he whispered.

Ariette opened her big periwinkle eyes, looking at Faaris with the sweetest renewal of hope. Faaris smiled and leaned closer so that their noses were almost touching, and their eyes were parallel. Ariette smiled, a certain sorrow still hiding in her eyes. As she blinked, another tear fell. Faaris smiled and drew her into a tender kiss—their first kiss as two humans.

"My love, my life, my saving light," said Ariette after their lips parted. "What do you think of our new life?"

Faaris smiled and shook his head. "Content I'll be forever more, knowing that my heart is yours. No more wishes, no more rhymes, now that you're forever mine. Greed and fear will leave you empty, but where there is love, wealth is plenty."

Ariette smiled at him. "The freedom that I feel inside, it comes from love and has no price. At last, I've found you, and now I see that you were my true destiny."

"Forever you shall have my heart," said Faaris. "My only wish now is that we never part. I've loved you since the night we met. My one and only Ariette."

EPILOGUE

ARIETTE SMILED OUT OVER THE cheering crowd as the crown was placed over her head for the first time. Her heart was beating faster than ever before. She reached to her side to dry the sweat from her clammy hands on the soft blue satin of her dress. She glanced to Faaris for solace. Faaris smiled, watching from beside Mehrzad. Ariette smiled back at him, feeling her heart begin to settle. She returned her focus to the crowd and smiled. It was a moment she would remember forever. All at once, it was as if all of the pain of her past had disappeared beneath a rush of happiness, peace, and hope. Her world, and everything she thought she had ever known about it, seemed different in the best way. It was new. *She* was new. She prayed that the rest of her life would feel this way.

Faaris stepped forward and took her hand. "People of Pernia," he called out over the crowd, bringing them to silence. "It's my pleasure to introduce to you the love of my life and your new queen, Ariette Setareh Aghasi."

The crowd cheered again, every face smiling up at Ariette. She blushed and couldn't help but smile back at them.

Faaris took a deep breath and looked out at the crowd. Ariette had never seen him this way, so regal and strong. For a moment, he took his eyes away from the crowd and looked down at her in a way that sent chills down her spine. It was as if all of the noise and excitement around them disappeared and it was just the two of them standing there, ready to take on whatever life had in store. Faaris smiled and returned his eyes to the crowd.

"Now," said Faaris. "Ariette and I will leave tomorrow morning to spend the next several months exploring all that we can of the westward kingdoms, but we leave you in good hands."

Mehrzad stepped forward and bowed to the crowd, which cheered with approval. The crowd cheered again and didn't stop until Ariette and Faaris disappeared from their sight.

THE SOUND OF THE CROWD WAS SO LOUD THAT it reached through every wall in the entire palace, even the dark depths of the dungeon, where Sanjar waited on the cold, damp ground. Not one, but two guards continued to stare at him as they had for the last several days, in shifts to preserve their alertness.

"You fools have the greatest job in the entire palace," Sanjar said with a grin, resting his shackled hands over his knees. "You have the privilege of staring at me from sunrise to sundown. I imagine your eyes must be sore."

The guards remained silent as they had every time he'd spoken to them before. The silence was beginning to drive Sanjar to insanity. They were like statues. Emotionless. Silent.

"I'll be king again, mark my words," said Sanjar. "And as soon as I am, I'm going to kill you both."

He sighed and looked up at the stars through a small window at the top of the prison cell.

"Curse you, Ariette," he said. "Curse all the stars, Faaris, and that stupid legend. When I'm king again, I'm going to destroy you all."

For a moment he was silent, staring up at them. He knew there was a chance he could die any day from now since slaying the Sima bird. An idea sparked in him and prompted a wicked smile. He huffed and looked at the stars with anguish.

> *"Roksana, my star, do you hear my call?*
> *I need to end this once and for all.*
> *Nothing on earth will stop me from winning,*
> *This is only the beginning."*

www.ingramcontent.com/pod-product-compliance
Lightning Source LLC
Chambersburg PA
CBHW021521250626
47154CB00006BA/1924